HE BROUGHT ME MUSIC

A MARRIAGE SURVIVORS CLUB BOOK

ANNETTE NAURAINE

This book is dedicated to my wonderful husband, Peter, who has encouraged me throughout my writing journey, and to my two sons, Lincoln and Ulysses, who understand what my writing means to me.

This series is a Valentine to St. Paul's on the Green and all the people I've met who've become my friends.
Remember: if you don't want to see yourself in a book, don't be friends with a writer.

PRAISE FOR ANNETTE NAURAINE

In the Beginning: Marriage Survivors Club Prequel

...Readers will identify and empathize with the characters, who, in turn, will become readers' friends as well.

I enjoyed this quick and fun prequel to the Marriage Survivors Club series. You get to meet six women, who I assume will each have her own novel, at the moment their friendship begins. A great concept, and so refreshing to have a book about women older than thirty!

Short and funny novella about friends who meet at a funeral. This story sets up an entire series, so I can't wait for each novel about the women in the Marriage Survivors Club. Great banter. Looking forward to the rest!

About Do-Over Daughter

...I am looking forward to the rest of Annette's books in this series. The characters draw you in, and you want to find out what happens next!

...A nice, inspiring women's fiction read with lovely characters.

About Kissing the Kavalier

...This is the kind of wonderfully written book with several side plots and good character development that adds to the over all feeling of a well-written novel.

...Read this book if you love romance and the pain people must go through to get it.

...This is truly a great story that I found to be easy to read, fun and entertaining. I enjoyed the chemistry and the realisticness they brought to the story. I highly recommend this book.

...All the lush historical and cultural details and the rich textures woven through the story pulled me in and made me feel like I was right there, experiencing everything right alongside the characters.

SYNOPSIS

Piano teacher Hélène Charbonneau turned her back on her former life after a crushing public humiliation. Even her beloved fellow members of the Marriage Survivors Club know nothing of her past. But when a desperate father asks her to teach his eleven-year-old son, Darius, a selectively mute piano prodigy, Hélène faces a choice: help a wounded little boy or risk exposure.

With music, Hélène changes the lives of father and son. To her surprise, their love heals her own broken heart. But then Hélène's old nemesis reappears, threatening Darius' future, and Hélène's newfound relationship with his father. Left with no alternative but honesty, she turns to the Marriage Survivors Club to help save the love and music these two lost men have brought her.

From the Ionian Community

Dear Lord, please give me a few friends who understand me and remain my friends.

Addendum by the Marriage Survivors Club:
And who will tell me when I'm full of bullshit.

CHAPTER 1

Let the one among you who is without sin be the first to cast a stone.
Jesus Christ

"Wat, I'd love to help, but my piano studio is full," Hélène hissed to Wat Crabtree.

They were standing in her music studio, whispering so the father and son waiting on the other side of the French doors couldn't overhear.

Wat, choirmaster and organist-extraordinaire of St. Paul's Episcopal Church, hissed back, "At least let me tell you about him. Darius is eleven, a child prodigy. Played Chopin at five."

Yeah, right. everybody thinks their kid is the next Lang Lang.

"Then he's out of my league," Hélène lied.

She glanced through the French doors, where the boy, Darius Harding, and his father, Bryn, waited on the parent's bench in her entryway. The boy, with a shrub of mad, wiry hair on his head, was made mostly of bones with the translucent complexion of a kid who spent all his time indoors. Beneath thick, straight brows, his somber, dark eyes stared at the floor as if he were deep in another world. In his shirt buttoned to the neck and khakis with a knife-edge crease, he looked like a little old man in need of a hug.

"Just hear him," Wat said with his usual vibrating energy.

"You should have been a salesman," she said, laughing. "And I don't have time today." She gave Wat her disarming smile. "You know I only teach beginner students."

Wat's brows shot up.

She turned away so she didn't have to see the skepticism smoking in his eyes.

Wat was a charmer, persuader, and Pied Piper, making him formidable and, in this case, dangerous.

He kept talking. "When his father moved to Norwalk for a job, he needed a piano teacher. He called Father Gabriel and asked if I could take him on, but when I heard him on YouTube, I thought of you."

The hair at the nape of her neck prickled. Why did he think of her?

"If he plays Chopin he's way beyond *me*." She forced a smile. "But I'm happy to call around to see if other teachers have room in their studios."

In spite of her protests, she felt the stirrings of temptation that happened when a talented student showed up. What would it be like to nurture a truly gifted student? To share music at a high level again? She glanced through the glass panes of the door once more.

On the parent's bench, Bryn's knee jiggled up and down at a *presto* tempo. Probably forty-something, he reminded her of Ichabod Crane with his knot of an Adam's apple. He was a pale-haired, slightly balding man with an elongated face and an anxious, roaming gaze. Bryn tucked his big head forward as if searching for something on the carpet. Engagingly shambolic, he had a stretched-out body, and the bones of his shoulders poked sharp angles in his goofy, short-sleeved Hawaiian shirt. He looked perfectly helpless, but helpless didn't mean harmless.

Father and son sat next to one another, but there was a chasm between them. Even through the closed doors, she sensed desperation and loneliness swimming around their ankles, threatening to pull them down.

They needed a life preserver, not a piano teacher, and certainly not her.

"But Darius needs someone kind and patient, like you." Wat squinched his nose, pushing his glasses up.

"Like me? Why?" Suspicion tickled the back of her mind.

"Darius is selectively mute. About a year ago, he stopped playing and talking. He refused to speak to therapists or speak in school. His poor father is on his last nerve. He thinks getting him to play piano will get him talking again."

She glanced at father and son again. No wonder the pair looked forlorn.

"And what about the mother?" she asked.

"I didn't want to pry, but I get the idea that she's not in the picture for some reason."

"He sounds intriguing, but if he won't talk, what he needs is therapy. Thanks for thinking of me anyway." She moved toward the doors to shoo Wat out.

Wat raised a hand to stop her. "Look, they're here. At least meet them. What can it hurt?"

A lot. It could hurt like holding a flame in her hands. Hurt she knew about. She could smell it like a toxic spill, and these two were Chernobyl and the Exxon Valdez combined.

Wat's movements were almost stealthy as he met her in the crook of the piano.

He whispered, "Hélène, I know who you really are."

CHAPTER 2

For nothing is hid, that shall not be made manifest; nor anything secret, that shall not be known and come to light.
Luke 8:17

Hélène stared at Wat, her blood frozen in her veins like ice.

"I have no idea what you're talking about," she stammered.

"I know you're *Hélène Noire et Blanche*." Wat jutted his chin at her black and white hair—a result of Mallen streaks. "I know your hair and your incredible playing gave you your nickname."

Cold crept into every pore, every muscle, making her bones creak, freezing her in place.

Wat said, "Don't worry. I haven't told them—or anyone—for that matter. I'll never tell. But please, I'm not asking for me, but for the boy and his dad. You're empathetic and patient. You have the technique to be able to help him." Wat glanced back through the glass doors. "I suspect Dad's not the most psychological kind of guy, but he's trying to help his son in the only way he knows how. Once you hear him, you might change your mind about accepting him as a student. He's truly amazing."

She did not need amazing. She needed anonymity. She needed Wat and this father and son out of her house. She needed a glass of wine.

Her chest had a concave feeling, and she had trouble getting her breath. She'd been scrupulous about scrubbing her identity, old bootleg recordings, and videos off the internet. She'd been careful to keep her past and her abilities a secret but her damn hair was a dead giveaway for anyone who dug deep enough. If Wat found out who she was, others might too, and then all hell would break loose. How trustworthy was he? People gossiped. Her mind raced toward the only thing she knew: running. Sell the house, move, change her last name again, disappear, and leave everything and everyone behind. She'd done it once, and she could do it again.

Her knees went weak, and she sank onto the piano bench. She shook her head. "I'm sorry..." Like gravel stuck in her throat, the words wouldn't come.

"Just meet them," Wat said.

He was the Napolean of music directors. She had dealt with the most egotistical, domineering conductors, but Wat wheedled in an irresistible way that made you think he had your best interests in mind.

"Are you all right?" he asked.

No, and she wouldn't be all right again for a very long time.

She recovered herself and bobbed a short nod. She stood and opened the doors to her studio. In spite of the coal black darkness welling in her gut, she smiled. "Hello, I'm Hélène Charbonneau."

Darius regarded her with troubled eyes that seemed to have seen things only grown men should see. He tucked his hands under his arms and swung his gaze away. His silence felt to Hélène like a protective shield. The hungry ache rolling off him made her want to gather him in her arms.

Bryn Harding leaped off the bench. Grinning supplicatingly, he stuck out his knob-wristed hand and engulfed Hélène's hand in his own. The man was all knuckles and joints.

Radiating the hopefulness of a man grabbing at a life preserver, Bryn spoke without coming up for air. "Hi, I'm Darius' dad, Bryn Harding, I'm pleased to meet you I'm so happy to meet you Darius is really talented, but he's had a tough time in the last year, and well, with the move, my changing jobs, and everything else since he won't talk I've had a hard time finding him a teacher—"

She could hardly understand his onslaught of run-on words. It was as if he was afraid he would be interrupted and unable to make his point. As he prattled on, the thumb and forefinger of his right hand flicked in a nervous gesture.

Hélène held up her palm. "I'm sorry. I'll give a listen and recommend someone better suited to him than me."

Behind her, Wat coughed.

She suppressed the urge to jab him in his Adam's apple.

Darius still sat on the bench, but now he was staring at her with the alarming intensity of a hungry little bear cub.

Bryn's face practically caved in, and she wanted to give him a comforting pat on his sharp-edged shoulder. He drew a deep breath and swung his hands wide and back together, making a big clap. "Okay, okay, that's a start, that's something to go on. I can work with that I think you'll be impressed when you hear him."

She slid Wat a smile that threatened murder, and she thought he blanched a bit. "I don't have time to hear him today."

"When can you?" Wat interjected.

"I can hear him on Saturday at four," she heard herself say. "Then we can talk more."

Please, God, let them not come back. Let them find someone else. Make them go away. I have a life here. Save me, God! Save me!

"Sure, sure, sorry—didn't mean to barge in or anything, I understand we'll be here," Bryn burbled.

Darius unfolded himself, and Bryn wrapped an arm around his son's shoulders and pulled him in. Bryn bent his angular frame down and kissed the top of his son's head. The loving gesture made Hélène instantly like this man who spoke too much and too fast. Few men openly showed such affection for their children, particularly their sons.

Bryn said, "There, Darius, now you've met her and you won't feel shy when we come back on Saturday, okay?"

The boy tipped his head back to gaze up at his skyscraper father and nodded.

The look that passed between them made her heart squeeze.

When they all left, Hélène locked the door behind them. Then she went to the kitchen and poured herself a large glass of wine. Hopefully, the aching boy and his desperate father wouldn't return, and her life would go back to the way it was before they walked in her front door.

She took her wine and went upstairs. Googling Darius Harding, a YouTube channel came up. As she listened, a cold, hard knot twisted in the pit of her stomach.

The kid was a genius, and he sounded just like she had at the same age..

CHAPTER 3

In the sweetness of friendship let there be laughter and sharing of pleasures. For in the dew of little things, the heart finds its morning and is refreshed.

Khalil Gibran

Like always, Hélène was late for dinner at Paella, the best tapas restaurant in Norwalk, and where the Marriage Survivors Club could be as noisy as they wanted, which was usually pretty noisy.

She grabbed a chair next to Bianca Treviso. The other club members had already swilled down two bottles of Rioja. The table was spread with a wide selection of cold and hot tapas, plates of cheese, a basket of crusty bread, and bowls of olives.

The six fifty-something women called themselves the Marriage Survivors Club because they'd all escaped—some more than others—unscathed from the institution of marriage. A few of them had fallen in love, but they were still allowed to attend their twice-a-month drink-and-debauch sessions.

They had all met years ago at St. Paul's Episcopal Church at the funeral of Flicka's fourth and last husband. Since then, they laughed, drank, cursed, and prayed together. Their motto was "All for one and no bullshit for any." If anyone of them was fooling themselves, the others immediately called out "bullshit!" It had proven an effective strategy. And besides, it was fun.

Even these women—whom Hélène would have killed for and who would have done the same for her—didn't know about her past. Now that Wat knew who she was, Hélène felt like she was in freefall and waiting to see when she hit the pavement.

"About time, Frenchie," Bianca Treviso said.

Bianca poured Hélène a glass of wine. Hélène nudged the bottle, filling her glass to the top, aware Bianca was giving her the hairy eyeball.

"Sorry I'm late, but I have a genuine excuse today," Hélène said.

"You always do," Flicka said, pushing her flaming red hair back from her sculpted, surgically enhanced face.

Frederica "Flicka" Cole Williamson Strada Kolinsky Whitehall was once a New York socialite who retired to Connecticut when her fourth and last husband died, leaving her rich enough to live as she pleased and get laid as often as she wanted. She was White, tall, gorgeous, with dyed red hair and a sense of humor like a longshoreman.

Bianca clawed at her messy dirty blond hair, leaving behind a trail of breadcrumbs. "So, what's your excuse for being late this time?"

Bianca was White, with rounded edges, and a divorce attorney. Hélène suspected she carried a switchblade stuffed in her sock—a blade she would wield to defend any of them. A sports fanatic and blurter of inappropriate comments, Bianca had seen enough marriages devolve into shit-slinging that she had sworn never to marry.

Hélène took a long sip of wine before answering. "Wat brought me a new student and asked me to take him."

"Any good?" Flicka asked.

When she'd seen the YouTube videos, Darius reminded her of herself so much that the temptation to teach him was nearly irresistible. But that would mean playing for him, and she wouldn't do that for anyone. Hélène answered, "Yes, but there's a problem."

"No hands?" Bianca blurted and pulled her hands into the sleeves of her sweater until they disappeared.

"Lord, Bee!" Tiny Olivia laughed her big laugh and rolled her eyes.

"He doesn't talk," Hélène said.

"Guess he won't come up with lame excuses for not practicing," Flicka said.

Hélène related the story of Wat's visit to her house, about Darius and his father, who looked like he was made out of pipe cleaners.

"Wat must think I'm some kind of magician because he wants me to get this kid to play *and* talk." Hélène smeared fig spread on a slice of bread. "I only teach beginning students, but I've agreed to hear him on Saturday and try to find him another teacher. Somebody who's a better fit."

"Why isn't the kid talking?" Bianca asked. She dabbed at a dribble of oil on the front of her Red Sox jersey. "At that age, I couldn't get my nieces and nephews to shut up."

"They took after you," Flicka teased and bumped Bianca's shoulder with her own.

Hélène selected a piece of Manchego cheese and passed the plate to Bianca. "I didn't have time to talk to ask the dad."

Frankie flipped her mass of tiny silver-and-black braids over her shoulder. "Of course, once they turn into teenagers, all they ever do is grunt, so it's not so different."

Frankie Carter was biracial with smooth, medium skin and dark, laughing eyes. She was the mother of two adopted teenagers, one of whom was autistic. She owned a thriving renovation business called Women's Work and possessed a will equal to the force of water gushing out of a busted dam. She never met a problem she couldn't solve.

Olivia said, "Usually, children stop talking as a result of trauma. It's their only recourse. Maya Angelou was mute for years after an assault as a child."

They all teased tiny Olivia Maxwell that she was only as big as a twelve-year-old. With porcelain white skin and bright blue eyes, she looked like she might be a china doll, but she had a core of steel. Since marrying Jack O'Grady, Olivia had literally let her hair down and it had grown into a mass of silver-blonde curls. She was the most emotionally astute of all the Marriage Survivors Club, the one who saw past heartbreak to healing.

"How awful," Flicka ground out, her green eyes flashing with angry fire.

"Something terrible must have happened to him," Carolina Singh said. "Maybe if you take him as a student, he'll tell you."

Hélène felt the blood drain from her face. If Darius had stopped speaking due to trauma, she wasn't prepared to help him. She could barely remember to feed herself. She would have killed a stone if someone were naive enough to give her one. It was why she'd never had plants or pets. The best she had to give was a quick hug or a high-five.

"Maybe God brought him to you because you're used to dealing with little kids. If anyone can help him, you can," Carolina said hopefully.

Carolina's unfailing faith bolstered the faith of the others the way a book propped up the leg of a wobbly table. She had inherited her dark, expressive eyes and sienna-colored skin from her

Guyanese father. A research librarian at Yale, she was the one who could find an answer to any question.

"Why did Wat bring this kid to you?" Bianca asked. She swabbed the bottom of a dish with a wad of bread.

Hélène shoved a slice of cheese into her mouth so she didn't have to answer.

"Because she's kind, supportive, gentle, and loves music," Olivia said.

Bianca jerked back and made a dramatic scowl. "We talkin' about the same person?"

They all laughed, and Hélène felt her insides loosen up.

Carolina raised her eyebrows and said, "Sooo ... Hélène, I need your help."

"I will say yes to you, you know that," Hélène said. Saying no to Carolina would be like saying no to an angel.

Carolina looked around the table at each of them. "So, Wat's asked me to chair the next fundraiser for the shelter."

Aside from drinking, eating, and joking, tonight's meeting was to discuss the next fundraiser for St. Paul's LGBTQ+ youth shelter.

Frankie's dream of an LGBTQ+ youth shelter had been taken up by the Marriage Survivors Club and St. Paul's. LGBTQ+ youth were at increased risk for suicide, homelessness, alcoholism, and drug addiction. Father Gabriel Ayliffe, the Rector, had laid the foundation for welcoming everyone to St. Paul's without exclusion and the shelter was a perfect way to extend the church's mission into the community.

Carolina said, "Will you be my vice-chair for the fundraiser? Wat thought we would work well together."

Merd.

This was not what Hélène had expected. She blamed it on the wine, making her head fuzzy. She said turned to Flicka. "Remind me next time to ask what I'm saying yes to."

"It's your turn," Flicka intoned, waggling a finger with an olive stuck on the end.

"What are we raising money for this time?" Bianca asked in a drawn-out groan.

Carolina said, "Furniture for the apartments. Father Gabriel thinks it's better to be specific so the congregation knows where their money is going." She turned to Frankie. "What's the status of the construction?"

"Cam said the foundation will be poured in two weeks." Frankie laughed. "You should see him with all his blueprints, making phone calls, wheeling and dealing. He's like a three-year-old with a new toy."

Cam Simpson, Frankie's perma-fiancé, had moved in with her and her boys. He was developing the condos where the shelter was located. Cam had donated two condo units for the shelter because he'd fallen hopelessly in love with Frankie and would have given her the moon if she'd asked.

"Whatever fundraiser we have, I hope it involves plenty of booze," Bianca said.

"What are we going to do this time?" Olivia asked, passing the dish of grilled Galician octopus down the table.

Carolina said, "Wat thought a piano concert would be an excellent choice."

Hélène felt a sizzle of wariness. Did Wat think she would perform? "Jazz, right?" she asked.

"No, classical," Carolina said. "Like Mozart. That's why Wat thought you would be good on this fundraiser."

Hélène's fingers tingled and went numb. Her wrists felt like blocks of wood. Even if she'd wanted to play in public, this was what happened when she even thought about it.

"I've heard of that Mozart guy," Bianca said with a playful grin. "Can we get him?" She cleared a spot on the table for the big pan of paella that Jaime brought out.

Carolina laughed. "Wat thinks he knows a big name we can get for free. Someone who would be enough of a draw to fill the church sanctuary."

And who might that be?

A new panic slid into place behind Hélène's breastbone. Wat was deluded if he thought he could coax her out of the shadows. First, the boy wonder, now this? She wasn't a woman given to violence, but right now, she wanted to break every one of Wat Crabtree's organ-playing fingers.

Hélène felt something snap inside of her. She slapped a palm on the table, making the flatware jingle. "Who? Who does he know? Wat doesn't know anybody good enough who can fill the sanctuary."

Carolina looked shocked.

"What are you so jacked up about all of a sudden?" Frankie asked, leaning back in her chair and scowling at Hélène.

"I'm not jacked up," Hélène said, feeling her cheeks growing hot. She had to kill off this idea before it went too far. She forced herself to speak calmly. "We can't charge a lot for tickets unless we raise Franz Liszt from the dead."

"Anybody know a gravedigger?" Bianca said as she dished up plates of paella and passed them around.

"No one wants to hear a classical piano concert anymore," Hélène scoffed. "It's a dumb idea."

"I don't think so," Flicka countered. "People love great music and superb musicians. I used to love going to Carnegie Hall."

"You had to go because one of your husbands paid for the stage renovation," Olivia said and smiled.

"I would have gone even if he hadn't," Flicka said.

"When was the last time you went to a classical concert, eh? In New York?" Hélène gestured to them, one by one, with her wineglass. "And you? When? No one wants to hear Beethoven or Chopin or Scriabin."

"Who's that last one?" Olivia asked.

"Russian late nineteenth-century composer," Carolina said, eyeing Hélène. She was a research librarian so, of course, she would know who he was.

Hélène had said too much. Maybe she was jumping to conclusions about Wat and his motives, but she wasn't going off high alert yet. She poured herself another glass of much-needed wine to steady her nerves.

Bianca frowned at her and wrenched the bottle away from her. "You still have to drive home, and I'm not bailing you out if you get picked up for DUI."

"Maybe Wat knows people from his days at Juilliard," Olivia said as she passed the seafood paella to Hélène. "You know how Wat is; he's not afraid to ask anybody to help."

Hélène set the plate of delicious paella in front of her, but, unlike other nights at Paella, she had no more appetite.

"None of the rest of us know the difference between a good and a bad pianist, but you do. You could work with Wat on finding someone," Carolina suggested to Hélène.

Not on your life.

Hélène chomped into her roll and ground it between her back molars like gravel. She had the distinct impression that Wat intended to use her friends to pressure her into performing. And that infuriated Hélène. She knew Wat couldn't be trusted.

Frankie said, "The rest of us can manage the logistics: tickets, printing, posters, publicity, programs, selling ads, and stuff like that, but you're the only one who knows about music."

Hélène's fingers wouldn't cooperate, and she felt the wine glass slipping from her fingers. She gripped it with both hands and held it shakily to her mouth. She set her glass down and angled her body away from the table. "Why don't we do something else? The barbecue last spring was fun."

"Except when the Chittam-Howell House almost burned

down," Olivia said. Her eyes were wide as she remembered her fear when her son, Taylor, leaped to the roof and put out the fire.

"What about a magic show or a comedy night?" Hélène suggested, scrambling for any idea but a piano concert. "We wouldn't have to worry so much about selling tickets. Classical music is such a hard sell." Hélène turned to Carolina. "Let's talk Wat into something else."

"What about a burlesque show featuring ladies of a certain age?" Flicka suggested and fluttered her eyebrows.

"And how you gonna hide all those plastic surgery scars?" Bianca asked her.

All of them except Hélène laughed.

"I don't think we can change Wat's mind. He's committed to this," Carolina said. "And everybody else thinks it's a great idea."

Bianca raised her wineglass. "To a piano concert with Mozart."

The others raised their glasses and touched them together with a clink. Hélène joined them even as humiliation shriveled her insides.

CHAPTER 4

Coincidence is God's way of remaining anonymous.
  Albert Einstein

Darius recognized Hélène the minute he saw her black and white hair, gigantic dark eyes, wide mouth, and tall, thin figure. Her last name wasn't Charbo-whatever. She was *Hélène Noire et Blanche.*

It was like meeting God or Taylor Swift.

Into the search engine of his browser, he typed in "*Hélène Noire et Blanche.*" It took a while and some searching, but finally, an old picture of her popped up on the screen. She was younger, with long, flowing hair, instead of the short flipped up the way she wore it now, but the Hélène in the picture and the one he'd met were the same. He expanded the photo to see if he could spot the mole on the back of her hand, but it was too blurry.

The Wiki site was in French, so he clicked "translate."

Hélène Villancourt, legendary French pianist, was nicknamed "Hélène Noire et Blanche" for her white-streaked black hair, a metaphor for the piano's black and white keys.

"That's her, isn't it?" he said aloud to his mother.

She nodded. She sat in her chair, glowing like she was made of moonlight. He could smell her perfume, just like when she tucked him in and kissed him goodnight. The necklace with a gold heart he'd given her when he was six twinkled around her neck. He'd saved up for it for her birthday, and she'd been happy when he gave it to her. She wore it every time she came. He loved making her happy. He would do anything to make her happy again. He hadn't meant for it to happen, and he was sorry. So sorry.

He felt the sore spot behind his eyes and the heavy pressure in his chest. "Can you come more often, Mom? I need you to give me the music."

He leaned forward, listening closely because her voice was so quiet.

She smiled. "Hélène."

He turned back to the monitor. "There's not much stuff about her here. Here's a picture of her with some old guy it says was her husband. He was like, some French conductor."

He scrolled down the list of about ten recordings and read Hélène's sketchy biography. Taught by her mother, debuted at ten playing Mozart piano concerto ... solo recordings at thirteen ... cult following ... studied at the Conservatoire de Paris ... death of her father, two-year absence from concertizing, married the conductor guy ... disappointing return to the stage.

Disappeared.

Darius cocked his head and did the math in his head. "She hasn't played in public or made any recordings for thirty years."

"And now she is yours," his mom said.

She shimmered like a handful of glitter tossed into the air and disappeared.

CHAPTER 5

Memory ... is the diary that we all carry about with us.
   Oscar Wilde

In the damp, musty-smelling basement of their house, Bryn sat on an upturned plastic milk crate. He opened a large cardboard box. Inside was a hastily packed jumble—swim towels, some CD recordings he made of Vivianne, notebooks about pianists, a string of Christmas lights, a a box of colored pencils cookbooks, Vivianne's pink bedroom slippers, and Darius' childhood toy, a stuffed lamb.

Bryn rubbed the soft fleecy lamb against his cheek. He closed his eyes and inhaled, imagining the smell of baby powder, formula, and whatever scent they used on diapers to disguise poop. He remembered what an adorable baby Darius had been. More so than any baby that ever lived. Talented, bright, eager, chatty, chubby. His wobbly legs had carried him across the floor right to Vivianne's lap and the piano.

They both knew how unusual he was and she had poured all her energies into him. The two of them lived in a land of music

Bryn couldn't enter because he didn't understand music like they did.

Instead, Bryn spent all their marriage trying not to rock the boat, doing whatever he could to make Vivianne's teaching Darius easier. And it had worked.

As Darius grew, everyone said the same thing over and over: "Astounding, amazing, brilliant, talented." Vivianne started a YouTube channel of Darius' playing that got thousands of views. Bryn was proud, but Vivianne made it abundantly clear that he had nothing to do with his son's gifts.

And then she died and his magical, beautiful boy went silent.

Now Darius was always gazing into corners or at some blank space as if he was looking for someone. It was a bit unsettling, but, Bryn reasoned his son was still grieving.

Never in a million years did Bryn think he'd be so far out of his depth as he was now. But Hélène Charbonneau was the answer. All Bryn had to do was convince her to accept Darius as a pupil. If Darius started playing again, he might find himself and come back to Bryn, to music, to life.

Bryn carried the little lamb, cookbook, Vivianne's slippers, and one of her CDs back upstairs. He put the cookbook on the kitchen counter and the other things in his bedroom.

In the kitchen, Bryn opened the cookbook and found the page for Vivianne's favorite red sauce. He inserted the CD of Vivianne playing Beethoven's last piano sonata. Bryn had always loved hearing her play. Before Darius was born, he had bought top-of-the-line equipment to record her. Now, he was glad he had because he could listen to her whenever he wanted.

As always, Beethoven filled Bryn with wonder and hope in the eternal goodness of mankind. After she'd died, listening to her CDs made Bryn feel close to her, as if she was speaking to him somewhere in the notes and rests. He had done everything he could to make her dreams for a career come true. It just hadn't been enough.

He swore he wouldn't make that same mistake with his son.

The water for the pasta had started boiling when Darius appeared in the kitchen. He frowned at the CD player. Bryn felt stupid that he hadn't realized the music might upset Darius with memories of his mom.

"Hey, I'm making pasta for dinner, that okay with you I'm using your mom's recipe that's your fav right? What do you think of Hélèneshe has a pretty French accent, and she seems nice, like she could inspire you to play again." Bryn saw a flash of something—irritation, anger—in Darius' eyes and forced himself to pause his motor-mouth. He said, "It's what your mother would have wanted, you know, for people to hear your wonderful talent."

Bryn babbled, "I like this sonata, don't youwhat do you think about your mom's playing, great, right?"

Darius frowned.

Bryn dumped the whole box of linguine into the pot of boiling water. It was a lot for the two of them, but they could eat the leftovers for the rest of the week in different sauces or in soup. He turned the burner under the sauce down a notch.

Darius went into the living room to the piano and returned to the kitchen with Vivianne's score of Beethoven's sonatas and sat at the kitchen table. He opened to the music, and his eyes moved across the page as he followed Vivianne's playing.

Bryne was thrilled; this was the first time since Vivianne died that Darius had even opened a music book.

"Can you show me the notes in the music where she's playing?" Bryn asked because, unlike his magical son and wife, he could not read music.

Darius nodded.

Bryn sat next to his son, grateful to share this with him.

Darius put his long, slender finger under a row of black notes and moved along the page. As Vivianne's fingers flew across the keys, Bryn heard spots where he thought she stumbled.

The sonata ended, and Darius leaned his head against Bryn's shoulder. They sat like that for a few minutes, not speaking or moving. Tears came to Bryn's eyes as he hugged his son and laid his cheek against his curls. Bryn's chest burned with longing for his son to play again, for him to speak, for him to come back to the world. His son's grief was like a heavy door shutting him off from life, but Hélène was the key to that door.

CHAPTER 6

All water has a perfect memory and is forever trying to get back to where it was.
Toni Morrison

Hélène shut the French doors of the studio, Liszt's *Don Juan* already playing in her mind and itching at the ends of her fingertips. Once, she'd been known as a Liszt specialist. One critic wrote, "She came, she played, she slayed."

The ebony, matte-finish Bösendorfer piano she'd gotten in the divorce settlement sat in the room like a massive ship waiting to set sail for a distant, unknown destination. Everyone in Norwalk believed she was a mediocre pianist at best so whenever anyone asked why she had a piano that cost as much as a small house, she said it had been her mother's. She'd repeated the story so often that no one asked anymore. She planned to be buried in the thing.

She slid her hand along the lid and felt a familiar thrill of expectation. When she played the piano, even if only for herself, it was like throwing open the windows of her soul. Her heart became a whirlpool of all the emotions she usually held in check. Playing was when she was most herself.

The wood-lined studio had the warm sound of an intimate recital hall. Later, during the editing process on her computer, she could add whatever extra ambience or reverb she wanted. It had taken her years to get back to playing for herself. Her YouTube fans knew her only by her online *nom de guerre, La Pianist.*

She regularly Googled herself to keep track of anything that might reveal her whereabouts. She seldom found anything new until, oddly, about six months ago, an old bootleg video of her playing Liszt's *La Campanella* at Carnegie Hall popped up on YouTube. It was easy enough to flag the video as copyright infringement and have it taken down. She hated the video and sound quality, though her playing had been superb.

The week after that performance, her father died suddenly, and she canceled the remainder of her American tour and flew back to France. As a kind of homage to him, she never played the piece again. She was still mourning when Yves got his clutches on her, leading to her ultimate downfall.

Her music studio took up most of the first floor of her house. The rest of the first level had her spare eat-in kitchen, the entryway with the "parent's bench," and the powder room. Upstairs were the three bedrooms, one which contained book-shelves stacked with piano scores, numerous CDs—many of which she'd recorded right in this room—and her editing set up. She slept in the second and smallest bedroom and had outfitted the third bedroom with a sofa and TV for use as a sitting room.

She unlocked the cabinet at one end of the studio and removed the microphones and camera. She placed the micro-phones around the studio in spots that best captured her play-ing. The video camera was attached to a boom positioned above the keyboard so only her hands showed.

Tonight, she would record Liszt's *Don Juan*. She wanted it to be the pinnacle of every other recording floating around on YouTube. But it had to sound more mature, more considered, and more profound than her past performances. YouTube allowed her to perform at a high standard, keep up her technique, and remain anonymous. The ad revenue also nicely supplemented her modest income from teaching.

She sat down on the bench and, for some reason, for the first time in a while, Yves' voice rang in her ears: *"Without me, without my ideas, you are nothing! What makes you think you have any talent? You aren't an artist!"*

Her heart clawed up into her throat. Her fingers seized, and her wrists cramped. She squeezed her eyes shut tight, clapped her hands over her ears, and shook her head a few times, trying to dislodge his denigrating voice. He reminded her of her mother. Perhaps that's why she had fallen prey to him.

She kissed the triangular mole on the back of her hand like her father always had before she went onstage. She always performed this little ritual before she played to remember him. He'd been a simple man, but he'd loved her with a fierceness she never again knew.

Her mother, Monique Démoulin, had been an astounding pianist with brilliant technique and a reputation as a fiery interpreter of Ravel. She was frustrated teaching piano in their small apartment in the Montmartre section of Paris. Her marriage to Hélène's father, Theo Villancourt, had been miserable for both of them. Her mother was a ranter, but Papa was a mild-mannered man who only once raised his voice.

Her mother's greatest frustrations erupted when she taught Hélène, and it seemed impossible to please her mother or her teacher. Having her mother as her teacher had been a deadly combination. When she died, Hélène didn't return for her funeral.

Everything changed one day when Hélène was six. She hadn't learned the assigned Mozart sonata to her mother-teacher's satisfaction. Monique struck Hélène with the flat of her hand, leaving a red imprint on her cheek.

When her father arrived home that evening, he saw the mark and threw a chair through a glass door. He shouted at Monique, railed at her, and threatened that if she ever touched Hélène again, he would throw her out the window. All three of them had been shocked at his vehemence.

The next day—a school day—he took Hélène by the hand and walked with her to the Ecole d'Musique. He found her a new teacher, for which Hélène was eternally grateful. Her mother had given her technique, but her father had given her love.

Feelings are all that matter, Hélène reminded herself. She hated to remember this phrase Yves had drilled into her but connecting her playing to this one idea had helped to keep her terror at bay and allowed her to find and play what was in her own heart.

She warmed up with scales and arpeggios. Her super-fast reflexes allowed her to execute runs at a pace once described as "machine gun over silk." She felt herself riding a lightning bolt, the sound of thundering chords, and filled with a kind of release that came only when she allowed herself to be carried away on the notes.

When she was finished, she sat back, satisfied, and smiled to herself. She was still *Hélène Noire et Blanche.*

At least when she was alone.

CHAPTER 7

The life of the dead is placed in the memory of the living.
Marcus Tullius Cicero

Darius climbed between the cool sheets of his bed, eager to talk to his mom sitting in the armchair, resting her chin in her hand. She usually came every night and he had so much to tell her.

His dad pulled the covers up to Darius' shoulders and plopped onto the edge of the bed, his weight pressing the mattress down. His hair was plastered down on his forehead, and sauce was splattered on the front of his shirt.

Darius nestled up against his dad for a minute. He was big, warm, and solid, even if he talked a lot. And he made good spaghetti sauce.

His dad patted the covers down. "How did you like Hélène I thought she was great seems really nice And that black and white hair, such big eyes, I'm sure once she hears you she'll take you as her student," his dad blabbed.

Darius reached up and patted his dad's cheek to get him to stop talking. He loved his dad but wanted him to go so he could talk to his mom. Those nights when she didn't come, he had the Bad Dreams about the blood and the snow and the cold. He couldn't tell his dad about those dreams because then he would be sad, too.

Those stupid therapists all said he quit talking and playing piano because his mom had died, but that wasn't it. He was listening for her but she was very quiet so he had to listen hard. He wanted to talk with her about music and how feelings were all that mattered, to hear how much she loved him. But mostly he wanted to tell her that he hadn't hurt her on purpose, but he was still waiting. He couldn't figure out how to make it so she was happy and not mad at him anymore.

"What are you thinking about?" his dad asked, brushing Darius' hair off his forehead. "I wish you'd talk to me you don't have to talk to anyone else, but if you told me what was on your mind, maybe." He kissed Darius' palm and held his hand between his gnarly fingers. "I want to understand why you stopped talking and playing piano your mother would want you to play. She loved teaching you and thought you were wonderful, so do I and so will a lot of other people if you play again."

His dad had never been like this before his mom went to the in-between place, but now he wouldn't shut up. It was like he was making up for Darius' not talking.

His mom glowed like smoke lit from the inside. Darius was afraid she was getting ready to leave. He balled the sheets up in his fists.

"Why are you looking at the chair?" his dad asked.

Darius burrowed deeper into the covers.

"Okay," his dad said and kissed Darius' forehead.

Secretly, he loved it when his dad did that because it made both of them feel less lonely and scared.

At the door, his dad stopped and turned to look at Darius

with his sad, lost-man eyes. "I miss her too," his dad said with a catch in his voice.

Darius waited until his dad's footsteps disappeared, then, he slipped out of bed. He sat on the arm of the chair. The dull pain in his chest felt better now that she was here. The little gold necklace with the eighth note twinkled around her neck. He'd bought it for her for Mother's Day when he was six and she never took it off. It was like their secret signal.

"What did you think of Hélène?" he whispered.

His mom said, "Marvelous. She is the one for you."

"I know she was your favorite, and you always tried playing like her. Is it okay if I study with her?"

When he was little, Darius and his mom had listened to Hélène Villancourt's recordings all the time. His mom had tried to imitate her, but she couldn't, but Darius could. He could play just like Hélène. She was the most fantastic pianist he'd ever heard. Like him, she'd been a childhood prodigy; then she disappeared all of a sudden, and no one ever said why.

"Yes. She will help you," his mom said.

He yawned broadly. His eyelids felt so heavy. "But you've always been my teacher. I can't play without you."

"She is your new teacher, my sweet," she said, her smile making his heart feel like an allegro movement in a Mozart sonata.

My sweet. He loved hearing her call him that, just like before she'd gone to the in-between place. He laid his head on her shoulder like he'd always done. "Will you come to my lessons?"

"Yes, I will be there."

He noticed that she held a music score in her lap. "What's that?"

"My copy of Chopin's *Second Piano Concerto*," she answered.

"Why did you bring that?" he asked.

"I want you to learn it," she said, handing him the score.

He took it and riffled the pages. "Am I ready?" he whispered.

She nodded, the soft, straight strands of her brown hair brushing her cheek. "Hélène can teach it to you."

He didn't want her to get mad or feel like he was shoving her aside in favor of Hélène. "All your markings are in here," he said. "I can just look at this and learn it by myself. It will be almost like you're teaching me."

His mom rose from the chair. "Hélène will help you," she said.

He slid off the arm of the chair onto the seat where her body had left a depression in the cushion. "If it will make you happy, I'll do it. Please don't be mad anymore." He pulled the comforter from his bed over himself and curled into a snail in the chair.

"Don't go yet. I'm sorry. I didn't mean to do it." He was so sleepy he could hardly get the words out.

She raked her fingers through his hair, but as hard as he tried, he couldn't feel the warmth of her palm. As he drifted off to sleep, he heard her voice, watery and thin, humming the first theme from the concerto's first movement.

Bryn set Vivianne's pink silk slippers under Vivianne's side of the bed. He lay down, fully clothed. He rested his hand on Vivianne's side, where the sheets were cool and unwrinkled. He stared into the darkness, fear and despair fighting against the hope he was placing on Hélène.

"I'm trying, Vivianne. I'm trying everything I know," he murmured into the night.

He wasn't the most insightful guy, but he had done everything for Darius that he could think of. He spoke to a neurologist, psychiatrist, and Darius' pediatrician. He took Darius to several therapists who said if he refused to talk or respond, they couldn't help him. No one offered any better answers than Bryn had himself.

But Darius was made of music and had to play piano. Bryn had searched for a new teacher, forwarding the YouTube links of Darius playing Chopin, Mozart, Bach, Beethoven, Liszt, and the Grieg piano concerto. The responses were always enthusiastic until he told them Darius didn't speak. Then ... crickets. So Bryn stopped mentioning that. Whenever Bryn told Darius they were going to try a new teacher, he didn't make a fuss. But when they got into the studios, Darius threw unholy tantrums. The experiences made Darius retreat even further into himself, left the teachers terrified, and Bryn disheartened. But he refused to be defeated.

He had thought that moving out of the house where Vivianne had died would help Darius talk again, but nothing had worked. Bryn was counting on Hélène to work a miracle.

When he heard Darius play, Bryn felt like angels were carrying him, as if he were standing in a shower of apple blossoms. It would have been all right if Bryn had never experienced that again, but Darius *needed* music to live, breathe, and speak. He was drowning, and Bryn would do whatever it took to keep his son afloat.

Darius was everything: the past, tomorrow, the breath, the beating of Bryn's heart. If it took setting himself on fire to save his son, Bryn would do it.

CHAPTER 8

If you find it in your heart to care for somebody else, you will have succeeded.
Maya Angelou

On Saturday, Hélène was disappointed to see Darius and his gangly father reappear at the appointed time. She held the door open for them, inviting them in. "Hello, Darius. Bryn. Nice to see you again," she said.

She'd been lying for so long that she'd become a virtuoso.

"Hi great to see you again thanks for taking time to hear Darius I think you two will hit it off," Bryn rattled on. He was carrying some music books under his arm.

Darius laid a hand on his father's forearm. Bryn glanced down at his son and went quiet.

"Let's talk a bit before I hear you, Darius," she said, avoiding the father's pleading, hopeful eyes.

She gestured to the bench and the pair sat down, as different as salt and pepper.

She watched the shifting emotions on Darius' face, which, despite his silence, he didn't seem able to hide. By nature, she wasn't a hugger, but she only just held herself back from gathering him in her arms. She was surprised at herself. She didn't even know where that impulse had come from.

She smiled down at Darius. "How long have you been playing the piano?" she asked.

The YouTube videos told her all she needed to know, but she wanted to see if Darius would respond to her with a look, a gesture, a nod—something that said he was in there and, with a bit of prodding, would emerge.

Nothing.

Darius held his arms stiffly at his side and gazed past her. She wasn't certain he even wanted to be here.

Bryn answered as she expected he would. "His mother was a classically trained pianist, and when he was two he insisted on sitting on her lap and she would play something and he would imitate."

She folded her arms and smiled. "Mhm, children's tunes and so on?"

"Uh no, Mozart, Bach, classical things." Bryn had a sense of awe in his voice, as though he wasn't sure it was true.

Bryn launched ahead before Hélène could speak. "Viv started teaching him, and he just raced ahead and played anything he heard or could get his hands on, didn't you, bud?"

That troubled her. She knew firsthand how perilous it was to bind one's musical identity to a parent. It was like giving your soul to another person. When that person wasn't at your elbow, you could feel adrift. Her father's decision to find her a new teacher had set Hélène free to become the pianist she was—or rather, had been.

Bryn was still speaking. "He could hear something once and

pretty much play it back mostly perfectly, like it just came into his head fully formed he's always been special that way and he remembers everything, don't you?"

Darius just glanced up at his dad.

Hélène couldn't hide her skepticism. Her own memory was prodigious; she never forgot what she'd played, but she had to study the music before it became part of her brain and hands. She'd only ever heard of a few other pianists who could hear something a few times and then play it.

"I see," Hélène said.

Looking at Darius, he seemed to be holding himself at some great distance. "Can you talk to me?" she asked. How could she even send him to another teacher when he didn't talk?

"I think because his mom died, maybe it's just a stage he won't talk—I thought maybe a fresh start here in Norwalk would help," Bryn said, the words gushing like water from an uncapped fire hydrant. It was like he wanted to get every word out before she changed her mind.

Darius stared at the Bösendorfer and she saw in his gaze, a true pianist's hunger. He'd probably never played one before. Perhaps the lure of playing it might make him talk.

"Do you want to play for me today?" she asked softly, resisting the urge to brush his wild hair off his face.

Finally, Darius looked at her, flicked a single, dark, straight eyebrow up, and nodded once.

That's something, she thought. She opened the doors to the studio, and as Darius stepped passed her, she touched him lightly on the shoulder, trying to communicate safety and warmth.

Bryn began to follow, but she held up a hand. She kept only one chair for herself in the studio because she never let parents in, relegating them to the "parent's bench." In this case, she thought it might be best for Bryn to leave the house altogether.

"Maybe go for a drive and grab a cup of coffee. I'd like to hear him privately," Hélène suggested, trying not to add to the man's worry. "We should be done in an hour."

Bryn looked stricken until Darius took his dad's hand. The ghost of a tender smile lifted a corner of his mouth. Bryn's eyes softened, and his face filled with adoration.

It was how her father gazed at her before she went on stage —complete love.

"You're sure?" Bryn asked.

Darius squeezed his father's hand, a conversation passing between them in glances and touches.

Bryn folded his lanky frame and kissed his son's temple. Like the first time she'd witnessed Bryn kiss his son, Hélène's heart softened with sweetness and compassion for these two. Bryn loved his son deeply and was desperate to help him.

But she wasn't the one who could do the helping. Her identity as a teacher for beginners was well-established. She would hear Darius, give Bryn the names of a few teachers, and send them on their way. Someone more emotionally capable should care for this bruised boy and his dad.

Bryn handed Darius his books and clasped his shoulder. "I'll be back you have your phone, call me if you need anything, okay?"

Darius nodded, followed her into the studio, and set his music books on the piano: Beethoven sonatas, Chopin Ballades, and Rachmaninoff Preludes—all challenging for even adult pianists.

He stared off into a corner as if looking for something.

"So, you aren't a talker." She crossed her arms and smiled down at him. "Unlike your father."

One corner of his mouth curled, which proved he was at least listening and understood.

"You ever play a Bösendorfer before?" she asked, caressing the piano's massive ebony case.

He surprised her by nodding. Bösendorfer's were rare, usually found only in major concert halls and kids rarely had the opportunity to play an instrument of this size or quality.

"Where did you play one?" She settled onto the chair beside the piano bench.

No answer.

"If you don't speak, how does this work? Do you write your answers on a piece of paper?" She tried a small laugh hoping to ease the tension. "Morse code? Semaphore?"

He turned to her with eyes full of endless dark galaxies of grief and pain, of unspoken words and unplayed music. His emotions were so clear and raw it was like a slap to Hélène's heart. Something had severed his ability to speak and play piano; the two most important avenues of expression for anyone, particularly an artist of his caliber.

She held her hand out to the piano as though offering candy. "You can play anything you want," she coaxed.

It was killing him not to play. His YouTube videos made it obvious that he needed to play like anyone else needed to breathe. She knew the need to make music gnawed at you with a kind of animal hunger, and she saw ravenous desire on his face. But how could she get him to play even a scale?

He pointed at her, then at the piano. He wanted her to play.

"Oh, no, you don't. This is your lesson, not mine," she said, laughing. "And besides, how do you know I can even play?"

He stared back at her and pointed again.

What could it hurt to play for him? He didn't know who she was, and because he didn't talk, he'd never tell anyone what he'd heard. If he did, no one would believe him. Even playing for one person was a way of touching them. It might inspire him to play again. It was a one-off risk, and when she sent him and his father on their way, they would never darken her door again, which would be best for everyone.

Ordinarily, when she even thought about playing for anyone, her fingers, wrists, and hands became paralyzed, but now her fingertips itched for the keyboard. Laudatory comments on her YouTube channel were nice but playing live transformed both listener and musician. It had been thirty years since another living soul had heard her play live, and she missed that invisible connection.

What could it hurt?

"If I play, then will you play?" she asked.

He nodded and light flickered into his eyes.

"All right. Me first, then you," she said.

She moved to the piano bench. She closed her eyes, let her head fall back slightly, and lifted her hands. The presence of the piano felt like a monolithic, pulsating creature before her. She launched into the Chopin Mazurka, Opus 50, number 3, in C-sharp minor. Playing felt like being tossed about in the center of a hurricane and loving it.

When she finished, she let her hands fall into her lap and stared at the keyboard. It was thrilling to play for even one person. She even thought she heard applause. She opened her eyes.

Darius was clapping and grinning. She grinned back at him.

Shaking a finger at him, she said conspiratorially, "You tell no one, not the teacher I find for you, not even your dad. That is for you and only you; do you understand?"

He blinked his agreement, and she knew she'd made the right decision. She rose and gestured to the keyboard. "Now you," she said, adding, "if you dare."

Darius took a step back and shook his head, the smile gone.

She lifted one eyebrow. "So, that's the way it is? I thought our deal was I play, then you."

He didn't move. It was time for tough love.

Picking up his music books and handed them to him. "I can't *make* you play. This is the only chance you have. I told your dad I don't have room in my studio for you. Play or don't play; it's up to you. If you do, I can at least help you find another teacher. If you don't, I can't even do that."

He looked up at her, the silence between them singing as eloquently as a symphony orchestra at full throttle.

"Last chance," she said in a sing-song voice.

Sagging as if defeated by an invisible opponent, he made a combination of a groan and a sigh. He sat on the bench.

She offered him the books. "Do you need your music?" she asked, certain Bryn had been exaggerating as proud parents sometimes did.

Darius didn't even glance at her before he launched into the Chopin Nocturne in C minor, Opus 48, number 1, playing from memory.

As though his emotions were buried only skin-deep, the muscles in his face shifted and twitched as he transformed into a dreamy, rapturous magician of sound. Even with his odd hand position—high wrists and fingers nearly vertical—he was breathtaking. He was poetic, with purling runs, a caressing touch, and delicate fluctuations of tempi. He handled the big chords with command. He possessed total emotional, musical, and intellectual command. His enormous heart contained universes of emotion he gave without restraint or hesitation. At eleven, he had the emotional depth and musical gifts of a thirty-year-old. Much of his interpretation of the Nocturne reminded her of herself.

Tears pressed against the backs of her eyes. Her heart expanded, twisted, and ached in her chest. Her lungs felt like she was at an altitude where the air had thinned, leaving her light-headed.

This boy-genius wasn't merely a prodigy; he was a *phenom*.

"Well..." she said when he had finished. She tried to marshal her feelings into thoughts, to rein in her galloping heart.

Here was a gift—the sort of student every teacher dreamed of discovering and cultivating. He was the kind of student who, at one time, would have sought her out and whom she could have trained for a career.

But for her, he could prove a curse. Bonds formed between teachers and students and between teachers and their parents; closeness held the danger of discovery. Father and son were like a pair of moths with tattered wings seeking a flame to warm themselves. She wanted to teach Darius, but that meant unmasking her technique and most likely, her identity. Those costs were too high. She was satisfied, if not happy, with being anonymous. Why destroy all that she had built now?

Gazing at him, Hélène tried to disguise her amazement with warm frankness. "Your playing is stellar, but you already know that. But you don't speak. I'm not the right teacher for you because I'm not a psychol—"

He nearly knocked her off the bench when he threw his arms around her and buried his face against her shoulder. His fragile body trembled as he gasped and sobbed silently into her collar.

To play for her, he'd faced some terror, and now, he was terrified she would let him down. She couldn't do that to him. He needed her—not just anyone, but her. No one had ever needed her before, and it scared the daylights out of her.

Her throat grew thick and words wouldn't come. She gingerly wrapped her arms around his bony shoulders and held him until he stopped shaking. She rested her cheek on his crown and the soft waves of his hair were like puppy fur. His body was warm, and he smelled salty and peanut buttery, the way little boys should smell.

He had chosen her, whether she wanted him or not. With one hug, he had undone her.

Bryn stood on the other side of the French doors, tears coursing down his long cheeks.

It might be a disaster. She might regret it. It would only be temporary. But for now, she could not turn these lonely, love-starved, aching, brokenhearted men out of her life.

CHAPTER 9

Pick up the scent of God when there is nothing else to go on
   Anonymous

St. Paul's Mass had finished, and Hélène and the Marriage Survivors Club were outside on the lawn with other parishioners celebrating the Episcopalian Sacrament of Coffee Hour. The snack and drinks table had been set up in the shade of a spreading maple tree and nearly everything had been consumed. The Marriage Survivors Club was on clean-up, which often as not, meant eating whatever was left.

Black musician's robe flapping behind him in the breeze, Wat strode up. To no one in particular, he said, "Hey, ladies! I wanted to check in to see how the planning's going for the fundraising concert."

Wat, who spoke in exclamations, operated under the assumption that his wishes would be executed by the parishioners. Since everyone loved his outstanding music program, he was usually right.

Carolina answered, "Hélène's agreed to be my co-chair."

Hélène made a grumbling noise of assent.

Frankie, who was in charge of ticket sales, said, "We can probably fit three-hundred-fifty in the church. Of course, what we make depends on how much we can charge."

Carolina said, "But how are we going to sell that many tickets?"

Wat eyed the cookies. Unlike Father Gabriel, who consumed sweets at an astonishing rate, Wat was perpetually dieting and it was the only thing he seemed to fail at.

"We just need to bring in a pianist people are dying to hear," Wat said, avoiding Hélène's narrowed gaze.

Her fingers went tingly and numb, causing her to drop a plate of leftover cookies onto the grass. If Wat thought she would come out of hiding to play the concert, he was deluded. She wasn't doing that for the Marriage Survivors Club, St. Paul's, or anyone. She'd already cracked the door for Darius, and she wasn't about to throw it open for general ridicule.

"I still say a classical piano concert will be a hard sell," Hélène said as she stacked some clean paper plates together.

Bianca said, "I would have thought that as a pianist, you would be happy we're doing something classical. Instead, you act like we're inviting people to a public flogging or to see tattooed, rapping strippers with snakes."

They all laughed.

Hélène snarked, "That might make us more money."

Olivia's husband, Jack O'Grady, and Cam Simpson, Frankie's fiancé, stepped over to where they stood.

To Olivia, Jack said, "We're going to take all the kids bowling. I'll see you at home later, okay?"

Jack kissed Olivia, and she glowed like a tiny firefly.

Cam pulled Frankie to him and kissed her against the side of her neck until she dissolved into giggles. Something Hélène had never seen her do.

In a caveman's gruff voice, he said, "You need a big, strong man to take this inside for you." The two men made a great show of carrying the lightweight plastic table into the church.

Watching the two couples, Hélène felt regret saw across her heart. She would never experience that kind of love. She was too broken, too skittish after her disastrous marriage, to trust another person. She didn't have love, but she had music, at least for herself, if not to share.

Wat rounded the table to stand at Hélène's side. "Darius' dad emailed me that you got him playing again! That's fantastic!"

"I can help him a little because, as you know, I'm only a beginner's piano teacher," she said, repeating something they both knew was false.

Wat said. "You'll have him talking in no time!"

She dumped a cold cup of coffee at his feet, and he jumped back just in time. "I'm not a therapist. If he plays for me, I figure that's progress."

Carolina gathered the half-empty cups scattered about on the table and tossed them into the trash. "Wat, you mentioned you might know someone to play the concert. Have you found anyone?"

Hélène caught Wat's gaze shift nervously away. She got a knot in her stomach, and she glared at him. *Not a chance.*

"I'm ... still looking," he said. He took a bite of a brownie, rolling his eyes with obvious delight.

Olivia mused, "You said Darius was amazing, Hélène. Might he be able to play?"

Music had given Hélène great fulfillment but also her greatest heartache and humiliation. She wouldn't wish that journey on anyone. None of the others knew anything about classical music or performing. They'd all grown up like normal kids with friends. They went on dates, had boyfriends, and experienced the angst of adolescence. They didn't know how a performer's ego and sense of self hung in the balance of each performance. She knew what it was like to play for crowds: the pressure, the preparation, the mental stress. She knew firsthand what it took, the grind of it all. She'd played Paris, Toulouse, Geneva, Lisbon, Carnegie Hall, Royal Albert Hall, and New York Phil, all before her twentieth birthday.

She remembered butterflies in her gut as she waited to go onstage. Her father patting her shoulder. The stamping feet making the floor vibrate. Audiences demanding encore after encore. The thousands of autographs she'd signed. She had slept in hotels on Christmas, Easter, New Year's, and her birthday. Darius wasn't up to that, and he might never be.

After her father died, she'd folded in on herself, unable to continue concertizing. Two years later, she was back at it, pushed onstage by that snake charmer, Yves, until her spectacular flame-out.

None of her friends knew the shame of public humiliation. The shame of letting yourself be emotionally abused.

Hélène reached for the pitcher of ice water and prepared to dump it. "Just what we need! To be known as the church that whores child musicians."

Wide-eyed, Olivia's head jerked back. She took a step away.

Bianca stopped chewing and stared.

"Whoa," Flicka muttered.

Frankie's eyes popped wide.

Carolina paused at her task.

"People are forever looking for some child prodigy to parade around like a freak." Hélène was only vaguely aware of waving the water pitcher back and forth. "Did you bring Darius to me so I could get him in shape to play a concert here?" she snapped at Wat.

"Easy, girl," Bianca said in her lawyerly voice. "Put that pitcher down and no one will get hurt."

Hélène set the water pitcher down on the table with a *thunk*. "I will not allow that child to play a concert here or anywhere. I don't know why, but he's too fragile, too hurt."

She was surprised at her fierce protectiveness. Darius had gotten deeper under her skin than she'd realized.

"Sorry I brought it up. I was only thinking out loud," Olivia said, pushing fluttering strands of gray-blonde hair behind her ear.

Wat's steady gaze was meant to assure her that her secret was safe. He spoke with more kindness than she deserved. "I brought Darius to you because I knew you would take care of him. Care for him. Help him. That he and his dad could trust you."

Hélène blinked into the luminous sunshine. What had come over her? It wasn't like her to bite her friends. She cared about Darius, but she was determined not to care too deeply. She would soon send him off as she did all her other truly talented students. She wasn't going to get attached to him.

Or his dad.

Carolina clasped her hands together and raised them to her chest. "It's clear you don't want Darius in a situation that might hurt him. Neither do any of the rest of us. We were only batting ideas back and forth."

Bianca heavily slung an arm over Hélène's shoulders. "Don't worry about having the kid play. We can always get rapping strippers with snakes."

CHAPTER 10

O Morning Star,
Splendor of light eternal,
And sun of righteousness,
Come, enlighten those who dwell in darkness,
And the shadow of death.

Advent Antiphon

Next to his dad, Darius bounced on the bench in Hélène's entryway. He'd waited all week to see her, and his fingers felt like racecars at the starting line. It was only his third lesson, but he loved coming here and playing. Today, he'd brought the Chopin Second Piano Concerto to play for her, like his mom said. Hélène would teach it to him and his mom would be happy about that.

Hélène came out of the studio. "Hi," she said, and he gave her a nod.

She had a wide, stretchy smile, and she smelled good. Her

black and white hair—her "signature" Wikipedia called it—fluffed out from the sharp bones of her face. He thought she was way prettier in person than those pictures on the internet.

"You want to warm up, and I'll be right in," Hélène said.

Darius went into the studio where his mom, in full color, stood in the corner. She smiled, showing her one crooked upper tooth. The gold necklace with the eighth note twinkled in the bright lights of the studio.

He held up the Chopin to show her what he'd brought. *See! I brought it like you wanted me to.*

She closed her eyes, smiled, and nodded.

In the entryway, his dad was blabbing on and on. "I'd really love to stay and listen I miss hearing him play; it gives me so much joy I haven't heard him play in ages, but if you want, I can go do something else while you two have your lesson—what do you think?"

Why did his dad have to talk about his feelings so much? It was embarrassing. *Feel* this, *feel* that. Nobody wanted to hear about his dad's feelings, especially Darius. His feelings came out in his piano playing, so he didn't *have* to talk even if he wanted to. When he wanted to say something to his mom, all he had to do was think.

Adults were like weird plastic creatures. Every time his dad talked to Hélène, he looked like he was lit up from inside by a nuclear explosion. He could tell how his dad felt, even if he didn't talk about it. The way he laughed: embarrassed or trying too hard. Flicking his fingers: nervous. The spot between his eyebrows wrinkling: thinking hard about something. Leaning from side to side: nervous. Crying at night when he didn't think Darius heard him: sad. But Darius had made him happy by playing

Darius went back to the entryway where his dad and Hélène stood and, with his fingers, played a five-note scale on her arm.

He wanted her to hurry up and come in so he could play for her.

She laughed softly. "Oh, yes, sorry to keep you waiting, maestro. Coming."

Maestro. *Cool.*

She touched his shoulder the way you'd pet a kitten. Momish. He liked it.

When he finished his scales, she said, "Excellent. Now, the thing I think is most important is this: feelings are all that matter, so whatever you play—scales, warmups, everything—do it with feeling."

That was what his mom always said. She said her teacher had said it to her. He thought that it must be something piano teachers told their students.

"What did you bring to play today?" Hélène asked.

He smiled at his mom in the corner and ripped into the first movement of the Chopin Second. His fingers flew over the keyboard, making explosions of colored sparks. Making an earthquake. The heaviness in his chest disappeared, and instead, starlight and a sweet wind filled him up.

He finished, and Hélène shot up out of her chair like her butt was on fire, her face looking like she might puke.

"Why did you bring this?" she asked.

He stared at her, confused. He'd played great so why was Hélène so freaked out?

"You're too young to play this." She rubbed her fingers and her wrists.

Even though she'd never recorded it, Hélène debuted with it at thirteen and he wasn't that much younger.

His mom smiled from her spot in the corner. At least she was happy.

Hélène shook her head, making the feathers of her black

and white hair shiver. "Another concerto, the Grieg or the Chopin First maybe, but not the Chopin Second."

What? How come?

Her accent was thick, probably because she was upset. He could hardly understand her. He felt like he was lost in a crowd of people who were going to trample him, and he couldn't scream.

Hélène was shaking. "I'm sorry, we can't do this piece."

His heart twisted in his chest. His neck felt like someone was choking him. He didn't mean to make Hélène upset, but he didn't know what he'd done, either. There was a stinging behind his eyes. He looked for his mom but she was gone. Mad because Hélène was refusing to teach him.

His dad came in, flicking his fingers, his face all pinched up. "Everything okay?"

Hélène rubbed her forehead with her fingertips. "I'm sorry; it was a mistake for me to agree to teach him. I'm just a beginner's teacher. If he wants to learn that, he will have to go somewhere else."

His dad looked like he was going to keel over. To Darius, he said, "What did you do if you said something mean or rude, you need to apologize right now."

Darius got off the piano bench and wrapped his arms around his stomach because he had a sharp pain there, like the time a kid in the third grade had punched him.

His dad's words came out in one long stream. "But he wants to study with you, and you said you would take him, and you guys were getting along really well he's played more for you than for anyone else this is only his third lesson I'm not asking for miracles, just someplace he can come and play whatever he wants, please, he'll listen to you." He bit his bottom lip, and Darius was afraid his dad was going to cry. "He needs you."

Darius was such a loser. He made everybody miserable: his mom, his dad, and now, Hélène.

Hélène rubbed her hands together. She spoke fast. "I can't teach him the Chopin Second. I will give you a list of other teachers."

"What Chopin?" His dad looked at Darius, the place between his eyebrows wrinkly.

Amazingly, he stopped blabbing and waited, staring at Darius like he expected him to talk. Darius backed up against the wall. The blackness came inside again. The pain in his stomach spread up through his chest like octopus tentacles squeezing his heart.

Why was Hélène acting like he wanted her to teach him how to play slashing heavy metal or the banjo?

"But wait, can't we talk about this, can we figure out something, can't we? I'm sure there's a compromise," his dad said, flicking his fingers like crazy.

His dad rested his big, heavy hand on Darius's shoulder, bent down, and spoke quietly but urgently into his face. "Is that okay, son, can you play other things you have lots of repertoire; maybe you can play the Chopin some other time, but now—*Blab, blab, blab.*"

Darius tuned his dad out and shrugged off his hand. His mom was in the in-between place, he couldn't lose *Hélène Noire et Blanche,* too. Mom wanted him to learn the Second and he wanted to make her happy but Hélène was refusing. How could he do both things at once?

"*Blab, blab, blab.* Don't waste this opportunity to study with Hélène," his dad was saying.

Darius laid a hand on his dad's arm, and he quit talking. Darius looked a long time at Hélène, then he nodded.

His dad gave him another one of his mushy hugs and head kisses.

Darius missed how his mom used to do that. His dad started doing it after she went to the in-between place. Sometimes, Darius missed her so much that he just wanted to melt away. This was one of those times.

Hélène's face went back to normal, like when a cat's fur goes back down when it's done being mad.

"Okay?" his dad said to her. "He can stay if he doesn't play the Chopin?"

Hélène whispered, "Okay, we'll see how ... I have to see how things go."

"It'll be fine he's a great kid I know once you guys get over this, it's going to be okay," his dad said in that jolly Santa way he had when he was even more nervous than usual.

Darius picked up the Chopin score and walked out the front door. He wasn't giving up. He'd just learn it by listening to Hélène's own recording.

CHAPTER 11

When I am afraid, I put my trust in you.
   Psalms 56:3

Hélène felt as though she'd only just escaped being run over by a subway.

In the kitchen, she poured herself a glass of wine, even though it was only five in the afternoon. She stared out the window, waiting for the light to leave the lavender sky and turn dark. As if that would hide her secrets.

If she never saw the bloody Chopin Second Concerto again, it would be too soon. Once musical ideas, words, commands, edicts, demands, and negative emotions infected a piece of music, it was nearly impossible to erase them from an artist's heart and mind. The concerto and her ex were like two strands of barbed wire that had wrapped around her and cut her in two.

On the internet, she had found other musicians who had been torn apart by well-meaning "teachers," "coaches," and the most voraciously egotistical of the musical species, the conductor. Some could never again play a certain piece of music and some had lost their love of music altogether.

After having been flayed to shreds, it was a lifelong task for any artist to reconstruct fragile self-confidence, and sometimes, it was impossible. How could she—if it was even possible—put Darius back together? She was barely holding herself together.

She had been stupid to play for Darius and accept him as a student. Someday, he would talk. Then the fans, the stalkers, the weirdos, the *paparazzi*, maybe even Yves, would track her down just for the pleasure of throwing her public melt-down back in her face.

The thoughts made her top up her glass of wine. Though he could only play for her, she knew Darius was a once-in-a-generation pianist. Even if he did speak, the responsibility of teaching him was enormous. As it was, she would have to handle him with kid gloves. If he spoke again, if he became strong enough, there would be competitions, auditions, performances, probably recordings. There would be forms to sign, and the press would inevitably come calling. People would want to know who his teacher was. Pianists would want to study with her. Someone would recognize her, and everyone would remember how she'd humiliated herself.

Darius, the silent boy, needed to be loved, to trust and be allowed to flourish as a person first, a pianist second, but she didn't have the kind of love he needed. If someone gave her a goldfish, she would end up drowning it.

She remembered her hand in her father's the first time they walked to her new teacher. How she took comfort from the certainty of knowing he would take care of her, even though he knew nothing about music or piano. He had saved her so she could become *Hélène Noire et Blanche*.

Like her own father, Bryn was trying to save Darius. They both needed her help, but how could she do that and still keep her past a secret? Which was more important, the child or her past? If she was careful and didn't play for him again, checked that everything about her was removed from the internet, then maybe she could take a chance. She could help Darius and his sweetly odd father.

A talent like his, a boy like him, a father like Bryn, demanded she try.

She was fairly certain that Darius's silence had something to do with his mother. Asking him might push him further into his world of silence, but asking Bryn would draw the two of them into a dangerous duet of mutual trust.

She had trusted Yves, and look where that had gotten her.

CHAPTER 12

Love is like a virus. It can happen to anybody at any time.
Maya Angelou

As the two of them waited in Hélène's driveway, Bryn nervously flicked his thumb against his forefinger, clawed his fingers through what was left of his hair, and checked the time on his phone repeatedly.

They were ten minutes early for Darius's lesson. Hélène was getting him to play again, and maybe, eventually, he'd start speaking again. He would be happy if all Darius said was, "Leave me alone."

Bryn said, "I love—" Darius placed a light hand on his forearm, and Bryn shut up. He knew he chattered uncontrollably, but otherwise, all he heard was the silence of his son's grief.

He was a precise man, a software engineer who worked in strings of logic that produced exact outcomes. With only a few lines of code, he could ensure the end users had the same predictable, seamless outcome every time.

Being unable to help his son was agony. Vivianne's teaching had created Darius, and her death had eviscerated Darius, the musician, the boy, the son. Hélène was Darius'—and Bryn's—light at the end of the tunnel.

Bryn checked the time on his phone. "Okay, two minutes until five; let's go, it's your turn."

Bryn watched, dumbfounded, as Darius rocketed out of the car and tore up the walk. He wasn't sure who was more excited about these lessons, him or Darius.

They stepped into the entryway just as Hélène came down the hallway wearing a sleeveless, body-hugging magenta dress and ... elbow-length yellow rubber gloves. Her bewitching face bore a look of frustration.

Bryn had been trying to think up a poetic metaphor for Hélène, and he'd decided she reminded him of sun-glinted water with mysterious ripples below the surface. Of the breath of sleeping birds. The fragrance of a forest in winter snow.

Her black and white hair swept away from her face, and he saw again how unusual her beauty was. She had high cheekbones, a sharp, almost chiseled jaw, and enormous dark eyes that looked like she could see at night. She was beautiful, but more than that, she had the kind of face that you couldn't look away from. Looking at her knocked him sideways.

She pulled off the gloves and made a face of disgust. "My kitchen sink's stopped up."

A grin spread across Bryn's face. "I can help I fix lots of stuff if it's okay, I'll take a look." He bit the tip of his tongue to force himself to shut up.

"Are you sure?" Her wide, expressive mouth curved into a smile.

If she had handed him a spoon and asked him to dig to China, he would have been thrilled.

He said, "Sure, I'm happy to help I like to be useful, point me in the direction unless you have somebody else to help you I don't want to step on any toes."

Hélène pointed down the hall. "There is no one else. I would consider it an enormous help if you fixed it. Kitchen's down there past the powder room."

"No one else."

Bryn wanted to cheer. He rocked back and forth on the balls of his feet. "Great, not a problem. Happy to do it, I'm just a nerdy man with a hammer Nerdy Hammerman, that's me."

Shut up, shut up, shut up! Stop!

She laughed, and even that sounded like a musical melody.

To Darius, he said, "Have a good lesson," and bent and kissed his son's head.

Darius rolled his eyes.

Bryn rubbed the side of his nose with a finger and laughed softly. "I know you're too old to be kissed, but I can't help myself."

It was strange how Bryn didn't feel the least embarrassed to show his affection for his son in front of Hélène. Whenever he did, Hélène gave a soft murmur, and her eyes, those star-reflecting black pools, softened.

Darius wrapped an arm around Bryn's waist and leaned against him, something his son hadn't done in a year. Bryn only just caught the emotion building in his chest before it escaped. Hélène was having a healing effect on the pair of them. Though he still wasn't speaking, Darius was more relaxed, and so was Bryn. Music was his words, and for now, that was more than enough.

Hélène held an arm out to Darius, gesturing toward the studio. "Shall we, maestro?"

Darius practically skipped into the studio.

Hélène's kitchen was an afterthought crammed into a corner of the house with seasick green cabinets and 80s linoleum on the floor. It was a stark contrast to her studio, with its gleaming blond wood interior, polished floor, and piano the size of a tugboat. The only things on the yellow Formica countertop were a two-cup French Press coffee maker and cardboard picnic-style salt and pepper shakers. In the corner sat two chairs at a forlorn Parisian-style, black wrought iron café table.

He'd seen campsites with more amenities. No wonder loneliness floated around her like a kind of perfume.

Three inches of murky coffee-colored water and vegetable scum filled the chipped enamel sink. He flicked the switch for the disposal and got only a hum—the sound of being stuck—in response. He made quick work of loosening the disposal with the hex wrench he found. He stood, flicked the switch and the disposal coughed to life.

Turning on the sink to wash down the residue, the faucet produced only an unenthusiastic dribble. She needed a new faucet. Since she had no one to fix this kind of stuff, he could help her fix anything she needed him to.

He opened a crooked cabinet door to see if he could tighten a screw and make it hang straight. Inside, there was only a bottle of soy sauce and a jar of Dijon mustard.

That's it? It's like she doesn't even live here.

Curious, guiltily, he opened another cabinet. There were two water glasses next to a dozen mismatched wine glasses. On the shelf above were two soup bowls, two salad plates, and two dinner plates.

Her house wasn't a home but an ascetic hideaway. No paintings, no pictures, no decorations. It was as if every emotion she had was locked up in that studio.

She didn't just live alone; she wanted to *be* alone.

The more he tried to figure her out, the more enigmatic Hélène Charbonneau seemed, like a bug in a software program he wanted to track down.

"I thought I heard the disposal. Were you able to fix it?" Hélène stood in the doorway.

He jumped, his face going hot. He was sure she knew he'd been poking his nose where it didn't belong. "I fixed it wasn't hard, there was just some gunk in it I can show you how to do it yourself next time it gets stuck so you can do it yourself."

Shut up!

She went to the sink and turned on the dribble of water. "*Magnifique!* How wonderful you are," she sang out. "I thought I would have to use the bathroom sink to wash my dishes. I've been waiting for my friend Frankie to come and fix it, but she's been so busy, and I didn't want to bother her."

Her pleasure made him feel as though he'd slain a dragon. She was even more beautiful when she was happy.

"I see you could use a new faucet, too I noticed it's slow, if you want, I could put that in for you," he said.

Her big eyes grew wider. "Really? You can do this kind of thing?" She was as enthusiastic as if he'd said he could fly.

He could tell she was genuinely grateful, not just fishing for free labor. He leaned against the counter, trying to act nonchalant. "Sure, no problem, I do little repair stuff like this all the time I'm a software engineer, but I like fixing stuff and helping other people." He pressed a finger to his lips. She didn't care about that crap. She just needed a new faucet.

"I would give you a discount on Darius' lesson fee," she said, her smile making his knees weak.

He waved his hands in the air. "Oh, no, no, no, that's not necessary—"

"I insist. Now, I have to get back to Darius." She turned to go.

"Wait," he said.

He didn't want her to go, but he didn't want to ask the question he had in mind, either.

She paused, her stillness as lyrical as her movements. The

lilt of her voice, the languid movement of her arms, her elegant fingers: she was music on the hoof. When he saw the tiny pulse below her ear keeping rhythm, he almost couldn't find words.

"How is he?" He swallowed the emotions welling at the back of his throat. "Has he spoken to you yet?"

"No, I'm sorry," she said, her eyes softening. "He hasn't yet, but at least he's playing."

"He doesn't play when I'm at home but when I get back from work or shopping, I park the car and close the car door quietly, then I tiptoe up the sidewalk so I can hear him through the door. I feel like I'm slowly getting my son back. Before we came to you, I'd ask him to practice or play, but he'd get up, stomp off to his bedroom, and slam the door. I really miss hearing him play."

"I can understand that. Music is the voice of the heart and soul, and his are enormous and old," she said. "I think he may find his way back to his words through music."

"Those are beautiful words," he said, becoming aware that he was whispering. "Thank you for teaching him; it means the world to me ... I want to do whatever I can to help him."

"Don't worry. He'll get there. Give him time," she said and patted his arm.

He laid his hand over hers, and her enormous eyes met his. He felt sharp pings of electricity snap where their skin met.

She made a sharp intake of breath, and her eyes widened. He might be mistaken, but he thought something unspoken yet genuine had passed between them. She seemed flustered, and something like fear flickered across her features.

He dropped his hand and stepped back, his face burning.

She smiled. "Thank you for fixing the sink. Now, I should get back to him."

She was at the kitchen door when he said, "Wait!"

She turned back, those exotic brows arched in question.

"I'd like to take you out to coffee and talk to you about

Darius." He bit his lower lip to force himself to stop talking, but he held her gaze.

"All right," she said.

After she'd left the kitchen, he clenched his fists and punched the air in triumph.

CHAPTER 13

Every new beginning comes from some other beginning's end.
Seneca

Bryn and Hélène were outside on a warm, sun-drenched, cloudless day at Café Pause on Wall Street. Their small round table was intimate, and Bryn had to turn sideways to keep from banging his knees into Hélène's. Big cups of cappuccino with biscotti sat before them.

Her bright green dress hugged her fatless body so she looked like a willowy leaf. When she looked at him, he felt as though the moon and stars were drawing him into an orbit far out of himself. His heart hammered inside him, but oddly, her dark eyes settled his mind and slowed his words.

Bryn licked the foam off his upper lip. "Thanks for letting me take you out for coffee—*take a pause*—I know you're really busy, but I wanted to thank you for helping Darius, taking him on and everything."

"You don't have to thank me," she said. "In the last couple weeks, you've done so many honey-dos, I feel as if I've been paid twice for teaching with him. You fixed the disposal, the faucet, the light outside my front door."

"I'm glad; I like helping out. I like to feel necessary because when I was married, Vivianne's life was all about music, and I was completely unnecessary. It was a space I didn't..." He spread his big, clunky hands. "I didn't understand." He was embarrassed at having shared too much.

He sipped his coffee, and for once, he didn't feel as though he had to shove his thoughts out to keep them from clogging up inside him like Hélène's sink. Her concentration on him was like floating in warm bath water. It wasn't like when he'd talked to Vivianne and felt as though he was cheating Darius out of her time.

He wanted to tell Hélène how he felt about her, but it had been such a short time since they'd met. She was Darius' teacher, which made it awkward. He didn't want to take someone away from his son when he'd only begun to play again. If he asked Hélène out on a real date, Darius might get upset and that was the opposite of what Bryn wanted.

"I don't want to pry or be nosy, but can you explain a little bit more about Vivianne teaching Darius?" She looked down and turned her cup around in the saucer.

Bryn said, "She taught him from the time he could sit on the bench. They spent hours together at the piano. Music was like a secret language Darius and Vivianne shared. They went to concerts without me because I was working a lot of overtime." He dipped his biscotti in his cappuccino, took a bite, and swallowed. "They'd come home and talk about music and composers and how someone had performed and stuff. I didn't understand any of it."

He felt the same old hollow in his chest. Loneliness.

He went on, "I read about music and listened, of course, but the two of them shared something I couldn't share. In a way, when it came to music and Darius, it was like Vivianne was an only parent."

Hélène had been leaning forward in her chair, but now she sat back and crossed her arms and frowned.

Perhaps he'd made a mistake bringing up Vivianne, like when divorced men talked about their exes on a first date. But Hélène had asked so she could understand Darius. She and Darius lived in the same untouchable world that Vivianne and Darius had. Even so, Bryn sensed that Hélène would understand his sense of excommunication.

She twisted her mouth to the side. "She could have included you in discussions if she'd have wanted to. Sounds to me as though she wrapped him in a cocoon, and you weren't allowed in."

He detected a thread of anger in her voice.

"I'm sorry," she said. "I don't mean to criticize your deceased wife, and I am not a therapist. But I doubt one parent shutting the other out of something important is good for the child."

For the first time in ages, he felt as if he had been heard and understood. Pieces of his life that had eluded his understanding snapped into alignment like strings of computer code. His shoulders felt lighter, and he felt less alone.

"I welcome any advice or help you can give. Since his mother died last year," Bryn toyed with his spoon. "I've been ... kind of lost. I didn't know what to do with him anymore."

"Have you tried taking him to a therapist?" she asked.

He gave a defeated laugh. "Only about six different ones," he said, feeling like a failure all over again. "He wouldn't speak to them and they said if he wasn't going to engage, it was useless."

"The two of you have been through a lot," she said.

"It's"—he let out a noisy sigh—"been a challenge."

"What was..." She took a bite of her biscotti, and he watched her think. "Vivianne's piano training?"

"She studied hard and even went to Paris to study for a while after we were married and before Darius was born. Performing was everything to her, but the career she dreamed of never happened. Instead, once he was born, she became devoted to Darius. For years, he couldn't sit down and practice—actually practice—what was in the book for more than twenty minutes. Eventually, of course, he did." Joy bubbled up through him, and he laughed. "Since you started giving him lessons, all he wants to do is practice."

She asked, "Did Darius stop talking and playing when she died?"

"Yes." Bryn hesitated to go on. She was getting to know Darius as he was now, and Bryn didn't want to screw that up by disclosing things he didn't think weren't necessary. Things Darius might not want revealed. When Darius and Hélène formed a tighter bond, the truth would come out in time.

The events surrounding Vivianne's death were best buried and forgotten so Darius could move on.

Her eyes narrowed. "Was she still teaching him when she died?"

Bryn was afraid he'd already said too much. His fingers flicked. "Yes," he said, "she was the only teacher he ever had; after she died, I took a new job and moved here because I thought being nearer to New York, he'd have a better chance of finding a good teacher."

He clutched his hands into fists and made himself slow down. "I took him to a few teachers, but he threw tantrums at the lessons. Then he refused to play at home, even." He felt a deep soreness in his chest. "I felt like he had died, too."

"When she died, he lost his mother *and* his teacher," Hélène said softly. "That's a double death for a musician. Some musicians never recover from the loss. Some never perform in public again. Van Cliburn never played in public again after his mother, who was his teacher, died. That was a terrible musical loss to him and the world."

The prospect of Darius never playing again made something in Bryn howl. It would be like the sun never rising again, but for Darius, it would be death by silence.

"I begged her to let him study with someone else, but Vivianne insisted she was the only one who understood how he made music." All over again, he felt the sense of exile that their camaraderie had imposed on him. He chomped a bite out of his biscotti and chewed before continuing. "The two of them had their own private world."

Hélène sat back in her chair, and he recognized what he thought to be disgust in the lifted peaks of her eyebrows.

He said, "I don't mean to make Vivianne sound like a grasping stage mother. She'd been a good mom. She sacrificed a lot for Darius." But his existence with Vivianne had been a lonely one.

Hélène went on, her tone increasingly biting. "You were right to try to pry them apart. Vivianne should never have continued to teach him after a certain point. When she said she was the only one who knew him, it made it impossible for Darius to study with anyone else."

"I ... I don't understand," he said, feeling like a musical and an emotional ignoramus.

Her eyes were bright with intelligence and warmth. "Teachers give students a language with which to communicate with the world. It's like a secret language they build together, a connection and relationship built around creating something out of thin air. When his mother died, he lost his language, his words, his voice. You were right to try to get her to let him study with someone else." She leaned her forward and spoke earnestly. "Studying with someone else would have cushioned his loss a little."

For the first time, Bryn felt someone was helping him solve the mysteries of Vivianne and Darius's relationship.

Bryn was a man of machines, computers, and tools. Vivianne had been artistic, and he'd been a clunky humanoid tied to Earth; a nerdy hammerman. Vivianne had made him feel like an emotionally bumbling man, and he wasn't, and he had done something right. He had loved Vivianne so much and had done everything humanly possible to help her career, including using his retirement fund to let her go to Paris to study.

When Darius was born a month "early," Bryn pretended not to notice. He'd loved Darius from the moment he knew she was pregnant.

As if reading his thoughts, Hélène said, "You're a good father, Bryn—a good man. You love Darius, and that's all that matters. He's playing, and I think he'll eventually speak again. Just remember that I told you I'm not really up to teaching him for a long time. I think of myself as a stopgap, until he feels strong enough to study with someone who has the skills to teach him."

He wished she didn't have to keep saying that and he hoped that Darius could change her mind.

Or that he could.

"Let's not think about that yet," he said. He looked away and swallowed, hot cinders swirling in his chest. "Thanks for everything." Without thinking, he reached across the table and lightly touched the back of her hand.

Her eyes widened, her gaze falling to where his hand lay on hers. The air between them became an earthquake of heat and thunder. Her lips formed a silent O and she inhaled but didn't draw her hand back.

With a nervous laugh, he yanked his hand back. "This is supposed to be a thank you. I feel like this turned out to be more about me than you." Fumbling, he reached into his pocket and laid the red envelope before her on the table. "Here, this is for you," he said, too shy to look at her.

Smiling, she picked it up between her magical fingers. "Shall I open it now?"

"Oh, no," he said, mortified. "Wait until you get home."

Her face took on a playful, inquisitive look. "What is it?"

He shuffled his feet and let his gaze roam over their surroundings so he didn't have to look into her soul-seeing eyes. "Oh, you know just ... I ... something. You'll see."

"Thank you." She placed her hand over his, and he felt that electrical snap again.

As he drove home, Bryn sang the melody from one of Darius' piano pieces at the top of his lungs. He felt fuller and yet lighter than he had in months.

CHAPTER 14

The child must know that he is a miracle, that since the beginning of the world there hasn't been, and until the end of the world, there will not be, another child like him.

Pablo Casals

It was the end of a long day of teaching. Hélène was weary of listening to botched scales, half-learned pieces from Bach's *Anna Magdalena Notebook,* of parents anxiously waiting for her to turn their children into pianists without practicing.

Soon, she would have to tell them she couldn't teach Darius anymore. They would both be disappointed and hurt, but it was for the best. Best for her, anyway.

Bryn's envelope crinkled in her pocket. She pulled it out. She had been carrying it since she'd had coffee this morning with Bryn.

She set it on the counter and stared at it like a bomb, waiting to go off.

It might contain a little cash, a thank you for the extra time she gave Darius. It might be a thank you card. It could be something completely innocuous but judging from the way Bryn had stared into her eyes, she expected that the contents of the envelope were much more.

His gaze had pulled at her, not for his neediness, but for a different kind of hunger. That look worried her.

At first, Yves' eyes had that look. He'd caressed her knuckles with his thumb, smiled, and charmed and encouraged. After they married, his encouragement became demands, his opinions about her playing scalding. He browbeat her into learning music faster and to perform it before she felt ready.

Stupidly, trustingly, she had tried to be the kind of pianist, the kind of woman, he could love. She knew those looks.

When Bryn was near her, she felt as though he threw sharps and flats into her smooth internal melody. He made her jangle inside.

She opened the cabinet door and prepared to toss the envelope into the trash when she noticed a new plastic tray under the sink, the sort to keep chemicals from spilling or a leak from damaging the wood.

Bryn's work and she hadn't even asked him. She smiled. It was a thoughtful, nearly invisible way for him to care for her without her even knowing. Giving her something without—yet—asking for anything in return.

She would miss Bryn noticing what she needed without her asking. Miss his rumpled shirts and eager smile. Miss Darius' moving playing and his aching heart. Miss the way Bryn looked at her as though he knew who she was without her explaining anything.

She tore open the envelope. Inside was a single sheet of heavy paper, each word carefully hand-written in elegant, old-fashioned cursive.

To Hélène

Where longing is the landscape
And darkness the blanket
Music is a howl
Until the sun rises
And hope shines through
The eye of a needle
Bryn

The words left her breathless. She reread the poem, and each time, her heart expanded until it felt like a singing violin. Never had she been anyone else's hope, only their disappointment, their fool, their disaster.

How could she dupe this generous man whose words rushed out of him like an open faucet? Who loved his son so deeply that he changed jobs and moved to another state to help him? Bryn was falling for someone so broken that she couldn't be honest, trust or love. He thought she was just like everybody else.

Darius knew she could play—a bit—but if he discovered her deception, his ability to trust would be shattered just when he was finding himself.

She had hoped to teach him a few more months, but Bryn's poem meant time had run out. She would have to find Darius another teacher. She had warned them she wasn't up to his level of playing.

She didn't know how she would break it to them, but she could make the excuse that Darius wanted to learn the Chopin Second, and someone else was better suited to that. She put the letter back in the envelope, picked up her cellphone, and made the call.

CHAPTER 15

Between rightness and wrongness, there is a garden. I will meet you there.

Rumi

Hélène paused at the back of the church to watch the Marriage Survivors Club tidy up the garden around the labyrinth. Bianca said something, and everyone laughed uproariously. Flicka, who didn't know a shrub from a flower, was striding around giving instructions, which the others ignored. Frankie was placing packs of annuals around the area they were replanting. Carolina was snipping the dead blooms off a rose bush.

Hélène had missed them. It had only been a few days since she'd snapped at Olivia—snapped at all of them, really—but she had felt bereft, cut off. They were the only family she had, and she had found belonging in their circle.

Hélène made her way to where they were working. Staring down at the dirt, she cleared her throat. "I want to apologize for snapping at all of you about Darius and the concert."

She went to Olivia, who was on her knees digging little holes with a trowel and laid a hand on her shoulder. "I especially want to apologize to you, Liv."

Olivia smiled up at her, and Hélène felt her friend reading every inch of her face, still caring for her. "It's okay, Frenchie. We're women. We'll fight to the death to protect those we care about," Olivia said.

Carolina stopped snipping and, with her forgiving eyes, gazed at Hélène. "We all know you have Darius' best interests at heart."

The others were smiling at her with humor and affection, and just like that, Hélène was sewn back into the fabric of their friendship.

Bianca wiped her hand across her face, leaving a smudge of dirt. "C'mon, Frenchie, don't think you're getting out of helping with this."

"I wouldn't dream of it," Hélène said.

She pulled on her gardening gloves, dropped to her knees, and set to work, but no matter where she dug, she hit stones and rocks. She gouged them out of the soil and hurled her bitter crop deep into the scrub brush.

"How's it going with Bryn and Darius?" Olivia asked as she patted a purple petunia into a hole.

Hélène said, "Darius is amazing. It's like the piano is an extension of his fingers. He's phenomenal." She stabbed her trowel into the dirt and hit more rocks. Apparently, she had chosen an abundant spot. "It's the first time in a year Darius has played."

"Something in your voice says you're worried," Olivia said.

Hélène's trowel slipped, and a small volcano of dirt erupted, spraying dirt over her shirt. "He's still not speaking."

"Give it time. Thanks to you, he's playing," Olivia said.

"And how's the dad?" Flicka asked, smirking. She pulled up a garden chair and crossed her beauty-queen legs.

Hélène smiled to herself. She wanted to share her news with them before it became irrelevant.

She pictured Bryn's brow furrowed in concentration as he repaired something, the ladder of his spine running up his long back as he bent beneath the sink, the way he seemed to rev to life when he saw her. Caring for other people was second nature to him, and he'd decided to take care of her. All this endeared him to her. All that, too, would end.

"I ... like him," Hélène said. "He's very sweet."

"You're grinning, so that says to me you think he's more than sweet," Flicka said and laughed so loudly the birds fluttered out of the trees.

"Bryn wrote me a poem." Then, she felt a hard poke right over her heart. There would be no more poems, either.

"A poem! He wrote you a poem?" Olivia said. She sat back on her haunches and looked at Hélène with envy.

Carolina closed her eyes and sighed dreamily. "How romantic. No one ever wrote me a poem or even a letter. All I ever got were emails."

"I used to get notes in school, but you couldn't have exactly called them poems," Flicka said. "They were mostly invitations to meet a boy behind the school." She laughed again. Even her laugh smacked of smut.

Bianca snickered. "And I'll bet you went every time."

Playfully, Flicka tossed a stick at Bianca, which she caught with an easy backhand.

"What did the poem say?" Carolina asked, returning to deadheading the roses.

"He said I was his hope," Hélène answered. Quickly, she added, "But I think it was more about hoping I can find a better teacher for Darius."

"Sounds to me like he's falling in love with yooou," Flicka crooned.

Hélène rolled her eyes at Flicka.

Frankie dropped a container of pansies beside Hélène. Frankie said, "How sweet; a home repair-poetry-writing-computer-genius."

It described Bryn perfectly.

"Sounds like both Darius and Bryn want to connect with you," Oliva, the emotion thesaurus, pointed out.

And that was the problem. "Darius will only be my student for a little longer," Hélène said.

"How come?" Frankie asked.

"He needs a more advanced teacher," Hélène said. She tried planting a pansy and hit another stone.

Flicka said, "At least screw the dad once before you kick them to the curb."

"Take the advice of an expert," Bianca said and nicked her head toward Flicka.

Everyone else laughed, but Hélène pressed her mouth into a thin line. She'd already said more than she should have. The friendship among the Marriage Survivors Club had a way of making all of them do that.

"What happened to the mother?" Frankie asked.

Hélène said, "She died a year ago, but I didn't ask Bryn how. I don't want to know. It feels too intimate, particularly since I have to find Darius another teacher soon."

Coffee, the poem, Bryn's doing things for her, Darius' joy when he flew in the door for a lesson. Those things all bordered on a building intimacy——something she couldn't return.

Carolina paused her work and gave Hélène a perplexed look. "But you care for Darius. Isn't that enough reason to keep him as your student?"

"It's for the best," Hélène said.

"Best for whom?" Carolina asked, not archly, but with touching concern.

Frankie said, "I agree with Carolina. You should keep the kid."

"And the dad," Flicka added.

Olivia crumpled the empty plastic container. "It's a devastating loss to lose a mother, no matter your age. Darius is just a child. No wonder he stopped speaking or playing. And now you want to kick him out?" Olivia's voice was laced with unusual harshness but Hélène didn't want another fight with her friend.

"I'm just not a good enough teacher, and he deserves better. He's only been with me a short while, and I don't want him to get too attached," Hélène said.

Olivia didn't look at Hélène when she said, "Who don't you want to get too attached? The poetry-writing dad, or the grieving little boy?"

Olivia dangled you over your rationalizations and made you look into the abyss. Hélène knew her plan wasn't ideal for anyone, but she didn't see a way out.

"He'll bounce back," Hélène said as the pansy she was trying to plant came apart in her hands.

"And what about Bryn and you? Will you two bounce back, too?" Carolina asked.

CHAPTER 16

The most important question in the world is, 'Why is the child crying?'

Alice Walker

The minute Darius saw Hélène's smile, he knew something was wrong. Usually, her smile made his insides feel like he just drank a big mug of hot chocolate, but today, she wouldn't look at him.

"Hello, Darius. Your dad didn't come in?" she asked.

Darius shook his head.

"Come on in. I have something I want to talk to you about before we start your lesson," she said, talking really fast and walking like a robot.

He frowned and followed her into the studio. In the corner, his mom was bright orange with jagged edges, like she was mad.

"I wanted your dad to be in on this, but we should just get it out of the way." Hélène stood at the end of the piano.

He stood with his back pressed hard against the wall. *Cold. Blasting winds. Ice. Too dark. Snow drifts. Sleet.*

"We've been working together for about a month now. When I accepted you as a student, I played for you, so you know I can play…" Her fake smile showed too many teeth. "Some."

She rubbed her fingers and wrists like they were cold. She was blinking her big eyes in a funny way. "But I can't teach you much more than I already have. You're beyond me."

Why was she lying?

"I know you want to learn the Chopin Second and I think I found someone who can teach it to you!"

His insides turned to fire, lava, a burning skyscraper. Why was she kicking him out? He'd promised not to play the Chopin Second so this was just an excuse to get rid of him.

In the corner, his mom flared up to the ceiling.

Hélène smiled a fake smile. "I made a phone call to a friend of mine, another teacher. He's performed the Chopin Second several times, and I think you two will get along fine."

She hadn't asked him if he wanted another teacher! Why did adults decide stuff and not even ask you? They just did whatever they wanted: died, moved, went places without him, talked and talked and talked, without even thinking about him.

He blew air out his nose in big, hard wheezes.

She pumped her hands at him in the air. She came toward him, but he backed away from her. "Darius, Darius, I can see you're upset, but that's not what I meant to do." Her voice was like a cartoon, jerky and squeezed. "I just want what's best for you. I know your dad does, too, and my friend is an excellent teacher."

Darius shook his head. *Liar!* She could teach him everything he needed to know. He needed her. He couldn't lose her, too. He stared at her, trying to burn a hole in her forehead with his eyes. It felt like the Bösendorfer was sitting on his chest. His back teeth made a grinding noise.

Hélène's eyes were round, and her voice wobbled. "I didn't

think you would get so upset or I would have waited until your dad was here. I'm going to see if he's back yet." She hurried to the front door, looked out, and came back. "He should be back soon, and then all three of us can talk it over, okay? If you don't like this other teacher, I can——"

She put her hand on his shoulder, but he jerked away from her.

Be careful! Don't hurt anybody again! Remember what happened last time.

He pounded his fists on his head, on the wall.

"Don't do that, you'll hurt your hands!" Hélène pulled him into a bear hug.

He didn't care if he chopped off his hands. He twisted and squirmed out of her arms.

Don't hurt her!

Animal noises came out of his throat. He pulled his hair and tore at his clothes.

She put her hands over her mouth. "Oh, no, no, no. Darius, don't do this."

He ripped his music book to shreds and kicked it around the room. Someone was howling and screaming.

In the corner, his mom glowed red hot, whirling like a fire tornado.

I'm trying, Mom! Don't get mad. Don't go. I'm trying to study with her like you said. I'm trying to make you happy.

"Darius, stop! You have to stop this!" Hélène backed away and put her palms on either side of her head. "All right, all right. No other teacher, okay?"

He backed into a corner and grunted. He hauled his breath in, and sweat was running down his face. They stood staring at each other for a long time. Her eyes were big, scared.

She brushed back her hair. "Okay. Okay. But if I teach you, you have to do something for me, all right?"

His mom was less red now. If it made his mom happy, he'd do it.

He grunted again.

Hélène crossed her arms. "You have to speak in our lessons and at home to your dad."

A crashing like cymbals vibrated all through his bones and shook his spine. His teeth made a creaking sound. Spit sprayed as he heaved air in and out between his clenched teeth. He made growling, howling sounds. He screwed up his face and sucked air in and out through his strangled throat.

He clenched his fists and screamed "FUUUCK!" into her face.

Her face turned white, but she didn't run off like all the other piano teachers when he'd screamed at them.

"All right," he croaked.

"So ... you can talk," she said softly.

"Obviously, I just don't want to." His voice sounded weird and scratchy. "If you won't teach me, I'll quit piano forever."

"Okay," she said. "I will teach you, but tell me, why did you stop talking?"

"No! No deal!" He karate-chopped the air. "I talk, you teach me."

She was shaking. "Anything you want to tell me while we're having this long conversation?"

"Yeah." He swallowed, trying to make his voice wet.

He had her now. She thought she was so smart, but he knew. He'd known all along. Looking right into her big eyes, he said, "I know ... I know you're *Hélène Noire et Blanche,* black and white."

She looked like she was going to pass out. Holding onto the piano, she went to her chair and sat down.

He stalked after her, coughing away a tickle in his throat before he could speak. "A long time ago, you were, like, super-famous for playing Liszt. You lived in France, and then you disappeared all of a sudden. People all over the world are still trying to find you."

He grabbed her left hand and pointed to the brown triangle on the back. "There, that funny brown triangle. I saw it in an old YouTube video and it's in all the videos of Le Pianiste. I know that's you, isn't it?"

Her hand was shaking, and she pulled it back and hid it in her other hand.

It was hard to talk. His throat felt like he'd swallowed an old rug. "I saw all the videos. Liszt, Schubert, Schumann, Rachmaninoff, Beethoven, Chopin."

Her face fell down, and she looked tired. "Yes, Le Pianist is me." She rubbed the spot on her hand. In a sad, quiet voice, she said, "I thought I was careful."

"I knew it was you because I've listened to your recordings since I was a little kid. I didn't have to see your hands to know it was you."

She lifted one eyebrow. "That's impossible."

He was proud of how he could do it. It was a special thing he'd been able to do since he was a kid. Maybe it was because of all the times he and his mom had listened to her recordings. "Yes, I can. I can tell it's you. You're the best that ever was. Why don't you play anymore?"

She massaged her wrists. "Our deal was that I teach and you talk."

He didn't know he was going to do it when he fell against her and clung to her. "I won't tell. I won't ever, ever, ever, ever tell anybody. Promise."

CHAPTER 17

Death is not the greatest loss in life. The greatest loss is what dies inside us while we live.
Norman Cousins

When Darius left, Hélène was shaking so badly it felt as though her bones would rattle apart. She hadn't wanted to ask Bryn why Darius stopped speaking because it felt too intimate, but closeness was being forced upon her by the poem and by Darius' need of her. Her affection for him was, in part, because of his complete vulnerability when he played. The only way he'd been able to protect his inner tenderness was to close up like a clam.

Now that Darius knew who she was, she could give him the technical and musical instruction he deserved. No wonder his mother had wanted to keep him under her thumb; Darius was everything she could never be.

Darius would go when he chose, but for now, he and Bryn were staying.

After so many years of being alone, Hélène found Bryn's run-on sentences comforting. She looked forward to seeing his gangly figure, his sweet, laughing eyes. His eagerness to please, the way he took care of her in his quiet, almost invisible way and demanded nothing in return, charmed her. She wanted, against all instinct, to care for him, too. She wasn't sure when she had begun to feel this way about him. Bryn and Darius had shaken something loose in her, and she wasn't sure she could put it back together, even if she wanted to.

Like he did every week, Bryn rubbed a dust rag over the gleaming ebony grand piano in the living room, polishing it until every surface reflected the light. If he didn't clean anything else, he did this one thing. It was his way of keeping his guttering hope alive. He lifted the lid on the keyboard and played a few notes just to hear the sound. The piano had cost him a small fortune, but Vivianne and then Darius had needed an instrument of this quality.

Now it sat there like a felled tree, forever reminding him of his dead wife, of his son's lost potential, of all the ways he had failed his silent son.

Bryn had done everything he could think of, but it was Hélène who managed to get Darius playing again, but he still wasn't speaking. According to Hélène, if Darius never spoke again, his life would be limited when his talent was limitless. Bryn was out of ideas as to how to get Darius to speak again. Hélène said to be patient, but how could he be when he knew his son was holding back a part of himself?

Darius came up, leaned against Bryn, and slipped his long-fingered hand into Bryn's.

He looked down at his sorrowful, broken boy, whom Bryn was afraid would never heal. He felt a deep bruise on his heart.

Bryn wrapped Darius in his arms, smelling his chocolate chip aroma, feeling the fragile bones of his spine.

Bryn said, "I miss your playing at home I feel so lucky I get to hear you at Hélène's I hope you play at home again soon."

Darius rubbed Bryn's arm, making him slow down.

Bryn inhaled, exhaled. "I'm glad I found her. She seems like a great person, a great teacher."

Darius raised his chin, and a faint smile crossed his face.

Bryn savored the momentary change of his son's face from a little old man back into a little kid.

"I like her," Darius said.

Bryn froze and stared down at Darius. He was afraid to believe his dream had come true. Maybe it was a one-off and wouldn't happen again. What had Hélène done to trigger those three words after the long, heartbroken silence?

Bryn held himself in place when what he wanted to do was catch Darius up in his arms and swing him around the room. To hoot and holler, to shake his fists in the air and shout "Yes!" To run into the streets and shout that his boy was home.

"Did you talk to Hélène? Did she do something that made you decide to..." Bryn realized that his mouth had slowed, that the words weren't leaping out to fill a silent void. "You know, to talk?"

"She said I had to talk if I wanted to keep studying with her," Darius answered.

Hélène had loved his son back into existence, and Bryn had no idea how to thank her. A chunk of his grief broke off and blew away in the dust of hope and joy. A sound like clanging church bells resonated in his chest. His beloved boy was making his way back to himself and Bryn all because of Hélène.

Bryn did the only thing he knew how to do. "I love you," he choked out, blinking back his tears.

Darius stretched his spindly arms around Bryn's waist. "I love you too, Dad."

CHAPTER 18

"It is such a mysterious place, the land of tears."
The Little Prince
Antoine de Saint-Exupéry

His mom sat curled up in the corner of the sofa, conducting the phrases with her pale arms as Darius played the first Rachmaninoff prelude. With his eyes closed, he felt like he was walking along a forest path, the bright green leaves of the tall trees shivering in the breeze. Sun shone through the branches making patches of dark and light on the path. The air was cool and silky. Everything was peaceful, and he wasn't even thinking about the night his mom died.

He twisted around on the bench so he could see his mom. "Did you like that, Mom? Did I play it like Hélène plays it?"

She nodded, her straight brown hair swinging against her cheek. When she first died, he could smell the perfumy smell of her hair all the time, but now, even when he concentrated hard, he couldn't. He used to be able to picture the exact color and feel of her hair. Not anymore. He missed coming home from school and eating the snack she'd made for him, but he got his own snacks now. If she didn't come to see him every night, the Bad Dreams didn't come so often.

"Beautiful ... my favorite," she said.

"I know. I want to make you happy. Remember when we used to listen to Hélène's recordings? You said it was like sitting in the audience."

Back then, he could almost see the way Hélène's arms lifted, the way her fingers curved, the bend of her wrists. He heard her pedaling, the way she fluttered the tempi. From listening to her YouTube videos as *Le Pianiste*, she played better now than when she'd been young, and she'd been insanely good before.

In a voice as thin as smoke, she said, "Hélène ... speak ... Second Concerto..."

His chest tightened. "I've been really busy learning other stuff and besides, you know she won't let me play it. She freaked out when I brought it. I don't want to make her mad, too."

She wavered, her eyes becoming two blind holes. He used to be able to tell how she felt just by the way her eyes narrowed or the way she twisted her mouth to the side. Since she'd gone to the in-between place, he couldn't see those expressions.

He twisted the hem of his shirt. "Mom? Are you ... still mad because of what I did?" he asked.

She flickered like Christmas lights going off and on. "Chopin..."

His voice scraped against his throat and his eyes stung. "Mom, you and me can learn the Chopin Second together. You can tell me how I'm doing, right? I want to do it for you."

Parts of her disappeared and reappeared, her edges going all smudgy like she was being erased. Her words came out in a distant sound.

His words clogged up in his throat, and he could hardly speak. "Mom, I need you. Can you come more? I want to see you. Please, please! I'll learn the Second Concerto to make up to you for what I did. I promise I will!"

He scrambled off the piano bench, arms outstretched to her, but she broke apart into a flurry of tiny, colored sparks.

"Mom! Mom, don't go! Don't go! Please, don't go!" His breath came hot and dry, and he blinked the wet out of his eyes. "I'm sorry! I'm sorry!"

But she had vanished, leaving him alone, again.

CHAPTER 19

Kittens are angels with whiskers.
Alexis Flora Hope

"Okay, let's knock off early today," Hélène said to Darius.

"Why?" Darius jumped off the bench.

His face was radiant, with a mischievousness she hadn't seen before. She laughed. "Because you're incredibly wiggly today. What's up with you?"

Hélène handed him back his music book, which he didn't need. He'd heard it, looked at it once, and played it flawlessly from memory. Their work now was fine-tuning. She always scheduled him last, allowing them to run as long as he wanted, and they were now up to two-hour lessons, twice a week. She often tired before he did.

His progress was astounding, as were his sensitivity, expressiveness, insight, and the speed at which he learned. It was as if, after starving for piano for a year, he was getting his fill.

"You see my new shoes?" he asked, sticking his feet out to show off a pair of red sneakers with blue laces and soles.

"I did notice. They're great," she said. It was the first time he'd shown up in sneakers. He'd even begun wearing T-shirts and jeans.

Gazing down at his shoes, he twisted his mouth to the side. It was a gesture she'd never seen him make before. He said, "These are cooler than my old loafers."

"I agree," she said. He was changing from the old man who'd walked in her door into a real, live boy.

Grinning, Bryn stood in the entryway. On the floor was something bulky in a plastic bag.

These two were up to something. She sensed an excited energy bubbling around him. She liked that about Bryn, his inability to keep his emotions from showing on his face.

Darius motioned to Bryn, who bent to let Darius whisper in his ear. Bryn nodded and smiled.

Seen together, Hélène couldn't help but compare them. Bryn, with his pale, receding hair, short blonde eyelashes, and pale gray eyes, was all rattly bones. Darius was softness, mad waves of hair and dark, observant eyes ringed with extravagant lashes. Having never seen a photo of Vivianne, Hélène assumed Darius looked like his mother.

"We got you something for your birthday," Darius said, adorably hopping from one foot to the other.

How did they find that out?

"You did?" she said, a familiar lump of panic rising in her throat. She kept smiling even as her pulse jittered. "How did you know?"

"The cards on your kitchen table," Bryn said, his face practically neon with excitement. "We didn't know the exact date, so we just made a guess."

Her relief was so complete she felt blood rush back into her fingers and toes. "It's today," she said. "You guessed right."

Lovingly, Bryn laid a hand on Darius' shoulder. "Go get it."

Darius raced out to the car.

"How are you celebrating?" Bryn asked, smiling.

She couldn't help smiling back at him.

"I'm going out with some friends to our favorite restaurant," she said.

Bryn pulled an envelope from the pocket of his shirt. "Here, this is from me." He stared at the floor, avoiding her gaze, but his darling ears were scarlet.

She took the envelope, and an electric charge crackled through her. "Thank you. I'll read it later," she said and stuck it in the pocket of her dress.

Bryn shifted from one foot to the other, and she recognized Darius' same wiggliness.

Quickly, Bryn added, "I hope you don't mind ... my, you know, writing poems for you. I do it not only because I'm grateful to you--" He cleared his throat, and redness climbed to his cheeks. "But you inspire me, and I love being around you."

A delighted eagerness like a brush fire crept over her.

"I ... I don't mind," she said, looking into his sweet face. "It's nice being someone's inspiration."

Bryn took a step toward her, his open face filled with affection.

She tipped her face up and rested her hand on his chest. He laid his hand over hers, his head dropping toward hers.

She stretched up on tiptoe. Even as their faces were inches away from one another, she knew there were so many reasons this shouldn't happen.

Darius clattered back inside. As if in silent agreement, Bryn and Hélène sprang apart.

Darius was hauling a plastic pet carrier from which a pathetic mewling emanated. He opened the carrier, reached in, and pulled out a tiny kitten, entirely black except for two patches of white on his front paws so that they looked like little hands. The kitten had a long, pointed face and oversized ears. Glossy black fur lay flat against his body, and he had a little switch of a tail. Alert green eyes took in his surroundings.

"How adorable," Hélène said. Her heart melted.

Bryn's long face lifted in a grin. "Our neighbor's cat had kittens a couple of months ago, and Darius thought—"

"Daa—aad," Darius said in a two-tone interruption. Another first for him.

Bryn looked embarrassed and shoved his knobby hands in his pockets. "Oh, sorry, I'll shut up."

Darius handed her the kitten. She took him and perched it against her shoulder. They all laughed when the kitten batted her earring and tried to bite it with his tiny, sharp teeth. She nuzzled his soft fur, and he snuggled closer, his purr buzzing against her clavicle.

Darius said, "Isn't he cute? Feel how soft he is."

"Thanks for bringing him along to show me. What have you decided to call him?" she asked, stroking the furry creature with a single finger.

Darius and Bryn looked at one another.

"He's for you," Darius said, his eyes sparkling as though he'd swallowed an explosion of fireworks.

"For me?" She tried not to recoil in horror. The pulse in her neck jumped to *prestissimo*.

Once, Bianca tried to get Hélène to take a stray cat, but she had refused on moral grounds of being an unfit animal parent. She couldn't accept this *gift*. A coffee mug she could use during Darius's lessons; a scented candle, funny paper napkins, a music-themed notepad, but a *kitten*? A living, breathing thing that needed attention and affection, that would meow in the middle of a recording, or want to sleep with her or scratch her hands and face? A creature that depended on her.

Bryn was studying her. He stroked the kitten's head, his big hand dwarfing the kitten. "Darius, can you go out to the car again and bring in the bag of cat litter?"

"Sure!" Darius rocketed out the door.

As soon as Darius vanished, she said to Bryn, "I can't keep him." She desperately tried to peel the kitten off her neck.

"Are you allergic?" Bryn asked worriedly.

"No ... but ... he's utterly adorable," she said, wracking her brain for reasons she couldn't keep this animal that had instantaneously adopted her. "I'm not good at taking care of anything or anyone besides myself."

"Look how you took care of Darius," Bryn countered. "He's come so far in a short time."

She said, "But there's feeding and the litter box. It's a very generous gift, but I don't think I can keep him." She held the kitten out to Bryn. "Here, you'd better take him before he gets too attached to me."

Bryn didn't take the kitten. Desperation was written all over his face. "Please don't reject his gift," he pleaded. "I know it's not normal for people to give other people pets out of the blue, but it was his idea he said so using words and everything." Bryn pumped his fists in and out of his pants pockets. "Please don't hurt him by refusing the kitten he was so happy when he got it for you he's as excited as when he was six and won his first competition." His Adam's apple bobbed. "He hasn't been this happy in a year it would mean so much to him I'll change the litter box and scoop it when we come for lessons."

She was afraid he would cry. Or that she would cry.

Bryn paused to point at the plastic bag on the floor. It was as if he couldn't speak and move at the same time. "That's a litter box, and I'll keep you supplied with food and cat litter we even bought a box and a scratching post which the kitten likes please don't hurt Darius' feelings."

"Bryn ... I can't—" She ended with a pained sigh. She did not say "love anything," but the words were on her lips.

Darius returned, carrying a small bag of cat litter, and set it on the floor.

The kitten had curled up against Hélène's neck and seemed to be asleep. His body felt like a cashmere scarf around her neck. She said, "Darius, this was thoughtful of you." She glanced at Bryn, and she stopped because she couldn't stand to see the disappointment hovering in his eyes. She couldn't bring herself to break their hearts. If they thought she could do this, actually love something ... maybe she could.

Darius reached up and scratched the kitten's neck. "We got him for you because you live alone, and you need to practice loving something and having something love you back."

He steered his gaze sideways, squirmed, stood with one sneakered foot atop the other. "And ... like, and if you need somebody, you know, to talk to..." He tapped his fingers, as though playing piano on the seam of his jeans. "If you need somebody to listen ..."

He looked up at her, and in his eyes, she saw his silence, deep and all-encompassing, like her own. "You can talk to him."

Her heart broke for the pain she saw him carrying, that he was incrementally letting go of.

The kitten made a squeak of a meow.

Darius stroked the kitten's neck. "I think you should call him Liszt." He gave her a pointed look, which meant, "because you play Liszt like nobody else."

She looked at Bryn, who seemed about to burst. It was the most words she'd ever heard Darius speak.

This damaged little boy and his lonely father had seen right into her heart. She thought the healing had only been going in one direction, but Darius and Bryn were giving her something she had tried not to accept: themselves.

It was a futile refusal on her part because they had nestled into her heart like the kitten purring against her neck.

She bent and kissed the crown of Darius' head. "That's a perfect name for him. Thank you for getting him for me. He's beautiful."

After they left, Hélène didn't have to meet the Marriage Survivors Club for another half hour, so she carried Liszt upstairs to show him around. She found an old blanket and made a little nest for him at the end of her sofa. He padded in a circle, curled up in a furry black ball, and went to sleep as if he knew this spot was his. She sat next to him and stroked his downy-soft fur.

"Best birthday gift ever," she whispered to Liszt. "Just make sure you pee in your litterbox, okay?"

From her pocket, she withdrew Bryn's envelope. When she saw her name written in his hand, her heart bounced in her chest.

Because of Music
> *Your hands moving through air*
> *Stir a storm inside me*
> *Would that I could stand in the midst*

You turn to face me
> *And the sky envelopes me in light*
> *Blinding me like a saint in ecstasy*

The point of your bare elbow
> *Reduces me to the fevered state*
> *of a 19th century lover*

. . .

The crease behind your knee
  Intoxicates as midnight moonlight
  On a summer lawn

The hollow at the base of your throat
  Where I would lay
  My soul to eternal rest

Bryn

The desire of it undid her. This was a man who didn't filter his love any more than he filtered his words. It was like a gusher, dousing everything and everyone around him, including her.

She pushed off the sofa and paced the room, trying to throw off the emotions dragging her toward the precipice of something she hadn't allowed herself in years: love.

CHAPTER 20

I cook with wine, and sometimes I even add it to the food.
W. C. Fields

"Happy Birthday to you," the Marriage Survivors Club sang with their champagne glasses in the air.

Hélène was relieved when they finished. She adored them all, but not one could carry a tune, and listening to them sing was like having her ears stabbed with an ice pick.

Jaime, the long-suffering proprietor of Paella, had given them six dishes of flán with a candle planted in Hélène's. The Marriage Survivors Club always celebrated their birthdays at Paella because they could get as loud and rowdy as they wanted, and they wouldn't get kicked out, which had happened in two other places.

"Another great year," Carolina said. Her cheeks were rosy from the champagne.

"You don't look a day over fifty-three," Bianca said with a laugh.

"Don't rush things," Hélène, fifty-one today, said. She polished off her glass of champagne.

The bubbly was soaking into her limbs, softening her, loosening her tongue, making her likely to say things she shouldn't. But what the hell? It was her birthday, and with the Marriage Survivors Club, anything was acceptable.

"Did you buy yourself something fun?" Carolina asked.

They had long ago sworn off giving one another gifts since none of them needed anything. Instead, they usually made a donation to St. Paul's.

"I had the oil changed in my car," Hélène said. "Does that count?"

"Does in my book," Frankie said.

Flicka, who had been through four husbands, all of them rich, said, "I used to pick something out at the jeweler's, then when my husband went in, the jeweler knew which way to point him. Worked every time."

Hélène said, "Bryn and Darius gave me ... wait for it." She held up her hand in a stop gesture. "A kitten."

"Is it still alive?" Bianca asked.

"I've only had it an hour," Hélène said and collapsed in giggles against Bianca's shoulder.

"Yeah, but you work fast," Bianca said.

"How sweet of them. I always said you needed a pet," Olivia said. "Something to snuggle up to."

"Does that mean for my next birthday, you're going to give me a dark-haired thirty-year-old with the staying power of a bull?" Flicka asked.

Their guffaws attracted glances from a few other diners.

"What did you name him?" Frankie asked.

"Darius named him Liszt," Hélène said, wiping tears of laughter away.

"Do you have any pictures?" Carolina asked.

Hélène took out her phone and showed pictures of Liszt sleeping contentedly at the end of her sofa.

Carolina handed her the phone back. "He looks very happy. How was it you let them give you a kitten?"

Hélène shook her head. "I honestly don't know, but if you saw these two, you couldn't resist them either. They're so dear, and Bryn, he's ... well, he's honest, kind and gentle, chatty, lovely, caring. He can fix anything, and he loves that child like you cannot believe. Even Darius is beginning to open up. He's started talking to Bryn and I. Bryn said he's even talking a little at school."

"Congrats." Olivia raised her glass. "You've made a big impression on those two."

"They've made an impression on me," Hélène admitted. Her face warmed with pleasure.

The possibility of letting Bryn closer meant telling him the truth. Darius knew who she was, but Bryn didn't, and that would be a difficult bit of dishonesty to wriggle out of.

"Bryn sounds like a good man," Olivia said.

"I like him, but a relationship is impossible," Hélène said as she poked her fork into the flan's caramelly sugar crust.

"Why?" Flicka asked.

Hélène said, "Dating Bryn might make Darius feel betrayed and go silent again. I don't want to take that chance with him or his talent. Darius is the one who matters in this ... situation."

"Now that you've taught him awhile, is your opinion of Darius any different?" Frankie asked.

Hélène considered the question of Darius' talent, and she was stunned anew. "I've heard lots of young prodigies who flamed out, and a few who went on to big careers. I've heard plenty of adult pianists." Hélène turned her champagne stem between her thumb and forefinger. She looked around at each of them. "I think he could be one of the most important pianists of the century."

"You shitting us?" Bianca asked, drunkenly.

"I'm not exaggerating," Hélène said.

She should know. She'd been one of those important pianists; a brilliant flame, a stirring performer, influential and memorable. Except what people remembered most about her was her cringeworthy public meltdown.

Olivia said, "And he walked into your studio. How do you suppose that happened?"

"God works in mysterious ways," Carolina said, repeating another of the Marriage Survivors Club's sayings, which was said as often in irony as it was in sincerity.

Hélène wasn't sure if Wat, God, or the devil was to blame for Darius' appearance in her life, but she did think perhaps the angels had sent Bryn. She felt a hollowness pressing at the base of her throat. When he found out she'd lied to him, Bryn's affection would go up in smoke.

"How does a young pianist like Darius get noticed?" Carolina asked.

Hélène polished off the last bite of her flan and dabbed her lips with her linen napkin. "Competitions are the first way. The Norwalk Symphony has a Youth Concerto competition and I think he should enter."

However, she would have to figure out a way to keep her name from being attached to Darius. Perhaps Doris Grimmstein would play the orchestral part with him which would allow Hélène to remain anonymous.

"Can he win?" Frankie asked.

"Without a doubt," Hélène said.

Olivia, with her usual insight into the heart, asked, "Is Darius up to competing emotionally?"

"Little by little, I'll see what his stress tolerance is. Before the competition, I'll see if he's up to the pressure of playing for other people again," Hélène said.

"How will you know?" Carolina asked.

"Maybe do a small private recital at my place," Hélène said.

Flicka said, "I have to hear this boy wonder. Can we come?" She emptied her fourth glass of champagne. Hélène suspected that Flicka had a wooden leg.

"If he agrees to play, I was hoping you'd be the audience," Hélène said.

Frankie looked down the table at Carolina. "Speaking of piano, has Wat made any progress getting a pianist for our fundraising concert?"

Hélène coughed into her napkin. If she wasn't too drunk to walk, she would toddle off to the bathroom until this part of the conversation wore itself out.

"Wat's made several phone calls." Carolina gave a sigh of defeat. "But everyone wants a lot of money, and since it's a fundraiser, we need someone to donate their services."

With studied nonchalance, Hélène said, "We could hire a chamber ensemble."

"We can't," Frankie said. Always a careful drinker, she put her hand over her glass when Bianca offered a refill. "We've already sold one hundred tickets to a piano concert."

"Wat did come up with an interesting alternative to a big name, and this is the perfect time for us to talk it over. We can let him know if we want to move ahead with it," Carolina said. She giggled for no reason but that she was tipsy.

"As long as it's not a banjo player," Bianca said with an eye roll.

Carolina said, "He thinks we could hire the winner of the Norwalk Symphony Orchestra competition to play a concert the week after they win. It will create a synergy between the

Symphony audience and St. Paul's and give the winner significant public exposure right away."

Hélène's ebullient mood fizzled, flat as two-day-old champagne. If Darius won—it was almost impossible that he wouldn't—then he would play at St. Paul's, and, as his teacher, eyes would be on her. Was she willing to sacrifice her anonymity to do what was best for Darius? For St. Paul's and the Marriage Survivors Club?

"Great idea!" Olivia said.

Inside, Hélène's champagne-inspired fizz went flat.

"This sounds like a win-win," Frankie said. "I say we do it."

Not to Hélène, it didn't. It had the ring of doom exactly like the opening chords of Beethoven's Fifth Symphony. If he decided to play in the competition, he'd only play for the judges. At Hélène's, he would only play for her friends. Those were different circumstances than playing in public in an hour-long recital at St. Paul's. If he played well at the competition but tanked at the concert at St. Paul's, it could break him. Playing for the winner's concert with the orchestra wouldn't happen for almost a year; enough time for Darius to build up the stamina to perform in public.

The others nodded in agreement as Hélène let her limbs turn to butter and slumped into her seat.

Frankie said, "We can sell program ads to local businesses."

"Lots more people go to the symphony than to St. Paul's," Flicka said. Then she mused, "I wonder if there are any single men that go to the symphony?"

In an effort to steer the conversation away from the competition, Hélène asked Olivia, "Any luck getting your pal to donate linens to the youth shelter?"

Olivia frowned at Hélène's veering off topic. "Hans from Belgianhuis? Yes, he's going to do one set of sheets for each bed. We'll put an ad for him in the concert booklet."

"How big a budget do we need to purchase all the things we need for the shelter condos?" Hélène asked.

"Not sure yet, but a lot. A really, really, fat lot of money," Olivia said.

Carolina said, "Hey, maybe we could suggest concert tickets as a birthday or anniversary gift."

"Genius!" Flicka spluttered so that it came out as "geniutth."

"Maybe we can have a raffle, for say, a private dinner with the pianist," Olivia said.

"We could raffle off things like gift certificates to restaurants, art works; that kind of stuth—stuff," Flicka suggested.

"Maybe Flicka can donate a kidney?" Bianca said.

Flicka coughed dramatically. "I need another drink."

Bianca obliged her.

Bianca said, "I'll donate a divorce and Flicka can ask her plastic surgeon to donate a facelift. Like a two-for-one."

Flicka laughed harder than anyone.

Now they were onto the idea of the concert; there was no holding them back. Sometimes, Hélène felt as though the Marriage Survivors Club possessed a nefarious ability to siphon money out of anyone's pockets.

"Sell concert tickets *and* raffle tickets?" Frankie said. "Why don't we ask people to sell blood plasma and donate the proceeds to the shelter?"

Bianca raised her hand. "I'm in. Type B."

"I think we can raise our fundraising goal to around $25,000," Flicka said, and no one blinked an eye at the staggering sum. None of her four ex-husbands had stood a chance when it came to money.

Carolina looked up and down the table. "So we're agreed. We invite the competition winner to play a paid recital at St. Paul's?"

Frankie raised her glass, and the others joined her. In

unison, they repeated the Marriage Survivors Club's motto. "One for all, and no bullshit for any!"

Now, all Hélène had to do was weigh who was most important in this scenario: Darius, her, or the Marriage Survivors Club.

CHAPTER 21

It is easier to resist at the beginning than at the end.
Leonardo da Vinci

Hélène found Bryn in the kitchen washing his sturdy hands. His face was shiny with a light sheen of sweat, and there was a smudge of dirt along the line of his jaw. He looked delicious. He greeted her with a grin that made her heart thud a low C.

"You two done?" Bryn asked.

He'd stopped speaking in run-on sentences, and in a way, Hélène missed that about this man who charmed her with his kindness. He had become confident, but not in a way that made her wary. It was lovely to have someone care for her without demanding something in return, like everlasting fealty or the surrender of her musical soul.

She leaned against the kitchen counter and crossed her arms to keep from putting her hand on his back. "Yes. He's upstairs playing with Liszt. What did you fix today?"

When they were near one another, it was as though some high frequency passed between them. She hadn't allowed herself to sense that resonance in a very long time, but it acted like a string plucked inside her, putting her in tune with ... herself.

"Your gutter in the back was clogged with pine needles. I cleaned it, so it shouldn't overflow anymore," he said with a smile that ate her up.

Was she smiling at him the same way? She had schooled her face to neutral for years so men wouldn't engage with her, but Bryn's smile made her joints come undone. They were getting into a rhythm of familiarity around one another which could have been the normal consequence of seeing one another at Darius' lessons. Except the way Bryn made her feel was anything but normal.

"It's so nice of you to fix all these things. You don't have to, you know. You're already paying me to teach Darius." She handed him a towel to dry his hands.

He wiped his hands on the towel. "Are you kidding? You got my son talking and playing again. There's nothing I can do that would pay you back for that. Besides, I feel like I'm part of helping him get better."

She tapped his jaw. "Here," she murmured up at him. "You have a spot." She dampened a corner of the towel and took his chin in one hand.

He kept his gaze on her as she gently wiped the hard line of his jaw to clean the smudge. When she finished, he took her wrist and, keeping his eyes locked on hers, he kissed her palm.

She felt the touch of his lips right down her center. It had been ages since she'd allowed herself the heat of flirtation or anything resembling a relationship, but this wasn't simply an itch. There was a crescendo building between them, and even though she knew it couldn't lead anywhere, she wanted to ride it. He'd stirred up the desire she thought was neatly packed away. He made her feel warm and bubbly inside.

"Hélène," he said softly.

She took her hand back, closing it around the kiss. They stood staring at one another until she collected her usually organized wits.

She patted a gap on the front of his shirt. "You're … missing a button on your shirt."

Bryn had been shambolic and disheveled the first time she met him, as if he couldn't remember how to dress himself or comb his hair. Now, when they came for Darius' lessons, he appeared carefully assembled, even though he was wearing work clothes.

She also took more time choosing a bright, snug dress, making sure her hair and makeup were just right, and applying a spritz of perfume. It was so long since she'd allowed herself to feel attracted to anyone, to recognize that someone was attracted to her. It made her feel … fizzy inside.

He flapped his shirt front with a chagrined expression. "Oh, well, I guess that's it for this shirt."

She poked a finger through the buttonhole and drew him to her. His shirt was warm and soft from washing and smelled like pine needles and June sunshine. "Let me fix it," she said in a whispered exhale.

He dragged a single finger down her upper arm, sending a cascade of cold, hot prickles dancing across her skin.

In a voice lower and smoother than usual, he said, "I fix things for you because I like taking care of you. It makes me happy."

She wanted to pass the sizzle between them off as just the animal lust of two lonely middle-aged people, but his remark suggested he didn't think that. And she was surprised that his caring didn't scare her.

"Take it off…" she said, looking into his eyes, which had gone a darker shade of brown. "I mean, I'll sew on the button if you want."

He nodded. "Thank you."

She tried not to stare as he unbuttoned his shirt. He wore a blindingly white T-shirt underneath. Wiry arms met broad shoulders, and she saw that he'd been hiding a sculpted chest under baggy shirts.

He caught her sneaking a glance and held her gaze. She was pretty sure smoke was rising up in the space between them.

Forcing herself to look away, she dug around in her kitchen drawer until she found a sewing kit she'd kept from some long-ago hotel stay. She waved the packet at him. "Look, there's even some buttons in here."

He handed her the shirt, but when she reached out to take it, he held on. His eyes held such naked desire, she thought she might just melt. A sort of wordless noise burbled up in her throat.

He gave a throaty laugh and finally released the shirt.

She settled into a seat at the dining table, grateful that her fingers were steady as she threaded the needle.

He sat across from her. "You're fast," he said.

"My father was a tailor," she said.

"Really? In Paris?"

"Yes. My mother was a pianist." She had let it slip because she was beginning to trust him. A little, anyway.

"Was she ... famous?" he asked.

Her shoulders tightened. "A few more stitches, and I'll be done," she said. She tied a knot and bit the thread off. She popped out of her chair and handed him back his shirt.

He stood, slipped it on, and buttoned it. It took all her self-control to keep from smoothing his shirt front over his chest or running her hands over his decidedly not-knobby shoulders.

When she was young, she'd had dozens of lovers, but after

establishing her anonymity here in Norwalk, the risk became too great. Whenever questions arose or things were progressing from the purely physical to the emotional, she broke things off. She found herself wanting to tell Bryn things, but her past still stalked her. How could he truly care for her if he knew what she'd done? That she wasn't really who he thought she was?

"Thank you for dressing me," he said. He finished buttoning his shirt and stepped closer to her.

She didn't move back but stared up at him.

Bryn dragged the back of his fingers along the ridge of her cheekbone, her jaw, the arch of her brow as if learning the curves and angles of her face.

It was like being set on fire and doused with cold water all at once. She knew she should make him stop, step back, but instead, she closed her eyes and leaned into his hand.

He cupped the back of her neck and slipped a hand around her waist. He drew her to him, and she let him. This one moment of physical touch was a bone-deep relief. He kissed her forehead, her temple, and the tip of one ear while whispering, "Hélène, Hélène."

She rested her palms on his chest and let her body press against his.

It wasn't supposed to happen, Bryn becoming part of her life. She had always intended to be dedicated to Darius alone. Her resolve had been weakened by Bryn's kindness, his sweet, long face, the way he cared for her, and the way he loved Darius. She'd drifted off course into Bryn's arms, and it was a delightful journey.

She would right herself. Later. She had to because, in the end, Bryn cared for someone she wasn't.

CHAPTER 22

If you live to be a hundred, I want to live to be a hundred minus one day so I never have to live without you.

A. A. Milne

Darius sat up in bed, pillows propped behind him, waiting for his mom like he had all week. She hadn't come for almost a week. Sleep pushed his eyes closed. The digital clock on his bedside table said eleven p.m.

The notes of the Chopin Second appeared behind his eyes as clearly as if he was looking at the music. As if by themselves, his fingers played piano on the blanket. He heard every note, felt the music swim around his heart, felt his fingers as if they were on real piano keys.

His head bobbed forward onto his chest. He jerked it up, afraid he'd missed his mom.

Into the darkness, he said, "Mom? I'm learning the Chopin Second like you wanted me to. I love it as much as you did. I'm going to do it, I am."

The music was off now, silence in his mind, eyes, ears, and fingers.

He scooched back down on his bed and turned on his side so he could see her chair. "Mom, are you coming? Please come."

He waited.

Nothing.

"I know you can hear me." No matter how much he wanted to stay awake, sleep pinned him to the sheets. Like an answer, the curtains waved a bit.

"Mom, I think Dad and Hélène like each other. I mean, like, really, *really*, like each other. I hope that doesn't make you mad."

A blue glow appeared in the armchair, pulsing like a heartbeat. He thought he could smell her shampoo.

He yawned. "I like her, too," he added so quietly he didn't think she would hear. "What would you think if she was my mom? But don't worry, you'd still be my mom, too."

The blue light crept along the floorboards, into every corner of the room, stretched up to the ceiling, and lay over his bed. The blankets felt heavy and warm, his bed soft and safe. He heard his mom humming and felt her hand on his cheek. She kissed his eyelids. Or maybe that was Hélène kissing his eyelids. He wasn't sure...

"Darius, Darius. You have to get up."

He dragged his eyes open.

His dad was shaking him. "You slept through your alarm. C'mon, you have to get up, or you'll be late for school."

His dad had thrown back the curtains. Sun splashed on the floor, dazzling every corner of the room. The window had been left open a crack last night and now the air in his room smelled fresh. The curtains ruffled in the breeze again, and the flickering light was pale blue and calm.

"You have a lesson with Hélène today. Don't forget to be ready," his dad said.

"I know!"

Darius smiled, threw back the covers, and staggered out of bed.

CHAPTER 23

There are very few monsters who warrant the fear we have of them.
  Andre Gide

Hélène stepped out onto the deck with two glasses of ice water, one for her, one for him.

Bryn rose from the step he was repairing and took the glass.

She held onto it for a moment, looking up at him. Her enormous dark eyes caught at him.

"Thanks," he said, bending to kiss her lightly. She kissed him back, and the hot sun got even hotter.

"Welcome," she whispered against his mouth.

Outside, the brilliant June sun made the white streaks in Hélène's hair shimmer. She wore a pale blue dress with a pattern of flowers around the middle, so she looked like a walking vase of flowers. She was simply the most beautiful woman he'd ever known. Bryn couldn't imagine letting her slip through his fingers.

Hélène closed her eyes and lifted her face to the sun. She touched the cold glass to the hollow at the base of her neck.

He watched a single glistening drop of water slide down her neck into the collar of her dress. He tore his eyes away to keep from imagining what lay in the nether regions of her neckline.

"Can we sit down?" she said. "I want to talk to you about something."

Her pointed tone made his gut clench for a second. He unfurled the deck umbrella, and they sat together in the shade.

"Darius is playing beautifully and making incredibly rapid musical progress. How's he doing at home?" she asked, her dark eyes earnest and serious.

Bryn took a sip of the cold water. "Since we found you, he's doing so much better. He speaks to me a lot more, and he's starting to talk at school, too. He's not as sad as before, either. I'm hoping that playing more will get him to speak more."

"I've been thinking the same thing," she said. Her eyes held a spark of excited urgency. "I wanted to talk to the two of you about having Darius play a recital here for a group of my friends."

Bryn's face cramped into a frown. He had to choose his words carefully. Hélène knew best about piano, and he didn't want to insult her or stomp on their relationship—a relationship he hoped had a chance.

He stroked the tendons on the back of her beautiful hands. "He used to love playing in public. He played at school, libraries, and churches in recitals with the rest of Vivianne's students. I don't want to push Darius the way Vivianne did. I don't want him to shut down."

Bryn smiled, remembering how jaws dropped when his little boy played things the other kids would never be able to play, no matter how hard they practiced.

That was before Vivianne died, before the snowstorm, back when Darius was innocent and full of joy. He wanted Darius to have that joy again. Much as he trusted and adored Hélène,

Bryn didn't want to cede his parenting decisions to her as he had to Vivianne.

Bryn said, "What if he doesn't play well and it sets him back? What if he can't manage the pressure and stops playing again, maybe this time forever? I think it's more important that he plays for himself rather than for other people."

Hélène drew her hand back. "If he gets upset or wants to stop playing, my friends will understand. I only want to give him the opportunity, to test his nerves. It's a different kind of thrill, playing for other people than for yourself."

"If he has to stop in the recital, he'll be humiliated," Bryn said, feeling his fingers squeeze the glass until his fingers ached. "Why put him in that position to begin with? He's doing fine as he is, don't you think?"

Hélène slumped back impatiently in her chair, skepticism in the tightness around her mouth. "You really don't know, do you?" There was a serrated edge to her words.

Only the other day, she was in his arms and they were kissing so that he thought his hair would spontaneously ignite. Was it her intention today to make him feel stupid? Her tone reminded him of Vivianne's when she let fly with a snide remark about how he didn't understand music or his own son. Did Hélène think he didn't understand Darius?

"Don't know what?" he asked, letting his irritation show.

"How gifted he is. I don't want to jeopardize his progress either, but a talent like his is towering." Hélène's voice was awestruck. "Darius will raise the standards for pianists for a generation."

It was Bryn's turn to be awestruck. "He's ... that good?" Bryn whispered.

He knew Darius was unique, but he had a hard time wrapping his head around the idea that he, uncoordinated and nervous, had produced a child who could make that big of an impression on the world.

"He is, and he should be heard," she said with the kind of enthusiasm Vivianne had expressed when talking about Darius. Bryn had always wondered if Vivianne was letting her own thwarted ambitions drive the bus, but he hadn't questioned her because she'd convinced him he was a musical dolt.

Now, Hélène's words made Bryn sit back in his chair and stare at her.

"The way he plays music is what makes art come alive," she said reverently. "Hearing someone like him is what makes life worth living."

"But he's fragile." Bryn wiped his face with his forearm. "He may agree to play just to please you, even though he doesn't want to because he loves you. I'm not sure——"

"His gifts shouldn't stay inside your living room forever," she scoffed.

"Why not?" he retorted, spitting out the "t." He shoved his chair back from the table.

Her voice rising, she said, "You want him to be like Van Cliburn, one of the most talented pianists of the last century who quit playing after his mother, who was his teacher, died? You can't wait, or the anxiety and fear will become so ingrained he'll never play in public again."

"So what if he never plays in public?" he said.

The tendons in Bryn's shoulders were hard as rocks. He was torn between wanting to give Hélène what she wanted, protecting his son, and giving Darius a chance to be his best self. It was like being locked in a triangle he couldn't find his way out of.

Hélène gave an exasperated huff. "A studio recital is merely a baby step toward bigger choices, bigger opportunities." Her eyes flicked away and he sensed she had something even more risky in mind.

Sweat trickled down the back of his neck and into the collar of his T-shirt. "What bigger opportunities?"

Hélène stretched her long, pale, bare arms on the table. "Well, since we're discussing it, the Norwalk Symphony has a concerto competition for musicians under eighteen. It's not New York or Europe, but agents and impresarios come, and they hire the winners. Darius has an excellent chance to win first place."

Her eyes lit with excitement and he felt another stir of uneasiness.

She said, "The world needs artists like him, but if he can't even play for my friends, he can't compete and of course, I won't send in his application." She leaned forward in her chair. Clasped and unclasped her hands. "I only want to see if he can, that's all."

"Vivianne used to say that, too!"

"I'm not her!" she said.

"Well, you're acting like her. I don't think he's ready for a competition."

"This is the first step to seeing if he is."

Bryn rose, his chair scraping metallically on the wood. He paced around the deck, flicking his fingers. "He's just a kid. When he's grown up, will the world still want him? He's not some disposable commodity. I don't want him and his gifts treated like pork bellies or Texas crude. He's my son!"

"I would never do that to him. You know that."

"Do I?" Bryn stood at the railing with his back to her. The sun beating down on his neck matched the heat in his chest. He hoped their disagreement didn't kill their flirtation, but now, when it came to Darius, he was going to speak up, which he hadn't done with Vivianne.

Hélène came and stood next to him at the railing. "If he can withstand the pressure and loves performing as much as you say he does, he won't be just a child prodigy. I believe his gifts will carry him far into adulthood, but we have to start somewhere. Let him take it as far as he wants."

Bryn set his glass on the railing, and a water ring formed. "All right, let's ask him, but he gets to decide. And no arm twisting. He's just a little kid. He's fragile."

"I *know* he is. I want what's best for him, too," she said gently. "And the two of you can talk it over. He doesn't have to decide today."

Bryn rested his elbows on the railing. "I don't know about piano or competitions or anything. I only know my son."

She laid her palm on his back. "You don't just know him. You love him."

He exhaled. "And if he does the recital, let's not mention the competition until afterward, all right?"

"Agreed," Hélène said.

"You know, when I look at him, he seems like a perfectly ordinary kid. The kind who might play video games, ride bikes, and throw a football with friends after school, but he was none of those things. I don't know if he should or shouldn't be doing those things. Is Darius the pianist more important than Darius the kid? Is he missing out on a part of life? I don't want to take his childhood from him."

"You're not," she said but he didn't feel reassured.

"I don't want to keep him from being a famous pianist."

"You're not. And as for those other things, music is his voice. The more he plays, the more communicative he'll be. I want to give him the chance to express what's inside of him."

Bryn squeezed his eyes shut and rested his forehead on his fists for a full minute and considered what even a recital might mean for Darius. How much was too much for his boy to bear? How could he protect him and still let him be his best self?

Hélène and Darius had developed the kind of relationship Bryn had hoped for. If anyone could shepherd him through the twists of a music, she could.

He stood, feeling weary to his bones. "All right. You can suggest it to him, but if he says no, then it's no."

She pressed a hand to his sweaty cheek and kissed him again. "You're a good father, Bryn Harding."

He hoped he was good enough.

CHAPTER 24

The soul is healed by being with children.
Fyodor Dostoevsky

Hélène found Darius sitting cross-legged on the floor in the entryway, his back braced against the wall, tossing a catnip ball for Liszt.

Hélène sat on the parent's bench. "Your dad and I were talking about having you play a small recital here for a few of my friends. It would give you a chance to see how you feel performing again."

He grunted and slid a sideways glance at her.

"No grunting. The deal was you use your words," she reminded him. "I don't want to push if you don't feel ready. Just think about it."

She knew pushing, and this wasn't it. Pushing was like a hand at the small of your back, shoving you in a direction you didn't want to go, unreasonable demands, a grueling schedule.

He got a mischievous gleam in his eye and one corner of his

mouth tipped up into a grin. He said, "I'll do it, but only if you play, too."

Her knuckles throbbed as if they were being crushed in a vise. The pulse in her wrists beat an unsteady rhythm.

Guess I walked right into that one.

She massaged her knuckles. "Someday, I might play again, but not now."

Liszt brought back the catnip ball, and Darius tossed it again. He peaked at her through his thick, dark lashes. He whispered, "I didn't tell Dad about our secret."

At the thinly veiled threat, her body heated from the inside out. But she also felt guilty for colluding—like Vivianne—to keep Bryn out. Out of her relationship with Darius, in the dark about who she was.

"Thank you for ... not telling," she said. "You can think about it."

"I have to ask my mo——" He clamped his lips shut and hunched into himself.

The hair on the backs of her arms prickled.

"Were you going to say you have to ask your mom?" she asked in an offhand manner, suggesting this was a perfectly ordinary thing, talking to one's deceased mother.

"Yes." Darius picked up Liszt and snuggled his face into the kitten's fur so she couldn't see his expression.

An ice cube of fear slid up Hélène's spine.

Artists of every sort were fragile. Madness and artistic talent were often two sides of the same coin. Maybe he believed he could talk to his mother, or she hoped, engaging in some imaginary fantasy. He was still grieving for her, that much was clear. There was nothing to do but follow his lead.

She eased back against the wall. "What do you think she would say if you asked her?"

He gazed up at her with his dark, troubled eyes. "She says you should perform again."

Her chest tightened, strangling her breath. She heard her blood crawling through the artery in her neck.

"She's wrong." She said it lightly, adding a short laugh, but his serious gaze didn't shift. "I can't play in public. You know that. This is about you playing for a few friends, not me."

He stared at her in a direct, unnerving way. "Why not?" he demanded. "You played for me the first day I came."

That had been the second biggest mistake of her life. She wanted to play again, but she could never do justice to *Hélène Noire et Blanche*. She would never be anything but a pale imitation of the artist she had once been and everyone would recognize her as a fraud. One major disaster in her life was enough.

Bryn came in from the deck, pulling the slider closed behind him. He leaned against the wall, a mix of emotions on his face.

Darius' eyes flicked to Bryn and back to Hélène. An unspoken look of secrecy passed between them.

She raised her eyebrows and fixed Darius with another indicative look. "You don't have to decide today, but perhaps there's something that might convince you to play?"

"You mean like a bribe?" Darius said with a grin.

How do mothers ever get anything past their kids?

Hélène laughed. "Not exactly, but like a trade." She rose from the bench and stood close enough to Bryn to feel the heat of sunshine radiating off his skin. She wanted to lean against him, to let her head laze back against his shoulder, but Darius didn't know about them. Or at least, she didn't think he did.

"Okay," Darius said with a boyish, half-cocked smile. "But only if you go out to eat with me and Dad afterward."

Bryn's dear face spread into a grin. He said, "Great idea. We can celebrate!"

They were a pair, no matter how complicated her feelings about each of them were.

She said, "That's very sweet of you, but that's not necessary."

"Dinner with us after the recital or no deal," Darius said. His mouth set into a stubborn line she'd seen before.

She glanced up at Bryn and laughed. "You drive a hard bargain. All right, deal."

Darius jumped up off the floor. He hurled himself at her and wrapped his arms around her waist. His pointy chin poked into her ribs and his soft, warm body pressed against her. She embraced him and kissed the top of his fluffy head. It felt like being needed, but also like she'd been rescued from a loneliness she'd chosen for years.

Bryn's Adam's apple bobbed.

She held a hand out to him and when their hands touched, it was as though water turned to steam. His grasp expressed a world of emotions that she was beginning to sense in herself.

CHAPTER 25

When we dream alone it is only a dream, but when many dream together it is the beginning of a new reality.
Friedensreich Hundertwasser

Bryn took out the last screw holding the broken ice maker in. He handed the screwdriver to Hélène, lifted the ice maker out, and set it in the sink to drain. Upstairs, he heard Darius playing with the kitten.

"Were you like this as a kid, fixing things all the time?" she asked, turning the screwdriver over in her hands.

"That's called a Phillips-head screwdriver, by the way," he said, smiling at her.

"Thanks for the tool lesson," she said with a laugh. "But with you around, I'll never have to learn how to use it."

She sat on the kitchen counter, watching him replace her ice maker. It was companionable, having her hand him tools and pretending to be interested.

He kneeled on the floor and pried open the box containing the new ice maker. This put him at the level of her ankles, which curved up to shapely calves. Glancing up at her, he circled one ankle and slid his hand slowly up her calf to her knee.

Her eyes widened and caught fire.

He kissed her knee, and her face—usually creamy and pale—went red. Delight rose in her eyes.

She caressed his cheek, and he brushed it against the inside of her knee. She inhaled sharply.

"Dad, are you done yet?" Darius called from upstairs.

Bryn and Hélène laughed.

"Almost," Bryn hollered back.

"Okay, but hurry up," Darius yelled impatiently.

She smiled. "So, tell me, did you always fix stuff?"

He wrenched his mind out of the gutter and back to the task at hand. He pulled the new ice maker out of the box. "I was an awkward kid, terrible at every sport ever invented, including ping-pong. I hung around and helped my dad. Made me feel competent at something."

"You two were close?" she asked.

"Yes, we spent a lot of hours together. I loved learning things from him." Bryn remembered learning to change the oil in the car, repairing their furnace, setting a new toilet in the bathroom, and the dozens of small things his father taught him. The computer they built together one summer. They all made Bryn a nerdy man who could fix things, even though he struggled with humans.

Bryn laid the sheet of instructions out on the counter next to where she sat. He glanced at them to make sure he was on track, but her perfume—sweet and floral—made him stop and inhale her scent.

"Were you close to either of your parents?" he asked, already knowing the answer.

"Only my father," she said, then frowned and glanced away. That same shadow he'd seen before crossed her face.

He understood she didn't want to discuss it, so he said, "He taught you to sew a mean button."

"That he did," she said, and the lightness returned to her face.

He tore open the plastic bag containing the new screws. He gave her a sideways glance, and the warmth in her smile emboldened him. He took her hand and looked deep into her eyes. "I have something hard for you," he said in his sexiest voice. He dropped the bag of screws into her hand and they both laughed.

"Dad!" Darius yelled.

"He's hurrying," Hélène called back.

He hoisted the ice maker into place. He held out his hand, and one by one, she dropped a screw into his palm.

"My dad taught me a lot of stuff and it made me feel like I was good at something. Built up my confidence. Phillips."

"Yes, Doctor," she said and slapped the screwdriver into his outstretched palm.

"I was never the delicate interior boy that Darius is."

"That's how you think of him, delicate and interior?" she asked quizzically.

He drove in a screw while he considered his answer. "Actually, I'm not sure what kind of boy he is," he said, flummoxed. "It's been on my mind how different Darius and I are."

"What do you mean?"

He felt a sharp pain up under his ribs. "I feel we're so different that I'll never understand him. Vivianne understood him best because of all the hours they spent together talking about music and piano and stuff."

"Rubbish." She gave a huff of disgust. "Your worship of Vivianne annoys me. The woman treated you like an ill-fitting suit to be tossed in a corner."

Her anger made him feel cared for, like she was on his side.

"I don't worship her. I just feel like I'm such a nerd and Darius isn't."

Hélène hopped down from the counter, scooped up the plastic packing materials, and jammed them into the empty box. "She acted like you were too stupid to understand music, that you had nothing to offer your son. You know him. You know how much he loves and needs the piano. You know his heart needs mending. If you feel like you don't know him, just wait. He's a kid and won't be the same person next week he is today or tomorrow."

Bryn shut the freezer door. "But I feel like he's so much more like Vivianne than like me. Sometimes, I even hear him talking to her at night in his bedroom."

Her brows knit. "I was going to mention something. When I asked if he wanted to play the recital, he said he had to ask his mom."

Bryn groaned and sank into a chair. "I hear him talking to someone at night and I suspected it was Vivianne."

"Why didn't you tell me?"

"Because I didn't want you to think I was a terrible parent?" he asked. "I've done everything I can for him, but some days I feel so lost. He still refuses to talk to a therapist. I don't know what else to do."

It was a relief to confess his insecurities. The last year had been filled with so many false starts and stops that he wasn't sure he had been an effective parent.

"You're not a terrible parent, and you've never been. We can only help Darius express himself the only way he knows how, and that's through piano," Hélène said.

There was a dull clack as ice cubes fell into the ice maker. Even if he didn't know how to help Darius, at least he could fix broken stuff around the house.

Bryn said, "He always had Vivianne's artistic temperament."

She spoke quietly but with sharp intention. "Don't look for Vivianne in Darius. Try to find the boy who is trying to find *himself*. He needs you to help him find himself."

"How?" he asked.

"You could share your poetry with him. Show him how to fix things, whether he likes it or not. It will give him something to feel capable about besides piano."

Bryn leaned against the counter, grateful for her support.

She took his big, fumbling hands in hers. "You can give him another way to see himself. You're the most powerful person in his life and you have things to offer him she never could. You're alike in that you're both very sensitive, creative, and in touch with your own hearts. Your poetry is an example of that. Don't miss the opportunity."

"But he's not interested in the things I do," Bryn said.

"Don't let him push you away," she said.

He slowly pulled her down onto his lap, and she rested her cheek against his. He felt her warmth through his shirt. Holding her felt like he'd won a prize he hadn't known was there.

CHAPTER 26

Having children is like having a bowling alley installed in your brain.
Martin Mull

Bryn sat on the edge of his son's bed, petting Darius' thick, dark curls. His son's twig-like arms lay on top of the covers and his feet made little sweet hillocks at the end of the bed. When Vivianne died, Bryn met a stranger who happened to be his son but since Hélène had lit their lives, Bryn no longer felt as though he was stumbling around in the dark.

Bryn knew he needed to ask Darius about his nighttime conversations with Vivianne, but what if he said the wrong thing? What if Darius needed to talk to Vivianne in order to play? Should Bryn play along with Darius' fantasy or kill it? He wished Hélène was here. She seemed to think Bryn was up to this.

Bryn caught the mad, whirling anxiety inside himself and forced himself not to chatter. "I heard you talking to somebody last night. Were you..." Bryn stroked Darius' bony spine. "Were you talking to your mom?"

Darius pulled the covers up to his neck and spoke to the wall. "You think Mom will be happy I'm playing a recital for Hélène's friends?"

Bryn's heart clenched. Darius spoke of her as if she was still alive. Bryn chose his words carefully, but lovingly. "*If* ... she was alive, she would be happy, but if you don't want to do it, you don't have to."

Darius stared up at the ceiling. "I think she'll like it."

"Honey, your mom's de—"

Darius clapped his hand over Bryn's mouth. "Stop! Don't say it!"

Bryn peeled Darius's hand off his mouth and held it in his own. "Okay, I won't, but you know it's true."

"I'm going to play the Chopin Nocturne in C minor Opus 48, number 1." Darius yawned. "Mom liked it. I've been working on it with Hélène."

Bryn asked, "Okay, what if I videoed your performance for your YouTube channel? We haven't uploaded any new stuff in a long time."

Darius' smile was gentle and sleepy. "That's good." He curled up like a snail and mumbled, "Will you read to me?"

Bryn's chest filled to overflowing. Darius' eyes were already sagging into the middle ground of sleep. He hadn't asked Bryn to read to him since he was five or six. Bryn had always loved it. Reading had been the smallest door through which he had squeezed to connect with a boy who confounded him. His son was inviting him to step through the door again.

"Sure, I'd love to. What shall I read?" Bryn asked softly.

"Anything," Darius said sleepily.

If he read his poetry to Darius, like Hélène had suggested, maybe they could find a crossroads on which to bump into one another. Maybe if Bryn shared his feelings, it might help Darius understand that talking about sharing feelings was a good thing.

The bed creaked when Bryn stood. "Don't go anywhere. I'll be right back."

He returned with a spiral-bound notebook. He sat next to Darius' form huddled under the blankets and leaned against the headboard.

Bryn flipped through and found one Darius might understand.

When he read poetry, Bryn had no trouble slowing down, savoring the words. Softly, he said, "I wrote this about you."

"A shining sound,
an immeasurable gift,
Each chord a vibration
of the undiscovered universe of your heart
Unknown galaxies revealed in your fingers
Melody closing the light years between us."

Darius' eyes were closed. Thick dark lashes brushed his cheeks, which were losing their little boy chubbiness. His lips were slightly parted, his mint-scented breath slow, his face slack with slumber.

"I love you, son," Bryn whispered.

He kissed his son's temple, quietly eased off the bed, and slipped out the door.

CHAPTER 27

Music is the shorthand of emotion.
  Leo Tolstoy

Hélène and Darius sat side by side on the piano bench, playing the Rachmaninoff duet, *Polka Italienne*. When they finished, they lifted their hands simultaneously and looked at one another. The playful twinkle in his eye tickled her heart. It was the way pianists were supposed to feel after playing something so joyful.

"That was fun," he said and giggled.

"Wasn't it?" she said and laughed too.

She hadn't allowed herself to play like this since her meltdown. Playing like this felt dangerous, glorious, and unrestrained. The intensity of making music with another person, trading rhythms, sharing the intimate space on the bench and the keyboard, elbows brushing, and awareness of their unity was like a conversation she had missed having.

"Can we play more duets?" Darius asked.

He inched closer and gazed up with a grin that made her laugh. She put her arm around him and laid her cheek on his crown. "After your recital, you can have them as a reward, but only when we're here alone."

She felt instantly guilty for ensnaring Darius in her deception, but how could she keep her secret and keep Bryn?

As if in answer to her question, Bryn tapped on the studio door. How much had he heard? Did he know how much skill it took to play the duet? Did he suspect she wasn't who she said she was? Had heard her demonstrate for Darius before? If so, he'd never commented.

Darius launched off the bench and opened it.

She pivoted off the bench, her face hot. Her fingers went numb and her knuckles curled into claws. Her arms turned to dead, dry wood. "Did you get the, uh, part ... uh, the doorknob?" she stammered.

Bryn laughed. "Doorknob was Monday. Today was the new dryer vent."

She forced a smile, hoping she didn't look as rattled as she felt. "Oh, right."

"You play wonderfully, Hélène," Bryn said, but he didn't look all that surprised.

She touched the back of her neck. "Oh, that's just an old piece I used to play with my mother. It's easy and hard to forget," she said in an offhand way. She tore her gaze away, ashamed of lying to him. How long could she do that?

Mercifully, Bryn fixed his attention on Darius. "All ready for Saturday, bud?"

"Yeah, it's no problem," Darius said.

She noticed him glance into the corner, and that strange, elusive smile flashed across his face.

"Excellent," Bryn said. "I know you'll do great."

She was touched to see how proud and excited Bryn was. She was almost as excited as he was. If Darius passed his tension test of playing for a little group, they would apply to the

Norwalk Symphony Concerto competition. She found it impossible not to dream of the endless possibilities for Darius, but he would need protection so he never again went silent. After her father died, she'd had no one to protect her, and she would make certain no one like Yves ever got their claws into Darius. She had come up with the idea of dying her hair and perhaps donning some fake glasses. That way, she could maintain a presence in the background of his career, and no one would be the wiser.

"Where are we going for dinner after the recital, Dad?" Darius asked.

She smiled, pleased that the restaurant was at the top of Darius' mind, not the pressure of performing.

Bryn leaned from side to side like a tall tree swaying in the wind. He said, "You want Italian, Mexican, or Chinese?"

"Italian," Darius said excitedly. "Fancy Italian."

"Fancy Italian it is." A glance passed between Bryn and Hélène.

Bryn said, "Darius, can you please bring in Hélène's trash cans and put them in the garage? I forgot to do it."

"You guys aren't going to fight or anything, are you?" Darius asked, his thick eyebrows knitted.

"No, not at all," Hélène said.

"Okay," Darius said, looking nervously from one to the other. Affecting a whole body slouch, he ran out to bring in the trash can.

This was it. Bryn was going to ask about her playing. Ask why she didn't play more. He was going to ask why she'd lied to him. The thought that he might end things between them was so enormous that had a physical effect on her, as if the lid of the piano had crashed down on her fingers.

Please, dear God, don't let him ask!

Bryn shut the studio doors and lowered his voice. "Is he ready for this recital?"

She was so relieved she had to take a few breaths before she could answer. "He's confident and musically, he's in top shape, I promise. We can only wait and see if he gets nervous in front of other people."

He moved closer, and it felt like a fire moving around her. "Okay, I trust you," he murmured.

She hadn't intended to trust him or for him to trust her. Bryn had moved into her heart with the slow, steady practice of caring, kindness, and trustworthiness. Except when he found out everything about her, he would be hurt and worse, disappointed in her, the way Yves had been after her debacle.

With a voice shadowed with desire, Bryn said, "We couldn't have done it without you. Get him talking and playing again." He took her hands in his and kissed each of her fingertips. "You and your magic hands."

The heat in his eyes lit her own desire, her adoration for him. She stretched up on tip-toe and kissed him. His hands slid down and cupped her ass.

She giggled. It had been ages since a man had done that.

"After the recital, we should tell him," Bryn said.

"About what?" She patted his chest and felt the heat of his skin beneath his shirt.

He tilted his head. "About us."

Oh, no. How has this happened?

She didn't want to extricate herself from what was happening between them, because that would be a little like ripping her own arm off with her teeth. These two had brought her love and music in a way she had forgotten existed. How could she break those precious gifts? Darius and Bryn needed her and as much as she was afraid to admit it, she found herself needing Bryn. And Darius's music had resurrected in her yearning to perform and make music that felt raw and alive.

But humiliation loomed over her, breathing its hot laughter down her neck. She could never be *Hélène Noire et Blanche*. She'd allowed herself to believe that she was worthy of the kind of love that Bryn offered. Like she'd been unmasked before, he would find out she was not.

Just not yet, she prayed. *Just not yet.*

CHAPTER 28

Music is only love looking for words.
Lawrence Durrell

"Darius and Bryn should be here by now." Hélène was unnecessarily scrubbing the sink and counter as she and Carolina waited for the others to show up.

"What are you worried about?" Carolina asked. Her calm demeanor eased the tightness in Hélène's chest a tiny bit.

"I told them to come a little early so I expected them already," Hélène said. With her sponge, she scrubbed hard enough to remove the enamel from the stove. "I hope I haven't made a mistake having Darius do this."

It was strange that, after convincing Bryn this was right for Darius, she was the one with sweaty palms and a swirling stomach. Hearing Darius might tip off the Marriage Survivors Club that she could teach at Darius' level added to her anxiety. But he needed this opportunity, so she had mentally collected excuses and prevarications to deliver in her own defense.

Mostly, she'd convinced herself to lie to her friends. It was a good thing Episcopalians didn't believe in sin.

"I'm sure he'll be fine. If he doesn't come, we'll just open a bottle of wine like always," Carolina said.

Hélène rubbed an old stain on the even older countertop. "I just want him to be able to share his music again, so he doesn't become a musical recluse."

Like me.

"His talent, the responsibility of caring for him, guiding, cultivating and supporting him." Hélène stopped her nervous scrubbing and whispered, "It frightens me, you know?"

"You're his angel. You love him and that's what he needs most." Carolina patted Hélène's arm. "It'll be all right."

Hélène's near-panic subsided. She put away her sponge and wiped her hands on a dishtowel and went to the front door to wait.

The Marriage Survivors Club members arrived and clustered, chatting, in the music room. Hélène scanned the street, looking for Bryn's car. The tendons in the small of her back grew taut. Her jaw was a vise and the muscles in her neck twitched. She texted Bryn—twice—but got no answer.

After a few minutes, Bianca came out of the studio. "It's past two. Did we get the time wrong?"

"No, no, I don't know where they are." Hélène pinched the seams at the sides of her dress. She choked out the words, "Maybe he got cold feet."

Bianca patted her shoulder. "Chill. Bryn would have called you if that was the case. You know what you're doing."

But maybe she didn't. "Thanks," Hélène said on an exhale.

"But if he doesn't show up, can we watch the Notre Dame basketball game?" Bianca asked hopefully.

Hélène laughed, grateful for the distraction of her dear

friend. Without a word, she pointed Bianca back toward the studio.

Hélène paced from the entryway to the kitchen, peeking out the front door every few minutes, checking her watch, smoothing her skirt, chewing the inside of her lower lip.

When Bryn pulled into the drive behind her car, she thought she would pass out from relief.

He unfolded himself from the car. Even from this distance, his body language was tense, and she saw his fingers flicking away. He met her gaze with a worried one of his own.

It wasn't unusual for parents to be more nervous than their kids. A performance was a mark of all their child's hard work, all the lessons paid for, the enrichment, the driving back and forth to lessons. A public performance was the BIG PAYOFF. To the kids, it was a chance to show off.

Darius, his face somber and aloof, walked calmly up the drive, something flat, wrapped in a plastic grocery bag, tucked under his arm.

He looked distinguished in a crisp white shirt, creased black dress pants, a blue blazer, polished new black loafers, and an endearingly crooked red bowtie. He had combed his mad hair back from his face. He seemed to have grown up even since the last time Hélène had seen him.

She wanted to grab him, hug him and tell him everything would be all right, but his demeanor was reserved, self-assured, his chin lifted with confidence. That thousand-mile stare meant he was already in the music, that the world around him wasn't even in his awareness. She knew that faraway gaze; her own had been much the same.

She pressed a palm to steady the butterflies in her stomach. Darius had an ironclad memory, a seasoned artist's emotional, technical, and intellectual maturity.

And his little heart was broken. Hopefully, this would be a way to stitch it back together.

Opening the screen door, Hélène smiled encouragingly, hiding every trace of her stripped nerves. "I thought maybe you'd changed your mind," she said to Darius.

He gazed up at her, unsmiling, his eyes solemn. Without a word, he proceeded toward the studio.

"What's in the plastic bag?" she asked in a low voice.

He passed through the French doors and into the studio without acknowledging she had said anything.

Harried and on edge, Bryn bustled into the foyer. His hair stuck up in back, and a corner of his shirt collar was turned up. One of his pant legs was caught up in the top of his sock.

He looked like she felt. "Is everything okay?" she whispered as she straightened his collar.

Bryn wiped a hand across his eyes. He was more rattled than usual because he wasn't speaking in complete sentences. "Sorry–got here as soon––I thought he wouldn't come–– bedroom talking to Vivianne––maybe cancel he seems––forgot video equip––"

She patted his arm. "Don't worry, you're here now. I set up my video equipment. Slow down and take a breath. Everything's going to be okay," she said, although she didn't think it was. "Did you say, 'talking to Vivianne'?"

Bryn took a deep breath and looked only slightly less panicked. He hissed, "He insisted on bringing her photograph in the plastic bag. Says he wants her to attend. He says he needs her to be able to play. I told you I didn't think he wasn't ready."

Her breath felt like she was breathing in ice fumes. Had she been so ambitious for Darius that she'd ignored the obvious signals? Would Darius fall apart, tumble into a place from which they couldn't pull him back? If he didn't at least try, he might never test his capabilities, and they would never know what he could do. Better he collapse here, amongst friends, than anywhere else.

"Should we stop him?" Bryn said.

Hélène glanced into the studio, prepared to reconsider her plan, but Darius was already setting Vivianne's photograph on the piano.

"Looks like it's too late to worry about any of that now," she said.

She tugged Bryn's pant leg out of his sock. She looked into his worried, sweet face. "It's all right, it's all right. If he can't finish or even start, it's not a problem. They're all my best friends and they'll be blown away. They'll love him." She squeezed his forearm. "Are you all right?" she asked.

Bryn cupped her cheek and kissed her softly. "Now I am," he said, recovering himself.

There was a crash and the sound of breaking glass.

CHAPTER 29

Who hears music feels his solitude peopled at once.
Robert Browning

Darius saw the world burst apart into a million shards of glass. He stared at his mom's photograph where he'd dropped it on the floor that seemed so far down.

He smelled smoke from the fireplace. Outside, a winter wind whistled and howled. The house shuddered from the force of the wind. Icy sleet and snow peppered the window. It was too dark to see the neighbor's house. He shivered and his fingers were stiff with cold. The house was cold, and he wanted another blanket to wrap up in. Everything was dark because the electricity was out.

Someone was holding his cold, cold hands in their big, warm ones and talking to him. "Darius, Darius, are you okay? Did you cut your hands?"

He blinked, and his dad was kneeling on the floor in front of him. "Honey, it's okay. Do you want to just go home?"

Darius' face felt wet. Why was he such a crybaby? He looked

at the corner where his mom usually was, but she wasn't there. He'd forgotten to tell her the time of the recital. Did she forget to come?

On the floor, she was smashed in bits of glass and a broken wooden frame. Her smile was crooked because the picture had bent.

His voice came out like a sob. "I'm sorry, Mom. I didn't mean to make you mad. I didn't mean to drop it or for you to get hurt. I didn't mean to."

He wanted her to hear him play today. For her to be proud of him. Like before, he'd ruined everything.

Hélène was bending down to look into his face. Her voice was calm and kind. "It's all right. She knows you didn't mean to drop it." She held up his mom's photo. "See? The picture is fine; only the frame is broken. We can easily get her another frame. Don't worry about playing," she whispered to him. "Feelings are all that matter. It's okay to be upset. We can do this another time."

Closing his eyes, Darius sagged against his dad and he put his arm around Darius. They stood like that for a minute, Darius sucking in air until he felt a strange calm in the room. It was like someone had turned on the sun, like the world had stopped rocking back and forth.

He opened his eyes and saw that Hélène's friends were all smiling at him. He felt their love flying toward him like a flock of orange monarch butterflies. Looking into the eyes of each one of them was like being lifted and carried along in a fuzzy blanket.

He looked at Hélène and his dad, and his insides felt like melted butter. They loved him, separately and together. They understood that feelings were all that mattered.

The icy wind stopped, and he flexed his fingers and rotated his wrists. The sound of the ice and snow ticking against the glass vanished. He could smell the heavy scent of the pink star-shaped flowers Hélène had put on a table.

The small lady with the brown hair and a kind smile was cleaning up the broken glass. When their eyes met, it was like a hug. Even she loved him, and he didn't even know her name.

Darius took his mom's photo from Hélène. He wiped his face with his sleeve. In the picture, his mom's smile was crooked, and her eyes stared past him. Could he play without her in the room or in her frame?

He blinked at his dad with his long, worried face and eyes like handles Darius could grab onto and pull himself along.

His dad said, "Let's go home, bud."

But Chopin, Bach, and Rachmaninoff were whirling around inside him, pushing against his heart, tingling to escape from his fingers. The music was sparks and the night sky, the rolling ocean, the swift-moving clouds, and the smell of apple pie and hot chocolate. The music filled his chest with trouble, curiosity, intensity, fury, and happiness.

Feelings are all that matter, he heard. And he wanted to share those feelings.

Darius wiped his eyes again and said, "We can't go home, Dad. I want to share my feelings and my music."

"Are you sure?" his dad asked.

"Yes." Darius strode to the piano, sat down, and played.

As he played, Hélène peeked at her friends.

Olivia's jaw hung open, her hand over her heart as though holding breaking pieces together.

Frankie's eyes widened, damp with tears.

Bianca leaned forward, elbows braced on her knees, staring with an intensity she reserved only for playoff games.

Flicka was as still as Hélène had ever seen her.

Carolina closed her eyes, tears slipping down her face during the most tender passages.

When Darius finished, they clapped with gusto, as Hélène had known they would. Bianca even put her fingers in her mouth and made a shrill, earsplitting whistle. At the end, they demanded an encore, and Darius granted them a moving rendition of Rachmaninoff's Prelude in E-flat Major, Opus 23, number 6.

When the last note died away, Hélène wanted to sink to the floor with relief.

The Marriage Survivors Club rose and congratulated Darius, who absorbed every moment like a pro.

Bryn's eyes were dull with exhaustion. To Hélène, he mumbled, "Thank you. I can't thank you enough." He folded her in his arms, and she let herself lean against him. He rested his cheek on her crown.

"He's so gifted he did it mostly on his own, you know. I didn't do much," she said, trying to divert attention from herself. "He's ready for the competition."

Bryn stiffened a little. "He just got through this."

She kissed him and unwound herself from Bryn. Together, they watched Darius chat with his adoring fans as if he'd been doing it for years.

She had the best friends in the entire world. They were her warriors of love.

Flicka asked Hélène, "Is this the one kid who makes owning such a gigantic piano worthwhile?"

Darius' head pivoted, fixed Hélène with an unmistakably accusing gaze. "She plays too," he said.

Hélène's heart pounded like a kettle drum in a Mahler symphony. What was he up to?

If it hadn't been Botoxed beyond movement, Flicka's face would have frowned. In a voice dripping with irony, to Hélène she said, "Imagine that. How come we've never heard you?"

Hélène threw Darius a glare and turned away, busying herself with putting away the video camera.

Enthusiastically, Bianca said to Darius, "You know, if you ever want to play at St. Paul's, they'd love to hear you."

Darius turned and looked up at Hélène with a wicked gleam in his eyes. His mouth lifted in a half smile and he said, "Maybe me and Hélène can play some of our cool duets."

Bianca raised an eyebrow at Hélène. "Huh. Really? How come we've never heard you?"

Hélène pretended not to hear Bianca. She forced an overly bright smile. "Thanks for coming! See you all on Sunday."

Even Bianca took the hint and the Marriage Survivors filed out while Hélène threw a murderous scowl at Darius.

CHAPTER 30

Hell is full of musical amateurs.
George Bernard Shaw

After Darius' rascally revelation that they played duets together, Hélène was relieved to have dodged questions from the Marriage Survivors Club. Bryn had been busy putting away folding chairs so he hadn't overheard Darius.

When Bryn had stored away the last chairs, Darius said to her, "Don't forget you promised to go out to dinner with us." The grin on his face turned him from a prodigy back into a kid.

"I keep my promises," she said.

Bryn slung his jacket over one slumping shoulder. His cheeks were slack with exhaustion, but his eyes shone bright with pride. Her nerves were equally fried, but she was thrilled, too. She rested a hand on Bryn's arm in a silent gesture of shared accomplishment. Together, they had gotten Darius far enough that he could play for a few people. His confidence was enough to enter the concerto competition, where he undoubtedly would slay.

If Darius could pull it together after dropping his mother's picture and still play like a god, his career and legacy could be limitless. She would do everything she could to protect him for as long as he needed her.

Bryn's eyes spoke of his gratitude when he gazed down at her. "Thank you," he whispered.

Darius broke the spell when he said, "I'm starving, Dad. Where are we going?"

Bryn said, "I made reservations at Tony's on Main Street. I'm ready if you are."

A celebratory dinner was the perfect time to talk about the competition when they were all flush with success.

As they prepared to leave, Bryn said, "Darius, did you leave something on the piano?"

Darius frowned for a minute. "Oh, yeah." And he returned to the studio to retrieve the picture of Vivianne.

Bryn and Hélène shared conspiratorial smiles. Darius had almost forgotten about his mother. They were all definitely making progress.

Tony's was a lovely place with quiet music in the background, candles on the table, and mouth-watering aromas.

Hélène took a sip of wine and set her glass down. "You played beautifully, Darius."

"Yeah, I'm proud of how you played. You were amazing!" Bryn said.

"Thanks for helping me," Darius said, around his fried calamari.

He was a genius but a humble genius—a rare combination that would serve him well in his career when greeting fans. Hélène realized that she was already mapping out his future as a pianist—one that would be much like her own had been, only with independence and resilience built in.

"Next, I think we should focus on the Chopin First Piano Concerto." She glanced at Bryn, whose brows lowered.

"I like the Chopin Second better," Darius said, sliding her a sly sideways glance.

Her spine stiffened. She jabbed at a piece of lettuce. "We've been through this. No Chopin Second Concerto."

Darius said, "Why do we need to practice a concerto, anyway? I'm not playing one any time soon."

Hélène smoothed her napkin on her lap. "The Norwalk Symphony has a concerto competition for young musicians, and I think you have an excellent chance of winning."

"What do I have to play?" Darius asked.

She said, "For the first round, the musicians play the first movement of a concerto. The finalists are required to play their entire concerto with the orchestra."

Darius' gaze turned inward as he considered the possibility.

Bryn's fork scraped the bottom of his dish, and a muscle in his jaw twitched.

"Bryn, I know you have reservations about—" she said.

Bryn shot ahead before she could finish. "He brought his mom's photograph. He can't do that for an important competition, can he?

She reached under the table and rested her hand on Bryn's knee, and she felt him settle. "You're right, he can't. I don't mean to wipe out his success with another hurdle, but we don't have much time to prepare a concerto." She turned to Darius. "That's why I suggested the Chopin First for you."

Darius' mouth twisted to the side. He gave a grunt. "I don't like it as much as the Second."

She ignored the remark and said, "We need to decide soon because the application deadline is coming up."

"If I decide to do it, I can get it ready in time," Darius said in a way that made Hélène think he relished the challenge.

Bryn's words poured out of him in an anxious stream. "But it's too soon it's too much pressure I don't want him to stop playing again, what if he loses—"

Darius laid a hand on Bryn's arm. His voice was ragged with anxiety. "Dad, it's okay. I can get it ready really fast."

"I don't think it's the right time," Bryn said bluntly.

Darius was stricken. "Dad, you and Mom used to fight about my piano playing all the time. Don't wreck it with Hélène."

Bryn and Hélène glanced at one another. They'd tried to be discreet about their growing affection for one another, but Darius was astute and tuned into emotions. He was bound to sniff them out.

"We'll all think about it, okay, Dad?" Darius said.

Hélène adored the way Bryn's eyes softened when he spoke to Darius.

Bryn said, "It's okay, buddy. Sometimes, couples disagree, but that doesn't mean they're fighting. We both want what's best for you and we have to figure out what that is."

Couples. He was tearing back the curtain on their ... what exactly was it between them? She didn't have time to come up with an answer because Darius piped up. "But a couple means two, and we're three; that means a triple." He dipped his calamari into the red sauce.

Bryn smiled at her, and she wished she could lay her head on his chest right here in the restaurant. For a second, her secret past hardly seemed relevant.

She wasn't sure when it had happened, but she had lost her heart to both these men. They made her feel like she was hearing a lovely, heart-lifting melody after a long, cold silence.

But Darius knew who she was, who she had been. Bryn did not, and there was no way she could keep those opposing truths from colliding. She was guilty of doing what Vivianne had done:

shutting Bryn out of her relationship with Darius. If Bryn found out she and Darius had kept a secret between them, he would be crushed. She would lose both of them, and the long, cold, lonely silence would engulf her again.

CHAPTER 31

Next to the Word of God, the noble art of music is the greatest treasure in the world.
Martin Luther

Darius bounced in, and Hélène shut the studio doors. "Congratulations again on playing so marvelously at your recital last week," she said to Darius. He surprised her by throwing his arms around her waist and hugging her. Delight buzzed through her and she hugged his warm, wiry body to herself.

"Thanks," Darius said with a tossed-off confidence. He released her and plopped onto the piano bench.

She didn't mention the incident with the photo. He had overcome his shock and gone on to play his heart out; the mark of a true performer.

Now, she fixed him with her most scorching, sneaker-melting scowl. "After the recital, you should not have hinted to my friends that I can play. You know I don't play in public."

Darius adopted a face intended to portray innocence.

How did kids do that?

He said, "You *can* play, you just don't *want* to. You're *Hélène Noire et Blanche*. You can play anything." Her glare had been ineffectual because his tone was mildly insolent.

She leaned into the crook of the piano. "I'm not *Hélène Noire et Blanche* anymore."

He sat on the piano bench and adjusted it to his height. "You should play in public again," he said.

"I'm almost sorry I made your lessons predicated on speaking again." She bugged her eyes at him, intensifying her glare for maximum effect.

"I've heard your live performances. They're way better than your studio recordings."

It was as if she'd been stripped of her skin, every sinew and bone exposed. She had never listened to her own early recordings. It was too painful to remember who she'd been ... before Yves.

"How did you manage that?" she asked, the words nearly choking her.

He hitched one shoulder up and let it drop. "Mom's old bootleg recordings."

"That was a long time ago," she said.

She allowed herself a moment to remember the heady days of her past; the applause, the chanting of her nickname, the thrill of walking onto the stage and seeing not a single empty seat. The frisson that had run through her veins when playing for an audience was what had made her *Hélène Noire et Blanche*. Those days were past.

She pushed the bruise of loss away. "That is closed history," she said and took her chair. "Tell me what you and your dad have discussed about the competition."

He shrugged, "We haven't decided. Why should I do it, anyway? It's only a local thing."

She said, "It's not a local thing. It's regional and prestigious.

One way for musicians to get noticed is to compete. First regionally, then nationally, and eventually, internationally. Agents and conductors come to the finals, and they often hire the winners. And, if you win this, you get a chance to play the concerto with the Norwalk Symphony. This competition is a stepping stone to bigger things."

A shadow of emotion crossed his face.

"You played for my friends but are you afraid of playing in public?" she asked.

"No, are you?" he shot back.

She shifted in her chair. He was like a persistent fly, zooming in and around her.

"Let's get started. Did you bring the score for the Chopin First Concerto?"

He rolled his eyes and sighed in perfect adolescent impatience. "Yeees, but I keep telling you the Chopin Second is better. Why can't I do that?"

She ground her molars and pitied mothers everywhere who had recalcitrant children.

Because she never wanted to look at it again. "Someday, you can, but right now, the First is a better fit for you."

"Your debut was with the Second," he challenged. He seemed to know all about her. Her debut had been in New York City with the Orchestra of Light. Right after, orchestras from around the world came calling. She was offered a contract to record Chopin's First and Second. It was what she hoped for Darius and the First would do that just as well as the Second.

She turned her face away from him and blinked hard. Turning back, she held out her hand. "The score, please?"

He pouted and handed her a battered copy of the Chopin First. It had Vivianne's name written on the cover. "Do your warmups, please," she said.

Darius' playing demanded her attention as his fingers flew

over the keys in a blur, each note silken and clear. Even these ordinary exercises were alternately sensitive, insouciant, introspective, demonic, or playful. He was fearlessly emotional, never holding back his heart.

She had been just as brave once, before she knew what it was to be broken by someone you loved, by shame and humiliation. After she'd left France, it had been an arduous journey to excavate her own heart, even for her YouTube recordings. Her black Bösendorfer piano had been a source of despair and heartbreak.

As he zipped through his scales, chords, and arpeggios, she once more turned over in her mind the risks of entering him in the competition. If he didn't win, he might stop talking again. If he did win, he might leave his silence behind for good. The concerto required someone to play the orchestral part, and if she practiced with Darius, Bryn would hear and have questions.

Without stopping, Darius tore into the first movement of the Chopin First.

This emotionally bruised, phenomenally gifted boy needed her to be brave again, but her courage had all leaked out. Giving up her anonymity scared her more than she could express. Once everyone knew who she was, there was no going back.

A solution tumbled into her mind. Perhaps she could get Doris Grimmstein to play the orchestral part and then Hélène could merely stand back and watch Darius' magic.

Relieved to have found an answer, Hélène followed along in Vivianne's score. As he played, something about the pencil markings and notations niggled at the back of her mind. The handwriting, the accent marks, the slashes that nearly tore the paper, and scribbled notes were all eerily familiar, but the reason was hiding just out of reach. Many of the notations were quirky or wrong, as though someone was stupid enough to try rewriting what the composer wanted.

Vivianne's talent hadn't matched her ambitions, but Hélène didn't think she'd been stupid.

Darius played with blazing technique, but for the first time, his execution felt rote, cold, and cerebral—entirely unlike him. He'd memorized the markings at the expense of his emotions. Correcting those oddities would take a significant amount of time they didn't have.

Darius let the final notes of the first movement die out. He glanced into the corner of the room and smiled.

At someone? Only then did he look to Hélène for comments.

"Beautiful," she said. "If you decide to compete, you could do very well with this, but there are a few things to go over." She indicated several spots in the music where he could improve his performance.

His bushy hair flopped down over his forehead. Without even glancing at the score, he said, "The writing on the top of the sixth page says to be more meditative."

Hélène frowned and pointed to the page in question. "Someone just wrote that in. It's not what the composer wrote. Most of these markings are just plain wrong."

"But that's how my mom played it," he said. He rummaged through his hair, his eyes flicking to the corner in that ticky way he had.

She said, "You have to play with your ideas, your heart, your soul, but with the composer's directions. Playing according to these markings will not win a competition. I know you can have this performance-ready by the competition, but not the way this is marked up. That is, if you decide to do the competition."

A naughty gleam that meant trouble appeared in his eyes. "I'll do the competition if you play in public again," he said slyly.

Why did you send this boy to me, Lord?

Her brain fired off a string of French curse words, which she was sure God wouldn't mind.

So that was his game. She'd walked right into his snare. He didn't just play the piano; he knew how to play her, too. She'd been stupid for underestimating him. He understood what competing could do for him and that she wanted it for him.

Somehow, his intuition extended to recognizing that she wanted to play in public again, even though she said otherwise.

She thought of a concert hall filled with people and they were all laughing at her. Her fingers tingled, and her knuckles ached. The tendons along the backs of her hands felt tight as piano strings.

A smile danced at the corners of Darius' mouth. "Are you chicken?" he challenged.

Yes.

"I am not a chicken," she said. He knew that about her, too. Maybe, for him, and him only, she could be brave. She could play for him here in the studio.

Give me courage, Lord, she prayed. *And I won't ask for a parking space for a month.*

She leaned back in her chair and folded her arms across her chest. "If you agree to compete, I won't play in public, but I will play here. For you. But only when your dad's not around."

"The big stuff," Darius said, eyes wide with excitement. "Rachmaninoff, Beethoven."

"Do you know what a con man is?" she asked.

CHAPTER 32

Please write music like Wagner, only louder.
Samuel Goldwyn

Trying to stay awake, Darius rubbed the sleep out of his eyes with his blanket. "Did you like how I played at the recital, Mom?"

She sat weightlessly on the foot of his bed. It had been a while since she had come. Tonight, she was see-through, and he had to squint just to see her outline.

Not looking at him, she nodded *molto adagio*.

"Sorry about dropping your picture." He wished she'd say it wasn't a big deal, but it was probably just one more thing she was mad at him for.

"You happy I'm doing the concerto competition? 'Cause I want you to be happy. You know that, right?"

She hummed the tune for the first movement of the Chopin Second Concerto.

He pulled the covers up to his chin. "I know you want me to play the Second, but Hélène is making me play the First."

His mom pointed to the floor where her score to the Chopin Second lay open. "How'd that get there?" he said.

He hopped out of bed, the cold wooden floor shocking him fully awake. He didn't pick up the score but sat in the chair and looked at his mom. She was doing the blinking off and on thing again.

"I know, I know, I know. I want to do it for you." He hadn't brought the score to his lesson since Hélène had a meltdown.

He loved his mom and wanted to make her happy, but he loved Hélène, too. It was like being stretched in two directions. He loved making music with Hélène, the way she smiled at him or sometimes pushed his hair out of his face. How she understood him and his music and how she seemed to know they weren't the same thing.

"How am I supposed to get Hélène to let me play it for the competition? I'm learning it from her recording, but she won't let me play it."

She pointed to the score again with glowing red fingers. "Ask her ... ask her why ... doesn't..." Her voice crackled to a stop.

"Doesn't what?"

"...play anymore."

"Of course, I want to know, but she's not going to tell me. I'm just a kid."

He yawned, picked up the score, and lay back down in bed. He switched on his bedside lamp and opened the score. He didn't need to see the printed page because he saw the score in his mind, but he liked to read his mom's markings, the words of her Paris teacher scrawled in pencil in the margins. He remembered her telling him about the Eiffel Tower, her brilliant teacher, taking a boat down a big river, museums and concert halls. When she talked about her time in Paris, it was obvious she'd been super happy. Happier than she was with him and his dad.

"Tell her," his mom said.

He whispered into his pillow. "Tell her what?"

"...Second ... or no..." There was the flap of fabric, and the damp smell of night floated through the half-open window.

"No what?"

Her words had the sound of the left hand on the sixth page. Bright and exact. "Or you don't play."

"Okay," he mumbled.

And just like that, it was morning, and the Chopin score wasn't even in his room.

On the way to school, Darius asked his dad, "Did you take a music score out of my room last night?"

His dad frowned. "No, why?"

Darius looked out the window where the wind fluffed the leaves on the trees. "I just couldn't find it is all."

"Which score?" his dad asked. "Maybe I can find it in the house."

At a stop sign, Darius saw a bird on a branch. It was singing the theme from the slow movement of the Second Concerto, the notes dancing on the shafts of sunlight. The air had a velvety feel against his cheek, like when Hélène would pat him.

"Never mind. I don't need it anyway," Darius said. "I have it memorized."

CHAPTER 33

Do not withhold good from those to whom it is due, when it is in your power to act.
Proverbs 3:27

After Sunday service, Father Gabriel Ayeliff, St. Paul's Rector, stood at the coffee hour table greeting his parishioners. The Marriage Survivors milled about chatting and joking.

Bianca elbowed Hélène. "Watch. He's going to sneak a couple of cookies into the pocket of his cassock."

Sure enough, Hélène watched him slip three chocolate chip cookies into his pocket with the practiced expertise of a thief. She and Bianca laughed at his attempt at subterfuge, which no one was taken in by.

"Let's go head him off at the pass before he becomes a diabetic," Olivia said.

Flicka sashayed up to Father Gabriel. "Father, I met the cutest waiter at a restaurant the other night."

Father Gabriel paused the cookie, which was halfway to his mouth. "Thanks, Flicka, but I've sworn off dating for Lent."

"It's not Lent," Frankie said, poking a piece of celery into a hummus dip.

"I'm getting an early start," Father Gabriel said and chomped a bite out of his cookie.

Carolina laughed and said, "You're going to have to stop trying to get him married, Flicka."

"I can't," Flicka said. "I'm on a mission from God."

"More like a mission from Satan," Bianca cracked. Flicka laughed the loudest of all of them.

Hélène saw a young person in combat boots, ripped tights, orange hair, and a lace tutu slip shyly up next to Father Gabriel. The person carried a heavy Hello Kitty duffle bag.

Father Gabriel, with his famously youthful looks, didn't look much older than the young person. The two of them exchanged a few words so quietly that Hélène couldn't hear.

Darren and Sam Wanamaker joined them at the snack table. "Hey, ladies," Sam said.

"Who you callin' a lady?" Frankie said, and hugged Sam and then Darren.

Father Gabriel glanced at the young person, who gave a wavering but brave smile.

"Folks, this is Haley," Father Gabriel said. "They're going to stay with Darren and Sam for a few days."

Bianca was the first to stick her hand out. "Hiya, Haley. How are you? Welcome to St. Paul's. Glad you're here."

Haley's eyes widened in surprise, and they answered in a shaking, whispery voice. "Thanks." They swallowed, and Hélène saw tears well in their eyes.

Sam said, "You're welcome to stay with us as long as you need to, Haley."

Hélène smiled reassuringly and said, "And you're always welcome to be who you are at St. Paul's." Haley stared at Hélène with such relief and gratitude she thought she might weep.

Haley said, "I'm hoping my parents will get used to the idea of who I am, and I can go back home."

Hélène knew that Haley's hurt at her parents' rejection probably felt like they'd been hurled against a rock wall.

When Hélène had fled Paris with only a few possessions, it had been, more or less, her own choice. It had taken all her reserves to start over, alone. The warmth of the Marriage Survivors Club and St. Paul's had saved her from a permanently broken heart. Hopefully, they could do the same for Haley.

Darren said, "You can stay with us, as long as you stay in school."

"I imagine school hasn't been easy," Olivia said. She always knew the right thing to say to make someone feel understood and seen.

Haley shook their head, and their orange bangs fell over their eyes. They pushed the lock off their face, chin lifted, a defiant gleam in their eye. "School's pretty terrible, but I'm toughing it out. I want to get my education so I can help other people like me when I'm an adult."

"Whatever we can do to help, we're on it," Flicka said warmly. "And I love that color of lipstick, by the way."

Haley gave the first smile Hélène had seen, and for a moment, they looked young and carefree, the way kids their age were supposed to look.

"It's called Hot Harlot," Haley said, and a light broke over their face.

"Perfect color for Flicka!" Bianca said.

Their laughter was so loud that the entire crowd of parishioners turned to see what was so funny.

Hélène watched as Darren and Sam shepherded Haley out the door. They would take good care of Haley. God's mission wasn't always easy or clear, but that's what people at St. Paul's did. While she was a reluctant shepherd, she felt the same responsibility toward Darius. God, she knew, didn't give you a choice when he demanded that your beliefs direct your actions.

Father Gabriel's young face took on a look of deep, compassionate concern, and in that moment, he had the face of a wise old saint. Hélène wanted to pat his back and tell him not to worry.

He stared into his coffee mug as though pulling his words together. Somberly, he addressed the Marriage Survivors Club. "I know your plan for the concert is to have the competition winner play, but I was hoping for a guest pianist that would sell out the house."

Carolina's face glowed like she carried an inner candle. "We think we can do that, Father."

He nodded. His thoughtful gaze took all of them in, but Hélène felt his eyes rest the longest on her as if he *knew*. It took all her self-possession not to cringe into herself.

He said, "Kids like Haley are why we need to raise as much money for the LGBTQ shelter as possible. For those kids, it's literally a life-and-death issue. We need to call as much attention as possible to the concert so that people everywhere, not just here in Norwalk, know why we're doing this. If there's a chance to add a famous pianist to the concert, it might raise our profile to a national level. Let people know how much need there is to protect these young, vulnerable people."

"If we can, we will," Frankie said. The certainty in her voice was what inspired the people of St. Paul's to believe in this mission in the first place.

Panic speared through Hélène's center.

Before she'd come to church, she had glanced at the comments on her YouTube channel. As always, they were raving with compliments.

Except for one.

Sounds like Hélène Noire et Blanche *back when she could play.*

I was at her last concert. What a joke! Good thing she retired when she did.

That morning in church, she had prayed hard, but the only thing she could think of to say to God was *Help!*

Carolina squared her shoulders. "We'll keep looking for someone, right, Hélène?"

Hélène could only nod as she tried to swallow around the lump in her throat.

CHAPTER 34

There is no greater agony than bearing an untold story inside you.
Maya Angelou

Darius slapped down the score to the Chopin Second on the piano. "I've decided I want to do the Chopin Second for the competition."

Hélène's face froze like a glitch on a livestream. Her words shot out like nails out of his dad's nail gun. "I told you the Second is off limits."

He tapped his heart with a finger and forced himself to grin. "But I feel the Second more, here. Plus, it's more flashy and exciting."

She gripped the edge of the piano, making her knuckles turn white. "You've already learned most of the First Concerto, and you couldn't possibly get the Second ready in time."

He walked to the end of the length of the piano and tried to look serious. "I've already been working on it by myself."

"But we haven't even worked on it together," she said, giving him her most pissed-off glare.

The sides of his neck felt tight, and he tried relaxing his shoulders, which were up around his ears. "I know how you want it played because I've worked on it by listening to the recording you made when you were thirteen. I play exactly like you but with my own feelings, like you said. Feelings are all that matter, right?"

He looked to the corner where the cloud of blue-grey smoke that was his mom wavered in the air. Her papery voice said, "Tell her."

I'm trying to, Mom!

"Why can't I do it?" he said.

The room was hot and sticky, and a trickle of sweat ran down his spine.

"The Second is for a more mature pianist," she said. She massaged her fingers the way she did whenever they talked about the Second.

The boiling inside him pushed out the daggers of his words. "But I'm mature! I want to do it. You did it at thirteen, and I'm eleven! That's almost thirteen."

"No, it's not. Two years makes a big difference at your age," she snapped.

His fist balled up. "If I can't play the Second, then I'm not doing the competition. I'm not! I'm just not!" he yelled.

Hélène crossed her arms. Her eyes were on fire as she stared at him. "Can you explain why the Second is so important to you?"

In the corner, his mom drifted into thin ribbons of smoke, and she disappeared.

Everything in him twisted into one giant knot. *No, Mom! Don't go. I want to make you happy. I'm trying, I'm trying! I'll do it for you!*

He couldn't make them both happy! He kicked the piano leg, and pain shot up his leg.

"Darius!" Hélène jerked out of her chair.

He couldn't hold in the explosion brewing inside him. He stomped around the room. "I have to! I have to play it!" Without warning, hiccupy sobs burst out of him. "I have to play the Second because it was my mom's favorite. If I play it, she'll be happy. She wants me to play it." He squeezed his eyes shut and pushed his fists against them, but tears leaked out anyway.

He felt Hélène put her arm around his shoulders. She smelled nice, and her arm was soft, and her voice was gentle. "What do you mean she wants you to play it?"

He swiped his sleeve across his face and looked into her eyes, which made him tell her things. "She tells me."

She was gentle when she said, "When does she tell you?"

He wiped his face with the bottom of his shirt. He didn't want her to think he was crazy, but the words tumbled out of him. "When I talk to her and see her."

Her big eyes got even bigger. "Does that happen very often? That you talk to her?"

"Kinda."

"Does your dad know that she comes and talks to you?" she asked.

"No and swear you won't tell him either."

She breathed out and didn't speak for a few minutes. "Why shouldn't I tell him?"

"Because he's happy now, and I don't want him to be unhappy."

It was hard, trying to make his mom happy, make his dad not be sad, and make Hélène not get mad at him. He felt like a pretzel inside.

Hélène held him against her, and she spoke softly. "When she died, you stopped talking and playing. Can you explain to me why?"

He whispered, "Because she talks real quietly, and it was the only way I could hear her."

Hélène hugged him close. "And you think she'll be happy if you play the Second Piano Concerto?"

He tipped his head back and wailed at the ceiling. "Yeees! I have to play it for her so she won't be mad anymore about what I did." His body was shaking, and he had so many feelings inside that he could have played the piano for hours, and they still wouldn't have gotten out.

She led him back to the piano bench and pressed his shoulders until he sat. She sat next to him so her hip touched his. She held a tissue under his nose like his mom did when he was a little kid. "Why do you think she's mad at you?"

He buried his face in her shoulder so he didn't have to look at the disgust he knew was going to show on her face. "'Cause of what I did."

She petted his head. "Darius, neither you or your dad has ever told me how your mother died. I should have asked, but I didn't..." She stopped and didn't finish her thought. "Can you tell me what happened that makes you think she's mad at you?"

Uh oh.

He didn't want to tell her because he loved and needed her. When she knew, she might leave him too. But he was so tired; tired of waiting for his mom to come see him, of carrying the secrets, of trying to make her happy. He let his entire body slump against Hélène.

She laid her cheek on the top of his head. "Darius, how did she die?"

Cold tightened around his throat. His head thundered with the sounds of snow pelting against the window. His feet were numb, and his toes ached. He yanked out of her arms and paced around the studio again.

"I don't want to talk about it anymore." He banged his fists on the sides of his head to try to stop the sound of his mom's moans. "No, no, no, no! Stop moaning. Stop it!"

All his insides, his brain, his blood, and his breath were shaking so that he might crack wide open. He couldn't get enough air to fill his lungs. His teeth chattered from the cold. Howling wind clacked the tree branches together. Swirling snow blacked out everything outside.

She stopped moaning. She was so still. He covered her with blankets, hoping she would wake up if he kept her warm. But the blankets weren't enough. Her lips were turning blue, and her beautiful hands were as white as the snow outside.

"It's so cold." He jumped up and down and rubbed his arms, trying to get warm. "It's so cold and dark. The wind is making snow drifts," he said through chattering teeth. "It's so cold. So cold."

From some place faraway he heard Hélène say, "I'm right here. If you tell me, you'll feel better."

His teeth chattered, the words breaking up. "It was snow—snow—snowing. It snowed for hours and hours and hours."

"There was a snowstorm?" she asked.

"Y-y–yes," he said. "I tried. I tried all night, but the phones didn't work."

"I'm sure you did," she said.

His head felt light because he was breathing fast and jumping to get warm. He screwed his face closed and held his hands over his ears.

She came to him and pulled him close to her. "It's all right, it's all right," she whispered into the top of his head.

He could feel the warmth of her breath through his hair. His breathing got easier, and he felt safe and finally warm against her stomach and chest.

The words gushed out of him. "Big snowstorm all of a sudden. No-no electricity. Furnace didn't work. It got cold. See–

see–me and Mom, we had this fight because..." He touched his temple. "She–she had a headache all day and wanted to see a TV show, but I wanted to play Xbox. We were arguing, and I pulled the controller, and––" A long, thin wail threw his head back against Hélène's shoulder. "She fell ... she fell down-she fell, and her head, like the back of her ... her head." He touched the place where the bright red blood had poured out. There was so much. A big puddle almost.

"She hit––the brick fireplace. I put a towel on the back to stop the blood, but it kept coming and bleeding, and I couldn't get it to stop. I tried to wake her up but she wouldn't open her eyes. I tried calling 911 but the cellphone didn't work because of the snow, and I couldn't get them to come. I tried. I tried really hard."

The words ran together in a sloppy, snotty, sobby jumble because his mouth was twisted out of shape.

"I thought if I could make the blood stop, she would wake up, but she didn't. I tried to lift her up and lay her on the couch, but she was too heavy. I put blankets on her but she got cold anyway." An earthquake of shivering shook his whole body.

Hélène pulled him closer.

"I was supposed to go to the neighbor's house if anything happened, but I couldn't see their house because of the snow, and I didn't want Mom to be so cold and all alone. I stayed with her and held her hand. It got so cold, her hand. I held ituntil Dad came home the next day, and he called the ambulance. I didn't want to leave her alone."

He paused to get his breath and wipe his nose on the back of his sleeve. "See, so when my mom comes, I tell her I'm sorry. I want to play the Chopin Second because it was her favorite, and she won't be mad at me anymore if I play it for her." He sucked in air, his sobs hiccupping. "I'm really sorry I made her fall and hit her head and die. Please, please, I didn't mean to do it, I didn't mean to do it. I'm sorry. I'm sorry."

"It was not your fault," she said from somewhere far away. "It was nobody's fault, least of all yours." She held him close, and he stopped shivering. "She's not mad at you, and I'm sure she doesn't blame you for her fall."

His entire body felt empty, like somebody took out all of his bones and muscles, all his feelings and thoughts. He was sorry for making Hélène cry—sorry for all of it.

She led him by the hand back to her chair, and even though he was kind of too big, it felt good and safe to sit on her lap, where he stayed until he stopped crying.

CHAPTER 35

"For I know the plans I have for you," declares the LORD, *"plans to prosper you and not to harm you, plans to give you hope and a future."*

Jeremiah 29:11

Hélène sat on her sofa, stroking Liszt. Hearing what Darius had endured and how much he blamed himself had smashed her to bits. She wished, not for the first time, that she could hash over her experiences with Bryn and Darius with the Marriage Survivors Club, but that would only lead to questions she couldn't answer. She wasn't ready and probably would never be ready—to tell them about her disastrous past. They would ask her all the same questions she'd asked herself over and over: Why didn't she leave him sooner? Why did she marry him in the first place? Why did she let him drive her into hiding? Why had she been so weak?

"I should have asked Bryn how Vivianne died," she said to Liszt. He glanced up at her with his bright green eyes.

"I can't believe I'm talking to a cat," she said and scratched his ears. "Bryn would have told me if I'd asked how Vivianne died, but I didn't. If I had, I would have felt obligated to trust him more." She sighed. "I made Darius suffer in silence because I'm a ... chicken."

Confessing to the cat didn't make her feel any less guilty.

Darius belonged not to his dead mother, his father, or her, but to music and the world, to all the people he could move and touch with his playing. He trusted her to help him do it, and she couldn't refuse him.

He needed her, and she'd never been needed by anyone before. Because she'd made sure never to give anyone the opportunity to trust her. It would have meant she trusted them, and she wasn't going back down that road to hell again.

"I have to teach Darius the Second Concerto." The kitten kneaded her shoulder, and his tiny claws pricked through her shirt. "Even though it's like facing a musical guillotine."

She stopped petting Liszt but pushed his head under her hand, and she resumed petting. "I've heard it said that kittens are angels with whiskers," she whispered against his silky neck. "And I know you won't repeat anything I say."

Lizst twisted round so his tummy showed, and she stroked his soft underbelly. His eyes were closed when she heard a voice that sounded like Bianca at her most belligerent.

Someone, God or the angels, has sent Darius to you, and you can't send him back.

"I'm going nuts. I'm talking to my cat and hearing voices," she muttered.

CHAPTER 36

Oh, how miserable it is to have no one to share your sorrows and joys and, when your heart is heavy, to have no soul to whom you can pour out your woes.

Frederic Chopin

Hélène stomped into the kitchen. "Why didn't you tell me how Vivianne had died? About Darius staying with her all night? You should have told me as soon as you brought him to me."

It was a few days after Darius' heartbreaking revelation, and Hélène had had plenty of time to gin up her temper. Now, she paced back and forth in the kitchen, glaring at Bryn's back where he was kneeling over a loose bit of flooring. In the corner, Bryn wrestled a tube of something into an orange tool.

She wished he'd stand up so they could fight like a real couple.

But you're not a real couple, she reminded herself. *This is all temporary until he knows.*

She considered telling Bryn that Darius "talked" to Vivianne, but she didn't want to betray his confidence. At least that was one secret she thought she could justify keeping to everyone.

He didn't bother to look up at her. "If you really wanted to know, why didn't you ask me or him? What were you afraid of?"

He had her there. Like a balloon poked with a pin, some of her anger left her.

With a tenseness she hadn't heard in his voice before, he said, "Was it because you would have had to feel something for him?"

She wiped at a non-existent spot on the counter. "I care about all my students."

He thumped his fist on the loose flooring to press it down. "He's not like your other students, and you know it. You'd have had to love him—really love him—if you'd asked about Vivianne's death."

His words arrowed into her heart. When had he gotten to understand her? Vivianne convinced Bryn he was an emotional dolt, but with Hélène, he was the equivalent of a heat-seeking missile shooting down her self-delusions.

Her temperature lowered, she stopped pacing. "Okay ... I should have, but at least I would have understood him better, so why didn't you?"

Bryn looked over his shoulder at her. His face registered the overwhelmed confusion she'd seen there when they had first met.

"Because I felt like a rotten parent. Because I wanted it to go away. Because I felt horrible that I hadn't been there that night. Because I couldn't help him get over it. Because I was protecting him." The anguish in his voice intensified as he spoke. "Because I let Vivianne push me out. Because I was afraid you would think he was crazy and kick him out." He roughly elbowed a chair out of the way, and it clattered against the table with a kind of violent jarring. "And *that* he never would have recovered from."

She remembered how she'd wanted to give Darius to another teacher and cringed at her own selfish fear.

"He needed you, even if you were scared."

She wasn't scared, just private. Well, okay, she was scared.

Bryn stood and screwed the lid onto whatever goo he'd been using. "You could have asked him yourself, but look at how you live, Hélène. You're like a hermit. Like you don't want anyone to see you or to see anyone else. Like you don't care about being with people." He waved the orange tool around like an accusing finger. "Like you want to be alone. Like everyone is an imposition on your privacy. Like Darius was too much for you." He stared hard at her, red-faced, his body tense with a demanding challenge that demanded an answer. He added, "Even if you aren't a fantastic pianist. Tell me why you keep everyone at arm's length."

Heat flooded her face. She touched her collarbone and angled herself so she could see the trees in the backyard instead of the simmering anger in his eyes. She had to catch her breath and find the center herself. Bryn and Darius both had the ability to knock her off her center with a look, a word. A kiss.

Bryn had poked holes in the ways in which she'd protected her heart over the years. He saw her in a way she hadn't thought possible. He saw things in her she hadn't been willing to admit to herself, and that left her feeling scrubbed raw.

She turned back to him, unable to deny his accusations. His face was lined with the pain and anger of a man who had given his all and resented being found lacking. But there was something unreadable in his eyes and in the taut lines of his face that unsettled her.

"I've done everything I can to be a good father since Vivianne died. Anything to save my son," he said, chin lifted like a boxer. "Neither of us wanted to talk about why he was silent, so don't make it sound like I was pulling the wool over your eyes. I thought you and I were past cowardly finger pointing."

He had called her on her bullshit but with the love of a man who cared and was willing to overlook her fear. Not that she was willing to reveal the source of that fear.

And she wanted him. Wanted to keep him close, to give him a small part of her broken heart. As long as he didn't push too far, too hard.

"I'm sorry I hurt you," she said, quietly. Comfortingly. Not taking her eyes off his, she crossed the kitchen to him. "You are a good man, Bryn Harding, and a good father, and I should have asked."

"Would it have made a difference?" he asked, dubious.

"I ... honestly don't know. But I do know that I love Darius," she said. "And not just because of the way he makes music. You have raised a lovely boy. And..." She slid her hands up the front of his shirt and felt his heart thrumming in his chest.

He trapped her hands in his and kissed the fingertips. A wave of desire made her knees give way, so she leaned her cheek against his shoulder. "The two of you make me feel braver than I've ever been." She could give him that.

"We all seem to be doing that for one another," he said, sliding his arm around her waist. "You make me feel like I understand him. Like I'm a decent parent. Like I really can be a part of the music in his life."

When he kissed her, her brain shut off entirely. A welcome development.

Darius raced into Hélène's studio, which gave Bryn the time he needed to take the folding stadium chair out of the car trunk where he'd put it earlier. He might be just a nerd with a hammer, but Darius was his son, and he wanted in.

Inside, while Hélène and Darius watched with curiosity, Bryn opened the French doors to the studio. He opened the chair and set it in the center of the doorway, sat, and stretched out his legs. Grinning, he folded his hands over his belly as if he were settling in to watch a sports game.

Liszt the cat meandered past. Bryn scooped him up, set him in his lap, and petted him. The kitten's purr was like a tiny lawn mower. Cats were like instant love. No wonder people liked them. Bryn had grown up with dogs but Vivianne hadn't liked cats or dogs, so they'd never had one.

Bryn decided that he and Darius would get a cat or dog of their own.

"What are you doing?" Hélène asked Bryn with a lilt of amusement.

"Listening," Bryn said as if he'd always done this.

"Like always, you can listen through the closed door," Hélène said, her teacherly imperiousness softened by a smile. A smile with a flicker of flirtatiousness in it.

Darius stared at Bryn, his dark eyes popping in irritation. "Dad, don't be a weirdo!"

The kitten jumped down off Bryn's lap, ambled across the studio, and jumped into the open piano. As he walked across the strings, his steps produced a series of *twangs*.

Hélène frowned. "Ugh, now see what you've done? He'll get hair in the piano." She rose and plucked the kitten out of the piano. "We have to close the doors to keep him"—she summarily dropped Liszt into Bryn's lap—"and nosy parents out."

Bryn nestled Liszt against his shoulder. "I want to listen with the doors open." This was one way to learn about what his son was playing, so in a way, it was as much Bryn's lesson as it was

Darius'. Bryn shot her a meaningful look. "I'm not going to be shut out."

She arched one dark eyebrow, and tiny muscles in the corners of her eyes twitched with tension.

Darius growled, "Dad, can't you just cooperate?"

Bryn fought a smile. "Insisting on something you want doesn't mean a person is being uncooperative," Bryn said mildly. This was a good lesson for Darius. One Bryn should have taught him when Vivianne was alive.

"In this case, it does," Darius whinged.

"You know I never let parents in the studio," Hélène spluttered.

Bryn gave her his innocent smile. "I'm not in the studio," he said.

She jammed her fists on her skinny hips. "Well, you might as well be," she said.

Bryn kind of liked the way her dark eyes sparked with emotion.

Her voice was growing increasingly agitated. Having spent his entire marriage trying not to upset anyone, Bryn felt the power in insisting on what you deserved.

"Dad, you are too in!" Darius said. His exasperation was a newly acquired trait. Annoying, but a necessary part of growing up.

Bryn unfolded himself from the stadium chair and waggled his eyebrows at them.

He stepped into the studio. "In."

He stepped out. "Out."

He repeated this, sometimes with a hop or skip, each time saying, "in," "out," "in," and "out."

Intrigued, Liszt tried climbing up Bryn's leg.

Grinning, Darius finally got into the spirit of the joke and played chords for each of Bryn's iterations.

Finally, Hélène laughed and threw up her hands. "Oh, all right, then, have it your way. But don't blame me if he has a lousy lesson."

Darius ran his hand from the top of the keyboard to the bottom—*glissando*—his version of a laugh. Then he gave an actual, full-throated laugh, the first since Vivianne's death.

Pride burst over Bryn. He had given Darius that frothy moment of joy. He had disarmed both Darius and Hélène and made them laugh. It was like being Superman and Batman all wrapped into one, and Bryn wanted to live the rest of his life filled with moments like this. Maybe he wasn't just a nerd with a hammer.

Bryn met Hélène's gaze. Her eyes radiated like bits of stars that had fallen to earth just for him and he thought his heart would pound its way out of his chest.

CHAPTER 37

Music fills the infinite between two souls.
Rabindranath Tagore

Darius played the final notes of the Chopin Second and lifted his hands from the keyboard in a springing motion. He waited for Hélène to say something, but her eyes had a thinking-about-something-else look, and her body was stiff, like a stick.

"Hello, Earth to Hélène," he said, waving a hand in front of her blank-eyed stare

She blinked and said, "Oh, sorry, my mind drifted for a minute. You played that well."

He bobbed his head from side to side. "Except for that mistake on the third page."

"Yes, maybe you should start there and play it again," she said absently.

He huffed. "I didn't make a mistake. You weren't even listening!"

She gave her head a little shake. She stood and walked around the studio. "Sorry, I guess I lost track for a minute."

"Why do you hate the Chopin Second so much?" he asked.

She turned to him and frowned. "I don't hate it," she said. But he totally did not believe her. She was doing that thing again where she rubbed her fingers and wrists.

Since they'd started working on the Second, he'd noticed Hélène didn't smile as much, and her face pinched up. It was like poison to her.

Then, it dawned on him. Why hadn't he thought of it before?

"You played it on your last concert, but there's not even a bootleg of that concert. Afterward, you quit playing. How come?" he asked in an annoying voice, almost guaranteed to get an answer.

Her eyes got bigger. "Is there anything you haven't looked up about me?"

"No, but I still haven't been able to figure out why you quit," he said.

"Let's try this again," she said.

"Why? You've hardly said anything to me while we're working on this anyway," he said irritably. Then he went for the kill shot. "Don't you even *want* me to win the competition?"

She sat back in her chair and wrapped her arms around her waist. "All right," she said, her face set like someone ready to swallow some nasty medicine. "Start from the beginning, and I'll pay more attention."

He crossed his arms and stared at her. "No. Tell me why you don't like it."

She dropped her head into her palm. "Darius, what am I going to do with you?"

He lifted his hands up in question. "What?"

"Play already," she said.

He scrambled off the bench and closed the keyboard cover with a *thump.* "I want you to tell me why you quit playing. I mean, you were *Hélène Noire et Blanche.* You're one of the best ever. Why won't you play? People everywhere wanted to hear you. They still do."

"No, they don't," she said in a soft, sad way. "That Hélène is gone."

"No, she's not. But she only plays on YouTube." He let his hand hover before letting it come to rest on her shoulder. "I told you about my mom. It's only fair for you to tell me why you quit."

She stared off for a long time. Her eyes were dark and afraid, like she was sinking in the ocean and couldn't get out. "I really shouldn't tell you."

"I know, but you want me to play the competition, so you're going to," he said, as certain of her ambition as he was of his own.

She twisted her mouth to the side and made a long, noisy exhale. "All right. My father died. He was everything to me, sort of like your mother was to you. I was sad and missed him very much."

"Okay, but what's that got to do with you stopping playing? I mean, you could have started playing again."

She touched her long fingers to the side of her neck. "A few years later, I married a conductor who was older than me."

"Like really, really old?" he plopped back onto the bench and watched her out of the corner of his eye. Her face was so sad that his heart felt like it was being squooshed into a pancake.

"Only really old," she said. Her hands twisted in her lap.

She blinked hard. He was afraid she might start bawling, and then what would he do? He hadn't meant to make her sad, but he wanted to know. He wanted her to play again because people should hear a great pianist like Hélène.

"And what'd he do, this old guy?"

She swallowed. "Well, at first, he got me all kinds of work; concerts, recitals, recordings, ensemble work, but I had to learn new music lightning fast. I can learn fast—like you—but it was a lot of pressure." Her skinny shoulders bent toward her chest as if she was protecting herself all over again. "Many times, I didn't play well, and I was disappointed in myself for that."

"It wasn't your fault," Darius said. Just in case, he pressed a tissue into her hand. "But what happened at your last concert with the Chopin Second?"

"As you've figured out," she pressed the tissue under her eyes for a moment. "I was playing the Chopin Second, and he was conducting."

Darius had to look away from her sad, sad face. He felt like *he* might start bawling.

She went on, her voice cracking every few words. "Our plane was late that night, and we had to rehearse right before the performance. It was pouring rain, and my fingers ached with the cold." She rubbed her fingers and her wrists again.

Her head hung down until her chin touched her chest like she wasn't strong enough to hold it up. "He'd booked the concerts too close together, but this was a gala concert with lots of rich, important people coming. He never wanted to pass up an opportunity like that. Then, at the last minute, he insisted on new tempi and dynamics. He criticized me in front of the orchestra and insisted I play a cadenza I hadn't practiced in a while."

He was mad at the stupid conductor-husband for doing that to her. She was *Hélène Noire et Blanche,* and nobody should have made it so that she couldn't play her best.

"But you have a photographic memory. Couldn't you just play it?" he asked in the gentle way his dad did when Darius was upset.

"I could have if I hadn't been so tired and stressed." Her hand was shaky when she tucked a feather of her white hair behind her ear. "I think he wanted to see how much pressure I could take. We'd been touring, recording, and rehearsing for eight weeks solid, and I was exhausted."

"He was a dumbass," Darius said, angry that someone would treat her like that.

One side of her mouth turned up, but not in a happy way. "I really shouldn't be telling you this," she said, her voice trailing off.

"Yeah, but I have to play the Second, and I need you to help me if I'm gonna win, and you're not paying attention because you don't like it," he said. "I guess this dumbass conductor ruined everything for you."

She didn't hear him but stared off toward something that wasn't there.

Her body sank lower and lower in her chair like she didn't have any bones. "That night, I played terribly. The notes were a jumble in my head. I made mistakes. Stupid mistakes. Once I stopped completely, I got off a measure, I missed a rest, I played wrong notes, my pedaling was sloppy, my tempi jerky, my dynamics were all wrong."

It must have been terrible because *Hélène Noire et Blanche* would never play badly. No wonder she didn't want to ever see the Second Concerto again. He knew he'd feel rotten if this happened to him.

She tipped her head back up, and her face was bright red. He wished he could give her a hug like moms did when their kids came home all upset because of bullies on the playground. He wished he could kick that conductor guy in the nuts. He'd ruined *Hélène Noire et Blanche.*

"It was ... a disaster," she said in a chokey voice. "After the concert, he screamed at me about how terrible I'd played, that I'd ruined his career, how I was nothing without him, that if I'd listened to what he said, it would been so much better. The reviews were brutal and, well, I just kind of ... collapsed." She lifted her hands from her lap and let them fall back down like she was giving up. "Afterwards, I didn't think I was good enough anymore. I couldn't face playing in public anymore. I was sure the audience would laugh at me. That critics would write terrible things in the newspaper. People would find me and ask what happened. I'd be a joke on social media. I was afraid he would do the same thing to me, over and over. I had to get away."

"But how could you give up everything you worked for your whole life? You played in public when you were six and made your debut when you were thirteen," he said. "You were already rich and famous. People would forget if you played bad just one time."

She shook her head. "I guess I was broken," she said. "I left France and never played in public again."

"So that's why you hate the Chopin Second. It's why you got freaked out when I brought it in the first time," he said. Now he understood.

She nodded.

His mom was in the corner smiling, her shape like a white fire that lit up the room.

Maybe that was why his mom insisted he learn the Chopin Second. It wasn't for Hélène.

CHAPTER 38

Beware of missing chances; otherwise it may be altogether too late some day.

Franz Liszt

"Listen, you two," Hélène said. "I'm pretty sure my clothes are getting snugger because we eat out after every one of your lessons."

Bryn leaned in and whispered, "The better to see your curves."

Tonight, they were at Burger Barn on Main Street. It was mid-week, and the place was quiet. She and Bryn were sitting next to one another in the booth, and where their hips touched, she felt as though a tiny flame smoldered.

She saw him sneak one of his signature red envelopes into her purse. He gazed at her with a combination of naked desire and care—care she knew was reliable and freely given. How long had it been since she felt the inner calm of knowing someone cared for her without demanding something in return? Particularly when she didn't deserve his trust and care.

She hated to disturb the pleasure of eating and chatting aimlessly together, but she had a sticky problem. She had accepted that Darius needed to play the Chopin Second, but she had to find a way to steer into safer waters. Doris Grimmstein was the oar.

Hélène said to Darius, "We need to discuss who will play the orchestral part with you in round one of the competition."

Darius' gaze swung toward her with raw fear. "Aren't you playing?"

She lifted her brow and gave him a "you know why" look. "I'm not good enough," she said and wiped a smear of ketchup off his cheek with her napkin.

Bryn said, "I don't get it. I thought a concerto was with an orchestra, so why do they need a second piano?" Under the table, Bryn ran a toe up the side of her leg.

Her breath caught, and heat spread across her face.

Nonchalantly, Bryn kept his eyes trained on his burger.

It was as if she had to think simultaneously in two separate trains of thought, one to push Darius back and one to bring Bryn closer. Her hormones, jolted by Bryn's flirting, made her brain stumble. It took a moment before she could answer his question.

She said, "Two pianists play the first round."

Bryn's toe found the back of her calf, and she giggled into her napkin.

Quizzically, Darius frowned up at her from beneath the thick slash of his dark brows.

She took a moment to gather her thoughts which Bryn had scattered. "The soloist"—she pointed at Darius with her fork—"that would be him, plays the solo part. The second pianist plays the orchestral part. It's impossible for all the entrants to practice with the entire orchestra and conductor."

"Oh, okay, makes sense," Bryn said. "But why can't he at least practice with you?"

She would have loved to play the orchestral part, but she didn't trust herself. Lately, she and Darius had been playing more duets, and that required her to send Bryn to the hardware store for screws, washers, nails, and touch-up paint. She was running out of things for him to fix.

It was rare that two well-matched pianists got to play together, and the chance to accompany a pianist of Darius' talent would never come along again. But she wasn't prepared to risk being unmasked, either.

"I'm not capable of anything as challenging as the Chopin Second," she said, fixing Darius with a warning stare. "But my fellow teacher, Doris Grimmstein, is. And you need to start practicing with her as soon as possible."

Even if she could play with Darius, she didn't trust herself. An attack of nerves might cause her to make a mistake that could throw him off his game, and that was the last thing she wanted. Moreover, if her identity was discovered, it could divert attention from Darius.

Bryn took a sip of beer and set down his glass. "But do the musicians ever get to practice with the orchestra?"

She said, "Yes. The morning of the concert, the three finalists rehearse with the orchestra and in the evening, they play in a concert with the orchestra. Those three will be ranked first, second, and third place."

Bryn chewed his burger, making little happy humming noises. He set his burger down. "But if you practiced you could learn it you're smart you've taught him for a long time he's comfortable with you might make the whole thing more enjoyable I bet you're really good—" He jammed his napkin to his mouth as if to stop himself saying anything more.

He hadn't spoken in that firehose way in a long time and

Hélène attributed it to his nervousness at Darius' participation in the competition. She adored him for his faith in her supposedly meager abilities. His face was filled with such affection that she almost reversed herself. She patted his leg under the table, and Bryn gave her a moony smile.

Darius jutted his chin at her like a cranky donkey threatening to bite. "Why can't you just do it?" Darius asked, knowing the answer perfectly well.

"The orchestral score is challenging, and even if I was up to playing it"—she took a steadying sip of wine and narrowed her eyes at Darius—"I don't have a second piano. Doris does."

Hélène kept her eyes focused on her food so Bryn wouldn't see her subtle duplicity. That Darius knew who she was and Bryn didn't was one more thing that required a split in Hélène's thinking. One more way she was betraying Bryn's unwarranted trust.

"I don't want to play with someone else. I want you," Darius said stubbornly, which she had expected.

Juice dripped down his fingers, and Hélène handed him his napkin. "Here, wipe your hands."

Darius scrubbed at his hands, his scowl never leaving his face.

She flicked a warning eyebrow at him. "Doris Grimmstein is a wonderful pianist, and she'll do an excellent job accompanying you for the competition." She picked an olive pit out of her salad Niçoise and set it aside. "Doris has two pianos that you need to practice. I don't." She smiled at Darius, trying to communicate both finality and threat.

Darius looked up at her with trouble-making eyes. "No, you."

She said, "I'm not sending you to her forever, just for the competition. We can work together on your solo part."

"I need you," Darius said, and she caught the plaintive, almost panicked tone in his voice.

"You don't need me," Hélène said. She reached over and tucked a strand of his mad hair behind his ear. "The music is inside of you. Feelings are all that matter. You'll be fine."

Darius shoved his plate back, nearly spilling his glass of milk. Only her fast reflexes kept it from toppling.

"Great reflexes," Bryn said. Then, "Can't we rent a second piano? I'll pay for it."

This caught her off guard, and she struggled for an answer.

Darius popped straight up in his chair. "See, you can play!" he said with wicked glee.

In her stomach, Hélène's salad was beginning to solidify into a rock. "Doris is better than me," she lied. "Which means you'll be in much better shape to win."

"Can you play with this other teacher?" Bryn asked Darius. Bryn swabbed his burger through a puddle of ketchup as he watched Hélène.

"Nope." Darius took on the mischievous look that always made Hélène wary. "I need someone who can play the black and white keys," he said, hinting at her nickname.

Hélène was tempted to kick Darius under the table, but that would have probably qualified as child abuse.

Her faith was a nebulous thing she only called upon for parking spaces and in emergencies. This qualified as an emergency. *God, help me out of this one!*

In his seat, Bryn shifted in a way that made Hélène uneasy. "I heard you two play a duet that sounded perfect I'll bet if you practiced hard you could do it but only if you want to," he said in a flood.

She felt him searching out her gaze but busied herself refolding her napkin.

"She just doesn't like to play in front of crowds," Darius said with a ketchupy grin.

She glared at Darius again, but his smile dared her to tell the truth. "I simply am not that good. And besides, I get stage fright," she said primly, which wasn't *exactly* a lie.

Darius stretched his gangly body toward Bryn. "Daaaad, will you please get her a second piano so we can practice together?"

Before she could object, Bryn said, "Sure." Then, to her, "Practice hard and decide later whether or not you feel up to playing the first round with him. You might even think it's fun to play for an audience."

With raw yearning, she remembered how electrifying it was to play live. She'd felt most alive, and the whole world dropped away. Worry, anger, frustration, rage, loss, and insecurity disappeared as the music flowed out of her soul, as effortless as an exhalation. The temptation to play in public again was as powerful as a gravitational pull.

Darius leaned back in his chair and crossed his arms. "Okay, here's the deal. If you don't play, I'm not doing it."

"Oh, Darius!" Bryn barked and threw his napkin on the table. "Don't be a *prima don!*"

When had he learned those words?

She narrowed her eyes at Darius and lowered her voice to an icy edge. "First, you refuse to compete unless you can play the Chopin Second." Hélène threw up her hands. "And now you insist I do something you know I can't do."

Darius narrowed his eyes back at her. "Because I love you, that's why."

There was no arguing with that.

Now she knew why Bryn frequently felt like an ineffective parent; kids made you do crazy things when you loved them like crazy. And she did love Darius, despite his being an *enfant terrible*. These two had wrenched her heart open. At every turn, Darius had managed to get her to do what he wanted. All along, he had been inching her toward playing in public when she'd spent years hiding and lying. He had figured out that she would do whatever he needed to make him successful, secure, and feel loved.

Silence fell over them all. She folded her arms and scowled at Darius.

The first round was ordinarily played behind closed doors for just the judges. Probably none of them had ever heard of *Hélène Noire et Blanche.*

What if...

Maybe just the first round...

Her hands rested on the tabletop. She flexed her fingers, and they didn't freeze up. Her wrists remained supple. She didn't break into a sweat, and her stomach didn't twist into knots.

Darius noticed her opening and closing her hands. He raised his eyebrows in expectation.

Bryn's mouth twitched at the corners.

Darius needed her. Could she do this one thing for him and Bryn?

She rolled her eyes, knowing what she was about to say was going to lead her straight down the road to hell. "I'm not saying I'll play the orchestral part, but I'll practice with you. If I can bring it up to a professional level"—she raised a warning finger—"I'll *consider* it. It will take me a lot of work, so I'm not making any promises. But you have to agree that if I say you have to play with Doris, that's it."

Saying yes to Darius while simultaneously lying to Bryn made both her heart and her head hurt.

Darius grinned. His entire face twinkled like it had been sprinkled with stardust. "So you're saying 'maybe'?" He was irresistible when he was excited.

Bryn smiled broadly and looked incredibly handsome.

She wondered if the two of them had planned this ambush. "I'm saying maybe," she responded.

"Okay, I agree." Darius popped out of his seat and came to

her. He threw his arms around her neck. What could she do but hug him and kiss his cheek?

He lay his head on her shoulder and whispered into her hair, "Thanks, *Hélène Noire et Blanche*."

"Thanks," Bryn said.

These two made everything perfect and perfectly scary. They were turning her world upside down and right side up.

But the tilt-a-whirl would come to a crashing halt when Bryn figured out that she wasn't Hélène the Lousy Pianist, but *Hélène Noire et Blanche*.

CHAPTER 39

Courage is being scared to death ... and saddling up anyway.
John Wayne

Three days later, Hélène, Bryn, and Darius watched the deliverymen huff, puff, grunt, and groan as they moved her Bösendorfer to make room for the second piano. Even on casters, it weighed over twelve hundred pounds. They wheeled in a 5'6" mahogany baby grand on a trolly, set it up, and tuned it.

Seeing the second piano sail into her studio made Hélène feel brave, as if she was performing open heart surgery or scaling Kilimanjaro.

It was final, there was no turning back. She was playing the orchestral part. She was afraid, but she was going to do it anyway. At night, she lay awake, excited about playing for an audience again, even if it was just the judges.

The day the second piano arrived, Bryn gave her a poem written in his signature careful script.

I imagine you
In the mornings
Waking
Dreams still in your eyes
returning from where I cannot follow
I am content to wait

The intricate silence of your smile
Your black irises a destination
More glorious than a sunrise
The journey between you and me
Enough adventure for a lifetime

Bryn

Nightly, she took out Bryn's poems from beneath her pillow where she slept with them and reread them, even though she had memorized them. With his words, he made her see herself in an entirely new light. He had given her a small part of himself —and of herself—with each poem.

Bryn trusted her with his son and his own heart. She hoped that one day, Bryn would understand what it cost her to play with Darius in the competition. She was giving Bryn a part of herself, even if she couldn't give him the truth.

To Bryn, she was an adventure, a future, and safety.

To Darius, she was *Hélène Noire et Blanche.*

To herself, she was a has-been who'd been manipulated, shamed, and browbeaten into public humiliation.

Vivianne had failed them both, but Hélène couldn't fail Darius, even if it cost her Bryn.

There wasn't much time for Darius to prepare, but with his lightning-fast ability to learn music, it wouldn't be a stretch. She was grateful she'd kept her technique in shape by making YouTube videos.

Time flew by. Three times a week, Darius and Hélène practiced together, adjusting tempi, playing off one another, matching dynamics and accents, nodding, and coordinating with a nod or a look. When she looked over Vivianne's score, the handwriting in it still bothered her, but there wasn't time to puzzle it out; they had lots of notes to play.

When Bryn was in the house, she intentionally made mistakes, fumbled entrances, and clumped along to maintain her fictitiously terrible playing. Her mistakes also served to prepare Darius in the event she actually did make a disastrous one in the competition. Nothing fazed Darius.

Bryn complimented her playing, but there was always tension at the corners of his mouth, as though he was sorry he'd convinced her to try playing the orchestral part.

The more they worked, the more confident she was that Darius would be one of the three finalists. As they practiced, she repeatedly challenged Darius to justify his musical choices. That way, he would be inoculated against the poison of having to play under the baton of a tyrannical conductor.

Someone like Yves.

CHAPTER 40

He has Van Gogh's ear for music.
Billy Wilder

Bryn checked the roast in the oven. It smelled fatty and juicy, the top was browning nicely, and the vegetables weren't drying out. He smiled to himself; he was getting the hang of this cooking thing. He popped a CD of Vivianne playing a Chopin Mazurka, and music filled the kitchen. He could picture her petite back bent over the keyboard, forehead creased in concentration, as she fought to conquer something beyond her ability. He felt sorry for her that she had been driven to achieve something that would forever remain out of her reach.

Darius shuffled into the kitchen wearing two mismatched socks. "Smells good. I'm hungry." He frowned at the CD player. "Who's recording of the mazurka is *this*?" he asked, wrinkling his nose. "Kinda sucks."

"Don't say that word. It makes you sound low-class."

"Whatever!"

Bryn shut the oven door and pulled the oven mitts off. "It's your mom. I made it when you were about, oh, say, five."

Darius curled his upper lip and arched one eyebrow with the disdain of a know-it-all kid. "I knew she wasn't great, but this..." His trailing off was as eloquent as anything he could have said.

Bryn listened closely. After a few measures, he was forced to acknowledge her shortcomings. "She doesn't have control of the tempo, and her right hand is a little ahead of the left. The balance between bass and treble seems off, and one high note is louder than the other notes. She's failing to bring out the melody in the left hand."

Darius grinned. "You're learning, Dad."

Bryn wasn't such a musical dolt after all. He'd supported Vivianne because he'd loved her and would have done so if he'd understood her limitations.

He handed Darius the water glasses to fill and put on the table. "I couldn't understand how she made her hands *do* what they did. I thought it was amazing how she could make me feel happy or sad, thoughtful or dreamy. Sometimes, I'd even laugh."

"Yeah, music can do that," Darius said as he set the glasses at their respective places. "As long as you're not laughing at the musician's playing."

"I thought what she was doing was ... magic." It felt a bit disrespectful, and Bryn wasn't sure he should say this, but he wanted to be honest with Darius. "When you started playing, it was clear you could play anything, and you sounded way better than her right off the bat."

Darius opened the silverware drawer and laid the flatware on the table. "Yeah, Mom tried hard, but she wasn't up to it."

Bryn stopped what he was doing and looked at his son, surprised—again—at his maturity and astuteness.

Bryn wiped a drip of grease off the counter. "Whenever your

mom talked about music, I felt like I was too dumb to get it. Now I realize she didn't explain things."

"Yeah, I know what you mean," Darius said. "When Hélène tells me something, I get it right away."

Bryn took the salad out of the fridge and set it on the table. This was the longest conversation he'd had with Darius since Vivianne died and the longest one they'd ever talked about music. This might be what it felt like to be an effective parent— one who'd saved their son.

"Mom acted like music was something only me and her could understand." Darius poured water into the glasses. "She used to say only special people like us could understand. She'd say you only understood computers and stuff but not music."

Bryn leaned against the kitchen counter, hoping it would hold him up because his knees felt like they'd been whacked with a golf club. He modulated his voice to keep his son from hearing the hurt stabbing through him. "Really? She said that?"

Darius put paper napkins beside each of their plates. "Yeah, other stuff, too. She said how we were making me into a world-class pianist, and you would have to get used to it. Like music was our way of communicating with each other, and you would never get it."

Not realizing he'd just run his father through with a dagger, Darius breezily added, "But I knew by the time I was, like, five, I could already do stuff other pianists couldn't. Stuff she couldn't do. Like play from memory music I heard only once." Darius dipped his chin, a gesture of shyness. "I don't want to sound all braggy and stuff, but I knew I was special, and not just because Mom told me I was."

Bryn's chest hurt with both sorrow and love. How had his son become so wise? How much had Darius lost out on because Bryn hadn't pushed against Vivianne?

Darius said, "Is dinner done yet? I'm starving."

"Oh, yeah." Bryn pushed himself off the counter and pulled the roast out of the oven. He sliced the meat, plated it, and set the potatoes and carrots alongside. They sat and dug in.

"This is good, Dad," Darius said.

"Thanks," Bryn said.

"Oh, yeah. Something's wrong with the blinds in my room," Darius said as he chased a potato around on his plate with his fork. "Can you fix it?"

Bryn remembered Hélène suggesting that he show Darius how to fix things as a way to share himself with Darius. "Be happy to. Maybe we can do it together. You can learn how to fix stuff yourself," Bryn said. "Comes in handy, knowing how to do stuff including play piano."

"Cool," Darius said.

They ate while Vivianne's bad mazurkas, clunky chords, uneven runs, and inexact rhythms played in the background. To think how much Vivianne had practiced. To think how much Bryn had sacrificed for her.

They'd listened for a while when Bryn decided it was as good a time as any to ask his son something that he'd wanted to for several weeks.

Bryn toyed with his knife. "I was hoping you'd start playing when I'm at home sometimes. It's been a long time since I heard you, and I miss it."

As he repaired things around Hélène's, hearing Darius play made Bryn feel serenely hopeful. Sometimes, when he'd gone out for some part or other, on returning, instead of going in the front door of Hélène's, Bryn snuck—there was no other word for it—around the back of the house. He would sit on the ground beneath Hélène's studio window, back against the wall, bows resting on his bent knees, listening to her play duets with Darius. Sometimes, their playing made Bryn cry. For joy, for relief, for gratefulness.

"Yeah, I want to rerun the concerto tonight," Darius said. He paused, fork halfway to his mouth. "Hey, there's this funny cat video on YouTube I want to show you after dinner."

Bryn patted his mouth with his napkin to hide his grin. "Sure. That'd be great. Right after you and I fix the blinds in your bedroom and after you practice."

After dinner, Darius ran through the Chopin Second Concerto while Bryn scrubbed the roasting pan with a fury.

Vivianne had actively put him down to their son. It enraged him that she taught Darius that his father was a musical dunce. Maybe Vivianne had been compensating for being ordinary.

Ordinariness was underrated. It allowed you to come home to the same bed, to have your things about you, to see the people you loved, to spend time with them, to have a routine, and to help others become their best.

But their ordinary life and love hadn't been enough for Vivianne. This crushed him because he had loved her and given her everything he could, and yet she made Bryn feel that he, not she, was the failure.

Bryn heard Darius' delicate touch in a soft passage in the concerto, the brilliance of his runs, the flawless execution. The singing melodies made Bryn's throat go so thick with emotion that he had to sit down for a moment.

When he'd finished cleaning the kitchen, Bryn stomped down the hall to his bedroom. He found Vivianne's pink satin slippers under the bed where he'd placed them. He snatched them up and crushed them in his hands. He raged out to the garage and hurled them into the trash can.

He wanted Darius to be the best *he* chose to be. Given the breadth of his gifts, it was hard not to push him. But Vivianne had treated Darius as though he were music and nothing else. Bryn wanted no part of that for himself or Darius. He was still unsure if this competition was right for Darius, but he trusted Hélène.

As much as he was able.

He took out the small notebook he carried in his back pocket and wrote.

To Darius

A road
A mountain
A river
A stream
Wherever you go
I will walk beside
As long as you need
And when you step into a land where I cannot follow
I will open my hand to wave you on
In wonder that I have made you
And that you have made me

This was the kind of dad he wanted to be.

CHAPTER 41

In the sweetness of friendship, let there be laughter and sharing of pleasures.
For in the dew of little things, the heart finds its morning and is refreshed.
Khalil Gibran

Bursting with excitement, and waving one of Bryn's poems, Hélène practically danced down the center aisle of the church.

"Wait till I read this to you," she said, eager to share her joy with the Marriage Survivors Club.

They were preparing the sanctuary for an afternoon wedding. Now, they paused and gathered around. Hélène, her heart whirring, read the poem.

Your light calls to me from the edge of the world
Beyond my final breath
Beyond my sightless eyes

Beyond my battered heart
Beyond my timid soul

Your hope breathes into my despair
Your eyes unearth my forgotten courage
Your heartbeats carry my staggering rhythm
Your soul frees my clipped wings
I am returned to myself

Bianca frowned at her phone. "So romantic I missed a three-point shot while I was listening."

"You have the soul of a rock, Bianca," Flicka said.

Hélène carefully refolded the paper, returned the poem to the red envelope, and tucked it back into her purse. She couldn't help smiling. She felt as though she was filled with the rainbow colors of the stained glass windows.

"We saw him at the recital, but you haven't talked about him much, " Carolina said. "What's he like?" She dusted a glass hurricane globe.

Hélène didn't have to think before answering. "Humble, caring, modest, thoughtful, smart, funny, sweet, and he adores Darius."

Flicka said, "And you, obviously."

Olivia said, "I'm going to ask Jack to write me a poem."

"He used to be a fireman," Bianca said. "He'll write about the flames of his desire." She made her voice throb with throaty seduction. "And about his long firehose."

Hélène laughed along with the others.

"Aren't you supposed to be polishing the brass candlesticks?" Olivia asked Bianca, who reluctantly took up a rag and polish.

Frankie settled a candle in one of the candle sticks bolted to the pew ends. "Sounds to me like you're falling for the guy, Frenchie."

Even though it felt like walking in the dark with her hands extended, Hélène was beginning to trust her feelings about Bryn. He hadn't tried to tell her what to do. He made no demands of her. She heard Yves' sarcastic, belittling voice less frequently. She had come to love having Bryn and Darius in her life. The little boxes of nourishing food Bryn left in her fridge, the red envelopes slipped into her handbag, a bottle of wine left on the kitchen counter, a single rose in a water glass on the kitchen table. They all made her feel cared for.

She'd fallen for Darius because he'd needed her, but she was falling for Bryn because she found she needed him. It was, quite possibly, the biggest surprise of her life. She'd made sure not to need anyone because that made her too vulnerable, but he believed in her and so made her believe in herself again.

She had started to consider that maybe she would never have to reveal her previous life. After all, she wasn't *Hélène Noire et Blanche* any longer to anyone except Darius. The past was someplace in the rearview mirror.

To Bryn, she was the future, a promise. All she had to do was let her memories quietly slip below the surface of the past, and she might find her future.

Hélène took up a cloth and helped Carolina to polish the hurricane globes.

Carolina asked, "Can you see yourself with Bryn?"

Hélène almost chuckled. "I think so."

Did I just say that?

Frankie laughed. "We'll have to give ourselves a new name, like the Maybe Marriage Club." She pointed to a box of candles. "Hand me one of those, would you?"

Hélène handed her one of the fat candles. "It's way too soon to talk about marriage, but Darius has hugged me a few times.

The best thing is that Darius has started speaking again, even in school. And he's competing in the Norwalk Symphony concerto competition."

Of course, Hélène didn't mention she was playing the orchestral part since she was only playing for the judges, and they wouldn't be there.

Carolina picked a bit of wax off of one of the candlesticks. "If Darius wins, he'll be playing here."

Hélène swallowed hard and let the comment pass. She could always listen from the back and slip out when it was done, and no one would be the wiser.

"I still think a strip show with women of a certain age would have been a sell-out," Flicka said. Their laughter echoed off the stone pillars.

"I've let all the planning for the concert fall on your shoulders, Carolina. I know its late, but what can I do to help?" Hélène asked, guiltily.

"Don't worry about it," Carolina said. "You have enough getting Darius ready to win."

"The Symphony sold another fifty tickets from their website," Frankie said.

"That's great, but we still won't make our fundraising goal unless we get the famous pianist Father Gabriel wants us to get," Flicka said.

Cold crept up the back of Hélène's neck.

"We'll just have to do more publicity," Olivia said. "And ask all our friends to buy tickets."

"Flicka doesn't have any friends," Bianca said with a laughing sneer.

Flicka said, "Except you!"

When she stopped laughing, Carolina said, "To answer your question, Hélène, we've already gotten Wendye Pardue Luxury Real Estate to underwrite the reception afterward.

St Paul's will pay the artist's fee. The Symphony is selling ads and printing the program. The Marriage Survivors Club is handling the publicity. As far as we can see, it's a win-win."

"Just think, everybody will know you're his teacher," Flicka said, her green eyes lit with excitement for Hélène.

Dread tightened around Hélène's throat like a noose. The glass globe she was holding wobbled.

Carolina caught it, steadied it, and gave her a look of concerned curiosity.

"Well, I really can't take any credit for that," Hélène said, holding the next globe tighter. "He came to me this way."

Bianca squeezed brass polish onto her rag. "What are you talking about? You should get some kind of trophy."

"You loved him and got him to play and speak again," Olivia said. "I'd say that's a pretty big accomplishment. If it weren't for you, he might not be playing at all."

"We're proud of you," Bianca said and put Hélène in a hug that resembled a headlock.

Frankie closed up the empty box that had held the globes. "Wouldn't seeing Darius' name on the concert poster be cool? We'll be able to say we knew him when. And Bryn and Darius should come to church, too."

Flicka said, "Did you get the posters printed, Carolina? We have to get our publicity machine cranking."

"Oh, I nearly forgot," Carolina said brightly. "I do have them. We all need to take some and post them around town." She retrieved a poster and held it up.

Norwalk Symphony Orchestra Youth Concerto Competition
    Final Round to be played at Norwalk City Hall
    Winner to play recital at St. Paul's on the Green

> *Norwalk Symphony Orchestra with guest conductor and finals judge*
> *Maestro Didier Morisot*

Hélène's head filled with a creaking, shrieking noise, not unlike the buckling of a giant metal structure collapsing in on itself.

Didier 'Yves' Morisot was her ex-husband.

CHAPTER 42

There are two means of refuge from the miseries of life: music and cats.
Albert Schweitzer

At three a.m., Hélène lay wide awake with Liszt curled up on the pillow next to her. The muscles in her neck were rigid with tension. Her legs twitched, her fingers curled and uncurled. She tossed and turned as she considered all the alternatives. Liszt, awakened by Hélène's restlessness, climbed up and settled on her chest and purred.

If Darius won the competition—which he was likely to—Yves would chop him up like an ax going through butter. "How can I protect Darius?" she asked Liszt, who only licked Hélène's chin in response. "I'm losing my mind, talking to my cat," Hélène muttered into the darkness.

She could pull Darius from the competition, but that would make him furious. Bryn would want to know why, after all her insistence, she had changed her mind. The only way to protect herself was by dropping out Darius' accompanist, but it was too late to ask Doris Grimmstein to play.

And if Hélène did drop out, she wouldn't be there to protect Darius.

Yves could toss Darius out of the competition just to get back at her.

Yves could destroy her relationship with Bryn.

Yves could destroy the life she'd built with four little words: *Hélène Noire et Blanche.* Everyone would know about her humiliation, how she couldn't play in public anymore, how she'd left her former life behind because she was too broken. She felt caught in a Chinese finger trap; the more she pulled, the more stuck she got.

"So the way I look at it, I can save my own skin or save Darius, but I don't see how I can do both," Hélène murmured.

It was as if the decision she had been propelled toward ever since Darius arrived, was no longer avoidable.

Liszt meowed and bumped his head under her chin.

Hélène had never been one to read her Bible or memorize verses, but for some reason, a verse from John 10:11 that Father Gabriel had preached on recently came to mind. *"I am the good shepherd. The good shepherd lays down his life for the sheep. The hired hand, who is not the shepherd and does not own the sheep, sees the wolf coming and leaves the sheep and runs away—and the wolf snatches them and scatters them."*

She stroked Lizst's silky fur. She could care for a cat and Darius, so she wasn't completely hopeless. Was she a shepherd or a hired hand? Would she run from Yves or stay and fight?

It occurred to her that she had already fought a series of life-saving battles. She had reclaimed music for herself, on her own terms. She had friends, a church, a home, students, a living, a job, and even a cat. All her life, love had been missing, but now it was within reach with Bryn. Just being around him made her feel as though she was resonating on a new frequency.

Yves might destroy all that, but she wasn't a "hired hand." She would fight for Darius because she loved him, and he needed her to be brave.

If Bryn left her because she'd lied to him, her heart would shatter, but she would eventually be ... okay.

She threw back the covers and leaped out of bed, the cool air hitting her skin. Going to the window, she threw back the curtains and stared out. The night sky was slowly fading, and only a smattering of stars were still visible.

Liszt padded after her and meowed. Hélène picked him up and pointed. It was a beautiful, glorious day to be alive. She had lots of love in her life. She had friends, Bryn and Darius. They would give her all the courage she needed. She was done being afraid of Yves.

An explosion of fire raced through her, blazed behind her eyes. Her heart, which had cowered in Yves' looming shadow, felt fierce and battle-ready.

She would accompany Darius and do her best to protect him from Yves. He had bent, but not broken her. She would take her life back from him, once and for all.

Bryn was underneath the kitchen sink when Hélène padded into the kitchen in her bare feet. They were the sexiest feet Bryn had ever seen, and he wasn't even turned on by feet!

He said, "A box of detergent had bumped the emergency switch and shut it off. It'll work now."

"You are a genius," she purred from above him.

He pulled his head out of the cabinet and shut the door. He twisted around and leaned his back against it. He'd thought about what to say, how to make himself slow down if he got nervous. They'd been flirting, touching, stealing kisses, but they were rarely alone for long. The way she was gazing at him, her lips curved into a smile, made his brain blow a circuit.

"Lesson's over?" he asked.

She nodded. "He wanted a break, so I came in for a drink of water."

She went to a cabinet and opened it. Seeing the new set of twelve glasses, she paused. The pleasure lighting her face made him feel like a giant. She really was so easy to please.

"Did you buy these?" She held a glass up to catch the light. "They're beautiful."

He unfolded himself from the floor. "You like them? You only have mismatched ones, and these reminded me of how your eyes sparkle." He laid a hand at the base of her spine and she leaned into him. He kissed the side of her neck. She felt breakable and fierce against him.

He thought they might need them if they were all together, eventually. At least he was restrained enough not to admit that.

She smiled, stretched up on tiptoe, and kissed him. She smelled of honey and lemon, of the inside of music books. He let his hands rest on her slender waist until she eased back.

"Thank you," she said. "But you don't have to buy me things."

"I know, but I want to," he said.

She filled the glass at the sink, sipped, and handed it to him. The simple gesture made him want to kiss every inch of her skin.

He set the glass on the counter. "Do we, I mean you and me, have a shot at a relationship?"

He'd intended to lead into the discussion, but things were going fast, and the competition was only days away. Things could change after that and he didn't want to miss his window of opportunity.

In the studio, Darius was playing a Scott Joplin rag—rowdy, joyous music. Bryn could hear his boy's heart dancing in the music.

Her cut-glass eyes went wide. "What if it's not good for Darius? He's just getting back to talking and playing. Neither of us wants to derail that."

Bryn said, "Darius loves you, and you must know how I feel about you. He loves having you in his life, and so do I." He stepped closer and pulled her to him. Laying his cheek on the crown of her head, he spoke into her black and white hair. "I want to see if we can have more than just a kiss here and there. If we can make it work."

"We don't know much about one another," she said against his collarbone. "What if I'm a vampire or a serial killer?"

He did want to hear what she had to say about her past and her divorce, which she'd barely mentioned, but that could wait. More than that, he wanted her.

"I know all I need to know about you. I'd still want you even if you were a vampire or a serial killer," he said.

She nuzzled against his neck, and it felt like someone had turned the oven on broil and left the door open.

"How do you feel?" He didn't want to push, but his feelings just fell out of his mouth.

She didn't look away, so at least he hadn't scared her.

She caressed his cheek with her fingertips. "You are the most extraordinarily kind, humble, gentle, devoted, honest man I've ever met. You are a wonderful father and a touching poet."

He felt like jamming his hands into the air like Superman, but he restrained himself. He settled for tipping her face up to his. Her lips gave under the pressure of his own, and her breath filled his mouth, the exhalation of air, sexy and fragrant.

It was like shutting down a nuclear reactor, but he pulled out of the kiss. "Look, I understand if you don't want anything more serious." He gave a shrug. "You're beautiful, settled, accomplished. But, like you said, this isn't just about you and me. You have to think of Darius, not just as a pianist, but as a person and as my son."

She shifted away from him and crossed her arms. The gap between them felt like the Grand Canyon.

He said, "I want to be a part of your life, hang out with your friends, go to St. Paul's with you. But I want someone who wants me, not just Darius."

He smiled, remembering his son, with his mass of curls on his head, toddling along in the living room. The way he held his chubby arms up to Vivianne to be set on her lap at the piano. How proud he'd felt, and later, how lonely.

"I can't compete for love with a kid who's as gifted as Darius." He shrugged. "I'm just an ordinary guy who programs computers and fixes stuff. I'm a nerd with a hammer, not a musical genius. I love music, it makes me feel things. I don't have any special talents, but I love taking care of you."

He drew Hélène to him again, tracing the slope of her hips with his hands, fitting her fragile body to his own. He leaned down and brushed his lips along the ridge of her cheekbone, finishing his journey at the warm skin beneath her earlobe. She sighed, and her entire body turned simultaneously soft and taut.

He whispered into her ear, "Now that I've found you, I don't want to lose you."

"Me either," she said. She kissed him so hard he thought the top of his head might blow off.

CHAPTER 43

The secret of life is honesty and fair dealing. If you can fake that, you've got it made.
Groucho Marx

At coffee hour, Hélène smiled as she watched Darius ease behind Bianca to reach for his third cookie. In his choice of food groups, he wasn't much different from any other kid. And, aside from his talent, he was beginning to act like other kids in other ways, too. He was wearing jeans with holes, had three pairs of sneakers, refused to cut his moppy hair, and expressions like rad, totally, and no way were frequent exclamations.

She had invited Bryn and Darius to Sunday morning service. As usual, they'd been welcomed in typical St. Paul's fashion.

Members of the congregation were gathered on the labyrinth behind St. Paul's. The sun was golden and warm, the breeze serene. The flowers that the Marriage Survivors Club had planted almost a month ago were a riot of purples, pinks, and yellows. Father Gabriel and Bryn were engaged in a discussion by the cookie tray. Children dashed around, squealed happily, their laughter singing between the pine trees. The scent of coffee mingled with the fragrance of lilacs.

Carol Baxter and Vic Carter, Frankie's dad, waltzed in the center of the labyrinth to music only they could hear. A loopy white woman and a handsome older African-American man, the world's most unexpected couple, embodied St. Paul's.

Bianca said to Darius, "Hey, you're doing that concerto competition next Saturday, aren't you?"

Darius glanced sideways at Hélène. "Yup. We are."

"Whose 'we'?" Bianca asked, alert to anything that might have escaped her notice.

Hélène held her breath and laid a warning hand on his shoulder. He smiled insolently up at her, and she knew she was cooked.

"Me and Hélène. We're both playing," he said around a cookie he'd stuffed in his mouth.

Olivia raised her eyebrows. "You're both playing? How does that work?"

Darius explained how Hélène would accompany him as the orchestral part in the first round. Right that minute, she wished a tree branch would fall on her head and knock her out.

"Really? Hélène is playing with you?" Frankie eyed Hélène with amused skepticism. "You sure that's a good idea?"

Hélène's ears became so hot she thought she might internally combust. "I've been ... practicing," she said, unconvincingly. "Alot."

Darius said, "In the final round, I'll get to play with the whole orchestra."

"So, you gonna win?" Bianca asked.

Darius took a deep breath and let it out, spewing a few crumbs down the front of his green tie-dye T-shirt. "I'm gonna try. I'm glad Hélène's going to be there." He grinned. "She's my lucky charm."

Hélène wanted to run, but instead, she smiled at him. "You don't need a lucky charm. Everything you need is in these"—she tapped her head and her heart. She wiggled her fingers. "And these."

"Can we come and hear you? Cheer you on?" Flicka asked. Her eyes were softened by a look of affection as she brushed the crumbs off Darius' shirt.

Her tenderness surprised Hélène. Flicka was the least motherly person she knew. Perhaps there was more to Flicka than her fake boobs, Botoxed forehead, and dyed red hair.

"First round is only for the judges," Hélène said quickly, glad for the easy dodge.

Darius frowned at her. "No, it's not. Dad called and asked, and they said people could come in and hear."

That meant Bryn would hear her. Hélène felt lightheaded. All she could manage to say was, "Oh."

Frankie smiled down at Darius and said, "We could all come. I'd love to hear you again."

Dread flooded Hélène. Once they heard her, depending on how she played, the Marriage Survivors Club would know she was either a hack or that they didn't know her at all. She blinked into the sunshine, trying to think up a way to say no.

Darius laughed at something Bianca was saying. It was the sound of a boy, carefree and light.

He was the one who mattered, not her. This was about nudging him toward playing in public and building his confidence. About putting him back together and making sure he was emotionally ready to play on a big stage. It was the first step in helping him inch his way toward the kind of career his gifts were meant for. The kind she had had, if he wanted it.

"You want to come hear us?" Darius asked. "Nobody's ever heard me in a competition before."

"We want to come to support you because you're one of us now, a St. Pauli," Carolina said with her guileless smile.

A question in his eyes, Darius looked up at Hélène. "I am?" he asked. "But we're not official members or anything, are we?"

Hélène heard the yearning to belong in his voice. He was still such a little boy, so tender, hopeful, and full of promise.

Frankie said, "Doesn't matter. St. Paul's takes everybody. If you want to be one of us, you are."

"Can they? Can they come?" he asked Hélène.

She found something incredibly interesting to look at on the ground.

"It'll be kind of like having your family come," Bianca said. "I'll even wear my Green Bay Packers cheesehead for good luck."

Hélène threw her a *don't-you-dare* look, but Bianca ignored her.

"Is it okay with you if they come?" Darius asked Hélène.

He asked because he was protecting her. He'd protected his mother when she'd died. He had protected Hélène when they had kept her identity a secret from Bryn.

It was her job to protect *him*. And she wouldn't let him protect her, over what he needed, deserved, and wanted.

"I think it's all right if they come," Hélène said, hoping and praying they wouldn't.

"I'm going to tell Dad they can come!" Gangled and uncoordinated, he bounded off to tell Bryn.

The sun was suddenly blisteringly hot for June, and Hélène felt queasy. "Let's stand in the shade. I'm feeling lightheaded."

They all moved into a shaded corner of the garden.

"You looked a little uneasy when Darius asked if we could come hear you," Olivia said. "If it's not okay, we won't come."

"But he'd be disappointed if we said we were going to show up and we don't," Bianca huffed, an annoyed scowl on her face. "We can't let him down now!"

Carolina nibbled around the edges of a brownie. "But it might make Hélène nervous."

"I have a little pink pill for that," Flicka suggested helpfully.

Bianca squeezed a muffin she was eating between thumb and forefinger. "Oh … sorry, I didn't think you'd get nervous, Frenchie. After all, it's only us. But look, the kid needs a family, people cheering him on, don't you think?"

"It's a piano competition, not a blood sport, Bee," Flicka said, her laugh turning heads.

Bianca squinted up at the sky, pretending to think. "We could probably find a way to make it one," she mused.

Bianca was right, for once. Darius deserved to be embraced by the same love that had saved Hélène.

"It will be all right. It will be okay," Hélène said, trying mostly to convince herself. Sweat dripped down her temples. The heat was making it hard to think clearly. "I haven't played in public in a long, long time."

Oops.

Quickly, she added, "But I never played this before. It's a big deal for me."

It wasn't *technically* a lie. She had never played the *orchestral* part of a concerto, only the solos. The Chopin First and Second Piano Concertos in New York and Tel Aviv at thirteen, the Brahms in Vienna at fourteen, and all five of Beethoven's concerti between nineteen and twenty in Prague, London, Madrid, Berlin, and Tokyo. She'd recorded five Mozart concerti and performed the Tchaikovsky and the Rachmaninoff First and Second Concerti by the time she was twenty-eight.

But this competition felt more important than all those times put together. She had an emotionally fragile, immensely gifted little boy and his adorable, sexy-in-a-nerdy-way father counting on her.

And Yves could make it all go to hell.

Or *she* could make it all go to hell.

She was still lying awake at night, trying to figure out how to protect Darius from Yves. She hadn't yet come up with a solution short of carrying a switchblade in her bra. And she was considering asking Bianca—who probably had one—if she could borrow hers.

When she slept, her nightmares were filled with nightmares. Trying to play the Chopin Second as the audience screamed with laughter and demanded their money back. Holding her hands up and seeing only shriveled crooked sticks where her hands were supposed to be. The Marriage Survivors Club in the front row with their faces stretched in horrified disgust.

Flicka said, "Darius was so amazing when he played for us, I can't wait to hear him again." She gazed to where Darius was swinging precariously from a low tree branch.

Olivia tilted her head the way a tiny, curious bird might. "I can't wait to hear you play," she said to Hélène.

Hélène's heart swelled with gratitude for how her friends wrapped Darius in their caring love. She just couldn't trust that they would understand that she had played *them*.

"We won't make you nervous, then?" Carolina asked.

Of course, you will. Hélène considered if maybe she would get hit by a bus.

"No, no, it's fine," Hélène said with a forced smile.

Bianca said, "Great! I've been waiting for the perfect occasion to wear my cheesehead."

CHAPTER 44

You have enemies? Good. That means you've stood up for something sometime in your life.
Victor Hugo

As he paced backstage at the Norwalk Concert Hall on the day of the competition, Darius' mind was wrapped in the music. He saw the notes racing across the page, heard the chords, saw his fingers on the keyboard, felt the glassiness of the melody inside himself

He scratched behind his ear. For some dumb reason, his dad had made him use gunk that plastered his hair down on his head. Never. Again. When he got home, he'd throw that tube in the trash.

As the competition got closer, Darius waited for his mom to show up at night, but she didn't, which kind of pissed him off. He'd agreed to study with Hélène and learned the Chopin Second because it was his mom's favorite. He'd spent all this energy trying to make her happy. The least she could have done was wish him good luck.

But Hélène was here, so he'd be okay.

Hélène's friends—who were now his and his dad's friends from St. Paul's—were coming. When he and his dad went to church, they all greeted them by name, and Hélène's beautiful, tall redheaded friend with the big boobs always slipped him a Snickers. Everybody wished him luck at the competition. It was like an instant family.

For the first round, most of the musicians played the first movement. A couple of musicians stupidly played the last movement, which was the flashiest but the hardest. It was where people crashed and burned. But not him. He and Hélène decided he should play the first movement of the Chopin because it showed lyricism, technique, and his feelings—all things he killed at.

He'd heard three pianists; one pretty good, but no real competition. One skipped two measures, and the other one totally went up in flames and came out crying. There had been a fantastic harpist, one trumpeter who was totally lit, and two awesome violinists. The cellist had been just *meh*, and the third violist had some screechy notes. There were still two more pianists ahead of him, but he wasn't sweating it. His head was too full of music to be bothered.

He dropped into the chair next to Hélène. She was frowning at the score in her lap. The edge of the page trembled a little.

He leaned in and whispered, "You don't have anything to be nervous about. You're *Hélène Noire et Blanche*."

She closed the score and leaned her shoulder against his. "Thanks for believing in me."

"Your friends, those—you know, those older ladies from church—what do you call them?"

"The Marriage Survivors Club? And I'm the same age as them, by the way." She laughed softly and fussed with the button on his shirt sleeve.

"Oh, yeah, sorry. Anyway, I saw them out there."

"Please tell me Bianca didn't wear her cheesehead."

"Nah, but maybe she'll put it on when it's our turn, though."

She laughed, and the tight lines around her eyes smoothed out. "It would distract me if she had."

He pulled back and looked at her, surprised. "No, it wouldn't. Once you get onstage, all you think about is the music."

She whispered, "How do you know what I think when I get onstage?"

"Because I'm the same way. Once we walk out, we only think about the music." He tugged at his bow tie, which was too tight. "Dad's out there, too."

She squeezed his hands, which were clasped in his lap. "He's excited for you, and so is everybody else. You've come a long way in a very short time."

He felt his ears get hot. "Because of you," he said.

Maybe today, his dad would figure out who she was. Maybe he would realize he shouldn't let her get away. They thought Darius didn't know they were all smoochy and stuff, but it was so obvious, it was pathetic. He was glad about it, though.

He frowned to himself. Maybe that was why his mom hadn't been around lately.

Hélène opened the score again.

"Why are you studying the score since you have a photographic memory?" he asked her.

She closed the book and drummed her fingers on the cover. "It gives me something to focus on. Where's your music score for the judges?"

"Under my chair where you told me to put it. Why?"

She flipped a page. "Mm, something is nagging at me." She sounded worried.

"Not like we're changing anything now," he said and reached under his chair, pulled out the solo score, and handed it to her.

She flipped through a few pages and made a soft *hu!* sound. "Why didn't I see this before?" she whispered to herself. Her face was white, and her eyes, which were already ginormous, were even bigger. Her mouth hung open. Her fingers twitched and trembled.

"What's wrong? You look like you're gonna keel over," he asked, worried he'd said something wrong.

Hélène's mouth smiled, but her eyes didn't. They looked scared. "Nothing, I'm ... I'm fine. There's just something familiar about the markings. This was your mother's score, right?"

He shrugged. "Yeah, same one I've been using the whole time."

"Where did you get it?"

"Out of a box in the basement where Dad keeps some of Mom's old junk."

"Her old junk?" she asked, her voice sounding kind of weird.

"Yeah, you know, junk like CDs dad recorded of her, old scores from when she studied in Paris way back in the olden days, way before I was born." He kicked his feet out. "She said her teacher told her the same thing you say to me, feelings are all that matter."

She breathed in shakily and whispered, "Oh God." The books slid off her lap onto the floor. She rubbed her fingers and her wrists.

Darius picked up the scores and set them on his seat. He didn't want to say anything else to upset her, so he got up and started wandering around again. He saw a poster about the finals concert on a bulletin board. The conductor's name was familiar. He ripped the poster off the board and crossed back to Hélène. He sat next to her and showed her the poster. "Is this the guy you used to be married to?"

Her mouth opened and closed, but no sound came out. She nodded.

Darius crumpled the paper and landed a three-pointer in a nearby trashcan. "Don't worry. I won't let him hurt your feelings again."

Hélène put her palm on his cheek. He liked it when she did that. It felt mom-ish.

"That's all right," she said. "You don't have to worry about me. Morisot probably won't even be here until tomorrow and by then, my job will be finished. He'll rehearse the orchestra and soloists in the morning and the final concert is in the evening, so I probably won't even see him."

"But he's here already," Darius blurted out before he could stop himself.

Her head turned so fast that her hair made a swoop. "What do you mean?"

"Oh, sorry, nothing," he said, trying to cover it up.

"What do you mean he's here?" Her voice was like somebody had their hands around her neck and she couldn't get the words out.

Idiot! Idiot! Idiot! You made her upset!

He was like his dad, blabbing whatever he thought of. "Nothing," he mumbled. "I shouldn't have said anything."

"Darius, it's all right. Tell me what you mean," she said.

She made him think of a little glass figurine he'd seen once in a store window. Like if you touched it with even one finger, it would break.

"I made a mistake, okay? Just forget it," he said.

She turned his face and made him look at her. Her face was so upset he wanted to give her a hug. "Darius, what did you mean 'he's here already'?"

Darius felt like dog shit. Why couldn't he just stupid keep his mouth shut? "That ... conductor guy? The one you used to be married to?" he said.

"Yes?"

He pointed to the auditorium. "He's out there. I saw him sitting in the audience."

CHAPTER 45

Choric Song

There is sweet music here that softer falls
Than petals from blown roses on the grass,
Or night-dews on still waters between walls
Of shadowy granite, in a gleaming pass;
Music that gentlier on the spirit lies,
Than tir'd eyelids upon tir'd eyes;
Music that brings sweet sleep down from the blissful skies.
Here are cool mosses deep,
And thro' the moss the ivies creep,
And in the stream the long-leaved flowers weep,
And from the craggy ledge the poppy hangs in sleep.

Alfred, Lord Tennyson

Hélène's insides melted as if she'd been hit by a blazing cannonball. Vivianne had studied with him in Paris.

Suddenly, Vivianne's score made sickening sense. The pencil markings carved into the paper, the jagged notations scrawled in the margins, the strange phrasing and accents were all in Yves' hand. it was a hand Hélène took years to forget. She didn't recognize it because she must have blotted it out of her mind.

Her brain faltered, the notes stuttering, jumping like radio static.

It couldn't be a coincidence that Yves was here before he had to be. Or that he was here at all. He never did anything unless it was in his own self-interest. Had he found out she was playing and come to jeer at her?

She bent forward and pretended to pick something off her shoe so the blood would go to her head. It had taken every ounce of her fortitude to convince herself that she could play in front of her friends and the judges, that Darius needed her. She hadn't counted on Yves being here, and she didn't have the courage to play in front of him.

What had made her think she could play the concerto that ate her alive, consumed her career, and spit her out like bones stripped of flesh? Her fingertips tingled as though frostbitten. The blood in her wrists congealed, frozen in place. Taking deep breaths to slow her heart, she straightened in her chair, aware Darius' eyes were on her.

He laid a hand on her forearm. "It's okay. You're going to play great. It's only the first movement and I'm playing the solo part now. You and me have practiced a lot, and we're going to the final."

She gazed down at him. Here he was, an eleven-year-old boy who had been through so much, comforting here. She pulled him to her, and his bony shoulder dug up under her heart. He smelled like sleep, fruity shampoo, and sugary breakfast cereal. Holding him, her heart settled.

She loved him. Not just the pianist, but the sweet, funny,

smart little boy who needed her. He and his dear father had brought music to her. They had claimed her when she hadn't even known she was tumbling about in the lost-and-found. She was scared, but her love for them turned her heart into a meteor, hurtling toward whatever, toward whoever was in the auditorium.

A middle-aged woman approached them. Tall and slender, with a smooth brunette shoulder-length bob, she wore over-large black horn-rimmed glasses that covered most of her face. Her bosom appeared to have been "excessively augmented," as Bianca would have said. In a way, her statuesque bearing reminded Hélène of Flicka.

The woman smiled encouragingly and said, "I'm Gwendolyn Concettini, President of the Norwalk Symphony. Thank you for coming to compete. Are you two ready?"

"You ready?" Darius asked, his dark eyes filled with sparks of light.

She nodded once. "Let's go kill 'em," she said and kissed his forehead.

He took her hand and led her toward the stage entrance. Before they stepped on stage, he paused and looked up at her. "Don't forget, feelings are all that matter."

Contests—even with a talent as monumental as Darius'—weren't a slam dunk, in Bianca's words. Points might be taken off if Hélène careened into a musical ditch and dragged him, even momentarily, after her. It wasn't likely, but not impossible. And even if they played spectacularly, Yves could derail them afterward.

They walked onstage, stood in the crooks of their respective pianos, and together, bowed stiffly from the waist. She avoided looking at the audience, fearing she would see Yves, lurking spider-like, waiting to see if she would humiliate herself.

When she had been performing professionally, any nerves evaporated when she laid her fingers on the keyboard.

Then, the world changed. The surrounding air stilled, the contrast between light and shadow intensified. The energy in the concert hall became a living, breathing thing that fed her. She heard nothing but the piano, orchestra, or other instruments, and she saw only the conductor. She became a kind of smelter's furnace for the music.

Today, her knees felt as though they might give way.

Then, Hélène heard the Marriage Survivors Club cheering wildly as though they were in a baseball stadium. Before she could stop herself, she glanced up, and there, in the first row of the balcony with the rest of the group, sat Bianca, her bright orange triangular cheesehead bobbing as she whistled shrilly.

Hélène nearly laughed out loud. Her taut nerves took on a kind of waveform as if their friendship and love sang through her body. They were smiling down at her, their love sailing through the ether. Their laughter, louche and unbridled as though Flicka had just shared an eye-watering joke, had its own echoing melody that filled the cracks of her courage.

She was loved now and would be loved afterward, no matter how she played. Their love warmed her fingers, and her wrists loosened. She felt charged as though a broken string inside of her had been replaced by a stronger, unbreakable, one. She sent a smile to them up in the balcony.

Thank you, God, for friends.

She and Darius took their seats. Across the space beneath the gaping ebony piano lids, they locked eyes. It was as though a match had been set to a dynamite fuse. Fire chased down her arms and out her fingertips.

Feelings are all that matter.

She breathed, leaned forward, and played the opening notes of the orchestral part. She was acutely aware the moment the audience's attention turned electric. Music fired along her nerve endings and she played like a demon. The notes passed before her eyes, the sounds of every orchestra instrument flowed from her fingers in cascades of sound. Her starved soul galloped over the notes. Joy flared up inside her, resurrecting the pianist she'd been, who she still was.

She was *Hélène Noire et Blanche.*

On page seven, Darius made his entrance. For the next eight pages, her part was easy, merely a whispering veil of clouds beneath his thunder. The fluidity of his runs, velvet tone, and gently fluttering tempi moved her even as she concentrated on the music. He was playing even better in front of an audience, the mark of a natural performer. His old soul merged with the melody and harmonies, every phrase a revelation, executed with no barrier between his heart and fingers.

His passion improved her own performance. They traded the theme back and forth, tossing the music between them like a leaf on a breeze. She was scarcely aware of her hands or her body until they reached the end and lifted their hands together.

For several long, astonished seconds, the auditorium was silent. Then, applause, hoots, and stomping erupted and roused her.

She assumed it was only the Marriage Survivors Club over-reacting, but when she and Darius rose, held hands, and bowed, the small audience scattered throughout the auditorium was on their feet, and even the three judges were grinning and applauding.

In the center of the auditorium, nodding approval behind his tented hands, was Didier Yves Morisot.

CHAPTER 46

I've always wanted to smash a guitar over someone's head. You just can't do that with a piano.

Elton John

As they left the stage, Hélène's body was zinging like a dragonfly on speed. She had done it! For years, she'd dreamed of playing in front of people again, and despite Yves being in the audience, she had finally, really, done it! She wanted to pump her fist in the air like she'd often seen Bianca do when her favorite team won.

To Darius, she said, "Magnificent." He smiled up at her triumphantly, and she added, "And thank you."

He tucked against her side for a moment and let her hug him. "You're still *Hélène Noire et Blanche*," he said in a low voice.

Bryn met them in the foyer of the City Hall. Hélène loved his funny, sweet face even more because of the pride shining in his eyes. It was because of him and Darius that she had been able to play today. Her plan had been to kick open the door for Darius, but he'd been the one to turn the handle and swing it open for her.

Bryn bent and hugged his son, then wrapped Hélène in a hug, which made her inner dragonfly flap faster.

"You guys were great amazing I can't believe how well it went you both played beautifully I said you could do it, Hélène knew you had it in you," Bryn said in his excited machine gun way.

"Oh, well..." she drew breath and exhaled. "It sure was a lot of work." It was as much of a fabrication as she could allow herself.

He thought he knew, but now, he really knows. But Hélène wasn't worried about that now. She was just content to bask in her and Darius' success.

"Now what?" Bryn said, stretching up on his toes.

"We wait for a little bit until we're all called back into the hall and they announce the finalists," Hélène said.

"I can tell them who they should pick," Bryn said with a delighted grin.

Hélène noted that Darius' dark eyes had the cast of a lost child. He clawed his fingers through his hair, making it spring out from his head in the way it was intended to be. He shoved his hands in his pockets and his narrow shoulders hunched forward.

Alarmed, she laid a hand on his shoulder and bent to look into his eyes. "What is it? Are you all right?"

He lifted his face, now that of a little boy needing reassurance, and blinked at her. "Do you think my mom's proud of me?" he asked. "She didn't come."

She saw Bryn's smile slip, and he looked at her sharply. He was worried about the pressure of the competition on Darius. Afraid that his son was retreating into his grief again.

She straightened and let Bryn gather Darius to him. Bryn

folded down and spoke into the top of Darius' head. "I think she'd be amazed at how you played, and I'm proud of you, too."

"Really?" Darius asked, smiling and hopeful. "You think she's happy now?"

Bryn's look was one of a man in desperate need of help, and she jumped in.

"You played with wonderful passion and sophistication." She laid her cheek against Darius' and said, "I'm very proud of you. But remember, I told you it's not always that the best musician wins the competition," Hélène cautioned. Though, based on how he'd played, she couldn't believe he wouldn't advance to the finalists' round.

That meant Darius would play under Yves' baton. She could only do so much to protect him. Hopefully, love, hers, Bryn's, that of the Marriage Survivors Club, of the people of St. Paul's, would give him the strength he might need.

"Hélène mentioned that sometimes winners are hired to perform," Bryn jabbered without stopping to breathe. Hélène tried to send him a warning glance, but he was too excited to notice and sailed right on. "Wouldn't that be great you might get to play with some of the big orchestras you deserve to win you guys were brilliant, fantastic."

Darius laid a hand on Bryn's forearm, and he clamped his jaw shut. Darius gazed up at Hélène. His solemn eyes weren't those of someone who had just killed it in the first round of a competition. He nodded toward the door and glanced intently at Hélène.

Turning, Hélène saw Yves. A hundred knives stabbed her insides. Fear fought to buckle her heart, but she gripped Bryn's hand and squeezed.

Her ex-husband, the man who'd destroyed every shred of her self-confidence, strode toward them, his glossy-skinned, surgically-modified face creased in a wide grin. He was as tall and imposing as ever, his shock of wild, bushy, once-dark brown hair was now snowy white and combed back over his skull. Even at his advanced age, Maestro Didier Yves Morisot retained his commanding presence. He dominated the room with the imperiousness of a man who made up for a mediocre talent with haughtiness and a terrifying, evil temper. He wore a starched white shirt and a black thigh-length designer coat that probably cost as much as all of Hélène's wardrobe combined. He still wore the gleaming, handmade Italian loafers he had always favored.

An impossibly young, statuesque, rail-thin blonde drifted along in his wake. Hélène recognized the look of adoration on the young woman's face and wondered what she'd had to give up to be Yves' "assistant."

When Yves had scraped her up off the sidewalk after her father's death, Hélène knew her own face had also born the same look of hero worship. Yves had promised to elevate her to a life of fame, money, and glitz, but only if she always did precisely what he told her to do, played as he told her to play.

And she'd fallen for it. *Fool!*

Hélène ground her molars, sending spikes of pain shooting down the tendons at the sides of her neck. Yves' approach felt as though a freight train was bearing down on her. Everything, her love for Bryn, Darius' potential, her secret, was going to unwind, and she didn't know how to stop it.

Instinctively, she moved Darius behind her, as if sheltering him from a gunshot.

"Young man, I would like to congratulate you," Yves said.

If you hurt Darius, I will personally gouge out your eyes.

CHAPTER 47

Little children, you are from God, and have conquered them; for the one who is in you is greater than the one who is in this world.
Jesus Christ, I John, 4:4

Bryn beamed in his irrepressibly enthusiastic way. She wanted to warn him that he was sticking his head in the mouth of a crocodile, but she couldn't tell him without revealing how she knew Yves.

Darius stared at the floor, his lips pressed shut. He raked his hand through his hair until his entire head looked like a baby lamb's brown fleece. He looked so vulnerable and tender.

Like slivers of ice, Yves' unsmiling eyes bore into Hélène, but she didn't let her gaze stray. She felt the wariness a soldier might feel waiting for an enemy to take their best shot. The air between them was like atomized gasoline, waiting only for a word to ignite.

Frowning, Bryn looked from one to the other, and she shot him a warning look. For once, he was quiet.

Yves clasped his hands behind his back and regarded Darius

like a vulture looking at a tiny, helpless animal. "You are a formidable talent, Darius."

Behind her, Hélène felt Darius squirm.

"You can tell that by only one movement of the concerto?" Bryn asked.

"Are you his father?" Yves asked all hale, hearty friendliness. This was the time to be most wary of Yves. It was easy to be lulled by his *bonhomie,* but Hélène knew a boa constrictor waiting to squeeze his victim to death lay coiled in his heart.

Bryn laid a hand on Darius' shoulder. "But I take no credit for his talent. It all came from his mother."

Please, God, don't let Bryn mention Vivianne's name.

Hélène didn't want Yves to connect Vivianne and Darius. The less Yves knew about Darius, the better.

"Ah," Yves said and offered his hand to Bryn.

Hélène wanted to knock Bryn's hand out of the way and say, "Don't touch him!" She didn't know why Yves hadn't acknowledged their mutual past, but it had to be a strategic omission on his part.

"I'm the conductor for tomorrow's finals," Yves said. "I flew in from Europe especially for this."

"Oh! Well, that's … that's just great!" Bryn said, impressed, as Yves wanted him to be.

Yves smiled superciliously. "I thought this competition would be a good place to find talent that can be cultivated. Take them to Europe, have them play with smaller orchestras in smaller venues, get their feet wet. I'm always on the lookout for malleable talent I can groom to become major stars." Yves puffed his chest out, and she wanted to deflate it by jabbing him with a metal barbecue skewer. He addressed Darius. "I found Yu Lin Lo when he was about your age. Madison Brightwell was fourteen when she debuted with me in Prague."

Yu Lin Lo and Brightwell had made meteoric rises and

flamed out, no doubt set afire by Yves' demands and browbeating. Yves would have to kill her before she let that happen to Darius.

"Hear that?" Bryn said to Darius. "Sounds pretty exciting, doesn't it?"

Darius clawed at his bowtie. Hélène unclipped it and slipped it into her purse.

Yves laughed. A low, rumbling noise that reminded Hélène of a predatory animal.

Bryn touched her elbow. "This is his teacher, Hélène Charbonneau. We're really lucky to have found Hélène. She's been a great teacher the last couple of months." He laid his hand on the back of Darius' neck. "Right, Darius?"

"Ah, those who can, do, and those who can't, teach," Yves said in a voice like an oil slick. It was an old adage, delivered to wound, which it did. "Charbonneau, is it?" Yves didn't extend his hand. "Hm."

He was toying with her, and she sensed the threat in his tone. "Yes," was all she said flatly, eager to end this conversation as soon as possible.

Angling his body away from Yves, Darius quietly said, "I'm thirsty. I want to get a drink."

"Don't you want to—" Bryn started.

"That's a good idea," Hélène broke in. She pointed down the hall. "All the way to the end."

Yves' icy glance flicked to Hélène.

Darius shuffled away to momentary safety.

Yves lifted his chin and spoke to Bryn. "I'm inviting the winner to play on a series I'm conducting in Dubrovnik next fall. Darius could do the Chopin Second Piano Concerto. Do you think he would like that?"

Hélène's gut twisted, and her brain shot off a round of

colorful French curses. At least Yves had the decency to wait until Darius was out of earshot before making his pitch. Yves knew she had disappeared because of what he'd done to her, and that was why he hadn't told Bryn who she was.

Yves wanted Darius in exchange for his silence about her meltdown. Even after all these years, he knew how to use shame to bend her to do his will.

Bryn looked like he was going to explode with happiness. Adorable man didn't even know what was coming his way. She stepped closer to him and touched his arm in warning.

Bryn flicked his fingers. Slowly, suspiciously, he said, "But Darius has to win first."

Yves made a dismissive wave of his hand. "Don't worry about that. I've taken care of everything."

Yves had fixed the outcome.

This sickened Hélène and made her long for an undetectable poison. Darius would win and Bryn would lose his son, and it was her fault. She was the one who had insisted he do the competition. She had raised Bryn's hopes. There had to be some way to slam the brakes on all of this.

Bryn's smile slipped, and his fingers flicked faster. "I ... see."

Without looking at the blonde, Yves gestured to her. "This is my assistant, Jillian. She'll get all your contact details so we can start planning on Dubrovnik. I want to get him signed before anyone else snatches him up."

Jillian smiled winningly, but her eyes had a dead look to them. Hélène felt only pity for her. She wondered how long Jillian would last and how damaged she would be when Yves tossed her aside for someone younger, prettier, and more subservient.

"Why don't we step over here so we can talk?" Jillian suggested to Bryn.

Bryn cast a glance of uncertainty at Hélène, but he followed the young woman off to the side, leaving Yves and Hélène alone.

Yves' presence was like standing in front of an open walk-in freezer. "What are you *really* doing here?" she growled.

CHAPTER 48

I wish the government would put a tax on the pianos of the incompetent.
Dame Edith Sitwell

"You think it's an accident that I'm conducting this third-rate community orchestra tomorrow?" Yves' friendly demeanor vanished now they were alone.

His eyes held contempt for her, and his voice had an edge as sharp as a meat cleaver. "I've been watching the boy develop over the years. Amazing what you can see on YouTube, isn't it? Before she died, Vivianne sent me videos of him and suggested I subscribe to his channel." He pulled down his cuffs. "I have my eye on several prodigies, but Darius has the most potential of any that I'm tracking."

Tracking like a hunter.

Hélène went cold inside. Vivianne had studied with Yves years ago, one of the supplicating musicians hoping for a leg up, but it was odd that he would have followed the recommendation of an untalented student like Vivianne.

Yves had come for Darius, but how had he known Darius was competing? Why come so far, so early, for one boy? It didn't make sense.

"I've seen him grow up and grow as an artist. Precocious, with personality to burn. A true musical genius. He's like me in every respect," he said breezily.

Why would he compare himself to Darius? "Unlike you, he has a heart and soul," she said.

"I can groom him," he said as if she hadn't spoken. "Give him a career, make him a star and he will make a helluva lot of money." His eyes swept up and down her figure like he used to do to indicate he wanted her on her back. He spoke smoothly, low. "Like you could have been, had you taken my advice. Instead, you chose to remain second rate."

She felt his words chopping away at her, trying to make her smaller and smaller until she disappeared. "You have nothing to offer him except misery," she spit out. "He's my student, and I won't let you near him."

Yves laughed and looked up at the ceiling as if searching for patience. "Oh, Hélène," he said tiredly. "You made your choices long ago. I didn't pursue you for the canceled contracts, which cost me a fortune when you"—he made a walking motion with his fingers—"ran away, did I?" His lips curled. "You can give me the boy."

She tasted bitterness in the back of her throat. "There's not a chance I'll let you destroy him like you did me."

He sighed with the air of a disappointed parent. "You buckled because you couldn't take it. No backbone, no endurance. I invested so much in you, and you disappointed me, but more than that," he said with his cold, thin smile. "You disappointed your audiences."

Chop, chop, chop, he went on knowing precisely where to do the most damage.

"No artist can tolerate the way you treated me," she said.

He gave a bitter laugh, dismissive as always. He turned his killer's eyes on her. "You've taught him well, though. I'll give you that. He sounds a lot like you did. Of course, those shallow ideas will have to be eradicated."

All his harsh berating, his belittling words, demands for sex, his public humiliation of her, rang in her ears like a screeching English Horn on steroids. Had she been second rate? Had she just fooled a lot of people because of her fast reflexes, her prodigious memory, her learning speed, and her work ethic? Had she fooled herself? Yves used to remind her there was always somebody better than her out there, begging for his help. Maybe he'd been right.

Maybe he *was* right.

She caught sight of the Marriage Survivors Club gathered in the area behind Yves. Bianca still wore her cheesehead. Tiny Olivia's smile belonged on someone twice her size. Flicka's laugh eased through Hélène like good wine. Sweet, trusting Carolina gave Hélène the blessing of her smile. The fierce, concerned tilt of Frankie's head reminded Hélène what strength looked like.

It was like seeing the cavalry ride in.

They loved her. They would back her up if she was storming the gates of the Bastille. They would love her no matter how big her failure had been. They were what love and friendship and support looked like, and she'd been a fool not to trust them. She needed them now more than ever. First chance she got, she would tell them about Yves, about who she really was. She would lay her brokenness before them and let their undeserved love pour over her.

She balled up her fists, her stomach filled with something poisonous. She would kill Yves before she let him "have" Darius. "I'll never let you get your hands on him. You'll burn him up the same way you did me. The way you did Yu Lin and Brightwell."

"What, and keep him in," he glanced around the atrium of City Hall with a smirk. "This quaint little backwater? I have the kind of connections that come from a lifetime of making music at an international level. I can do for him what you can never do."

"You're not interested in him for his sake. You only want to ride his back to heights you can't get to on your own." She stepped into Yves' space and thought she smelled sulfur. She lowered her chin and growled, "I won't let you near him."

"Oh, my dear, you can't stop me," Yves' said in a voice velvety with threat. He bent closer. "You see, he's my biological offspring."

He said it with the sly satisfaction of someone delivering the final blow to a bull in a bullfight.

She reached out to grab ahold of something to keep herself upright. His words made her dizzy and terrified.

Suddenly, it all made perfect sense: Vivianne was studying in Paris. Yves' marks in her score. Vivianne telling him to watch Darius' YouTube videos. Yves' early arrival to ensure Darius won.

She wouldn't put it past Yves to make some kind of public declaration that Darius was his son.

Did Bryn, her adorable, chattering, caring, kind, dear man, know Darius wasn't his? If he ever found out, it would crush him and all his illusions of Vivianne's love.

Or Yves might simply be gaslighting her the way he always had.

"You're lying." Hélène wanted to claw Yves' face off his head. She would not let him destroy Darius. She couldn't let him hurt Bryn, if indeed what he was saying was true. A firestorm ignited inside her. "Darius doesn't need you. He's pure magic."

He arched his eyebrows, and his face folded into an expression of withering disdain. "You think it's an accident I'm the conductor for the finals? Don't be *stupid*," he spat out. "You always were naive, Hélène." He jabbed a finger at her. "Think what people will say when I conduct my long-lost son's international debut. Think of the press. The orchestras offering for us to appear together. The offers for us to record. The concert tours. It will be the crowning achievement of my career, and some pitiful has-been like you is not going to stand in my way."

She pushed her words past her constricted throat, past her clenched teeth. "I won't let you near Darius."

"Try telling that to Vivianne's husband," Yves said with steely confidence.

CHAPTER 49

You write to become immortal, or because the piano happens to be open, or you've looked into a pair of beautiful eyes.
Robert Schumann

Darius, Bryn, and Hélène sat with all the other contestants, families, and teachers in the town hall's auditorium, waiting to hear the competition results. The tension was thick enough to cut with a chainsaw.

But she and Bryn already knew Darius' name would be called. Of its own accord, her knee jiggled, while next to her, Bryn's fingers flicked against his pant leg like a set of steel pistons.

Sitting between her and Bryn, Darius exhibited the calm that would serve him well in his career.

The Marriage Survivors Club lined up in the row behind them. Hélène expected one of them to lean forward and ask how she suddenly could play like that when, in church, she struggled to get through a hymn.

She would tell them as soon as she could and she sent up another prayer of thanks for their friendship.

Yves was nowhere to be seen. He had probably already slithered out. After all, he didn't need to wait for Darius' name to be announced to know he'd won.

Hélène didn't think she could generate any more hate for Yves than she felt right now. Her throat burned as though Yves had poured acid down it. Playing in the competition was the worst thing that could have happened to Darius, and she had done it to him. She wanted to get up and announce that the thing had been rigged, that they were withdrawing Darius, that Yves was something dragged out of the Seine. But Darius and Bryn had trusted her and she couldn't take this away from them; they would never forgive her if she did.

From his seat, Bryn looked over Darius' head and grinned at her. He had no idea his heart was about to get smashed, that his son, the boy he loved and raised, who was his own heart, was about to be launched into Yves' clutches. The pain of this knowledge, of her helplessness, scalded Hélène.

Gwendolyn Concettini stepped onto the stage. She pushed her gigantic glasses up on her nose. "Thank you all for coming and waiting patiently while the judges met and chose the finalists. The talent this year was astonishing and made the judges' decision very difficult."

Hélène overheard Bianca say, "Look, Flicka, she looks kinda like you."

"I'm sure she's older than me," Flicka answered.

Gwendolyn said, "And now, I'd like to introduce our wonderful Maestro Silverstein, who will announce the winners."

Maestro Wallace Silverstein, a dapper, jolly man who was the conductor of the Norwalk Symphony Orchestra, stepped out onto the stage. The air was charged with electric attention as everyone grew silent. He tapped some notecards against his hand.

Darius' name was written on one of those cards.

She whispered to Darius, "No matter what the results are, I want you to know you played amazingly. Everyone is proud of you, and you should be proud of yourself."

"Thanks." He rested his head on her shoulder.

She pulled him to her side. He was fragile and innocent. Short of murder, she would do anything to keep his sense of wonder and brilliance safe as long as she could.

Well, I might even commit murder.

The microphone rumbled as Silverstein tapped it to be sure it was on. "Before I announce the three finalists, I want to mention that the finals concert will be conducted by the eminent French conductor, Maestro Didier Morisot."

There was a smattering of lackluster applause. Hélène wanted to yell out a curse in French.

Silverstein's shiny round face beamed. "We are very pleased that Maestro Morisot found our competition and orchestra of sufficient importance to come to Norwalk."

The only thing of any importance to Yves was himself.

Silverstein went on. "Now, for the first round, all our contestants have played only a single movement of their chosen work. For the finals concert tomorrow, the three finalists must play the entire concerto. In the morning, they will practice with Maestro Morisot and then perform in the evening. And let me tell you, that is a challenge." Polite chuckles. "This is not ideal, but the maestro is a busy man, and we wanted to have our finalists play under his baton. This competition is very prestigious. At the finals concert, orchestra conductors, concert bookers, and agents from all over will be here. National Music, a recording company, called and informed me that they will also be sending someone."

Excited murmurs passed through the crowd.

Silverstein said, "The last six winners of this competition have gone on to impressive careers. This year, we have a new prize for the first-place winner: a paid concert at St. Paul's on the Green in their beautiful Gothic sanctuary. The other prize is a contract to play with the Norwalk Symphony in next year's season." Silverstein drew a big theatrical breath. "Aaaand the first place winner receives a cash prize of $5000, second prize $3000, and third prize $1000. We want to thank our generous sponsor, Wendye Pardue Luxury Real Estate, for funding the prize money."

Behind her, Hélène heard Bianca mutter, "Shut up and tell us Darius won."

Bryn and Darius turned around and grinned at Bianca. She put on her cheesehead, but with a snort of laughter, Flicka yanked it off.

"And now, without further ado, I'll announce the finalists." Silverstein cleared his throat, obviously enjoying the suspense. "From Montclair, New Jersey, Ms. Judith Waxman, harpist, will play the Glière Harp Concerto."

There were girlish squeals and another smattering of applause. Hélène curled her toes. She was torn between wanting and not wanting Darius to win. But of course, the judges hadn't had any say in that.

Silverstein said, "From Manhattan, Mr. Kwame Makawesu —" Hoots and hollers erupted from the middle of the concert hall, cutting Silverstein off.

"Wait, wait." Silverstein laughed and held up a hand. "Mr. Makawesu will play the Hummel Trumpet Concerto."

Hélène held her breath. She hoped her anxiety wasn't leaching out of her into Darius. She thought she heard Bryn's teeth grinding.

Darius looked up at her uncertainly and patted her arm. "It's okay. It's okay if I don't final."

No, it wasn't okay. But neither he nor Bryn knew how terrible it would be if he did win.

"And lastly, the Chopin Second Piano Concerto will be performed by Norwalk's own Darius Harding."

The Marriage Survivors Club vaulted out of their seats and screamed like they were on fire. Bryn hugged Darius and then her. Hélène bit her lip to keep from crying.

How could she save these men she loved?

CHAPTER 50

Creativity takes courage.
Henri Matisse

When Bryn and Hélène had dropped Darius at home after the competition, he had climbed out of the car, a sly, all-too-knowing smile on his face.

Goodnight and goodbye, she had thought. Watching him run up the driveway, she had swallowed a sob.

After what she had to tell Bryn, she would never squeeze Darius' bony shoulder, see the naughty glint in his eye, or hear his heartrending playing.

She would never again feel Bryn's breath on the side of her neck, never again feel the bit of fur that showed at the V of his collar. Never feel his arms holding her comfortingly against his chest.

Now, with her heart in her throat, she paced the length of the studio while Bryn sat on the piano bench with a confused look on his face.

"But Morisot could help Darius," Bryn said, opening his

hands imploringly. "He has the kind of clout to give him a career, get him recording contracts and more performance opportunities. It's everything Vivianne ever dreamed of for Darius. Why do you want to hold him back?"

Vivianne's name set off an explosion in her chest and Hélène whirled on him. "Stop with what Vivianne wanted! What about what Darius wants? What about what you, or even I, want for him?"

Bryn's face looked as if she'd thrown cold water in his face, and, in a way, she had. She looked into the eyes of the man she loved, and she almost changed her mind about telling him. She was about to destroy him and everything he thought was true. He might hate her for telling him, might not even believe her. If Bryn chose the career for Darius that Yves had dangled in front of him over what the two of them felt for one another, she wouldn't blame him. Lots of musicians had sold their souls for less. After all, she had.

Hélène opened Vivianne's copy of the solo part of the Chopin Second Piano Concerto and laid it on the top of the piano for Bryn. "See these markings?"

He rose, his brow furrowed as he peered at the score. "I don't know what they mean, but yes, I see them."

Hélène opened her copy of the solo score and laid hers next to Vivianne's. "See mine?"

His eyes flicked from one to the other. "They look … similar. The handwriting…" He made no mention of the fact that she had a score for a work as advanced as Chopin.

Her mouth felt as though she'd drunk sand. "They're not similar. They're the same. They were made by the same person, Didier Morisot." His eyebrows rocketed up, but she saw that he didn't—or chose not to—comprehend.

She patted the open scores. "These are Morisot's markings here, in Vivianne's score."

He flipped a few pages in the score, looking at them. "Yes, she went to Paris for a month to study the year before Darius was born..." He frowned in concentration. "I thought his name sounded familiar."

"His full name is Didier *Yves* Morisot." Sweat dampened her palms. "I studied with him as well."

Bryn's fingers flicked. "Why did you call him Yves?"

She closed the scores and laid them side by side on the piano. "Didier is his professional name, and he's Didier to his several ex-wives." She shelved her score so her back was to him. "I called him Yves."

"Were you going to tell me you knew him?" He didn't sound angry, or hurt, just curious.

"I'll explain everything, but first, we have to talk about something else."

"Okay, go."

She would try to gently nudge him toward recognizing the truth without hitting him over the head with it. "When Vivianne went to Paris to study, how long after..." She forced herself to look into his eyes. "...was Darius born?"

Bryn made a strangled sound. His eyes went from inquisitive to desolate. The contours of his face were like those of a man facing a firing squad. He was beginning to understand. To save Darius, she was going to have to crush Bryn and his feelings for her. She couldn't expect him to understand why she had lied to him for so long.

"He was born eight months after she came back." Bryn's Adam's apple bobbed. "She said ... she said he was early." Bryn rose from the bench and shoved his fingers through his thin hair.

She waited for him to say it, to be certain he understood what Vivianne had done. His eyes begged Hélène to tell him it wasn't true, and she wished she could. For the first time in years, she was going to be honest, no matter that it cost her his love and respect.

"Yves said Vivianne told him that Darius was…" She rode the hurt over the cliff's edge of her resistance. "Oh, Bryn, Yves told me Darius is his child."

Bryn's eyes widened. His knees buckled, and he dropped down hard onto the piano bench. He leaned forward and held his head in his hands. It was several minutes before he spoke in a graveled voice. "I didn't know it was him, but I knew it."

"Oh, honey…" she said and leaned down to kiss the back of his neck.

He raised his head from his hands, and the suffering in his eyes burned a hole in her. "I knew he wasn't mine, but I-I didn't…" he shook his head vigorously. "I didn't want to know whose he was. I never asked Vivianne. I loved him from the minute I saw him. I didn't give a damn. As far as I was concerned, he was mine." Fiercely he added, "He is mine."

She eased down onto the bench next to Bryn. "Of course, he's yours, but we can't let Darius find out Morisot is his biological father."

Bryn tilted his head, the gears of his mind spinning. "But why did Morisot turn up here in Norwalk?"

"He's been watching Darius' development on YouTube for years." Hélène looped her arms around Bryn's neck as if that would soften the next hammer blow she was about to deliver. "Vivianne sent Morisot YouTube links so he could keep track of Darius. She was willing to do anything to ensure Darius' success."

Bryn let out an outraged growl. "She kept in touch with him!"

It felt as though shards of glass had rained down around them, leaving no safe place to step and no way to save themselves from the ugliness that had swooped into their lives.

"I'm so sorry. But you can't let him get his claws into Darius. You have to protect him. Yves will destroy him."

"But why? Why would he do that if Darius really is his son and is so super talented? Wouldn't he *want* to help him? Do everything he can for him?" The despair in Bryn's voice was heartbreaking.

"Yves is a deadly monster. He will grind Darius up for his own purposes. He will use him to enhance his own fame. He'll take Darius' music and rip it out by the roots."

Bryn stared at her with a kind of willed naiveté in his eyes, waiting for an explanation.

What they had together would be smashed to save Darius, and it had to be so. She drove home the *coup de grâce*. She couldn't bear to see the color of pain in his eyes, so she stared straight ahead and prepared to lose the only man she'd ever loved.

CHAPTER 51

Your pain is the breaking of the shell that encloses your understanding.
Khalil Gibran

Hélène clutched her hands together and stared at a spot on the floor. "I used to be known as Hélène Villancourt, *Hélène Noire et Blanche,* Hélène Black and White. I was a concert pianist in France. I was..." She inhaled and prepared to say the words that had been true, once. "I was something of a legend. And I was married to Yves."

"Why didn't you tell me? I would have understood." He sounded almost as wounded as when she told him that Yves was Darius' biological father.

Hélène resolved to tell him everything. "I need wine for the rest of this."

She rose, took his hand, and led him into the kitchen, where she poured each of them a glass of wine.

They sat at her tiny café table in the kitchen, their knees intimately touching as she told him the whole sordid story of her past. Yves' emotional abuse, her meltdown, her shame, her escape to Norwalk, her anonymity. She included that Darius had known who she was from the very beginning, how she'd made him promise never to tell anyone, even Bryn. Over and over, she apologized for not telling him and hoping he would understand.

Bryn stared straight ahead, listening, not moving, occasionally sipping his wine. Everyone he'd ever loved and trusted had lied to him—and thanks to her—even his son. Her insides felt as though a pack of ravenous animals were tearing her apart. But at least she had finally been honest with him. She would miss him terribly. Miss both of them. After her confession, she took a long drink of her wine, but nothing eased the spike of loss twisting in her heart.

"That's why I never told you about Yves," she said, her confession thoroughly wringing out.

The air between them seemed to have a bitter, acrid smell of something burned to a crisp. It was as if they'd moved to opposite sides of the world.

Bryn huffed a bitter laugh. "Guess you never thought you'd run into Morisot again, did you?"

Naturally, he was more upset about Darius and Morisot than that she'd kept her history a secret.

She shook her head. "Never. But what I don't understand is, Vivianne's been dead, so how did Yves know Darius was even in the competition?"

Bryn screwed his eyes shut. "Fuckity, fuckity, fuck!" he ground out. "Because I posted an announcement on his YouTube channel."

"The channel Yves has been watching all these years," she said.

Bryn's face contorted so that he didn't even resemble himself. "Fucking YouTube. Fucking Vivianne. Fucking Yves fucking Morisot. I loved her! I *never* said anything about Darius not looking like me or that I knew the date of his birth didn't line up." His voice sounded like it was being torn out of his chest. "I loved her! I believed her! How could she do that to me? To Darius?"

Hélène wished she could comfort him and make this nightmare go away, but they had to save Darius. "I'm so sorry. I wouldn't have said anything, but I can't let Yves get ahold of him."

Bryn looked at her, distraught but enraged. "What should I do? Should I confront Yves?" he asked.

She shook her head. "No, then he'll make sure Darius doesn't win, and he deserves to."

Bryn sank back into his chair, the realization dawning on him. "That's what he meant when he said, 'Don't worry about that. I've taken care of everything.' He rigged the competition to get Darius into the finals."

She nodded. "What's worse is, Yves cheated Darius out of winning on the merits of his talent. The other kids are probably super, but Darius…" Flattened with amazement all over again, she shook her head. "He's in a class all his own. His heart is in every note, from the first note to the last. He moves people. For him, feelings are everything."

Bryn turned the stem of his wineglass. "Funny, that's what Vivianne used to say."

"Yves used to say to all the pianists he coached." She twisted her lips to the side and said, "Ironic, isn't it? Yves Morisot taught both me and Vivianne the single most important thing that makes Darius, at age eleven, a once-in-a-generation pianist: his unfettered access to his feelings and his ability to put them into the music." On a sigh, she said, "Feelings are everything."

Bryn polished off his wine and poured again. "Is Morisot evil enough to tell Darius that he's his biological father?"

Hélène wished she didn't know the answer, but the time for half-truths was over. "He's not above it."

He set the bottle down hard. "Maybe we shouldn't let Darius play in the final round."

"I've considered that, but Darius has worked hard and deserves to win. And he doesn't need Yves putting his thumb on the scale to do it."

"What are we going to do? I can't fix this with a hammer or a wrench. I don't know what to do." Bryn rubbed his hand over his face. "I don't want him to say anything to Darius at the finals concert that might upset him. He's so fragile that he might stop playing again."

If she could pull off an idea that had been fomenting in her brain, and if Darius won, it would be entirely on his own. She was willing to take her chances that he might—or might not—win. There would be other competitions, but without the jeopardy Yves posed. Her idea would ensure Yves Morisot would have nothing to do with the competition's outcome, either way.

"I think Darius is strong enough that he won't stop speaking and playing if he doesn't win."

She laid her hand on Bryn's, but he snatched it back. "You don't know that, and neither do I," he snapped.

"Do you trust me?" she asked this man who had no reason to do so.

His hot stare sliced through her. "It's not like you've been exactly open with me." The hurt in his eyes raked her conscience. "But do I have a choice?"

"I know, and I'm sorry," she croaked. "And yes, you do have a choice. You could go this alone and let everything fall where it falls. You could walk away from what you and I have, and I wouldn't blame you." She waited until her voice steadied. " It's up to you."

He was silent so long she thought he might walk, which would irrevocably and deservedly break her heart.

"Okay, let's set our differences aside and do what's right for Darius. Is there anyone who can help us figure a way out of this?"

Her phone pinged. It was a text from Bianca.

You two hit a home run today.

Hélène texted back. *Need help. Emergency MSC mtg my place @7.*

Bianca: *Will text others. Putting on my Batgirl cape. C U @7.*

She smiled at Bryn. "I know some people who can help us."

CHAPTER 52

Think where man's glory most begins and ends
and say my glory was I had such friends.
William Butler Yeats

Hélène sat down at the piano. The Marriage Survivors Club was seated in the folding chairs in her studio, holding glasses of an expensive white burgundy. If she got them drunk, maybe they'd be more understanding.

Flicka said, "So, why'd you call this emergency meeting, Frenchie?"

Heart beating a frantic rhythm in her chest, Hélène looked at her hands—her most valuable asset—and flexed them, willing them not to embarrass her. She had invested her life in these hands, and yet her best friends knew nothing about what they could do. Now, these hands would make her confession.

She drew in a long, shaky breath. "I have something to tell you that I should have told you a long time ago. I love you all, and you've been my friends. I should have trusted in your love. I didn't, and ... I'm sorry."

The banter quieted, gazes fixed on her.

Hélène said, "The best way to explain why I called a meeting is to play."

Bianca, who'd heard Hélène's intentionally botched renditions of hymns, muttered, "Oh, please don't." Flicka elbowed her.

Hélène ripped into a rollicking Chopin Mazurka, each note purling off her fingers. She felt as if she'd been raised from the dead, and her soul was unfolding, stretching its arms to the glow of a long-missed sun. She was throwing joy into the air, tossing it about and catching it. When she finished, she stared at the keyboard for a moment, letting the sparks dance inside of her.

She couldn't look at them yet. "That was a Chopin Mazurka."

The Marriage Survivors Club looked at one another, and the silence in the room was solemn.

"Name a composer," Hélène said.

"Um, Mozart?" Frankie tried.

Hélène narrowed her eyes for a moment, and pages of music popped up in her mind's eye and into her fingers as if it was merely waiting to be played. She played flawlessly, and they applauded when she finished.

Exhilarated, she allowed herself a smile. "That was the first movement of Mozart's Sonata K. 576. It's known among pianists to be the most difficult of his piano works. But if you don't like that one, I can play another."

"Oh, I'd say that was a touchdown," Bianca said with quiet reverence.

"Next composer?" Hélène asked.

"What about Beethoven?" Olivia said.

"All right, this is the last movement of the *Appassionata*."

Hélène tossed off the fiendishly difficult last movement. She was pretty sure lava was flowing through her veins.

Again, they applauded and murmured their astonishment.

"Anyone else?" Hélène asked.

"What's this about?" Flicka asked, skepticism written on her normally immovable face. "You've always made a big deal about how you were only a beginning type of piano teacher, that you weren't very good. We heard you play at the competition, so"—she glanced around at the others—"we were already a little suspicious. Now, you just played three difficult pieces from memory. What's up?"

Hélène's fingers felt as if she'd let them out of a pair of boxing mitts. After years of living in self-imposed silence, fear, and shame, her heart leaped to finally be heard.

"I have a photographic memory for music. I remember everything I've ever played."

"Well, *sheee-it!*" Flicka murmured with a southern inflection.

"I haven't been entirely honest with you guys." Hélène winced and closed her eyes, turning her face away.

"That's putting it mildly," Bianca muttered under her breath. "You're a genius."

"I ... there's ... I..." Hélène lifted her hands and dropped them back in her lap. She couldn't string the words together.

"Here, Frenchie, take my glass of wine," Carolina said. "I think you need it more than me."

Hélène took it and gulped it down. She looked into the faces of the women she loved the most in this world, the friends who'd loved her, to whom she had lied, whose love she had rejected because she'd been a coward.

"I was ... I was..." The words simply wouldn't come out.

Bianca threw up her hands in exasperation. "Just say it already! Unless you're Charles Manson in drag, we don't really give a shit!"

Hélène held her wineglass out for a refill, drank it down, and handed the glass back to Carolina. Hélène pushed the words out in a rush like Bryn so she wouldn't lose her courage. "I was a child prodigy I made my professional debut at thirteen I was known as *Hélène Noire et Blanche*—Hélène Black and White—for obvious reasons."

As the truth flowed, her hurt and humiliation dropped away like stones falling out of a hole in her pocket.

"...concertizing all over the world ... famous ... Morisot ... marriage ... wrecked my life ... catastrophic failure on stage ... hiding out in Norwalk ... anonymity...."

Their mouths gaped, and their eyes widened.

"So, you *are* Charles Manson in drag," Bianca quipped when Hélène had finished.

"Holy shit," Frankie muttered. "Did you shoot JFK?"

Carolina said, "I'm so glad you finally told us. You must feel so relieved." Her serene, angelic smile was like a prayer sailing right into Hélène's heart.

"Why did you keep it a secret from us so long? We're your friends," Flicka said. "Or so we thought."

"I know, and I'm sorry." Hélène had said that a lot today, and she probably wasn't done doing so.

"She did it because her heart was broken," Olivia explained lovingly.

"It must have been an amazing life to walk away from," Flicka said.

The wine had loosened Hélène's joints and given her courage. "Performing isn't as glamorous as it sounds," she said. "Lots of time in planes, trains, and hotel rooms. I spent hours in the practice room, which I used to love. I was so young when I started concertizing that my father held my hand until I walked onto the stage."

With each word, she pulled a scale off of the carapace she'd used to protect herself. It was as though she was becoming who she was meant to be, someone who could be trusted and trusted in return. Someone worth loving.

"You were only a child," Olivia murmured.

"My father did everything for me. He knew how to order a meal, manage the press, get a good hotel room, a private table in a restaurant where we wouldn't be bothered. He listened to me practice, made sure I got enough rest and ate well enough. When he died, I was entirely lost." To keep back the tears, Hélène squeezed her hands together, released them. When she had collected herself, she went on, "I got very depressed and canceled my engagements for the rest of the year. That was when Yves got a hold of me. He was forty, and I was only twenty-one. He was very persuasive with incredible charisma."

"He's sort of a musical predator," Frankie said. A muscle ticked in her jaw.

"Yes. I trusted him. He arranged performances and recordings, but he made me adhere to a grueling schedule. I found out later he was the only one who made any money. I didn't even have my own checking account because I didn't know how to set it up." Hélène shook her head. "I was so stupid."

"No, you weren't," Olivia said. "You were fragile, and he took advantage of that."

"How did you end up married to the shit?" Bianca asked.

"I was getting worn out and said I wanted to take a break. He countered by proposing and I accepted. We married in the registry office in Monaco."

"What a fucker," Bianca muttered, and Hélène appreciated the sentiment on her own behalf.

"When I finally got up the courage to leave him, I came to America with only my piano." Hélène patted the top of the

Bösendorfer. "And a suitcase of clothes. He broke my confidence and I haven't played in public since I came to Norwalk."

They were all quiet for what seemed like a long time. The room filled with a kind of grief, but for once, Hélène wasn't carrying it alone.

"That was an enormous loss for you," Olivia said, her blue eyes reflecting a compassion that made Hélène feel as though she was being hugged. It was the first time anyone had framed her history like that, and somehow, it made Hélène feel less guilty.

Flicka fiddled with her double string of pearls. "What's it like, playing in public?"

Hélène closed her eyes and let the memories tumble into her. "It's like being shot out of a cannon." She opened her eyes and saw their non-judgmental faces. "It's part of what made me..." She paused, not sure that she still had the right to use the word. "...a legend. I thrived on playing in public. Playing in front of an audience is like getting an infusion of life. There's nothing so exciting or satisfying. It drove my every decision. It was thrilling."

"Until he took it all away from you," Frankie said, clenching her work-strengthened hand.

Hélène nodded.

"Do you even *want* to play in public again?" Carolina asked.

Hélène pressed a hand to her chest, trying to hold back the emotions vying to explode. "It's been my dream for a long time. I only played at the competition because Darius refused to play otherwise. It was the most nerve-wracking and satisfying thing I've ever done. I thought it was only going to be for the judges, and no one would ever know."

Flicka arched a perfectly shaped eyebrow. "And then we showed up," she said.

"Yes, and I was never so glad to see anyone in my whole life," Hélène said.

"Does Darius know who you are?" Flicka asked.

"Yes, right from the beginning. Seems I was his mom's favorite pianist. One way he's learned is by listening to my old recordings. I couldn't say no. I did it for him."

Carolina asked, "Are you going to perform again?"

Hélène shook her head. "The competition was enough. I don't have the courage to play in public for a large audience anymore. I can't take a chance that I might fall apart playing solo."

"You didn't fall apart today at the competition," Olivia countered.

"No, but I don't think I could take the humiliation if I made a mess of a performance," Hélène said.

"Just now, your playing brought tears to my eyes," Flicka said, blinking her green eyes which shimmered with tears.

Bianca said, "Well, that's a miracle right there!"

They all laughed, and Flicka bumped her shoulder playfully against Bianca's.

"But what made you finally tell us all of this now?" Olivia asked.

Hélène said, "I know I don't have any right to ask you this since I didn't tell you the truth for so long, but—"

"Oh, forget it, we're already over that," Bianca said, and the others nodded.

Relief and gratitude washed through Hélène. They loved her, understood her, and forgave her. They had been there all along, and she could finally accept that it wasn't going to change. Her grief and shame lifted like a spiral of incense smoke on a Sunday morning at church.

"I need your help to protect Darius. Yves told me that he's

Darius' biological father. When I told Bryn, he said he knew Darius wasn't his, but he never guessed Darius' biological father was his wife's old piano teacher. He's heartbroken over it."

There were gasps, moans, curses.

Bianca clenched her fists and said, "This Yves dude just gets worse and worse."

Hélène gave them the background on Vivianne, Yves, the YouTube videos, and what Yves had said about Darius winning the first round of the competition.

"So, if I understand," Frankie ground out. "Morisot, who's conducting the concert tomorrow night, could make Darius win or lose."

"Or, if Darius wins, Yves could destroy him like he did you," Carolina said. Even she sounded furious.

Flicka said, "Or he could tell him that he's his sperm donor."

"We can't let any of that happen," Olivia said, glancing around at the others. For such a small woman, she had the unstoppable spirit of a Wagnerian Rhinemaiden.

"We's cud orduh a hit," Bianca said in her graveled *Godfather* voice.

"I was—" Hélène smiled. "Considering something not quite so lethal, but I need your help to pull it off."

Bianca got a sly smile. "Count me in."

"But you don't even know what she's asking of us," Carolina said. Hélène saw her fingers tremble slightly.

"If any of you don't want to help, I understand," Hélène said, holding up palms toward them.

"One for all, and no bullshit for any," Flicka said resolutely and raised her wine glass.

The others followed suit and repeated their motto.

Flicka said, "I'm in, whatever it is."

Frankie said, "We got your back, Frenchie. Nobody's going to hurt you or Darius."

"Could it get us arrested?" Olivia asked, her old nervousness reasserting itself.

"Only if we get caught," Bianca, the lawyer, said with relishing glee.

Frankie looked around at the others. "We need a plan."

CHAPTER 53

That inner voice has both gentleness and clarity. So to get to authenticity, you really keep going down to the bone, to the honesty, and the inevitability of something.
Meredith Monk

Hélène's stomach felt as though she'd swallowed a beehive as she waited for word that the Marriage Survivors Club had accomplished their mission. Bryn's fingers flicked as though on a hyper setting. It was possible that they both might spontaneously combust from a double case of overheated nerves.

In Norwalk Concert Hall, people were chatting and meandering to their seats. Orchestra musicians trickled onto the stage and began tuning their instruments. There was an electric air of anticipation as everyone waited to hear the three finalists.

Bryn mopped his brow with a handkerchief. "Is it normal for parents to be more nervous than their kids?"

Hélène pressed her hand on his knee. "Everything's been taken care of."

He gave her a quizzical look. "Should I be worried about something?"

She touched his cheek. "Not anymore."

"Will you tell me later what you did to take care of everything?" he asked.

She screwed her lips to the side. "Mm ... maybe."

"You think you're so enigmatic, Hélène Charbonneau," he whispered in her ear. Feeling his breath whisper against her skin sent a thousand tiny earthquakes through her.

Hélène kept watching for Olivia. She was to come and report on the "Plan." They'd all agreed on radio silence; no phone calls or texts that might prove incriminating. All communication was to be in person.

If anyone was caught, they'd all agreed to protect one another.

Please, God, don't let them get arrested.

Hélène tried to distract herself by reading the concert program. The trumpet concerto was first, then the harp. Darius' concerto was the entire second half of the program. After that, winners would be announced.

The lights flickered, signaling the audience to take their seats and quiet down.

Still no Olivia.

The house lights went out, and then dark. Olivia and Jack, her husband, edged into their seats beside Hélène.

Olivia clutched Hélène's hand and whispered, "Part one executed."

Hélène's body went rubbery with relief, even though they weren't yet in the clear. "Thank you," she breathed, so relieved she felt like crying.

Bryn looked past Hélène, where three seats were still empty. "I thought all the Marriage Survivors Club were coming."

She fixed her eyes on her program, trying not to giggle with a satisfied sense of long-awaited revenge. "Um, Flicka texted me that she, Bianca, Frankie, and Carolina will be in the balcony for the second half."

There was a clatter of applause as Gwendolyn Concettini appeared onstage. She flapped her program against her thigh, adjusted her glasses, and glanced repeatedly toward the back-stage entrance as if expecting someone. She introduced herself and launched into a preamble of sorts.

"Yada, yada, yada," was all Hélène heard over the pounding of blood in her ears. She squeezed her eyes shut and crossed her fingers and toes.

Then came what she'd been waiting for.

"There has been one small, unexpected development. Our guest conductor Maestro Morisot has"—the woman's face squinched up painfully—"has failed, um, to appear."

The orchestra members grinned at one another and seemed to sigh in unison. Yves managed to engender hate wherever he went.

Hélène avoided looking at Olivia or Frankie because she was afraid they would all burst into hysterical cheers. Thank heavens Bianca wasn't here or she would have.

The audience murmured and stirred. Out of the corner of her eye, Hélène saw Bryn's eyes widen.

"Oh no, will they cancel?" Bryn asked. His knee began to jiggle at an alarming rate.

"I don't think so," Hélène said. She dug her nails into her palms to keep from squealing in excitement.

Gwendolyn went on, "We've tried to reach him on his cell-phone, we've called the Norwalk Inn where he was staying, but they said a car picked him up over an hour ago, and as you know, it's only a block from here to there, so I don't think he got lost."

The orchestra laughed the loudest and someone said, "Don't be so sure," which elicited more laughter.

Gwendolyn looked horrified, and she rushed on, "So tonight's concert will be conducted by our own Maestro Silverstein." And, wisely, she fled from the stage.

The orchestra stomped their feet, and the string players tapped their bows against their music stands, the equivalent of violin applause.

Hélène felt Bryn's eyes on her, but she didn't dare meet his gaze. He leaned over and whispered, "You're grinning. Did you have something to do with this?"

She stared straight ahead and whispered out of the corner of her mouth, "Who, me?"

The lights went down, and Kwame Makawesu strode out with his gleaming silver trumpet in hand, an equally gleaming smile on his young face. The conductor gave the downbeat, and the evening sailed past. The trumpeter was marvelous and exciting. The harpist was winsome and charmingly angelic, sitting behind her gilded harp.

Darius was a marvel. When he finished, the audience let him know it by giving him the only standing ovation of the evening. Hélène and Bryn gripped hands as they announced the winners. The harpist took third, the trumpeter second, and Darius first.

Bryn hugged Hélène so tightly she felt his heart thumping in his chest. He kissed her, hotly, wildly. "I don't know what you did, but thank you, thank you, thank you," he said, over and over again.

She still hadn't decided if she would ever tell him.

It was the way of the world, Hélène knew, that conductors, coaches, and teachers often voted for their own students, and in some of the biggest international competitions, judges accepted bribes. But Darius had done it all on his own: his musicality, his talent, his heart, his soul, his technique.

Looking impossibly young and jubilant, Darius accepted his trophy, his check, and a bouquet of flowers. Silverstein stuck a microphone in his face and asked if Darius had anything to say.

Heat shot across Hélène's chest. "Oh no."

Bryn sucked in his breath. "What if he won't speak in front of all these people?"

But Darius took the microphone and, in his soft voice, said, "I want to thank my dad and my teacher, Hélène Villancourt." With that dangerous grin of his, he gave a little wave in her direction.

Hélène gasped. Her heart took on a death-inducing pace.

Silverstein's jaw dropped as he scanned the audience. A murmur went through the audience. Heads turned, looking for her. Hélène tried to slip down in her seat, banging her knees against the seat in front of her.

Olivia grabbed her hand and tried to haul her back up into her seat. "It's okay, it's okay," Olivia said. "It's over. No one can hurt you."

"You're acting like you're a wanted criminal," Bryn said.

After tonight, she might well be.

Silverstein said, "Hélène Villancourt? *Hélène Noire et Blanche* is your teacher? Right here in Norwalk?"

Like a comedic pro with impeccable timing, Darius turned and said, "Yeah, rad, right?"

On cue, the audience laughed. Darius grinned out at the audience, waiting until the laughter died down. He said, "At the winner's concert at St. Paul's, we'll be playing some duets we've been working on. I hope you guys can all come and hear me and Hélène. It'll be totally cool." He handed the microphone back to Silverstein.

She could have wrung his neck.

CHAPTER 54

Jump, and you will find out how to unfold your wings as you fall.
Ray Bradbury

In the lobby of the concert hall, Hélène glared down at Darius while Bryn stood by, exhausted by joy. "I may just have to kill you," she growled at Darius in a low voice.

In her scolding, she expected to discourage his pressure campaign against her, but he seemed to be, somehow, more grown up. He stood with his chin out, his limbs loose with a touch of swagger. He was anything but apologetic.

Mouth cocked in a rebellious smile, Darius handed Hélène the bouquet of roses. He said, "I got all excited and everything, so I guess I forgot." He shrugged, his eyes mischievous. "It just kinda, mmm, slipped out."

She bopped him on the head with the bouquet. "No, you didn't. You did it on purpose." She gave him her sternest *I-don't-even-remotely-believe-you* look. "And I am absolutely, positively *not* playing the St. Paul's concert with you."

He jerked his head up, eyes blazing. "Why not?"

She sighed. "Oh, honey. I know you mean well, but I can't because it's *your* concert, *not* mine."

"If it's my concert, I can have anybody I want, and I want you," he said belligerently. "I want us to do the duets we've played. It'll be fun."

"I want people to come to see you, not me. You're the star, not me."

"You're just afraid," Darius said.

"Can you two have this argument some other time? I'm beat," Bryn said with a sigh. He held the trophy and check and, in a way, he was a winner as much as Darius. None of this would have happened without his love for his son. Parents deserved trophies, too.

"It's not an argument. I'm telling him the way it's going to be," Hélène said.

Gwendolyn Concettini, in her windshield-sized glasses, glided around the corner, grinning. "Darius, I can't tell you how pleased we are to finally be able to award the first place prize to a local musician," she gushed. "You're immensely talented, and I know we'll hear more from you." She turned to Bryn and Hélène. "Are you his parents?"

"He's mine." Bryn settled a hand on Darius' shoulders. "But I can't take any credit for his talent, either."

"Well, you played divinely and the switcheroo of conductors didn't throw you off for a second," Gwendolyn said to Darius.

"Yeah, no problem," Darius said with the confidence of a seasoned pro.

Bryn slid a glance at Hélène. "What happened to Morisot?" he asked.

Gwendolyn was flummoxed. "We haven't the slightest! When he offered to conduct, we were excited and flattered, but then—*Poof!*" She made an exploding gesture with her fingers. "He's a no-show."

"How terribly unprofessional," Hélène gasped, trying not to overdo it.

"Isn't it, though?" Gwendolyn agreed.

Darius said, "Ma'am, can I have Hélène play with me at St. Paul's?"

"I guess that's up to her." Gwendolyn smiled at Hélène. "Ah, Ms. Villancourt, I understand you have quite a history. How is it we didn't know you were a Norwalk resident?"

Hélène felt her face heating up. "I go by Charbonneau now, and I prefer to keep a low profile." Hélène stepped to Darius' side and warned him by tightening her grip on his shoulder.

He wriggled away from Hélène's grip. "I want her to play with me at St. Paul's concert or I'm giving back the prize." His thick eyebrows lowered, and his mouth set in a pout.

"Darius!" Hélène hissed. She fixed him with a withering scowl. "That's not how it works."

This little pill had been trouble from the beginning, pestering her to play, pushing her to concertize, and outing her. As irritating as it was, she loved him for it.

Darius snatched the trophy and check from Bryn and held them out to the stunned woman. She looked desperately to Hélène for help.

"Darius, what are you doing?" Bryn said. His eyes were bulging, and his fingers flicked.

Hélène grabbed Bryn's hand as much to still it, as to take strength from him.

"This has never ... happened." Gwendolyn blinked, her face retaining its astonishment. "Do you know what you would be giving up, Darius?"

Bryn snatched the trophy back from Darius. Bryn's face was blotchy with a kind of fury Hélène didn't know he was capable of. "We'll discuss this at home," he snapped at Darius.

"No," Darius said.

Hélène saw all their hard work, effort, hopes, and possibilities flying out the window like escaping butterflies. Darius had wanted this as much as she and Bryn had, but now, as he had all along, Darius was dragging her kicking and screaming out of hiding. God may have sent him to her, but he was bedeviling her at every turn.

Hélène held up a finger. "One moment." She led Darius by the hand to a corner, away from the flabbergasted woman and his irate father.

She lifted his chin and spoke to him in her most convincing voice. "You won this all on your own. It's a prize you deserve. The world wants to hear you play, not me. My time is ... past."

His face shifted from adolescent tyro to scared child. "My mom wanted to play like you." He whispered, "I figure, maybe if she hears you play solos one more time, she'll be happy, and maybe she won't be stuck in the in-between anymore."

A fist of fear tightened around Hélène's throat. "Solo?! I thought we were talking about duets, and I'm not even playing those."

"Please?" he said quietly. Needfully.

Hélène dropped onto a bench. She pulled him down beside her and put an arm around his shoulder. He nestled into her side. His earnest plea made a tsunami of compassion sweep over her heart. He was a child struggling with adult burdens and demons, handling them in the only way he knew how, and he was asking for her help.

She didn't want him still fighting those demons when he was her age. Neither she nor anyone else could break the hold his mother had on his mind and heart. Darius had to *let* his mother go.

"Your mom would be so happy you won today. She'll leave the in-between when you don't need her anymore." She took his hand and placed it over his heart. "But she'll be forever in your heart. It's up to you to let her go, not me."

Her life might have turned out differently if someone had told her this when she was trying to find her way out from under the sway of Yves Morisot, back when she needed saving. Fleeing Paris, she felt as though Yves had strangled the music out of her.

On the other hand, if someone had rescued her, she wouldn't have Bryn or Darius or the Marriage Survivors Club. She caught the pleading look on Bryn's sweet face and thought that maybe her struggles had all been worth it.

Darius kicked his feet out. "I don't think of her or see her like before when I didn't talk or play. But Mom needs you." He leaned his head on her shoulder. "And I need you, too. You can so play in public. Mom said so."

She had?

Darius sat up. "So what is it, yes or no?"

"Where did you learn to be so stubborn?" she asked, crossing her arms.

He said, "I'm not stubborn. I just want to play the piano. With you. In public. That way, everybody can hear how great you are and how I play like you. And my mom will hear you. And besides, all your friends already know you're *Hélène Noire et Blanche,* so what are you afraid of."

He was right about that. Across the lobby, Silverstein had joined Bryn and Gwendolyn. The conductor was red-faced, clawing his hand through his hair, gesturing furiously at Bryn and a bewildered Gwendolyn.

Hélène held a hand to her forehead. "Playing for the competition was one thing, but you don't know what you're asking."

Darius stood. Straight-backed, arms swinging, he walked across the lobby. Loudly, he announced, "I'm not keeping the first prize. Give it to Kwame."

Hélène jacked out of her seat. "Wait!"

Darius turned back to her.

Hélène saw Darius watching her as she flexed her fingers and rotated her wrists. They were free and painless. Terror wasn't making her seize up. There was no guarantee they wouldn't or that she wouldn't humiliate herself again. But Yves wouldn't be there to laugh at her. If she did make a terrible mistake, her friends would still love her. If Bryn hadn't thrown her over when she told him how she'd lied to him, he would still love her. All that love buoying her up didn't mean she wasn't still scared. It had been a long time since she'd played in front of a big audience. She lifted her head and saw all three adults staring at her in desperate expectation. Saw Darius, his face set in an intractable mask.

"All right," Hélène said, feeling her head grow light, her body leaden. "All right. I'll play at St. Paul's with you."

CHAPTER 55

A dream you dream alone is only a dream. A dream you dream together is reality.
   Yoko Ono

Flicka's cherry-red Porsche was parked in the drive and the lights were on when Bryn pulled up to Hélène's house. Bianca and Flicka had waited for her. She couldn't wait to hear their story and share her own.

Bryn turned the car off, and they both leaned back against the headrests, exhausted. In the back seat, Darius was slumped against the door, dead asleep. She and Bryn exchanged glances —she couldn't ignore the familiarity—like two parents proud of their beloved, worn-out progeny.

"I remember how tired I used to be after a concert. It takes everything out of you," she said.

"I'll let him sleep in tomorrow," Bryn said. He jutted his chin at Flicka's car. "Who's here?"

"Flicka," Hélène said, gathering her pashmina and handbag.

"Kinda late for a visit," Bryn said, his voice low and silkily suggestive so that Hélène leaned over and kissed him long and hot.

She climbed out of the car and shut the door softly. Bryn did the same. He crossed to the passenger side and settled his hands on her waist. The pressure of their pelvises bumping together sent a pleasant jolt through her.

The grassy fragrance of late June, a green pungency of dampness and freshness, enveloped them. The glaze of moonlight across Bryn's features gave his ordinary face the sheen of a sculpted god. His brown eyes searched her face and his gaze fixed on her lips. He bent, cupped the back of her neck and brushed his lips across her temple, eyebrow, until he landed on her mouth. He kissed her, tenderly at first, then insistently. Her entire body lunged to life. She looped her arms around his neck and kissed him back, giving as good as she got.

When they came up for air, he said, "My feelings for you don't have anything to do with you teaching Darius. At first, I was afraid they were, but I want you. I want to take care of you."

She laid her head against the ridge of his collarbone, and his fingers caressed her nape. She said, "Neither are mine."

"Everything's happened so fast since I met you," he said. "Darius talking, playing, the competition, and my feeling like you switched on my own personal sun."

A wedge of light fell across the glass, and she saw the curtain in her front window fall closed. She laughed to herself. Some of the Marriage Survivors Club members were inside spying on her. She was excited to tell them that Darius won and that she'd agreed to play with him at the St. Paul's concert, but theirs promised to be the better story.

Bryn must have seen it, too, because he laughed softly, and she felt the vibration in his chest. In the wash of moonlight, he smiled down at her, one eyebrow cocked. "By any chance, did you and the Marriage Survivors Club have anything to do with Yves Morisot not showing up tonight?"

She stepped back out of his arms and adjusted her pashmina around her shoulders. "How could I? I was with you all evening. I never left your side," she said, sounding completely unbelievable even to herself.

He tilted his head, and she kept her eyes as wide as possible, meeting his gaze, because she'd read that liars always looked away.

"Tell me about it sometime?" he asked.

She glanced away. She didn't want to have to lie any more than was absolutely necessary to this man who made her heart take flight. "Mm ... could be."

He moved to walk her to the door. "I can walk to the door myself," she said, wanting to forestall any more questions.

He glanced over his shoulder at the house, then looked back at her, his suspicion an undercurrent flowing between them. "I'll talk to you tomorrow."

She nodded and stepped up the walk.

He caught her hand and pulled her back into his embrace. "And *Hélène Noire et Blanche*?"

The muscles across her abdomen tightened as if tensing for a blow. It unnerved her to hear him call her that when he held her in his arms.

He said, "Thank you for agreeing to play with Darius at the concert. I know it was a difficult choice for you."

Tension flowed out of her body. "Darius has pushed me to play from the first day I met him. He's impossible to resist." Against the solidity of his chest, she made a gesture of two fists. "Playing in public again has been a dream of mine that I've never felt ready to seize."

He kissed her, making her head swim. He whispered hoarsely, "You're not the only one with a dream."

CHAPTER 56

Mix a little foolishness with your serious plans. It is lovely to be silly at the right moment.

Horace

Hélène found Bianca and Flicka in the kitchen with a half-empty bottle of wine on the kitchen table between them.

"Va va va voom! That was some hot kissin'," Bianca hooted.

"Were you spying on me?" Hélène demanded, but she couldn't help smiling.

"Of course," Flicka said. "After what we pulled off for you tonight, don't we deserve a vicarious thrill?"

"Whatever you did to keep Yves away tonight, thank you," Hélène said. She felt as though every muscle in her body had been stretched to breaking. She dropped into a chair.

Bianca's smile was both rascally and triumphant. "It was kind of fun."

"We could do it again," Flicka offered. "But for money next time."

"Hope you don't mind that we let ourselves in," Bianca

said, stroking Liszt, who was curled up in her lap. "Once you've started, it's easy to slide down the path of illegal activities."

"We could start another group called the Episcopal Robbers," Flicka said and laughed.

Bianca used her *Godfather* voice. "The Episcopal Robbers could also kidnap, drug and break knees as part of their services."

"I'm in," Flicka said, giving a thumbs up.

"You'd be president," Bianca said with a laugh.

Hélène frowned. "Why are you wearing that weird brown wig?" she asked Flicka.

Flicka pulled off the wig and tossed it onto the table next to a pair of oversized black horn-rimmed glasses. "Pretty good disguise, eh? I look just like that Concettini woman from the orchestra."

Bianca's wavy blonde hair was dyed a ridiculous goth black, and her eyes were outlined in thick black liner. Her nose seemed oddly swollen. She wore a tight-fitting black suit, white shirt, and bow tie.

"And why did you dye your hair?" Hélène squinted at Bianca. "And is that a neck tattoo?"

"Fake," Bianca said. "It'll come off with baby oil, but I'm thinking of getting a permanent one." She peeled off a fake nose. "And so is this." Her cheeks were so puffy that she looked like she was having an attack of anaphylaxis. She spit two large buttons into her hands, and her cheeks immediately returned to their normal pudginess.

Hélène closed her eyes, grabbed hold of the counter, and braced herself. "Am I going to go to jail for whatever you did tonight?"

"Nah. We didn't get caught," Bianca said, "Let us tell you the whole scoop."

"I need wine for this," Hélène said. Giddy with exhaustion, she poured herself a glass.

Flicka, her eyes shining with a wicked glee, started. "I saw Gwendolyn Concettini's photo on the website. It wasn't hard to make myself look like her with the wig and glasses. Then I called Yves at his hotel and invited him for an early dinner before the concert."

"How did you get him to take you up on it?" Hélène asked.

Flicka smirked. "Simple: I just played to his ego."

"That would work with Yves," Hélène agreed.

"I told him I was an *enormous* donor." Flicka adopted a cooing tone. "Oh, I know how famous you are, Maestro Morisot. I would like to discuss future engagements with the symphony. I'm leaving town in the morning, and this is the only time I have. I'll send my limo driver"—here, Flicka hooked a thumb at Bianca—"to pick you up at the hotel. We'll dine at my home." Flicka lowered her voice to sound like a phone sex worker. "It will be more private."

"Took it hook, line, and sinker," Bianca said and touched her wine glass to Flicka's.

Bianca took on the story. "I got to be the limo driver. I borrowed my brother Vito's stretch and picked up Morisot at the hotel."

"Where did you take him?" Hélène asked.

"Olivia's wealthy client is out of town for the weekend. She gave us a key," Bianca said.

"Scaredy Cat Olivia was in on it, too? She didn't mention it at the concert," Hélène asked. Her astonishment at their ingenuity and ballsiness was growing with each twist and turn of the story.

Flicka said, "Of course. We all were. Olivia went to the house and laid out the best china, crystal, and silver, so the whole setup looked perfect."

"What about Carolina?" Hélène asked. It was hard to imagine her taking part in anything that wasn't strictly legal.

Bianca bobbed her head from side to side. "Uh, it took a little prodding, but we talked her into playing the role of the housekeeper."

Through her laughter, Flicka said, "When Carolina served dinner, she was shaking so much, I was afraid she might give us up."

"But how did you keep him from going to the concert?" Hélène asked.

"Mommy's little helper! I slipped a triple dose of Xanax into his wine," Flicka said enthusiastically.

"Carolina let me in the back door, and we waited until he passed out," Bianca said. "Then the three of us dragged him into the bedroom. Flicka and I stripped him and handcuffed his wrists and ankles to the bed."

"Where was Frankie in all of this?" Hélène asked.

"We'll get to that," Bianca said.

Hélène was torn between laughing hysterically and terrified they would all get caught. She wiped away tears of laughter. "Your disguises are pretty good, but what if he recognizes you somewhere and calls the police?"

Bianca's laugh made Liszt jump off her lap and run away. "Oh, I don't think he'll do that."

Hélène looked from one to the other of her friends.

Bianca and Flicka traded grins.

"Remember mine and Carolina's ex-husband, Al Kolinsky, the guy who was into leather, getting whipped and stuff?" Flicka laughed so hard, tears ran down her face and streaked her mascara. "We dressed Morisot in a spiked leather collar and handcuffs, then we left a bunch of sex toys laying around—" Flicka collapsed on the table in laughter, unable to continue.

Bianca picked up the story. "I took pictures, printed them out on the printer, and propped them up next to him where he could see them. If he goes to the cops, we threaten to put the pics on the internet. He'll never work again."

"How did he get out? And what about the owner of the house?" Hélène said.

"After the concert, Frankie went to the house and pretended to be the owner," Flicka said. It was clear she had enjoyed every minute of the evening's caper. Hélène was almost sorry she'd missed it.

Bianca said, "Frankie acted all outraged, let him loose, and told him if she ever saw his filthy face again, she'd report to the police that he'd broken into her house and had an orgy."

"Then, Olivia and Carolina came back and straightened up the house and put it exactly back in order," Flicka said.

Bianca rested her hand on her chin, a smile of satisfaction on her face. "It was great. I haven't had so much fun since I was a kid and I tied up my twin brothers and wouldn't let them go."

"I can't believe it," Hélène said with astonishment. "You guys did it. You actually pulled it off."

Hélène laughed until she cried. Then, she flat-out cried because her friends loved her enough to do this for her.

Because Yves Morisot had finally gotten everything he deserved.

Because Darius and his music were safe.

Because she had agreed to play in public again.

Because now her friends knew who she was, and they still loved her.

CHAPTER 57

*Man cannot discover new oceans unless he has the courage to lose
sight of the shore.*

Andre Gide

Hélène rubbed her forehead and said to Bryn, "I can't believe I
promised Darius to play a solo at the concert. What do you think
I should play?" Not that she expected him to name a piece, but
she wanted to hear his voice override the anxious bass notes
thudding doom in her mind.

They were in the car, alone, headed to Sunday evening cock-
tail hour at the home of Sam Wanamaker and Darren Houser, a
couple of parishioners from St. Paul's who threw amazing
parties on their deck. It was the first time they'd gone out
together without Darius. Hélène found the chemistry between
her and Bryn to have a simmering, sizzling effect that had only
ever lingered in the background. Tonight, it threatened to spill
over and catch fire.

Bryn smiled and shrugged. "Whatever you want. People will
just be glad to hear you."

He didn't understand what was at stake. For him, playing piano the way she and Darius did was miraculous, not a responsibility for giving people the experience of a lifetime. People would recount hearing the legend *Hélène Noire et Blanche* play—poorly or brilliantly. Her longing to play brilliantly went past her heart and soul; it went to the marrow of who she was. Who was she if she didn't play with all her old magnificent flair? Who would she be if she flopped?

"What do you want to play?" he asked.

She looked out the window at the late afternoon light fading at the old Victorians of the Golden Hill neighborhood where families quarreled, ate meals together, and shared their disappointments and successes. Maybe she and Bryn and Darius could have a life like that. A life where things didn't feel as if they hung on the sound of a single musical phrase or bad performance.

She said, "The Marriage Survivors Club wants to sell enough tickets to hold the concert in the town hall's auditorium, but that's such a big venue, it just adds more pressure."

Even though the jerk behind them honked, Bryn—a decent man if there ever was one—stopped at a light to let someone cross the street. "I thought this was going to be at St. Paul's," he said and went through the intersection.

She remembered Haley, the young person she'd met at St. Paul's coffee hour, who Darren and Sam had taken in. This concert was also for young people like them. "If we hold the concert at Town Hall, we can meet our fundraising goals for the shelter for the year. They've done so much for me, I can't turn them down."

All for one and no bullshit for any. Now it was time to pay the tab on all the bullshit she'd served them.

She recalled the laughter she'd shared with Bianca and

Flicka when they told her how they'd kidnapped Yves and left him handcuffed to a stranger's bed, what the Marriage Survivors Club had risked because they loved her. The least she could do was gather her courage and play in a larger space so as to maximize revenue.

He reached over and took her hand. A hand that felt so reliable, safe, and trustworthy. "I wish I could make this easier for you," he said.

"What was I thinking when I promised Darius I'd play a solo?" She studied Bryn's profile, his too-long nose, his forehead wrinkled with the intensity of listening. "Your son can talk me into anything, it seems."

He laughed softly. "That happens when you fall in love with your kid."

Love. To her, that word used to mean heartbreak, giving up who you were, enduring shame for the love of music. But with Bryn, like a key change in music, the word had modulated to mean opening your hands to catch the impossible light of hope. To become who you actually were. To trust that those who loved you would help you back up when you fell.

"You could do something easy," Bryn said.

"The audience expects *Hélène Noire et Blanche,*" she said with a resigned sigh. "That means something brilliant and flashy, Rachmaninoff, Liszt, Chopin. I can do those, but..." She clenched the seam of her skirt.

"You're still *Hélène Noire et Blanche,* but you're better." He stopped at a light. "Older and wiser."

She gave a single sad laugh. "I don't want to be known as *Hélène Vielle et Sage,* Hélène the Old and Wise."

The light changed, and she pointed out a place where he was to turn. "I don't want to disappoint anyone. If the concert is at Town Hall, I'll be the one who gets the attention, not Darius. It feels like an enormous responsibility to try to bring in all that money on the basis of my name. I've wanted to play in public again for so long, and all I feel is dread."

He frowned. "I don't think the Marriage Survivors Club expects that of you. It's your own expectations making you anxious. They want you to enjoy yourself. Didn't someone once say, 'Perfection is the enemy of expression'?" He grinned lopsidedly at her. "Or, more succinctly put, horse shit."

They laughed.

"What if people accuse me of trying to make a comeback? What if I have a memory lapse or make a mistake? What if they laugh at me or pity me? Or worse, what if they *ignore* me?" Her insides burned with the bitterness of shame. "You don't know what it's like to be loved and admired one day and a joke the next."

"You're right, I don't." He took her hand and rubbed his thumb across her knuckles. "But I do know that you can't be perfect and be an artist. Don't be the old Hélène. Be who you are today. Be Hélène the Magical. Hélène the Loving."

She adored him all over again for wanting to comfort her. She laid her hand on his thigh and felt the muscle tighten beneath her hand. "I've wanted to play in public again for so long, and all I feel is dread."

"Here it is," she pointed. He parked at the curb in front of Sam and Darren's rambling Victorian.

He shut the car off, turned, and looked at her. "You spent your life trusting what other people told you was best." He cupped her cheek. "They *broke* you. You've spent years putting yourself back together. Don't put the pressure on yourself to raise all the money in one evening. The Marriage Survivors Club can have other fundraisers. Play for your own sake, not for anyone else's expectations."

She stared at him, dumbfounded. "How is it you have gotten to know me so well in such a short period of time?"

His face reddened, his fingers flicked. "I'm pretty sure there's a lot more about you I don't know yet and I'm eager to learn all about you." He squinted at her with exaggerated suspicion and lowered his voice to a whisper. "Like, what did you have to do with Morisot not showing up to conduct?"

She felt heat around her ears and ignored his question. "So you don't think I should play Town Hall?"

He lifted her hand to his mouth and kissed the back of it. An electric spark ran up her arm and straight to her heart.

He said, "Not if you don't *want* to. One way for you to get *your* voice back is to say no. This is your chance to play because you love it. After that, see how you feel about playing as *Hélène Noire et Blanche*."

If Yves suspected she was connected somehow to his kidnapping, he might show up and try to sabotage the concert. She balled her hands into fists and clenched her jaw. *I am not afraid of you!*

"You're right," she said. "I gave up my voice for people like Yves and even, to some degree, my father. The most important people in my life know my identity. I can be who I *am*, not who I was." She saw a kind of heat in his eyes that strengthened her. "I don't have to be afraid, do I?"

"You can choose to be either that person or the person you are now."

"*Hélène la Vielle et Sage*." Feeling lighter, she laughed. "Doesn't have a very catchy ring, does it?"

He said, "I know you want to impress everybody, but when Darius plays one of his quieter pieces, it moves me more than when he plays something full of thunder and lightning." He kissed each fingertip of her hand. "Do you have a piece that shows you off?" He leaned closer, nibbling at her earlobe. "But also shows the tender, sweet, delectable part of you?"

He lowered his mouth to her neck, nuzzling and nipping. Her body went limp, and she breathed a sigh. "Ooooh, my god…"

He slipped a hand under the hem of her dress and caressed the inside of her thigh. "You make my brain shut off when I'm with you," he said hungrily.

Where had this Bryn come from?

"Oh, my Goood," she said and scanned the street for passersby.

He sucked gently on her earlobe and whispered, "Maybe you should call yourself Hélène Hot and Sexy."

Sensations galloped through her, and she could only moan in response. All her other mostly one-off hookups had been reminiscent of Yves. This was unbearably hot.

Bryn whispered, "Bianca and Darius will still be at the soccer match for another hour or so. What say we—"

"Yes," she hoarsely.

Back at her place, Bryn gave her a poem that she read as he unzipped the back of her dress. He slid it down over her shoulders, his hands drifting down her hips. Every inch of her skin was on fire. Her body was calling to her with a long forgotten all-consuming desire.

No smelter's furnace
Molten center of the earth
Or surface of the sun
Heat my blood
The way one touch of your finger does

No extinguishing star

Streaking the night sky
Breathing it's last
No arc of lightning slashing heaven
Eclipses the light in your eyes
When you look at me

Bryn

CHAPTER 58

When you wake up every day, it's like a new birthday: it's a new chance to be great again and make great decisions.
  Poo Bear

"This is great," Darius said to Hélène as he buckled his seatbelt. "Me and you going shopping for Dad's birthday present." His mom used to take him, but Hélène was doing it this year, almost like she was his mom. That idea made him feel light and bouncy, and he was sure his mom didn't mind, either. He liked that he and his dad were happy around her. He didn't know how she did it, but besides getting him to play and talk again, she'd smoothed their lives out.

"Where are we going, by the way?" Hélène asked.

"Carlin's hardware," he said. "Dad goes there for all the parts to fix stuff."

"Oh, yes, I know right where that is."

When he came home from a game with Bianca on Sunday, Hélène's and his dad's faces looked like they just got off a merry-go-round. She made his dad happy and that meant Darius didn't have to make him happy.

"When's your birthday?" she asked as she backed out of the driveway of their house.

"Next January. I'll be twelve. I want to go see somebody at Carnegie Hall for my birthday," he said. He knew it was kinda weird, but he didn't feel embarrassed telling Hélène because she got him.

"I'm sure that can be arranged. Anybody in particular you want to hear?" she asked.

"Yeah, you," he said and cackled at her.

"You talked me into playing at the concert, don't push it, mister," she said. "From now on, I'm going to play because I love music. I'm not going to try to be who I was."

He huffed out a breath. "That is so bogus! You're as good as ever. Probably even better."

"Do you ever give up?" she asked.

"Not if it doesn't cost me money, I don't," he said.

She laughed and shook her head. "Now, what sort of *cadeau* do you want for your father?" Her French accent was like a melody by Debussy with soft edges and mysterious colors.

"What's a ca-doe?" he asked.

"*Cadeau* is French for 'gift.' As long as we're together, you might as well learn a little French."

Her smile made him feel like when Liszt snuggled on his neck. "Will you teach me French curse words?" He grinned. She made him do that a lot.

"No," she said, and they both laughed.

At the hardware store, Darius wandered around checking out the screwdrivers, drills, shovels, hammers, nails, screws, plungers, grass seed, buckets, and trash cans. The place was totally random. He stopped in front of something called a "ram hammer." "This looks totally gnarly. Let's get this."

She read the box and frowned. "I don't think he needs that."

Chuck, the owner, was about his dad's age, with a shiny fore-head and brownish-grayish hair that didn't start until the back half of his head. He knew Darius because he came with his dad sometimes. "You brought your mom in today, big guy?" Chuck asked.

Trying to be cool, Darius hooked his thumb at Hélène. "She's Dad's girlfriend."

Chuck nodded. "Sorry about that."

Hélène's face and neck turned all red. "No problem," she said as she shoved the ram hammer back onto the shelf next to the lightbulbs.

"Looking for something special?" Chuck asked Darius.

Darius squinted at the shelves. "It's my dad's birthday, and we came to find something he needs, but he already has electric drills and saws and stuff."

"What's your budget?" Chuck asked.

From the front pocket of his jeans, Darius dug out the dollar bills he'd been saving and laid them on the counter. "I got sixty-two dollars."

Chuck waved for them to follow him down a cluttered aisle. He stopped in front of a big red and black toolbox and held it up. "What about this here? He could put his gear in here. Carry it around, you know. Pretty handy. It's sixty-five, but..." Chuck dropped his voice. "I'll let you have it for sixty-two as long as you don't tell anybody I gave you a deal."

"I'm good at secrets," Darius said. "I won't tell anybody." He looked at Hélène to see what she thought.

She nodded and smiled.

Darius said, "Okay, she says it's a go."

"The girlfriend says it's a go." Chuck carried the box to the cash register.

Hélène's face turned that funny red color again. He'd have to ask his dad why girl's faces did that sometimes.

Afterward, they stopped at Stew's grocery store for ice cream. They took their cones over to the animal pen to check out the cows, chickens, and sheep.

"Smells like poop," Darius said. Then he remembered. "Like *merd!*"

"Don't say that. It's rude," she said. She was using her teacher voice, but her mouth curved up at one corner.

He grinned. "Yeah, but it is cool to be able to swear in another language. My friend, Ahmed, is from Afghanistan and he can swear in Pashto."

She slid him a sideways look that he figured meant, "Yeah, but don't let me catch you doing it." He actually kind of liked it when she gave him those looks. It was because she cared about him, the person, not just him the pianist.

Sometimes, it used to feel like his mom only cared about him the pianist, but Hélène was different. She knew about the accident with his mom and didn't think he was a bad person for what happened. It had felt good to tell her and after, he thought the happy parts of his music were better. He felt the moodier parts deeper in his heart, and he could make them come out in the piano easier.

Darius licked a drip sliding down his cone. "So, like, are you and my dad going to get married or something?"

Hélène dropped her ice cream cone over the fence and into the pen. A black and white goat ran over and ate it.

They both laughed.

"Why do you want to know?" she asked.

"He *is* my dad, so I kinda want to know." He stopped eating and put his wrist to his forehead to stop his brain freezing.

"We're a long way from considering that." She scrubbed her hands with a wadded-up paper napkin.

"Don't wait too long. You guys are kind of old, you know."

Her ginormous eyes closed when she laughed again. "Don't buy me a wheelchair just yet."

He said, "It's good you guys are in love. I like you, and I know Dad likes you and—" Embarrassed, Darius stopped, until he remembered he could tell her stuff. "It'd be cool for you to be my mom."

A baby cow came over, stuck his tongue through the fence, and tried to get Darius' ice cream cone.

They laughed again. It was easy to laugh with her. Easier than it had been with his mom. He wondered if someday, he'd stop comparing them. They were different, but they both loved him.

Hélène nudged Darius back from the fence. "You think it would be ... cool?" she asked.

"Yeah, I think I'm ready for a new mom." It was hot and sunny, and the ice cream was melting. Darius licked faster.

"What about your mother?" Hélène's voice was soft and kind.

She didn't think he was a whack job for talking to his mom sometimes, and that made it easy to tell her things. "Mm..." He licked his cone. "Yeah, I think she's cool with it."

"Cool with it," Hélène repeated.

They laughed at a goat on the roof of the little barn. All kinds of kids did weird stuff.

"Do you see your mom anymore?" she asked.

"Not so much. If I try hard, I can." He broke off a piece of cone and tossed it over the fence to a goat who gobbled it up. "But I don't try that much anymore."

"Is it okay..." She paused and touched her fingers to her neck. "That you don't see her?"

He ate the pointy end of the cone. "Yeah."

She took out some more napkins and wiped at his hands. It was nice having her do that.

She looked down at him. "I couldn't be your piano teacher anymore if I was your mom."

He hadn't thought of that. Something way colder than the ice cream cone shot into his middle. "How come you can't be my mom and my teacher? My mom was."

She thought for a minute before answering. "You need to have a teacher who isn't your mother. It's not good for you. A teacher helps your music—not theirs—to grow in your heart and mind."

"We'll figure that out later," he said. "But it'd still be cool if you guys got married. You should kinda hurry up because Dad misses you if he doesn't get to see you."

Her eyes had fun in them. Happiness. "How do you know that?"

"Because, like, I'll be talking to him, and he doesn't hear me." Darius rolled his eyes. "And he's always writing those poems all the time, too. He goes like this." He squinted his eyes like his dad. "He stares and thinks, then he writes stuff down in his notebooks. They have stuff about your eyes and stars and stuff. He's totally in love with you." Realizing he'd given himself away, Darius stopped. "You won't tell him I'm reading them, will you?"

"No, but they're private," she said. "And you shouldn't read them, okay?"

"Okay, I won't," he promised.

A fat sheep *baahed*. A little lamb jumped off a rock and ran back to the fat sheep.

"I'll bet the big one is its mom. My science teacher said mother sheep know their babies because of the way they smell. They can find them even if they're with a whole bunch of other baby lambs."

She took his hand. A quiet warmth came over him. He'd like to have that feeling all the time.

He kicked at a clump of grass. "Do you think you could find me in a whole bunch of other kids, just by the way I smell?"

She pushed a fluff of hair behind his ears. "No, but I could find you by your hair, by your smile, by your intelligent, sweet face, by how tall and broad you're getting."

When he leaned against her, she had a soft mom-kind of feeling to her. It was the best afternoon he'd had in a long time.

CHAPTER 59

A poet is a nightingale, who sits in darkness and sings to cheer its own solitude with sweet sounds.
Percy Bysshe Shelley

When the restaurant waiters sang a version of "Happy Birthday," even Bryn knew they were catastrophically out of tune. He blew out the candle on his slice of chocolate cake. "Thank you," he said to Darius and Hélène. "This is one of the nicest birthdays ever."

Bryn sent Hélène a smile, and she smiled back, radiant as ever. He was with the two people he loved best in the world. It was a dream come true that he was celebrating his birthday with *Hélène Noire et Blanche,* and Darius.

Darius set a bulky gift on the table. Bouncing in his chair, he said, "Open your gift, Dad. Me and Hélène bought it."

Bryn laughed at his son's joy, which had been absent for so long. Thank God he had found Hélène. The change in Darius was amazing. He spoke at school, practiced all the time, laughed and told funny stories over dinner, rode his bike, and helped

Bryn with small repairs around the house. Most thrilling of all, Darius was excited about playing the concert at St. Paul's, which was in three days' time. A year ago, it was something Bryn couldn't imagine his silent son doing.

Bryn tore the paper off the box. "Wow, a new toolbox. This is great!"

Darius jumped out of his chair and came to stand next to him. He opened and closed the little plastic compartments, demonstrated how the trays inside worked, and suggested where to put this and that. "Look, I even put your nickname here on the tag." He showed Bryn the name tag. "Nerdy Hammerman."

"What a name!" Hélène said and laughed her musical laugh.

Bryn pulled Darius to him and kissed the top of his warm, furry head.

"Dad!" Darius said, pulling back. "Not in public."

Bryn would miss kissing his son, but it was a sign that he was growing up. Bryn said, "Thanks, Darius. I love this. You chose just right."

"Hélène helped me pick it out. I thought you could use one since you're always fixing stuff at her place. Someday, maybe me and you can put in a cat door for Liszt so he can get in and out." Darius glanced at Hélène with raw eagerness to be closer to her. He said, "Or we might have to build me a new bedroom there."

Hélène blushed, but she looked pleased. It was too soon to think about that, but for Bryn, it was what he wanted. He reached for her hand and kissed her unblemished, soft palm. "Thank you for everything," he said.

Darius made a noise of disgust, and Hélène chuckled as if she was used to his scorn already.

"Now my turn." Hélène handed Bryn a small, square, flat package.

In the candlelight, her eyes shimmered, making Bryn's mind hang up like a blue beach ball, spinning endlessly on a computer screen. Lately, his brain buzzed all the time with thoughts of Hélène, the way her naked skin tasted, how the ribbon of her spine felt beneath his fingers, the way her fingers dug into his scalp at the moment of her climax. He wanted to care for her. He'd never expected to fall in love with Darius' piano teacher.

Bryn shook the package next to his ear. He put on a thoughtful frown. "Hmm. What is it?" He sniffed it. "You know what this is?" he asked Darius.

Darius wagged his head.

Imitating Darius, Hélène bounced in her seat. "Hurry up, hurry up! I can't wait for you to open it. I hope you'll love it."

Laughing, Bryn ripped the paper off. It was a slim red book with the words *Love Poems of Bryn Harding* printed in gold foil on the cover.

A whoosh of air left him, and light gathered in the spot around his heart. He'd never thought to see his name on an actual book. He turned it over in his hands and stared, unable to disguise his astonishment at having created something. No one—including him—ever thought he was anything more than dad, husband, computer software engineer, fixer-upper, taxi driver, cook; a general services factotum. A Nerdy Hammerman.

But Hélène thought he was a *poet*, someone who moved people with his very own words.

Bryn felt his body grow weightless, as though he'd been catapulted to the moon, launched above the useful, utilitarian man he'd always been.

He had written poetry before Darius was born, but when Vivianne needed more time to spend with Darius, writing poetry became a kind of shameful, time-wasting secret, like looking at porn on the internet.

Bryn swallowed against the pressure building in the back of

his throat. "Well," he said, contemplating the book in his hands. "Well, I don't know what to say."

"What is it?" Darius asked, peering to see what it was.

Bryn showed him.

Darius looked from Bryn to Hélène and back again. Grinning, he said, "Oh, cool."

Bryn cleared his throat. He could hardly bear to not jump up and pull her to his chest.

"Say thanks, Dad," Darius said.

Bryn said, "Thank you."

She laid a hand on his arm. "I think your poems are beautiful. I think they belong in the world, even if that world is only ours."

Ours.

Was she communicating the possibility of a future together? In her eyes, he saw something he almost didn't have a word for, but he was pretty sure it was love.

Bryn leaned over and kissed Hélène. It was the first time they'd openly done that in front of Darius.

"Ew! Gross! Not in public, you guys!" Darius squawked.

Several diners laughed. Someone clapped. Bryn and Hélène laughed.

Bryn's heart swelled up in his chest. What he had to say *mattered*, if only to her. After the long, lonely desert of his marriage, *he* mattered.

"Cool." Bryn leaned close to Hélène again and whispered in her ear. "I think I love you, *Hélène Vielle et Sage.*"

CHAPTER 60

French is the language that turns dirt into romance.
Stephen King

Hélène met Bryn and Darius at her front door. Wrapping an arm around her waist, Bryn bent to kiss her. If Darius hadn't been there, they would have carried on.

Darius squinched up his face. "Sucking face is so totally gross."

"Says you," Bryn said and laughed.

Hélène touched Darius' shoulder. "You can play with Liszt for a minute. I need your dad to fix something."

"Awesome!" Darius raced up the stairs two at a time.

She yearned to hug Darius, too, but only when he needed her to. If things continued with Bryn as she hoped, Darius would need a new teacher, but not before he was ready.

Calling after him, she said, "And we have to go through the concert repertoire."

"I know," he hollered back.

"I'll bet I know what needs fixing." Bryn pressed his mouth to hers, his tongue languorously insistent.

The pit of her belly tumbled with desire, and she was loathe to stop. Between his nips and licks, she got out the words, "The upstairs toilet is ... ah ... oh... keeps running."

Against the side of her neck in a velvet tone that made her skin feel on fire, he murmured, "Okay, I'll show you how to fix the toilet."

"I never thought I'd get turned on by the repair man," she said and laughed.

He made her laugh all the time. No one ever made her laugh like he did. He made her feel like spring inside, like he was a wall she could lean against and it would never fall down.

"I'm a man of many skills," he said with a newly acquired wolfish grin.

Following him up the stairs, she admired his middle-aged man's flat butt and squeezed one butt cheek.

He guffawed. "Can I return the favor?"

"As soon as possible," she said.

In the bathroom, he lifted the lid from the tank. "See, look in here. The flapper valve's failing."

"I didn't do anything different from usual," she said, utterly bemused by the internal mechanism she'd never given a second thought to.

"It happens. They just wear out." He placed the tank lid on the floor. "Number one, never balance these lids on anything because you can never get a replacement if it breaks."

"Okay, I'll leave you to it." She inched toward the door.

"Get back here." He crooked his finger at her in such a way that she would have walked over hot coals to him.

He pointed to an oval silver knob behind the toilet. "Okay, now, bend down and turn that valve to the right."

She pegged her fists on her hips. "This does not seem like foreplay."

He laughed. "Next time, I promise. This time, I'm teaching you."

"Why?" Down the hall in her TV room, she heard Darius laughing as he played with the kitten.

"Because you've depended on men for too long, for too much," Bryn said. "I want you to prove to yourself that you can do hard stuff."

She laid her palms on his chest and felt the heat of his body through his shirt. "But it's so easy for you. You could do it in the blink of an eye," she countered.

He gathered her hands in his own and kissed the tips of her fingers, something he did often now. Laughter, not desire, danced in his eyes. "This is a perfect opportunity for you to learn something confidence-building," he said.

She scowled down at the knob he'd indicated. "But what if it breaks? Won't water spray all over?"

He looked at her with a lovingly withering gaze. "Darling, you have to learn to be self-sufficient. That's just the water inlet; it won't leak. Now, kneel down and turn it to the right."

"Oh, all right!" she grumbled.

Glad she had on stretch pants, she kneeled and squeezed herself between the wall and the toilet. She tried the knob, but it seemed stuck. *Good, let him do it.*

She twisted around to look up at him. "I can't, it's stuck," she whined pitiably.

He handed her one of her good hand towels. "Use this to hold on to it. It will give you a better grip." He stood back, hand on hip, watching like a foreman.

"I should have just called Frankie. She would have fixed it," she groused.

"You can fix it."

"I don't want to fix it! I want you to fix it," she pouted. "I'm not made for this."

He squeezed his eyes shut, threw his head back, and wailed, "Wah, wah, wah!"

"Oh, shut up!" she scolded and laughed. "It won't turn!"

"Try harder," he said with an insistence he'd never used on her before.

She applied more energy to the knob and felt a silly rush of satisfaction when it turned. "I did it! It turned!"

"It's only a knob, honey, not rocket science," he said.

"Don't quash my enthusiasm. I've never done this kind of thing before. I always just paid somebody to do it," she said in her most obnoxiously whiny voice.

"Quit whining or I'll teach you to fix the dishwasher."

"Then I'll switch to paper plates. My knees are getting tired. Can I get up now?" she pleaded.

He helped her up off the floor. "Okay, now flush."

"How long is this going to take?"

He pulled her into him and kissed along the line of her jaw to her earlobe. Laughing, he said, "Not as long as it takes you to complain, apparently."

She pulled back and looked into the adorable face she'd come to know almost as well as her own. "Why is it that, before, you did all these things *for* me? Now you're making me do them myself."

He smirked down at her. "Don't you remember telling me that if Darius learned to fix things, it would give him a sense of competence? I'm giving you a taste of your own medicine."

She raised an eyebrow. "Don't believe everything I say."

He pointed. "Flush."

She did and watched as the water whooshed down the hole beneath the dull red thing he called a flapper valve. "But now there's no water. Now what?"

He reached under the sink and pulled out a cardboard container labeled "Universal Flapper Valve."

"What's that doing down there?" she said. "I didn't buy that."

"I heard the valve trickling last week, so I bought it and stashed it here so we could fix it together."

"You set me up!" she said.

He reached around and squeezed her bottom. "Uh-huh."

She giggled into his chest. "I didn't think toilet repair made men horny," she said, keeping her voice low so Darius wouldn't hear.

Bryn tugged her shirt free from her waistband and reached up underneath her shirt. He cupped her breast, sending jolts of pleasure racing from his hand to her center. Her mind blanked as she concentrated only on the sensations he sent galloping through her.

"Wait until we clean out the garage," he said, his hot breath falling on her ear.

"You are an incurable romantic," she said in panted breaths. "But we have to ... finish ... floppy valve ... Darius ... get ready for ... aaah." She exhaled. "Concert." He let her go, and she wished he didn't have to.

In what felt like an hour-long task, but was really only a five-minute swap, they had changed the valve, turned the water back on, and made sure the valve was seated correctly.

"I'm so excited!" Hands clasped, she couldn't resist an excited squeal. "I've never fixed anything in my entire life. I fixed a floppy valve!"

"Flapper valve," he said. "Yeah, if this piano thing doesn't work out, you can always start a toilet repair business."

She raised her arms, settled them around his neck, and kissed him. He reached behind her and gave the bathroom door a shove. They pawed and squeezed and kissed for a moment before the bathroom door creaked open and Liszt walked in.

They jumped as far apart as they could in the space between the sink and tub. Her face was hot with embarrassment and desire.

In the open door stood Darius, his face a mixture of revulsion and joy.

Bryn snatched the hand towel and held it in front of him. "Hey ... son, hey, uh, what's up?"

Hélène smoothed her blouse and tucked it into the waist of her slacks. Using her driest, most teacherly voice, she said, "I'm just coming down for your lesson. We had to fix the toilet."

"Yeah, and swap spit," Darius said. He rolled his eyes and walked out of the bathroom.

Hélène looked back over her shoulder, and when Bryn licked his lips lasciviously, she nearly turned around and went back to him.

CHAPTER 61

Hell is empty and all the devils are here.
William Shakespeare

As Hélène warmed up for the St. Paul's concert, every minute muscle in her fingers snapped with energy. Her mind settled into the music, and her heart threw itself into every measure.

She hadn't wanted to overshadow Darius, but after intense lobbying on his part, she had decided to play *La Campanella* by Liszt. As Bryn had said, it was what happened when you fell in love with your child. *La Campanella* was the most demonically challenging piece she'd ever played, but it was a showstopper, and she could play the hell out of it.

Yves always told her she wasn't good enough. Even though it wasn't very Christian to think so, she thought, he could go where the flames were hottest.

She *was* good enough.

The Marriage Survivors Club moved about the sanctuary, setting up extra chairs for the sellout crowd, preparing the ticket table in the back, and arranging flowers. Their presence made

Hélène feel as though she were wrapped in a protective blanket of love. There was immense comfort in knowing that if she faltered or failed, they, and Bryn and Darius, would love her still. She had nothing left to prove. She was sharing her love for music, sharing her heart, supporting the cause of young people like Haley.

There was some commotion from the back of the sanctuary, and she lifted her head.

Yves, flanked by two policemen, marched down the aisle as if he owned the place. Gwendolyn Concettini scurried along behind, looking flustered.

Yves stopped in the middle of the church, pointing like the star of some crime movie. "There she is!" he bellowed, indicating Hélène.

Facing his wrath, previously, she would have frozen up, and her hands would have become blocks of ice, but that didn't happen. Instead, every knob of her spine felt as though it was made of iron. A righteous fury spread through her, from her scalp to her toes.

Yves' wild bush of hair flared about his head, giving him the look of a crazed serial killer. "Officer, this is my ex-wife. She had me kidnapped, so I couldn't conduct the Norwalk Symphony last week."

"What are you going on about?" Hélène snapped. How had he figured out she was behind it?

Father Gabriel stepped out of the chancel, where he'd been helping with the last-minute preparations. "Can I help you with something, Officers?" he asked.

Out of the corner of her eye, Hélène saw Carolina and Olivia. Worried he might recognize them, she moved in the opposite direction to pull the attention away from them. They didn't deserve to get in trouble for saving Darius. If it came down to it, she would take the fall.

"Hello, Father, I'm Sergeant Fowler," he said in a Bronxian drawl. He was a paunchy man with a walrus mustache. "This is Detective Slovik. We, uh, Mr. Morisot is making a criminal complaint against Hélène Charbonneau." He nodded toward Hélène.

"I'm *Maestro* Morisot, not mister," Yves snapped at the Officer.

Hélène gave a snort of derisive laughter.

Yves' eyes were ablaze, but she didn't flinch in the least. *I'm not afraid of you.*

"But how could that be?" Father Gabriel asked.

Detective Slovick had a head of unnaturally black hair and eyes that never seemed to stop scanning the sanctuary. He said, "He claims a woman that looks like Ms. Concettini invited him to dinner, drugged him, and tied him up in a, uh, compromising position."

The expression on Father Gabriel's baby face said, "What? The Marriage Survivors Club causing trouble again?"

"That's absurd," Hélène said. "I was at the Norwalk Symphony at the winner's concert."

Out of the corner of her eye, Hélène spotted Carolina scurry off. *Good. At least she'll be safe.*

When everyone's attention was on Father Gabriel, Hélène signaled to Olivia to stand behind a pillar. Olivia, her jaw set in determination, shook her head.

Slovik went on. "He says the owner of the home, a tall, rather fierce African-American woman, returned, untied him, and threw him out."

Father Gabriel's brows lifted. "I see." He glanced around the sanctuary, clearly looking for Frankie. He said, "This isn't really the time to bother Hélène. She's giving a concert in about an hour. Can we deal with this later?"

Yves had come to sabotage Hélène's performance, to chop her down to size.

Or he'd come to claim Darius as his own.

Hélène would strangle Yves right here before she let him hurt Darius.

Bianca strode in with the demeanor of a Valkyrie. Carolina followed in her wake, chin lifted pugnaciously in spite of the frightened look on her face.

"Good afternoon, gentlemen," Bianca said authoritatively. "I'm Bianca Treviso, attorney. Hélène Charbonneau is my client. Is this a problem that can be taken care of some other time?"

Hélène could have flung her arms around Bianca's neck. Her appearance was the equivalent of turning a rabid junkyard dog loose on a pair of Easter bunnies.

Hélène had to deal with Yves once and for all. She refused to be afraid. She had to stab the proverbial stake through his non-existent heart.

She wished she could stab him with a real stake.

"Says she kidnapped him," Officer Fowler said, his tone one of bored disbelief.

"Kidnap him?" Bianca snorted a laugh. "She weighs about a hundred pounds. What's she going to do, pick him up throw him over her shoulder, and cart him off? There must be some mistake."

"She was the driver!" Yves said, pointing at Bianca.

Bianca fixed him with a look that could have melted asphalt. "Officers, did you bring a mental patient in here to accuse my client *and me,* an officer of the court, of *kidnapping*?"

"That one. She was the housekeeper. She poisoned me with..." Yves took two steps toward Carolina. "Some weird dish!"

Carolina shrank back behind Father Gabriel's left flank. "I am not a housekeeper," Carolina said, incensed. "I'm a librarian."

"Who else is he going to accuse, our priest?" Bianca said and motioned to Father Gabriel. She guffawed with a derision that could have stopped a charging bull.

Gwendolyn Concettini stood there looking combustible. "I'm sorry, Hélène, I don't know what to say. He insisted *I* invited him to dinner, but I didn't. I have no idea what he's talking about. I thought I'd come try to help sort this out."

It was remarkable how Gwendolyn bore a vague resemblance to Flicka, who was slinking up the center aisle of the church like it was a strip club runway.

Officer Fowler turned, glanced once, twice, then stared openly at Flicka and her well-displayed rack.

"Why, Officer," Flicka said with her dazzling smile, "can I help in any way?"

The policemen appeared hypnotized. Hélène wanted to protect Flicka, but she was doing a fine job on her own.

Fowler blinked and dragged his stare away from Flicka. "Last Saturday, before the ...um concert, well—this guy says some ladies picked him up and took him to an apartment and drugged him with some kind of date rape drug."

Yves squinted at Flicka, then he looked back at Gwendolyn. He jabbed a finger at Flicka. "She's..." He was so apoplectic he couldn't get the words out. "I think she's the woman who promised to hire me. She tried to seduce me!"

Flicka's withering gaze swept down Yves' figure. In a Southern accent dripping with scorn, she said, "And *why*, in God's holy name, would I *evah* want to do *that*?"

Tiny Olivia stepped closer, looking like she might bite Yves on the leg.

Frankie emerged from the Lady Chapel gripping a folding metal chair. Hélène wouldn't have put it past her to clock Yves with it.

Yves raised a fist toward Frankie. "She's the one who said she owned the house! She threatened to have me arrested."

"I've never seen you before in my life," Frankie said. For someone so honest, she was a great liar.

"Don't you see," Yves shouted. "They're all in this together! Arrest them! Arrest them all!"

"Calm down, sir," Slovik said.

Bianca barked a laugh. "This all occurred before last Saturday's Norwalk Symphony concert?" she asked.

"So he says," Officer Fowler said with an air of exhaustion.

To Hélène's relief, Frankie set down the chair.

With a steady voice, Frankie said, "My friends and I were gathered for cocktails and book club. Afterward, we attended the winners' concert at the Norwalk Symphony. And I have the ticket stub to prove it." Her voice dropped to a level just above lethal. "And why would we want anything to do with this"— Frankie narrowed her eyes at Yves—"whacko?"

"What book were you reading?" Slovik asked.

"*Kissing the Kavalier* by Annette Nauraine," Carolina said. "A first-rate historical novel. I recommend it at my library." Hélène didn't think she'd ever heard Carolina lie before.

Yves blustered and blathered, but nothing intelligible came out of his mouth. It was very satisfying to see him so irate.

Yves spit out, "Hélène's behind all of this!"

Bianca shook her head and chuckled. "Officers, you got yourself a winner. Why don't you take him down to the psych ward at Norwalk Hospital and come back and enjoy the concert?"

Father Gabriel added, "We'll even give you two free tickets."

Bianca held up both hands. "Not a bribe or anything, just a friendly offer."

Father Gabriel's boyish face reddened, and he coughed into his fist. "Of course."

Hélène had needed this when she was twenty and utterly, desperately alone. Friends to stick up for her, to love her, to tell her, no matter what, they had her back. They would kidnap, lie, and protect her with their lives. A community that accepted her. The Marriage Survivors Club gave her the strength and resilience to be who she was now: not *Hélène Noire et Blanche,* but Hélène Charbonneau, parishioner, friend, teacher, lover, healer of the hearts of little lost boys. She loved a poet who loved her back. She didn't need old Hélène. Hélène *now* was better, kinder, more sensitive, less self-centered, more giving, wiser, and fiercer.

New Hélène could even fix a flapper valve!

After all these years, she saw Yves for what he really was: a pathetic, controlling monster. He'd spread his *seed* around to grow artists the way one might grow a plant or raise puppies. She had fallen under his Svengali-like spell and allowed him to squash her like a bug.

Well, that was over as of right now.

Yves turned on Hélène and snarled, "I made you a legend. You had that name because of your kookie hair. You were second-rate then, and you're even worse now. When this concert is over, you'll be a laughingstock on this entire continent." He flung his arm wide for emphasis.

Once, she thought if she saw Yves again, she would faint. Now he was her bullseye. Her vision telescoped until all she saw were the two ice-blue pools of his dead eyes. With slow, deliberate steps, never taking her gaze off his face, Hélène covered the space between her and Yves as if she were stalking prey.

She got within three inches of his face and lowered her voice to a growl. "You have no right to tell me what I or my music are worth. Once, I made the mistake of listening to you. You were as crazy then as you are now. But you know what?"

She was so close to him she could smell his sour breath, his three hundred dollar cologne. "That. Is. Over. *C'est fini!*" she yelled into his face, but he didn't jump. "I have a life, I have my music, and I have love." She gestured around her. "Leaving France and my career was the best thing I ever did. I found my friends and the place where I feel the happiest I've ever been." She put a forefinger, stiff and steady as iron, in his face. "Don't you *ever, ever* bother me again."

"Come on, Mr. Morisot, I think you've had your say," Officer Fowler said.

Then Darius and Bryn stepped into the sanctuary, and Hélène's heart stopped.

CHAPTER 62

Everyone has a plan 'till they get punched in the mouth.
  Mike Tyson

There was her dear Darius with his mad crop of wavy hair, pointy chin, and the little man slope of his shoulders. And Bryn, surprise registering in his eyes but protectiveness, too. And a certain grief of knowing.

Hélène had wanted to believe that Yves had been lying when he had claimed to be Darius' biological father, that it was only more of his egotistical bluster. But seeing them in the same place, even far apart, the resemblance was irrefutable: Darius was Yves' progeny.

Yves' eyes lasered in on Bryn and Darius, his expression triumphant.

Hélène's heart kicked in her chest. Her breath rushed out of her.

Bryn's face drained of color. He moved to back out, taking Darius with him, but he wasn't fast enough.

She saw his thoughts on Bryn's face, and she wanted to

protect both of them from what was barreling down on them. If it wasn't for her, Yves might never have tracked Darius down, might not be so vindictive. Though Bryn had always suspected, Yves' identity might have remained a distant quantity if she hadn't insisted on the competition.

She had done this to Bryn. She had broken his heart and Yves would break Darius'.

Hélène had been looking forward to Darius playing tonight, to hearing the roar of applause, the stomping of feet, screaming for an encore—for him. But, she admitted to herself that she longed as Hélène *Noire et Blanche* to shake the rafters and prove she could play for an audience again. Tonight was her chance not only to make her dream come true but to prove Yves wrong. Tonight was the night she had yearned for—and feared—for thirty years. She knew she could slay again.

But Darius and Bryn were more important than her simmering desire.

She would not let Yves ruin everything.

Yves moved toward Darius, roughly shoving Hélène out of the way. She stumbled, but Frankie grabbed her and steadied her.

Hélène stepped in front of Yves, blocking his path.

Yves yelled, "That boy is my—"

Hélène drew back her arm and drove it forward, throwing every ounce of her body into the thrust. Clenched in her fist were rage, discarded shame, the ragged pain of lost years, strangled self-confidence, and the certainty—which she now knew was wrong—that she had been unlovable.

Her clenched fist mashed into Yves' jaw with a force she didn't know she had.

She felt the distinct crack of breaking bones, a shattering like fine china, as her knuckles shifted out of place. She felt the ends of bones scraping together. Her wrist twisted unnaturally, the tendons stretched to tearing. A red-hot poker of excruciating pain shot up her arm. It jarred her shoulder and radiated up the side of her neck.

The two officers caught Yves before he hit the floor.

Shrieks of agony bounced off the stone surfaces, and it took a moment for Hélène to realize it was her. Tears flooded her eyes as she bent double and cradled her hand against her stomach. Black spots appeared before her eyes, and she thought she might pass out. The pain was so intense she wanted to vomit. Olivia guided her to a pew and sat her down.

Bianca stepped in between Hélène and the officers and spread her arms out protectively in front of Hélène. "You saw him assault my client," she said forcefully. "She acted in self-defense."

"I saw fear in her eyes, yes, I did," Flicka cooed, but her smirk said, "wish I'd have done that."

"He was about to hit her," Frankie said.

"She feared for her life," Olivia added.

"Oh, dear, in the sanctuary," Carolina said.

Using his angry-prophet voice, Father Gabriel said, "Please get this lunatic out of my church before I call the mayor and the chief of police! I can't have people coming in and shoving my parishioners!"

"You want to press charges, Mr. Morisot?" Officer Fowler asked Yves.

Except Fowler's gaze was fixed on Flicka's boobs because she had placed herself strategically in his line of vision.

Bianca said, "If he does, we will counter with charges of slander and attempted assault. We will make sure his *photo*," she emphasized the word, "and this story runs in every paper and on every website in the world. People will know just what kind of *pervert* you are!"

"Bluh, thhh," Yves blubbered through his crooked jaw. Blood streamed from his split lip and onto his white shirt.

Fowler hauled at Yves' arm. "Come on, Mr. Morisot, let's be on our way, shall we? Looks like your jaw's out of whack. You need to go to the hospital and have it wired shut. Or we could take you down to the station and charge you with assault. Your pick."

Officer Fowler winked at Flicka. She swiveled her hips and gave him her smuttiest smile.

"Buth ... kidnaps ... you hash ... a-west..." Yves burbled as the two officers half-dragged, half-walked him down the aisle.

Darius came to Hélène. "That dude is a total freakazoid! Are you all right?"

Hélène was bent over, cradling her hand. She met Bryn's gaze. Through teeth clenched, she said, "He won't bother any of us again."

"Oh, Hélène," Bryn said, his face unrecognizable with sorrow. He sat next to her.

"Are you going to be able to play?" Darius asked anxiously.

Tears flooded down her face. She winced and held her hand out. She couldn't open it. Her knuckles pulsated agonizingly. Bloody cuts ran across her knuckles where she'd connected with Yves' capped teeth. An eggplant-colored bruise was already blooming over her hand. She bent double again, breathing deeply to keep from passing out.

"No," she said on a moan.

Darius sat beside her on the pew and laid his head on her shoulder. The warmth of his cheek moved through her dress. "I need you," he said in a plaintive whisper.

Hélène forced herself to sit up slowly. Her entire body hurt. She put her good arm around him and laid her cheek on his crown. She wrenched out the words. "Tell me how it feels when you play."

Without hesitation, he said, "Like I'm a kite riding on the wind. Like fire is coming out of my hands. Like the world is full of new colors. I can say all these things I didn't know were in my heart. There's only the sound of the piano. I'm happy when I play." He gazed up at her with trust she finally felt she deserved. "And I'm *really* happy playing for other people."

She managed a smile. "You don't need me to feel that. You can make that happen all on your own," she ground out.

He whispered into her ear, "I don't see her anymore."

Hélène flicked her eyes toward heaven. "She's still listening, though."

Darius smiled his boy-man smile.

"Piano is not something you do, my little love. Piano *is you*, but it is not all you are." She tipped his chin up to look into his heartbreakingly vulnerable eyes. "You must learn to swim over all the challenges you will meet. This is just one of the first ones you will face as long as you play. Your father will help you."

"And Hélène will help you, too," Bryn added in a choked voice.

Darius puffed his cheeks and blew out a breath. "So, you're sayin' I gotta play the concert alone?"

"Yes. You can do it," she said.

"I don't want you to miss it," he said, sounding small and needy.

She closed her eyes against the pain hammering her hand. "I'll stay until the last encore to see about my hand."

He leaned against her shoulder. "I'm sad we don't get to play the duets tonight."

"Me too."

Suddenly, she was thunderstruck. She might never play again. All the hours she'd given to music, to the piano, all the sacrifices she'd made. It was all gone with one furious, love-driven slug.

It was worth it.

She panted against the pain, then said, "Can you play the Schubert Sonata to fill the time we were going to play together?"

"Yeah, sure." His voice was filled with the kind of bravado he deserved to have.

"Go on, play a bit of it," she said and nudged him gently with her shoulder toward the piano.

And he sat down at the keyboard and made glorious music.

CHAPTER 63

The truth will set you free, but first it will make you miserable.
James A. Garfield

During the concert intermission, Hélène sat slumped against Bryn in the sacristy, cradling her injured hand to her stomach while the ice pack leaked down the front of her gown and made a puddle on the floor. Her breath pressed in and out in shuddering gasps.

The sacristy was a cramped room where the priest and altar party prepared before church services. It was cluttered with brass candlesticks, incense thuribles, flower vases, robes, water glasses, and other ecclesiastical doo-dads.

Even over the incense lingering in the room, she smelled Bryn. Warm clothes fresh from the dryer overlaid with burned toast and, vaguely, of construction adhesive. It was intimate to know a man's scent. She couldn't identify when she felt connected to him, but they had chosen to belong to one another. Even with a mangled hand, she felt contentment hum through her like the long, low, vibrating note of a cello.

"Darius' first half was amazing," she said.

"They love him," Bryn said.

She suppressed a moan of agony, but he sensed it anyway.

"I wish you'd let someone take you to the hospital," Bryn said.

"I promised Darius I'd be here for him. It won't be any more broken in an hour than it is now."

"It must hurt like hell. Thank you for punching Yves." He laid a finger gingerly on the icepack. "I feel terrible that you may never play again."

"I know," she sighed and pressed her cheek into Bryn's shoulder. "But I have you, and Darius is safe from Yves, so it was worth it."

"Really?" he asked with a smile in his voice. "I feel like I'm supposed to be the one who drops the bad guy with a single punch, but you did it all by yourself. Kinda cool. How did it feel?"

Her hand felt as though someone had pounded on it with a tire iron. Her wrist throbbed and burned, and the bones of her knuckles scraped like sticks rubbing together. Even her shoulder was wrenched.

And she felt like a heavyweight champion.

She had sacrificed her dream of playing in public forever. In exchange, she was loved for who she was today, right now. All the poisonous things Yves had ever said to her were yanked out of her heart and mind forever, replaced by the love of the Marriage Survivors Club, of Bryn, and of Darius.

She'd do it all over again.

Hélène smiled up into Bryn's worried face. "Except for my hand, I feel pretty great. I might even take up playing something else."

He kissed her temple. "Like what?" he said.

"Steel drums?" she suggested.

"Marimba?" he said and laughed with a gentleness she had come to associate with him.

"Xylophone?" she said.

"What about those champagne glasses filled with water? Those are pretty cool," he said with both grief and humor.

Their laughter was careful, but she still bit her lower lip in pain.

"You need more ice?" he asked.

"I'm okay," she said, even though she wanted to lie down and die. "It's better having you right here."

She couldn't remember the last time anyone had worried about her. When she had trusted someone enough to let them worry about her. Loving and being loved meant letting people care for her when she needed it and trusting they wouldn't swallow her whole, that they didn't have a hidden agenda.

He whispered into the spot above her ear. "It took me so long to find you, I never want to let you go."

"I'm not planning on going anywhere," she said. It was romantic that he thought of himself as looking for her even before they knew of one another's existence.

He said, "I'm sorry I'll never hear you play *La Campanella* since you gave it up the last time you played it at Carnegie Hall. That night, your fast reflexes—"

He froze, and his body went rigid.

A sick, hot sensation filled her.

She pulled back and looked up into his stricken face. For a moment, she couldn't speak, not because of the pain but because of shock. "How did you know I played that at Carnegie? That I never played *La Campanella* again?"

"What? Oh, saw it on YouTube." His fingers flicked.

She narrowed her eyes at him and backed out of his embrace. "That was a pirate video. It only showed up on YouTube six months ago, and I had it pulled down for copyright infringement two days after it appeared. It only had ten views. You couldn't have seen it."

He shifted his weight from one foot to the other, his gaze sliding away from her. His words ran together in one long flood. "I don't know I guess I saw it somewhere on some website or some old review everybody said it was the last time everybody knew about your fast reflexes." Realizing he'd said too much, he squeezed his eyes shut.

"Oh my God," she whispered, barely able to get the words out. "Oh my God. That video. It was posted by..." Beneath her breastbone, her heart thundered like a piston. "By Nerdy Hammerman. That's ... that was you. You posted it before we met."

A sickness of the heart descended on her, killing every bit of light, joy, and love in her heart.

"You knew who I was when you came to me, didn't you? You..." She groaned as if every bone in her body was breaking. "You looked for me, didn't you?"

He was still and silent, his eyes pleading forgiveness. He looked as devastated as she felt. "Yes," he said in a voice gravelly with despair. "I did it for Darius."

Inside of her, there was a crashing, kettle drums thundering, screaming brass, the cacophony of cymbals, an entire orchestra screaming random notes at full throttle. The throbbing in her hand was nothing compared to the throbbing of her crushed heart.

"But why? Why did you put that video up?"

"I thought ... I, oh God." He put a hand to his face and shook his head. He dropped his hand and tried to look into her eyes, but she stared past him, unwilling to let his despair touch her. "I hoped it would flush you out, that it would lead me to you. When it was taken down, I knew—I was pretty sure you were still out there, somewhere. All I had to do was find you."

"Why did you *lie* to me?" she asked, her voice breaking.

"For the same reason I didn't tell you about Darius being with Vivianne when she died. I was afraid you wouldn't take him. I-I-I knew you were hiding ... I didn't know why—"

"I don't believe you," she growled.

Rapidly, he said, "No, no, that part is true. I did *not* know why you quit playing. That's the God's honest truth."

"You wouldn't know the truth if it bit you on the face," she spit out.

He breathed deeply before continuing. "It still took me almost a year to find you and yes, we moved here so Darius could study with you."

Everything she had allowed herself to believe, all her trust, dissolved in the acid of his lies. What was wrong with her that she believed men? Why did she let them get close, let them take care of her? There must be some broken string in her that she trusted men who didn't want her. They only wanted something from her. The relationships were never about her. It was *always* about *them,* their needs, their ambitions, their manipulations, what she could do for them.

"Why me?" she asked woodenly.

"Because you were Vivianne's favorite pianist. She said everything about your playing was perfect." He held his palms up and lifted his bony shoulders. "I didn't know a piano teacher from a baseball coach. It was all I had to go on to try and save my son."

"You knew," she accused. "All this time, you knew who I used to be. You pretended to ask Wat to recommend a piano teacher, you pretended not to know I could play, and all along, you knew! You lied every time you came in my house, every time you kissed me—" Here the words were burning coals of grief. "Every time we made love, you lied." She wiped her tears with the back of her good hand.

"No, no, that's not true. Please, Hélène—" He shuffled across the tiny room as though his lies hobbled his ankles, and he couldn't escape. "I meant to tell you—"

"Did Darius know why you came to me?" But then, she had connived with Darius to hide her identity.

Bryn shook his head vigorously. "I never told him, I swear it, but I think he figured it out for himself. He never said anything to me about you being *Hélène Noire et Blanche*. If he knew, he didn't know that I knew. We never, ever, talked about who you really were, until you told me."

She wanted to throw Bryn against a wall, to yell at him, to hit him with a gleaming brass candlestick for breaking her heart. She wasn't a violent woman, but she felt positively murderous. If her hand wouldn't have felt better if she cut it off, she would have punched him in the face, too.

"Vivianne wanted to play like you, so she went to study with Morisot. She had no idea that he was the reason you stopped playing, and neither did I. The video of you from Carnegie? It was a bootleg I bought for her birthday one year. She used your recordings as examples for Darius." He sounded like a man waiting for his execution. "When Vivienne died ... I thought the only way to save Darius was for him to study with you."

"You tracked me down because I was your dead wife's favorite pianist? Really?" A single harsh laugh scraped against her throat and he winced.

"I tracked you down because Darius needed you." His voice rose insistently. "He's always listened to your recordings and imitated them. He's not physically your son, but Darius is your *musical* child."

She rose from her seat and walked as far away from him as she could get in the tiny, cluttered room. She couldn't stand to look at his face, a face she once couldn't wait to see—a face whose contours she had unwittingly memorized by staring at him asleep next to her. A face she would never be able to forget, even if she tried for the rest of her life.

His voice was choked. "You represented a connection with Vivianne for Darius, and I hoped you could help him. And you did, you did." Bryn moved to her and touched her shoulder.

She violently shrugged him off, and he retreated to the other side of the room.

"I was trying to rescue my drowning son," he pleaded. "Any father would have done what I did. Darius is all I have. He's *everything* to me. I'd do anything for him."

"Including getting me to fall in love with you?" she snarled.

He dropped his head and spoke to the floor. "I never planned to fall in love with you. I couldn't invent feelings if my life depended on it. Why would *you* fall in love with me?" He laid his palm over his heart. "What would an exotic, brilliant, talented, worldly French woman like you see in a poetry-writing computer nerd who's handy with a hammer?"

She remembered the dreamy feelings his poems stirred in her. She'd even believed those. "The poems," she said, the words corkscrewing out of her. "Were those more of your lies?"

"No, everything I've ever said about how I feel, what I've written, is one hundred percent true."

"I wish I could believe you," she said.

"Hélène, do you really think I could lie in my poems? Those come from the deepest part of me."

She raised her good hand to silence him. "How did you even find me?"

His face colored bright red. "I'm ... it's embarrassing."

"You lied about knowing me," she scoffed. "What *else* is there to be embarrassed about?"

He jammed his fists into his pant pockets and pulled them out again. "I put an old photo from one of your newspaper reviews into the facial recognition software my company's developing. The software scrapes matching images from the Internet. It matched a picture of you from the Norwalk Hour at the groundbreaking for LGBTQ shelter. Your name was listed as Hélène Charbonneau, but once I saw it, there was no mistaking it was you. That's why I went to Wat. I didn't admit I knew you, but I hoped he would point us in your direction, and I was right."

She had been so careful to stay off social media and make sure most references to herself were removed. Yet her picture had appeared on the front page of the local paper for all the world to see.

"I never even thought I had a chance with you until the day you kissed me." He laid a hand on a table as though to steady himself. "That was when I thought you might actually like me for me."

His face was wrenched into an expression of agony and apology, but she didn't believe his pain was real.

"People admired Vivianne—and then Darius—but I was invisible. I was proud of them, but I existed in their shadows. People think I had something to do with Darius being who he is, but I'm just an innocent bystander who got struck with a meteor of a son." He took two steps toward her, his voice a low, urgent whisper. "But you? You're like a gift just for me. You see me like I am, not as an extension of Darius. You think of me as a poet, and you made me think of myself as one. You can't know what it's like to finally be seen for who you are." He rummaged through his thin, pale hair. "I'm sorry I lied to you, but I never, ever thought you would have feelings for me. That I would fall in love with you." He tipped his head back and stared up at the ceiling. "But I felt dried up, and you watered me back to life."

Everything she believed about this man had turned from hot coals to ashes. She let acid drip from her lips. "You must be so disappointed. You came looking for a legend, and what you found was me."

The sanctuary lights flickered, and they heard the audience stirring as they returned to their seats.

He fixed her with an unmoving gaze. "Precisely. You, Hélène Charbonneau, not *Hélène Noire et Blanche*. I don't need a legend or someone famous. I want someone who loves me for who I am, not what I can pay for, and not for Darius. I gave Vivianne everything I could so she could reach her dream of becoming a concert pianist." He swallowed hard. "Instead, she betrayed me. After Darius was born, I gave her everything so that she could concentrate on him." His mouth twisted to the side. "That was my mistake. You give everything for your kids, you know? I came to you for Darius, but you became mine."

He gestured to her broken, ice-wrapped hand. "You gave your hand for Darius. How could I have given him any less? I might have lied about knowing you, but that's all I've ever fudged."

"Lied about," she said, hoping her words cut him to the heart.

He hung his head. "Yes, lied about. I understand if you decide to push me away, but it will kill me. Darius loves you, too, but don't stay with me because of him."

She poured her scorn on him. "Why should I stay with a man who's betrayed my trust? Who pretended not to know me; who tracked me down? What reason would I have to stay with you?"

His eyes took on the soft light of adoration, and she nearly let that light set fire to her heart again.

He said softly, longingly, "Stay with me because I love you, Hélène."

His words almost convinced her.

The sanctuary lights flickered a second time, and the audience grew quiet. This was the moment Hélène had always liked best: standing in the wings, her heart flip-flopping, knowing they were waiting for her.

"We have to take our seats," she bit off.

She struggled to her feet, and he took her elbow to steady her. She jerked away when what she really wanted was to tumble against him and sob against his chest for all he had destroyed in her.

They took their seats in the choir stalls at the front of the church in the chancel, where they alone sat. The house lights went out, leaving only the spots shining on the piano. Hélène felt the suspended breath of the waiting audience.

Darius stepped through the door to applause, shouts, and Bianca's shrill whistle.

He sat down and played like a god. His depth of expression, his total command, and utter immersion in the music were breathtaking. He played from a mature connection to the music that few pianists ever achieved. As if his emotions were just beneath his skin, the muscles in his face twitched, his eyebrows flickered, his jaw flexed, his lips pressed, opened, and shifted with the music. He played at turns hauntingly, thunderously, humorously, and playfully. He executed not only what the composer wrote but what was intended to be *felt* by the listener so that when he finished, not a heart was unmoved. He even made Hélène forget the pain of her crushed hand.

The rafters shook with applause and shouts and foot stomping. St. Paul's had never seen anything like this, and never would again. It was a singular experience that would be recalled for decades to come.

Hélène wept when Darius came to her, laid a bouquet of flowers in her arms, and shyly kissed her cheek. It was, she knew, the last time he would ever kiss her.

CHAPTER 64

Your problem is how you are going to spend this one odd and precious life you have been issued. Whether you're going to spend it trying to look good and creating the illusion that you have power over people and circumstances, or whether you are going to taste it, enjoy it, and find out the truth about who you are.

Anne Lamott

Two nights after the concert, the Marriage Survivors Club barged into Hélène's house carrying wine, flowers, and bags of Chinese takeout. They gathered in the kitchen and Hélène slumped into a chair, gingerly holding her hand close to her chest so she didn't bump it.

Olivia eyed Hélène's bound-up hand with sympathy. "Ouch! How are you feeling?"

"It feels like a train ran over it," Hélène said, holding up the bandages for a group viewing. She had a cast to mid-elbow and her purple fingers were taped together.

"We thought you could use some cheering up," Bianca said. Then she added, "Whether you like it or not."

"It must hurt like hell," Flicka said, rubbing her own hand.

"That doesn't even come close to describing it." Hélène closed her eyes momentarily against the pain. "Even with the pain medication, it's agonizing."

What she really lacked words for was the pain in her heart. Volcano, skyscraper collapse, semi-truck careening off a bridge, and forest fire, came close.

Carolina set two bags on the counter. She removed the cardboard cartons, chopsticks, soy sauce packets, and fortune cookies. Frankie and Olivia set up folding chairs around the kitchen.

"I guess this is why we've never eaten at your place," Bianca said, flapping some paper plates.

Flicka placed six wine glasses on the tiny cafe table. "She has the most important dining implement." She poured generously and handed each woman a glass.

"All right, we're all dying to know, so I'm just going to ask," Olivia said with infinite gentleness. She paused as if to signal that what she was going to ask would hurt, but Hélène was beyond hurting. "What's the doctor say about your hand?" Olivia asked.

As if on cue, pain knifed through Hélène's hand. "Six weeks in the cast and then physical therapy. They'll see if I need more surgery after they take off the cast. I broke my wrist, thumb, several metacarpal bones, and my middle finger."

Bianca held up her bent middle finger. "Dang! That's the most useful finger. I don't think I could function if mine got broken,"

They all laughed, Hélène painfully.

"They'll know after that if I can play again," Hélène said, not bothering to keep the sadness out of her voice. They all shared a long moment of grieving silence.

"We'll pray for you," Carolina said.

"Thank you," Hélène said. "Ask for a miracle, will you?" She didn't really believe in miracles, but if anyone could pull one off, it was Carolina.

"Has Bryn been a lot of help?" Frankie asked. She scooped a lump of lo mein and two steamed vegetable dumplings onto a plate and set it in front of Hélène. At least it was okay to let the Marriage Survivors Club take care of her. Them, she could trust.

"Not exactly." Hélène was reluctant to admit she had, once again, been stupid enough to put her faith in the wrong man.

"How come? You broke your hand for his son's sake. I think he'd be over here on his hands and knees," Frankie said. She sat in a chair and balanced her paper plate on her lap.

The others began loading their plates with sesame beef, General Tso's chicken, egg rolls, dumplings, stir-fried rice, and lo mein.

Hélène unfolded the story of Bryn's betrayal, how he'd searched her out, how he knew all along who she was, how he feigned love for her. "I'm furious at him."

"Huh," Bianca said and chased down a piece of chicken she'd dropped in her lap. She popped it in her mouth. "So, you're pissed off at this guy because he wasn't straight up about knowing you. That he tracked you down? That he fell in love with you?"

"And you fell in love with him," Carolina added.

"Not like you were straight with him, either," Flicka said cuttingly.

Hélène felt a stab of guilt. Of course, Flicka was right.

They stared at her, their gazes amused, accusing, empathetic, annoyed, loving.

"Why be angry? It seems romantic to me," Olivia said.

"I guess I'm mad at myself for being so gullible. Here he was, this lonely man with this needy little boy and—" With resignation, Hélène shook her head. "I just couldn't help myself."

Carolina said, "I don't think you were gullible. I think you have a loving, compassionate heart, and you let them in. You have faith in people. That's a good thing."

Bianca said, "I've met lots of guys who said they loved their wives when they were bonking some bimbo. Bryn doesn't strike me as the kind of guy who could lie about his feelings even if you hit him with a bowling pin," Bianca said.

As a divorce attorney, she'd seen enough marriages implode that she had no illusions about love. She was as clear-eyed as they came and even she thought Bryn loved Hélène.

"I think not saying he knew me counted as a lie," Hélène said, looking for justification for pushing Bryn out of her life.

"Okay, I'll give you that one," Bianca conceded.

Flicka poured herself her second glass of wine, and they'd only been here for ten minutes. She affected an injured tone. "You know, I had this friend who lied about who she was because she thought I wouldn't love her if I knew the truth. I gave her my friendship and support, but she still didn't trust me." Flicka dabbed at the corners of her eyes with her napkin and sniffled loudly. "She thought I wasn't worthy of her trust. I feel so devasted."

Hélène felt herself growing smaller as, *snip, snip, snip,* Flicka cut her down to size.

"Huh!" Frankie pointed an egg roll at Flicka. "We know the same woman. I told her about how my mom abandoned me. At the time, she seemed sympathetic, but now"—Frankie scowled theatrically—"I think she was faking it."

Heat crept up Hélène's neck to her ears. She had entirely lost her appetite.

Bianca took a turn at making Hélène into a punching bag. "I thought we were friends, me and this one woman—probably the same one you guys know—but she didn't think I would understand how someone hurt her and drove her into hiding." With a wounded expression, she shook her head.

"And how did that make you feel?" Olivia asked, getting in on the act.

"Kinda like shit," Bianca said in her eloquent fashion. "Like I had been, you know, tricked into caring about someone I didn't really know. Made me question all my relationships." She glanced around the table. "Are you guys really who I think you are?"

Nobody laughed.

"Like Father Gabriel says, we are all human and all broken," Carolina said with her open smile. "We all fail each other and ourselves. We fail to do things and leave things undone. That's why we have to forgive one another. It's what loving requires."

Leave it to Carolina to offer a spiritual and religious perspective on things. Hélène didn't disagree; she simply didn't think her heart was big enough to forgive Bryn for lying, for making her fall in love with him.

"But you know what?" Carolina glanced around the table. "We forgive you for not telling us the truth, but I don't know why you didn't. You must have been suffering in great pain. We could have helped you. Shame is a powerful emotion and can make you do—" Carolina paused, searching for a word.

Bianca finished Carolina's sentence for her. "Dumb shit, like lying to your best friends and thinking you're the only one who's ever been ashamed or hurt."

"Yeah, and then you never have to take another chance at love. Unlike me, who has given love four chances," Flicka said with a smirk.

Hélène wanted to crawl under the table. She had taken their love and friendship for granted, failed to trust them, hidden what their love could have healed long ago.

Flicka set her wine glass on the table. "Sorry to call you on your bullshit, but you're crazy if you think we're going to let you get away with calling Bryn a liar." She fixed Hélène with the most serious look she had ever seen on Flicka's face. "Bryn loves you. He didn't when he started looking for you, but he grew to love you. Look at this place." Flicka waved her hand around. "No dishes, no artwork, never inviting your friends over, nothing in your life except that piano. You cut everyone off who could have helped you get over your past. We've been here all along, and you never trusted us. We won't let you throw Bryn and Darius out without facing them."

Hélène had nursed her hurt to make certain no one else ever hurt her. She'd been willing to be lonely to be safe. It had always —until now—seemed like a good trade-off. How much love had she missed out on because she'd been scared? Who had missed out on the love *she* had to give? She'd given all her love to her piano and that had broken her heart, too.

"You have to see Bryn at least," Olivia said.

"How do you know I haven't already?" Hélène said meekly.

Bianca *tsked* and banged a fist on the table. "You're lying again! What the fuck is it with you? You think we haven't already talked to him? The guy is devastated that you've kicked him to the curb. He loves you and wants to make up. You'd give him another chance if you had any guts—which we already know you don't."

"You don't have to be so harsh, Bee," Olivia said gently.

"Well, how could she be so thick?" Bianca ranted and tossed her hand in the air. She turned to Hélène. "From the first time I saw you two together, he was like a drunk in a liquor store. When he was around you, he lit up like Fourth of July fireworks." Bianca reddened and lowered her voice. "We all want someone to look at us like that." Bianca wiped the sauce stain on her shirt. "Sorry, it's just that, well, you know, we love you and want you to be happy. This is your chance at love. Don't fuck it up."

"Are you guys done lecturing me?" Hélène said, feeling utterly chastised.

"Only if we've gotten through to you," Frankie said, poking her chopsticks in Hélène's direction.

Great, hot tears ran down Hélène's cheeks. They were all quiet as she folded her arms on the table, laid her head down, and sobbed in hiccups. This was the kind of crying that made her want to hold a pillow over her head and howl. Someone rubbed circles on her back. There was a quiet clearing away of the dinner things. Another bottle of wine was opened.

Hélène lifted her head when she needed a tissue, and someone pressed one into her hand. "I don't know what my life will be like now that everything has gone to hell. I can't play, I can't teach, I'm alone. The man I loved lied. I don't have anything to offer anyone. If he loved me for being who I was, why would he love me now? How can I forgive him?"

Carolina threw away an empty takeout container. "What will forgiveness cost you? Your heart is already smashed up into little pieces. He loves you, and Darius loves you. They can help you put your heart back together. And I promise you, it will not be the last time he will hurt or disappoint you or that you will hurt and disappoint him."

"And don't forget, he has to forgive you for not being straight with him either," Frankie said.

Everything they said was true. She had hurt Bryn by hiding who she was. She had conspired with Darius to conceal her identity from Bryn. She had even denied her gifts as a musician by being afraid and holding onto the wounds Yves had inflicted. Now, she knew that, no matter how hard you tried, you weren't immune from disappointment, grief, or a broken heart. Art and music were invented to communicate grief, love, joy, pain, and heartbreak. They were all part of living.

And that terrified her.

"I'm worthless without my music," Hélène said, touching the fingers of her broken hand with the fingers of her good hand.

"Not to us, you're not. Not to God," Carolina said optimistically.

Olivia said, "Bryn can help you find out who you are and want to be without the piano. Playing isn't the only thing you can do. Give him a chance to love you. To heal your heart."

"Do you love him?" Frankie asked Hélène.

"And don't lie to us, either, Frenchie," Bianca said with a curl of her upper lip that made her look both as though she was laughing and also might bite Hélène.

Olivia rolled her eyes and made a huff of exasperation in Bianca's direction.

Hélène closed her eyes and recalled the way her skin tingled when Bryn's fingers caressed her back. How she couldn't wait to see him walk in her door. How a light switched on inside of her when he held her. How safe she felt when she laid her head on his chest and heard his heart beat a steady rhythm. The way his shy, self-deprecating smile made her want to kiss him. How the particular shade of his hazel eyes, for some strange unidentifiable reason, made her think of Brahms. Of his reliability and how he took care of her. How he didn't demand anything in return for doing so. How he made her laugh. How, aside from admitting he knew her, he was an open book. How she thought of him all the time. How she wanted to be with him. The way poetry came to him in the same way music came to her. The way he openly showed his affection for his son. How, when she was with him, she didn't feel lonely or scared. She respected Bryn's sacrifices, dedication, and selflessness for those he loved. Surprisingly, that included her.

Hélène's heart felt as if it would burst out of her chest. "Yes. Yes, I do love him."

"You know, the people we love the most have the ability to

hurt us the most," Frankie said in the way that someone who has been loved and has had to forgive would.

"I suppose I love him more than I've ever loved anybody. And I didn't know it until all this happened. I might not even have loved him if he had known who I was. I might have just been suspicious of him," Hélène admitted.

Flicka arched her plucked eyebrows. "Here's the deal: we'll all give you another chance if you give him one."

Hélène smiled weakly at her loving, ass-busting friends, whose love made her the person she was meant to be.

"One for all, and no bullshit for any," Bianca intoned, trying to sound solemn but sounding slightly drunk.

They all repeated their mantra and clinked glasses together.

CHAPTER 65

Grace be with you all.
    Hebrews 13:25

Even though Bryn's bones ached to see Hélène, he waited until he heard from the Marriage Survivors Club that they'd visited her. Waiting until she texted him was agony. He lay awake nights worrying if she was all right. He wanted to apologize, to thank her for everything she had done for Darius, to tell her about the agent who had seen a video of the concert and called about representing Darius, and that he'd turned the agent down.

He waited to tell her that he would understand if she chose to say goodbye.

Now, standing on the porch, his hand hovering over the doorbell, his stomach churned. Father Gabriel had given a sermon on grace the first time Bryn had gone to St. Paul's. They'd chatted afterward about the meaning of grace, which was basically opening your heart and loving the other person wherever they were on their emotional journey. It was about giving the other person the room to fail and be human. Bryn wasn't a praying guy, but all he had was this last Hail Mary.

I don't know if you're up there, God, but let her give me grace.

He shifted the bouquet of peonies, each one big as a softball, from one sweaty hand to the other. He smoothed back his hair and brushed his hand down the front of his dress shirt, which had taken him an hour to iron. He jerked his collar straight and shook out his pant legs. He reminded himself not to blab a mile a minute or press her on anything. Just to give her grace and hope she gave him some, too.

He jabbed the doorbell and steeled himself.

Hélène opened the door. She smiled but he saw how pain had sharpened the angles of her face and worn her entire body down so that she looked even more fragile. She wore a fuzzy pink bathrobe and leopard-spotted slippers that he found endearing. There were grey circles under her eyes that made him want to carry her up to bed like a baby. Her hair, usually so striking, stuck up in sweet baby-bird-like tufts around her head as if she'd been too exhausted to brush it.

Seeing her bandaged hand made him wince. He wished he could trade her injured hand for a good one of his. He clamped his arms to his side to keep from gathering her to him.

Shut up. Don't say anything.

She smiled weakly, and he thought his heart would break at the way her eyes shone light at him.

She opened the door. "Come in."

He stepped into the entryway and held out the bouquet of peonies. "These are for you." His fingers ached slightly from holding them so tightly.

She took them in her good hand. She closed her eyes and breathed in the rose-like fragrance. "They're beautiful," she murmured. "Thank you, but I can't manage to put them in a vase. Would you mind doing it?"

"Happy to."

In the kitchen, he pulled out a chair for her. "Want to sit down? You must be tired."

She nodded and sat.

"So, where's your vase?" he asked, knowing she didn't have one.

Idiot, you should have brought one.

One corner of her mouth curled up. "You know, I don't have an actual vase. Can you use a plastic water pitcher?" She pointed to a cabinet.

The pitcher was easy to find in the cabinet because there was nothing else in it. He wished he'd asked her why her cabinets were empty. Now, he might never have the chance. There were still so many things about her he didn't know and might never know. The thought was like someone slugging him in the chest with a ten-pound hammer.

He put the flowers in the makeshift vase and set it on the table.

She fingered one of the leaves. "Did you know pink peonies are my favorite flower?"

"I didn't know." He bit the end of his tongue, hoping she would go on.

"In the summers, I would go to my grandmother's in the south of France for two weeks. She had a lovely garden, and these were her favorites."

She stared at the peonies, and with the subtle shifts of her wide mouth and the delicate lift of her brows, he saw her remembering. He knew her face well enough to guess at her thoughts. This both moved and saddened him because this might be the last time he would ever see the changing light in her eyes, the startling shades of her hair, and the sharp peaks of her upper lip. He might never hold her to him again.

"Did you ... help her in the garden?" he asked carefully,

understanding she was giving him something precious of herself that she'd kept hidden.

She smiled with a certain innocence. "Oh, yes. I loved digging around and getting dirt under my nails. My mother insisted I be meticulous about taking care of my hands." A painful memory shifted behind her eyes. "She was my first teacher, you see. She was a concert pianist. She taught me a great deal, but I needed her to be my mother, not my teacher. Eventually, my father found me another teacher."

"That's why you knew how damaging it was for Darius to lose Vivianne."

She nodded and touched a flower petal with one slender finger.

He didn't want to press her for stories that she might later regret sharing, so he said, "So why haven't you ever planted a flower garden here? You have plenty of sun in front."

She sighed. "It's a lot of work, digging, watering, weeding, mulching, cutting things back, staking them up. And as my mother taught me, it's hard on the hands." Her smile was rueful as she held up her broken hand. "Guess that's not a worry anymore."

"Will you let me plant you some pink peonies? As a..." He swallowed back the clump of emotion in his throat. "As a farewell gift?" He was happy to know he could give her something that she would enjoy and, perhaps, when she saw them, she would remember him and Darius.

"Are you leaving?" she asked, the light in her eyes flickering.

Is this grace?

He couldn't look at her, afraid her anger would shoot out and crush what little hope he had left. That she would hate that he had come. "No, but I figured you never wanted to see me again."

She stared at the flowers.

In the long silence that stretched between them, memories

of holding her, of kissing the tiny mole behind her left ear, of the way her calves curved into her ankles, of the smell of her, filled his heart. If she said goodbye, how would he hold on to those memories? There was no box he could keep them in, no way to recall the feeling that surprised him every time she turned and glanced over her shoulder at him, smiling with humor and an unpredictable shyness.

Finally, she said, "There's a lot you don't know about me." She sounded scared, as if he could find out things about her that would make him dislike her, or worse.

"I know you helped my son. I know you cared—" He looked down at his two strong, whole hands. "At one time, you cared about me. You changed our lives, and I want you to know how grateful I am. And that I..." He screwed his courage to the sticking point. "And that I love you."

They sat quietly for a moment, and he was glad to be in her soothing presence.

"I'm sorry," she said finally.

He said, "No, no, I'm the one who should apologize. I shouldn't have come to you under false pretenses. I figured if you weren't playing publicly, there was some reason you didn't want people to know who you were. I wanted to respect that, but of course, I hoped you could help Darius. Then, as things went on, you and I ...." He fiddled with the button on his shirt and realized it was the very button she had sewn on for him. "Well, by then, there was no easy way out of it."

She looked him in the eye, and he saw trusting courage in her gaze. "I'm sorry I lied to you about who I was. Once I started having feelings for you and I knew you had feelings for me, I should have told you, but I didn't. I hope you can forgive me."

He felt his chest expand like a sky swept clear of dark, over-hanging clouds. Blue and sparkling with possibility. He adjusted one of the lily stems. "Of course I forgive you, but why didn't you tell me?"

"I was ashamed." She seemed to wilt in her chair as though finally laying down something she'd carried about her neck and shoulders for a long time. "I guess I didn't trust you to understand how awful I felt." She sighed with a weariness that went beyond the physical. "I was so used to hiding it was like the natural instinct of a scared animal."

"Are you still ashamed?" he asked, wanting to touch her cheek.

She shook her head. "No. My shame has been a huge burden for most of my life. I believed others would think I was a fraud, that they would dredge all that up if they knew my past. Because Darius kept pushing me, insisting I play with him, that I perform, I realized I'm still a fine pianist." The corners of her mouth turned down as she dragged a finger down her cast. "Well, I was a fine pianist."

"You were very brave to fight all your demons to play with him. But you didn't have to do it alone."

The look on her face was both vulnerable and scared. "I think I was inching closer to letting you know who I was. I'm sorry I didn't do it sooner."

Sun shone through her kitchen window and lit the room in a warm golden glow. The lower sash was raised, and outside, he could hear a riot of birdsong. He thought maybe he could hear the leaves trembling on their branches. A breeze stirred her hair, and she tucked it behind her ear, the movement of her hands making him want to kiss her palm.

"You did what you had to to live with yourself. I understand why you didn't tell me," he said.

"The Marriage Survivors Club, you, and Darius made me see that I can let go of the shame I have—I had—about my past. I'm working to accept myself just as I am." Her chest rose and fell with one great sigh. The lines around her mouth and creasing her forehead had released, and she appeared settled in a way he hadn't seen before.

Then, her beautiful wide mouth spread into a smile. She stood and moved toward him. "But now I know that you knew who I was, and you still loved me." She eased down into his lap and slipped her arm around his neck. "I'm looking forward to seeing who I become with you and Darius," she kissed his forehead. "If you'll have me."

The pressure in his chest eased as she pressed her lips to his. Every soft curve of her body braced against his own, and he inhaled the lavender scent of her skin. "Have we made up?" he asked, barely able to let himself hope.

"Yes, but I can't wait until we can make up properly," she murmured.

Thank you, God!

They sat like that for several minutes, feeling the other's heart beating and infusing love into one another.

"I'd like to spend the rest of my day like this, but I should go. I don't want to tire you out," he whispered against her ear.

She slid off his lap. "When will I see you again?"

He took her face between his hands and kissed her. "Tonight? I'll come and make dinner for the three of us."

"That would be nice." She stood on tiptoe and kissed his cheek. "And when I'm healed, can we plant those peonies together?"

"I'd love to," he said. He let his hands rest on her hips, not wanting to let go of his joy, his love. This was what grace was. He wished he could capture this feeling, but it would be like light in his hands.

She gazed up at him with limitless hope in her eyes. "And what if we start planning a bedroom for Darius?" she asked.

Driving home, he sang "Goin' to the Chapel" at the top of his lungs.

EPILOGUE

Rise up, my love, my fair one, and come away;
For lo, the winter is past, the rain is over and gone;
The flowers appear upon the earth;
the time of the singing of birds is come;
Arise, my love, my fair one and come away, away.

Song of Solomon 2:10-16

Six Months Later

On a cool Saturday morning, Father Gabriel married Hélène and Bryn in the Lady Chapel. Sunshine radiated through the stained-glass window and made diamonds of color on the stone floor. With Our Lady gazing down, the chapel was filled with a rapturous burst of joy that couldn't be contained within the walls but found crevices and cracks and flowed out into the world like a melody.

Hélène wore a white suit overlaid with black Alençon lace and a white pillbox hat. In her arms, she carried a bouquet of pale pink peonies. Bryn wore a morning suit with a tie, vest, and tailcoat, making him look distinguished and gentlemanly. He was carefully gentle when he slipped a gold and diamond ring over the twisted knuckle of her ring finger.

Darius was the best man. For Hélène's walk down the "aisle," he played a piano piece he had composed called, "Hélène Rocks." He wore high-top Converse sneakers and a T-shirt printed to look like a tuxedo.

The Marriage Survivors Club stood up for Hélène, and even Bianca, who did not believe in true love, shed a few tears.

And they all promised Hélène they would not eject her from the Club.

AUTHOR'S NOTE

The character of Darius Harding is based in large part on the brilliant, incomparable Russian pianist Evgeny Kissin. If you've never had the good fortune to score a ticket to a live performance, I recommend listening to him on your chosen digital medium, but with good speakers. His playing is amazing and moving. And yes, he is a once-in-a-generation pianist.

Performing is both stressful but also a musician's lifeblood. It takes hours of work to make something appear effortless. It demands hours of practice, teachers as gifted as the student, and the support of dozens of people. But once you are onstage, you are alone, your ideas and technique on display for all to see, to praise or ridicule. The mistakes are yours and yours alone. Many fantastic musicians never attain the kinds of careers their talents deserve. Others opt for more predictable, financially stable lives, but that doesn't make them any less gifted. Please attend live classical concerts wherever you live; live music touches the heart in ways that recorded music can't. Don't be worried if you don't "understand" the music. Just absorb, listen, and allow yourself to be transported.

I am a trained opera singer, and all of my musical experiences revolve around classical music. However, one doesn't have to be a peerless musician to benefit from lessons and practice. Studies show that children who play an instrument are better all-around students. Music allows the expression of emotions that can't be put into words, builds fulfilling collaborations, and community.

Not many people are still playing on community team sports into their fifties, but you can sing or play an instrument until health prohibits.

Kids always complain about having to practice because it challenges the edge of learning: incompetency pushes against mastery. That's how we learn. Some parents let their kids stop playing or practicing because they decide it's not worth the struggle and nagging. I assure you, it is. One of the greatest gifts you can give a young person is classical musical lessons. Not electric guitar lessons, not drum lessons, but classical lessons. Classical training exposes kids to music they would not otherwise encounter. It involves a rigor that other types of music don't, and teaches them to read music. Eventually, kids might branch out into jazz, or even pop or rock, but teach them classical music first. You don't have to own a baby grand piano or a solid silver flute, but make your kid join a band, choir, or orchestra or take lessons, the same way you make them take math and reading. Music isn't optional. Art illuminates and gives expression to life.

DOWN PAYMENT ON JUSTICE

Home is the place where,
When you go there,
They have to take you in.

Robert Frost

Sitting in the sanctuary of St. Paul's on the Green, Bianca Treviso checked the Red Sox score one last time on her phone and prayed the pitcher's arm would hold out until the final inning. She would have lit a candle, but she didn't know whose team God was rooting for. She tucked her phone back in her pocket.

Frankie had invited her to the monthly Race and Social Justice meeting because someone interesting was speaking, but Bianca would have preferred to be home yelling at the stupid umps on her TV. She didn't recognize many of the people because the group comprised residents from all over Norwalk.

Olivia Maxwell, Flicka Whitehall, Carolina Singh, and Hélène Charbonneau were also in attendance. Together, they made up the Marriage Survivors Club. Primarily, they laughed, drank, and chided one another, but here at St. Paul's, they were dedicated fundraisers for the LGBTQ youth shelter.

Father Gabriel Ayeliff—six-six, with touseled chocolate brown hair and looking like a sixteen-year-old in a priest's costume—rose and stood at the front of the church. The chatter quieted.

"Welcome to St. Paul's. After the meeting, please join us for a glass of wine and snacks in the Undercroft, which is Episcopal-speak for 'basement.' We're glad you're here, and you are welcome anytime."

Bianca leaned over to Flicka and said, "It's like having your little brother invite his friends for beer pong."

Flicka slid her a sideways look as her shoulders shook with irreverent silent laughter.

Bianca thought of each of the five other members of the Marriage Survivors Club as a sport, and Flicka was definitely women's roller derby. Much-divorced Frederica 'Flicka' Cole Williamson Strada Kolinsky Whitehall had a poof of dyed red hair and the figure of a beauty queen maintained by generous amounts of plastic surgery. In her designer clothes and saber-toed stilettoes, she looked every inch the New York socialite she'd once been. But her raucous laugh and smutty sense of humor played against type. She was her own red light district.

Flicka whispered to Bianca, "Maybe the next fundraiser for the shelter should be a beer pong tournament!"

Bianca snorted a laugh.

Frankie Carter flipped her silver and black braids over her shoulder. "Behave, you two, or I'll get you kicked out," she whispered with a grin on her face.

If Frankie were a sport, she would be a sword-wielding, problem-slaying gladiator. She banged away on any problem that arose until she found a solution.

"You just try it," Bianca hissed back with a laugh.

St. Paul's was the one place where she felt at home. Everyone in Norwalk knew St. Paul's as the church that took anybody, even people like Bianca. No one cared if she blurted out rude comments. No one cared if her dirty blond hair often looked like a nest of weeds. No one cared if she had a stain or snag on her clothes or made fun of her kankles. Unlike her dad when she was a kid, no one noticed that her splotchy pinkish skin was pockmarked from adolescent acne or that she was plump. The Marriage Survivors Club loved her because she was a shark: because they knew she had their back, no matter what. That she would do anything for any of them, and she knew the same was true for the others.

Father Gabriel said, "We'll start this evening with a prayer." He bowed his head. "Heavenly Father, thank you for bringing all of us together to fight for the cause of justice for all persons. Give us courage and perseverance until your Kingdom is realized here on Earth. Amen."

Father Gabriel made a gesture of invitation, and a handsome black man rose to stand next to Father Gabriel.

Something about the guy jiggled in the back of Bianca's brain, but she couldn't quite put her finger on it. The brawny man was middle-aged with glossy medium-brown skin, a gleaming shaved head, and intense eyes that stared with unwavering calm around the room. Shoulders thrown back and chin lifted, he held the audience's attention with his commanding presence. His face had the topography of a man accustomed to grief, but he had battled his way to the other side where dignity and indignation lay. He had the vibe of an ancient prophet sent to deliver a message. But Bianca wasn't in the mood for a message unless it was that the Red Sox had clinched the game.

Father Gabriel said, "Tonight's speaker is a Norwalk native and former prison inmate, now criminal justice activist. I'd like to introduce Reed Etheridge."

Bianca had been wondering what would be served at the reception afterward, but now, her mind snapped to attention. Every muscle in her body went taut.

It couldn't possibly be him. What was he doing at St. Paul's?

www.ingramcontent.com/pod-product-compliance
Lightning Source LLC
Chambersburg PA
CBHW011409310726
48972CB00011B/2906